Pax Germ

By Tony de La

Second Edition: April 2022

Edited by Ruby Street

The paperback edition first published in 2021

ISBN 978-168524566-5

US $13.72

9 781685 245665

51372

Contents

This book is dedicated to the men and women of all nationalities, races, creeds, and religions, who gave their lives during the First World War, 1914-1918.

Their names shall liveth evermore.

Prologue

The end did not come, but they were allowed to breathe for the first time in four years. All over the world, people began to breathe, and it felt like the first breath for a long time. What would happen tomorrow did not matter. The only thing concerning millions of people was the sharp intake of air that would fill the lungs as ears desperately tried to find another loud source of noise to compensate for the silence. Silence and air; that's what it really was.

No one expected the end to come. Even the optimists lying peacefully in their respective beds did not really consider the world to simply move on after four years of conflict. The higher-ups shrugged their shoulders when they learnt about who would dictate the peace thinking to themselves that at least someone was talking about it. Perhaps talk was peace; the top brass contemplated. Talk was a sign that people were listening, and they had not listened for so long. The dialogue of war, some thought, was all that the world now knew. Too much thinking, this time caused too much thinking.

Would the war to end all wars follow the talking to end all talking? Who knew that peace, if only for a moment, would ask more questions than it would answer? The fantasies of those deeply involved in the Great War had been feverish, especially in the last days before the end but now that the time had come to think about putting such fantasies into action, it made people freeze. One wrong move, one badly thought-out plan and the whole thing would unravel again. Such thoughts made more headaches than were once expected.

That is what peace felt like; a very muddled and breathy experience for everyone, on either side of the divide. It had been so easy for four years to run like clockwork because they knew what they had to do. Don't get shot, push them back, find the breakthrough and live to tell the tale. Try to lose less than them as well, don't forget that. Well, now what? What is the key display of victory now? What is the key sign of progress? Scratched

A

heads whirled with questions about the future. Would it be so bad to consider this halt in the fighting as unhelpful?

No, the show ended, and the restrained applause must be followed through. And amongst the breathing and the questioning one key little point danced around the minds of almost everyone, regardless of their role in the Great War from 1914-1918 was this; could it have been different?

The notion had been laughed at in small circles, careful to not let their views get into the public domain. Many believed in fate as it was fate that brought people the strength to do what they believed needed to be done. 'God wills it!' people thought they might as well shout; it made just as little sense to them anyway. No understanding was easy to come by when thinking whether something different could be done or could have followed.

And for the winners, the end was preordained. You don't fight a bloody war only to lose it in the end! It was always meant to be. God was on their side. The fates were on their side. They were the best shots. They had the upper hand. They had the right tenacity. They lasted the longest. They were the best, weren't they?

For the losers? It was easier for the higher-ups to console themselves with the thought that they were never going to win. They simply delayed the inevitable with their cunning, skill and determination. They made sure that the conditions for loss were suitably pushed into their favour so that the conditions for peace would not be so unduly harsh. Console, learn, and adapt.

Thus, it was on that unusually wet day in June, not too far from the anniversary of the death of the silly Archduke Franz Ferdinand, that the slow motorcade, previously the slow train which had to stop a couple of miles from the now-silent front lines, proceeded to a clearing in the woods outside of Spa in Belgium. The roads the motorcade took from the battlefield to the woods were lined up with silent men; some sitting and some standing, watching the silent parade pass through. Many would consider the sight rather pitiful, but shrugged shoulders and breathing people were in greater abundance. Someone had to be in the car, and it would have to go one direction or the other at some point. In the end, who cares which side it goes through? The damage had surely been done. To

B

many watching the scene it felt like children walking past their parents on their way to clean up their own mess. Some men looked away.

It could have all been so different. Such a sentiment was shared by millions, and millions more. It could have all been so different, but fate ordained that only one side could see what would happen next. Men had cursed fate for so long, yet fate would carry on delivering. It was delivering in front of their very eyes. Judgement had been passed and the sentiment was carried day after day after day. Perhaps it wasn't so possible? What's done is done. Frustrating, yet tantalising, the young ones shuddered, the old ones contemplated.

Men in grey suits, men in brown uniforms, men in grey uniforms, their eyes darting around the corridors and halls where the talking was making more waves than ever before, were wandering how it could have all been so different. People were asking whether it was healthy to even contemplate it still? Weeks were going by and still the sentiment remained. Why could they not get it out of their heads? It was infuriating! Some went mad with the mere thought and yet there it was. What if? What if? It was as if parrots were mocking everyone on street corners with the question. It caused some to scream at the top of their lungs in order to drown out the noise. Some simply took the distress with silence and thought.

Stay very still, for if you stay still then the bee won't sting you. If you stay very still, then the bee will simply pass you by. Did that also work with time and thoughts? The simple answer for most was no, but the more complicated answer was a resounding no with a bee sting on the arm. In the end, people had to choose; scream or silence. That was the only way to answer the question. What if? Who cares? Who knows? Nobody. Thoughts, thoughts, thoughts.

The truth would come out of the woodwork in time, but that time would come much later. For now, the reality was stark and true. Germany and her allies had won the Great War following decisive action in the mid-spring weeks of 1918. Peace would be dictated to by the swashbuckling adventurers of the new century, and they would dictate it as such. They would decide how the race towards the next catastrophe would come and they would decide what the peace would look like until the next great issue arose. For now, the German Kaiser, the young and meandering Austrian

C

Emperor and the quiet and nervous Sultan would sit expectantly, as the vanquished Allies entrusted to them the reins of power and thus the reins of peace.

No one, but no one, was kidding themselves. The real boss of the trio was the German Empire, and she would act as such, taking the reins of power from Britain who had held on to these reigns for over a hundred years. Responsibility was a heavy crown, but the Germans had paid for it with their own blood. The twentieth century would be theirs to mould for as long as they could. To many it looked as if a grumpy child had just been thrown an overgrown cloak, a sceptre too large to hold with one hand and a crown too heavy to balance. Maybe some pity was reserved for the winner as well, but that was all in the background. There were nerves being felt everywhere, no less atop the seats of the victors.

Some say they saw the German Emperor physically unable to sit still for any longer than twenty seconds. Some say that whenever he tried to speak, he had to clear his throat silently under his breath. Some say that they saw his withered arm twitch on his sword. It all contributed to the general feeling of unease being felt by everyone. What on earth was going to happen next and what would those who could decide things, decide upon? The truth was that nobody knew, not least the most powerful. They were still trying to answer the first question; could have it all been so different?

The era of Pax Britannica had ended. No longer would the British Empire be the final arbiter of world affairs. No longer would the British Empire have the ultimate sway over the entire globe. The era of Pax Germania had begun.

D

Chapter 1

The only good thing about the rain was that it was something else to listen to. That made anyone fighting in Belgium feel lucky; it was always raining. Farther down the line, more in France, it was known that the winter rains of the earlier months were less frequent than usual. Water slipping elegantly through the British lines seemed to be never-ending, one man attempted to see if he could get a piece of wood to float as far as it could down the slightly sloped ridge where his trench stood. There was no point looking out into no man's land, the Germans were probably doing the same thing.

The monotonous sound of the rain was what managed to soothe Major William Steele's mind to catch a few minutes of sleep. Those few minutes crept towards the hour mark as the rain intensified as did the sound it made, which played the music of sleep on. It was a welcome break for William, who had had quite a difficult winter to contend with. His sleep was well earned, as for too long he had burned the candle at both ends, but it was necessary. Sleep was always necessary.

He hadn't been a Major long. In fact, he was an acting Major in the line. He constantly felt the 'acting' part of the job. Several months isn't exactly the proper experience for a man in such a position, and why he was so close to the front also seemed ridiculous. But there he was, trapped between responsibility and necessity all the same. At least he got a few extra spaces between him and the next sleepy gentleman, and his bed had a few better springs, though the winter had rusted through most of them. His dugout had the overpowering aroma of damp, but as a man of creature comforts, he had done his best to deck the place out with a few home improvements. It was the greatest achievement of his winter.

William Steele was not a man well liked back at regimental headquarters. As he dreamt of being back home with his wife-to-be, a picture of the well-to-do woman pressed into his unwashed palms, the top brass was still thinking whether the acting Major was 'all they had'. That was the phrase uttered back at them by their commanding officer. "Winter slows the availability of adequate replacements" the overly moustached old-Etonian retorted to his sub-ordinates. It was the greatest line of defence for making Steele the acting senior officer for a large stretch of the line. The younger officers thought of Steele as a jumped-up farmer. The idea of a man who used to till the field in his youth, acting as a senior leader at the front had riled up the chaps at the back.

William was not a common farmer by trade. His family were well respected in the South-West of England, and he had attended a good school, but he was not part of the in-crowd who made up the majority of the senior respected officers of the British Army. He was a middleman, caught not only between military stations, but social stations also. He had the common touch but also knew how to drink tea properly, and that made him an outsider to both; if you aren't fully one of them you were against them. He was treated as such and knew it as such, but that wouldn't affect his sleep. At the age of thirty-two he was not too young to play the part of a Major, but he felt much more junior in the role than was perhaps necessary.

William did not feel alone. It was more luck than good-will that a good friend of his was posted in a similar senior role about a mile to the south of his posted area. Henry Forbes was similarly sleeping, but he had found himself a bit further back in the line. Henry was of suitably finer stock, a lawyer until he had seen the good sense to take a commissioned officer role in the army two years before the war. The most important thing about him were his connections, and he was suitably better kept than his dear friend, William. Henry had been in his role at the front for a longer period of time and had gained the key skill of getting other people to do the jobs he needed to do and was respected for it.

The two men met when they were younger, when William first arrived in London. William had moved there to work at the French embassy six months before the start of the war, a post he was grateful to have been given by an old acquaintance of his father, Lord Sheffield. He took up lodgings renting a room in a house owned by Henry Forbes's father, Giles. Henry himself was staying in the same house because his father thought that any son of his should not rely on his father's wealth in perpetuity and that included the roof over his head. The two men struck up a good bond

2

that was endearing if only to serve as a means by which they were able to live together; and it was enough for them to remain on good terms, and as the war took hold of the world, they had begun to write to each other.

In the end, it was this semi-friendship that caused Henry to recommend his friend William to take up the acting post of Major in the line. To William this post felt more of a curse than a stroke of good luck, but there was no ill will in Henry's mind. There was no need to. Henry wanted what was best for William, and this feeling was reciprocated, though Henry had the greater means to follow through on his wishes. To William, Henry was a lifeline and an area of support. Henry was also familiar with William's sweetheart, Emmanuelle. Once again, the recommendation for William's suitability was given by Henry.

William slept soundly in his little dugout, decked with imported wood to line the roof, the floor and the walls. It had come all the way from Scotland and was considered of good quality. It did not soak up the water like French or Southern English wood did. This was yet another small modicum of leniency that the soldiers in Belgium were afforded. William himself was afforded the extra time with his eyes closed as a Major. Acting, he kept thinking, acting.

If truth be told, William was missing the real Major, the one he was acting for. Major Rupert Haines had been William's commanding officer for over two years and had acted with impressive bravery, especially for a man of his years. Rupert was a man of the old world who had served the army all over the empire. He waxed lyrical about his experience drinking tea with Kitchener in Khartoum. The other ranks and non-commissioned officers used to call him 'roaring story Rupert'. None could quite believe if all of his stories were true. They seemed to get more fanciful and magical as time passed. There was a hushed word or two about his potential loss of sanity. To William, the stories were all real and they allowed a sense of escapism and wonder.

He was also a brave officer. He didn't hide from a fight and nor was he far from one. He was never entrusted with leading the main attack, but there was always space in the military plans for his brand of fighting. There was more than a touch of the mindless optimism that was rampant within the corridors of power, but many of the soldiers found it easy to forgive commander Haines for it. He had earnt the lenient treatment from his men he gave as good as he got, by not being as strict as he could have been, and kinder that he needed to be with the odd indiscretion here and there.

It therefore came as a regretful shame that he had to retire from the line, injured in the line of duty. Haines, Steele and around fifteen hundred men of the battalion were involved in the fourth waves in the third battle of Ypres, supporting the charge of the Canadian Corps who were bearing the brunt of the action in those final days of the offensive. In the ensuing melee around the area known as Passchendaele, Major Haines was wounded by shrapnel shards in his head and shoulder. Luckily, he was not very far away from relief and was carried back, though there was concern that for a man in his early fifties he was not in the greatest form to deal with the injuries. A medical orderly quickly brightened the present men's spirits up when they were informed that the injuries were only skin deep and that he would make a good recovery and would be able to tell his stories once again.

William admired Major Haines with great respect, but even as he slept in the dugout with the acting pips of his old mentor, he could never forget the sight of the man slumped between the arms of two soldiers being dragged from the ground to an aid station to a truck bound for grassier places. He had always believed that Rupert Haines was a strong man who looked far younger than his age. Within the space of ten minutes, he looked much older, and much frailer. He had finally reached the end of his tether as a strong demeanour as a leader in the field in the time it took to boil a cup of tea. William could never un-see the sight of the legs dragging his torso back, his head wobbling from side to side, his arms above his shoulders being carried in a most undignified manner to his place of refuge. His hair, often straightened to within an inch of its life, was a terrible mess. William didn't even have a chance to pat his old commander on the back and wish him a speedy recovery, time was of the essence and there was a schedule to keep to, even if they were a couple of months behind collectively within Field Marshal Haig's elegantly flawed master plan.

Acting Major William Steele remained for the whole winter and as the crisp cold air was replaced by a warmer spring-like atmosphere he felt as unqualified in his role as he did when he was first assigned the post. At least he could sleep a little longer. His dreams would remain the same, or rather the nightmares would remain the same. Often, he would wake up frightened from a memory playing out in his vulnerable mind from a previous battle, or maybe his mind would make it up, but it would feel all-too real. In the end, William did not care much for the post he was given. He felt just as bad as before, but the elbow room was welcome.

A corporal by the name of Jeffreys meandered into Steele's dugout at a later than usual time to wake the sleeping officer. The time keeping of men at this part of the line was already slightly more relaxed than it should have been. It was an uneventful period of the war for most of the division of South Essex light infantry, so discipline was slightly below par. It was the corporal's duty to wake up the commanding officer of the line when it was time, and he was doing his job. Luckily for William, this corporal did this duty in a rather lighter fashion and rather than making a loud noise, Jeffreys calmly set to heating up some water for a rather makeshift tea in the dugout. The underground room had enough ventilation for such a shaded comfort; it had two entrances with seven steps down to the dugout. Jeffreys had banked on a slow method of waking William up so he could spend a little longer in what seemed like the presidential suite in a hotel in the middle of a war.

William stirred himself awake, slightly faster than he desired and looked to see the corporal hard at work fixing together a rather watery breakfast. Before he could give his customary warm greeting, he glanced down to notice that he had fallen asleep with an old picture of Emmanuelle pressed in his palm. She would hate it if she knew that he used her memory to fall asleep, but that would be a secret he might keep to himself. He smiled with the memory of her, but that smile was stilted as it always was because the memory of this woman was not so straight forward. He had left things back at home rather less stable than he would have liked, and it was not all of his making.

William was of a slightly lower class to Emmanuelle's parents and though he would try to brush it off, it was always of great concern to him. The middle classes of England were not so well established as to attract the total acceptance of the upper classes, but it was William's persistence that allowed him to court the young girl. She had fallen for him and though it was some time ago that William had last heard her admit it, the feeling was still there. Emmanuelle's father was the real trouble and though not an authoritarian gentleman, there always loomed the threat of tutting in the daughter's ear. Emmanuelle was a woman of her own mind, but what time does to people William was all too familiar. William remembered with vivid accuracy one of the last moments he and Emmanuelle shared together before his most recent deployment to Belgium. Her father was there and was in a more unusual state of speaking his mind. "You cannot expect my daughter to wait around for your return, that might not come! Unburden her with emotion and let her go about her life in peace!"

It was not a shock for William to hear, but what was the shock was Emmanuelle's motionless response, passive as to suggest that she was not in full disagreement of her father. William noticed this and pleaded his case knowing full well that his words would fall on deaf ears. The final goodbyes exchanged between the pair betrayed hesitancy from Emmanuelle whilst William was just as sure about his feelings towards her as when he first saw her. He left on that day with doubt, and the time was only served to let that doubt fester in his mind. This was evident in the fact that the picture he was holding of Emmanuelle had a significant thumb dent in it from his more than stern grip on it. He was worried.

He fastened the picture into his breast pocket on his tunic and stirred awake. The cool air he expected to breathe was much warmer to his surprise, and this was not due to the steam from the kettle. The air was warmer and that meant the spring had finally arrived. To many this would be a welcome omen, and William would remember with fondness his parents and their happiness at feeling such a change. The fields would awaken once again ready for a great year of sewing and reaping. But this was war and the warmer weather only meant one thing; the general would try to make for another push.

That was the realities of the Great War. Good weather made for itchy soldiers, nervous as the dispatches from the rear would reach the front. It could be an order to stand fast. It could be an order to expect an attack. Worst of all, an order could come through to fix bayonets. No one envied the role of the dispatch runner, though there was the odd soldier that would be more than prepared to shoot the messenger after such a long time in the line.

William stirred for his morning drink. "Jeffreys, you've outdone yourself again."

"Thank you, sir,", Jeffreys responded, clearing his throat. "I'll have something warm for you soon. Mind you, you won't need to warm yourself up too much. Changeable wind, south-westerly". He noticed William's extra leg room on the bed and snorted a bit. He had noticed this before but didn't make a habit of remembering. William was a bit shorter than regulation beds accommodated for and was thus a bit shorter than most of the soldiers. It was always better to be shorter, less of you to hit, as one or two would say.

William swung his legs around dangling them over the bed, wishing for a moment that he was sitting on a wooden pier reaching into a river. Such wistful thoughts constantly plagued William. He knew they were useless and only served to remind him of home and curse his existence in the front line. It was always best to forget the better days; it was the only way to really survive where rats thrived. He stretched his arm out at the piping hot mug of tea and rested it on his lap. He looked around the room to check that it was still in order and the rain hadn't got through. He was house-proud and wanted to keep it that way, even if a corporal with very muddy boots was inside, messing up the décor and the mood. Too late to tell him to do something about it. The damage had been done.

Jeffreys noticed William glaring at his boots but decided not to say anything, hoping that avoiding the subject of muddy boots might get him out of trouble. "See they still haven't sent you your pips yet" he said as he gestured towards William. "Seems like you keep getting forgotten. Couple of the boys and I would be alright with trying to fashion a bullet or two into some shiny things to pin onto your jacket. They won't do but they'll at least make the jacket seem a bit weightier as if the real ones were there. They'd also take a good shine in the sun, lighting you up like a Christmas tree. Perfect for letting Jerry know where you are".

William gestured with his hand that he wanted Jeffreys to stop talking. William was far too engrossed in his tea to care about the thinly veiled barb that was coming his way. He stood up and made for one of the entrances and leant on the wooden wall, looking out. The rain smelt strong, indicating that it had been pouring for at least a good hour without

7

stopping. At least it would mean that there would be not much action going on today, certainly not around that part of the line. The clouds were dark, ominous but not untoward. William liked the rain. It made him feel cosy and it vindicated his efforts to make his dugout cosier than it needed to be.

He turned back in and looked at his desk. It had unfinished letters of condolences he had strategically left to do for later and thought it might be a good idea to finish them during the downpour. One soaking walk up and down a section or two and he would come back and get stuck into the grizzly business. He had taken the trouble to outline a bit more in his letters about the details of how people died thinking it would give the soon-to-be grieving families a sense of those final moments their son, husband or father had alive. Nothing would make this task better. He thought he might walk up and down a few more sections in the rain instead to delay this task. He slid his feet into his boots and gave them a good wiggle to bribe his circulation to hurry up.

"Any word from the bosses?" Jeffreys asked, giving away a slight tone of dread. William shook his head and went for his steel helmet. His officer's cap was still soaked through from his last sojourn in the deluge yesterday and it was still drying. His helmet was more cumbersome, but it would serve him better. He fastened the straps around his chin and looked outside.

"How are the lookouts?" William asked. He was always asking about the state of his men. He believed that grumbling men made for a lesser quality of soldier and favoured dealing with any grumbling immediately.

"They're to be relieved in just under fifteen minutes. It's chucking it down out there so they're probably checking their watches all of the time".

"Make it ten minutes until the changeover".

Jeffreys nodded and shuffled out into the rain. William looked on outside with his tea. He motioned to leave but realised that taking tea out into the rain was probably a bit of a mistake. So many things to do, he thought. He drank it quickly, retching a bit from its inferior taste and set the mug aside on the desk. He buttoned up his tunic to the top and stepped outside.

His trench was about fifty yards from the front lines, but he was by no means out of danger. The local section of the front was very flat, the land did not make for good vantage points against the Germans. His section was vulnerable to many forms of assault. They had owed their prolonged stay in this part of Belgium due to the winter months. It would not take a major German attack to dislodge the battalion from their winter digs. William often sighed at the hopelessness of this situation, knowing all too well that he would be back in Ypres soon. The third battle of Ypres that ended with the taking of a useless village a couple of miles to the north never seemed like a sustainable push and this was well known to Major Steele and his men. It made William's efforts to cosy up his dugout all the more bizarre.

William meandered around the trench, soaked to the brim with mud and wood. It seemed as if the entire trench was sinking into the Belgian abyss. The winter months had frozen the mud but now it seemed as if the whole process was recommencing. William passed by soldiers in great woollen coats leaning against wooden slats desperately trying to save their cigarettes from premature extinguishing from the rain. They nodded towards him in their customary lacklustre fashion as a mark of respect and the odd private would touch the rim of their helmet. William was used to this by now. After all, his hybrid status as a man too posh to be relatable to the other ranks and too common to be considered one of the well-to-do officers was well-known to all. But William had shown great valour in combat in his year and a half at the coal face of the war. He wore his medals and ribbons with pride. William had earned respect, but he never stood out and that counted for something with the South Essex boys. To make it all a bit more complicated, William wasn't even from Essex, and that was well-known too.

William trudged in his boots from section to section, giving the odd wet pat on the back to soggy soldiers as he passed by. He seldom said anything on these walks and today would be no exception. The rain was exceptionally heavy so people might not hear him anyway. William had a somewhat louder than usual voice, but he used it sparingly. The idea of people shouting 'what?!' to each other as they tried in vain to hear what each other was saying was enough to put William off opening his mouth outside of the dugout, especially if there wasn't anything worth saying.

The odd artillery shot could be heard far off but it was nothing that many took notice of. William was expecting some information to be passed as to where this was coming from as a curtesy note, but in this rain, he would forgive runners taking their time to deliver such a message. He instead walked through the trenches a bit closer to the line to see if he could hear anything in no-man's-land. He would never forgive himself if he had not done this every day just in case he missed hearing the cry of a German charge or the cries of a wounded man out there. He made this little journey almost every day for the last couple of months he was in the front line and not once did he hear anything of note. But he always thought that the one day he did not check would be the one day there would be something worth hearing. Today would be no exception.

As William shrugged his shoulders, loosening the uncomfortable feeling on his shoulders from his heavy tunic, he noticed the glint of the tops of a few rifle guns about twenty yards down the line. He thought it might be some late soldiers hurrying their way to their lookout stations ready to relieve the now-drenched observation posts. He thought little of it and carried on his soggy way through the communication trench. He looked back and noticed the rifle tops poking out of the top of the trench was coming closer to him and he could hear a bit of a scuffle. These things happened but he kept his gaze this time and raised the front of his helmet. They were coming closer, stopping every now and again and then making their way. This was irregular. He decided to alter his path.

He walked away from the front-line trenches back towards his own digs and peered down where the noise was coming from. The footsteps seemed urgent, and he heard the odd 'that way' murmured. He walked more purposefully and suddenly saw three soldiers in full rifle and pack, but their insignias gave away the oddity of the situation. They were from a different battalion further down the line. They had concerned looks and William noticed that they had hot-footed here for a good while as their boots were covered in mud. Behind them was an officer in a soggy cap. It was Major Henry Forbes, who similarly had a concerned look on his face. William smiled; it was good to see a friendly face. He had not seen Henry in the last two times he was on leave. William let a smile eek out.

Henry noticed William standing there in his helmet and tunic, unarmed and with a semi-grin attached to his face. He made straight for

10

the acting Major, overtaking the three men who were accompanying him. As he got closer William's smile vanished as Henry did not look like he was in any mood for a friendly catch up. It would be business and that would be all. Nevertheless, as Henry approached William stuck his arm out to shake Henry's hand. This was ignored.

"William. Good to see you. Urgent business, where is your dugout?" Henry dictated with no hesitation. William turned around and walked purposefully guiding the serious party back to his little welcome home. He went down the stairs first and they came in very soon after. He saw the party drag a lot of mud in and he sighed. Some people just didn't care about the house-proud.

Henry unbuttoned his tunic and revealed a map underneath that he was hiding from the rain. He cleared William's desk, knocking his still-warm tea mug off the table. Henry stretched out the map revealing its contents. It was a map of the entire western front with red marks hastily drawn on certain sections. One of the three soldiers weighed down the sides of the map with whatever he could find of William's things whilst the other two stood by each entrance guarding and looking outside every now and again. William glanced to the entrance and noticed Corporal Jeffreys poke his head round. They made eye contact, but William just shook his head, silently indicating for Jeffreys to go. He made for the desk, sighing once again at the mess the party had made.

"OK, William. It's bad. This is urgent stuff that's been happening for the last day or two." Henry gestured to the sector of the line in France close to where the British and French armies met. "The Germans are pushing, and they've done a damn good job of it too. Almost everything we gained around Bapaume is lost, Peronne is probably lost too. High command is ordering everything heavy be transported back over the Somme River. Albert is being evacuated of divisional headquarters and right now there is no telling just how bad this could be". At each point, Henry gestured to where he was referring to. William noticed the crude circles drawn. It was clear that this news had just been received".

"Why didn't we hear anything about this sooner?" William asked with a slight degree of urgency.

"The Germans have cut communication wires all over the place. That's what has **HQ** so worried. This is clearly a big operation. Jerry's really pulled out the stops for this. We tried to wire something to you, but nothing was getting through." Henry gestured to the map again. "Look how much we've already lost, William. They say there are thousands of enemy soldiers swarming all over the place. They've overrun strong areas before they've had a chance to fire back. I haven't a clue what's going on exactly here. It's as if they've discovered a way of just walking through us".

"What are our orders?"

"Retreat of all important personnel and material back. We will leave a strengthened skeleton force here."

William's eyes darted to Henry in an annoyed fashion. "Retreat? Where to? We've only been here a few months!"

"Back to Ypres. Our section is too vulnerable to enemy attacks so we're pre-empting it. We're too exposed here in this bulge in the line. General Gough and Plumer want us back in Ypres now. Make the necessary orders and then come with us. We can go together".

William felt a wave of depression hit him. His battalion had stayed here during the harsh winter months after a bloody battle in which he had to see his old commander hauled away and now it was about to be given back for nothing. He looked around at his dugout, his efforts wasted in his eyes. He knew he would not even be able to bring back a fifth of the things he had stored here. He looked at the now-muddy floor and thought to himself that the place was mildly ruined already. He had a consoling after-thought shoot through his mind with the sense of comfort that he was going to go back with his friend. Clouds and silver linings, he thought.

"We'll wait for you out by the aid station. Don't be long. We need to go now!" Henry barked the orders, pulled the map from the desk letting fly the makeshift weights and made for the exit with his party. As Henry left the sound of close-range artillery fire could be heard. Henry had truly brought bad news and bad omens with him. Henry's party vanished leaving William scrambling for his backpack, rifle and anything worth taking with him.

He grabbed for bullets and bandages, table cutlery and tinned meat. He hesitated to bring the tea after the less-than-desirable taste it left him with not long ago but thought of small mercies that were needed at this heightened time. After a few more necessities were packed in he reached for his diary, stuffed with noted and thoughts that he might find fun to read back in better times. In his haste he dropped the diary and it fell to the floor, opening itself as it collided with the ground. William slipped his thumb underneath and dragged the book back up and place it in his backpack. As he did, he noticed the page that it had opened. He glanced at the word 'Emmanuelle' that was written and for a moment allowed himself to peak in to see what he had written.

'*I think of her again and again. Her slightly raised nose that she hates, her brown hair magically getting lighter with each new summer, her eyes which are never half open, always fully as if to take in the magnificent aura of the day. To hear that voice that sounds like it sings again. I hope so too, my darling. One day she will write back to me. It is because of the cold. I can't wait for spring*'.

William's mind whirred again, anxious but for a moment less about the news of a German attack miles away, and more about the love of his life who he had not heard from. He had gotten through the days and weeks without hearing from her by blaming it on the cold and the idea of a fantastic message making up for lost time coming very soon. He worried that this sudden movement back to Ypres might cause such a letter to be lost.

He also let out a slight chuckle. He had long waited for spring to set in and at the time it finally had there seemed to be a German attack coming. How wrong he was. That chuckle was enough to dislodge the anxiety long enough for him to plunge the diary into his backpack. He hoisted his back on his back, took his rifle, buttoned his pistol to its holster and made to leave. He took one last look at his little winter abode and with a sigh turned his back on it, leaving it to enjoy the warm air inside it one last time.

William made for Jeffreys who was strategically standing away from the dugout. He was looking up and grimacing. "Looks like Jerrys sending us over some umbrellas. Aren't very good now, are they?" He joked. His humour was never perfect, and it was not going to break the anxiety William was feeling at the moment.

Jeffreys noticed William was decked out in his attire and frowned. "Off on a scavenger hunt, sir?"

"Corporal. Give the orders for two of the three companies to make ready and retire back to Ypres. Skeleton defence in force to remain. Got it?" William ordered in a sullen and apologetic tone.

"Yes sir, but, retiring? Why?"

"No time to explain. We will be back. This is a precaution, that's all". In fairness, William believed this to be the case too. Bad military news would always be followed by specific orders to spike guns and to burn papers. None had been given so this felt like anxious generals wanting to prepare better defences for attack and possible counterattacks should the matter require it. Jeffreys sighed and went his way up the line to relay the orders. William turned around and did the same going down the line.

Fifteen minutes later, as Forbes and his men waited impatiently by the nearby aid station, William popped out from the rear-most trench with more and more soldiers following behind. By this time artillery fire was raising its noise levels and wet mounds of earth began to jump up in the air a few hundred metres away. It caught the eye of most people around the aid station as wounded men were loaded onto red cross trucks with mechanics desperately trying to keep rainwater out of the engines. The artillery fire didn't feel like the prelude to a German attack, it was more designed to pepper the retreating parties that were spotted by German observation posts.

"Now's a good time, William!" Henry shouted. He was clearly impatient and getting concerned, more about the time they were expected back in Ypres rather than the sporadic artillery fire. William caught up to him and they made for the well-trodden paths back down the slightly sloped hill. William looked around and noticed familiar shell holes and mounds where he and his men had ducked and weaved around several months ago to get to where they were now leaving. The departing men didn't need to be reminded of the futility of this war, but the immediate thought couldn't help but pass through their minds as they made the half-day's walk back to the old salient.

Artillery shells fizzed overhead. William jogged over to Henry's side. "How have you been keeping, Henry?" He asked, attempting to take the opportunity to reconnect with his friend.

"Knee's been playing up a bit. Too much sitting around." Henry gestured to the ground. "Careful with the barbed wire there".

William looked down but that only made him press his foot into the little coil of wire which dug into his trousers, gently grazing the skin around his shin. He sighed with annoyance as he had to stop, letting Henry carry on ahead of him as he tried to untangle himself. He was less annoyed about his uniform getting scuffed than he was about being interrupted with trying to talk to his friend. This was a momentary setback, but he knew that would have half a day for him to try to reconnect.

As William tore himself free of the little stumbling block, he looked up to see where his friend was. Henry was thirty or so feet away. William blinked, and felt the force of a small explosion ahead of him during that blink. It was only small, but William mentally checked to see if he could feel anything. He was fine. Nothing felt warm or painful. He looked up. A couple of men were on the ground, not dead but shaken. Henry was down too but his leg was shaking. William rushed over to see what happened.

"Bloody typical. Bloody typical!" Henry exclaimed, clutching his left wrist. It was bleeding profusely. A nearby soldier applied a bandage to it.

"You alright there, Major?" One of his party asked.

"Yes, I can still move it, but it hurts like the devil!" Henry winced.

"Bad luck there, Hen." William tutted. William was never good at consoling people or finding the right words to say in stressful situations. He then realised he had forgotten the notes of condolences he had left on his desk. He blamed it on the fact that they were swept away during the map debacle.

The soldier kneeling by him inspected the bandage. "Yep, it's soaking right through. You'll have to be seen to". He gestured towards a nearby soldier with a red cross on his arm. "Take him back with you. The wound needs treating.

What annoying luck, William thought. He was now deprived of reconnecting with his friend. A selfish thought, but he felt like he was owed one or two. He watched Henry get hoisted into a red cross truck. Henry was driven away with the groaning chorus of the wounded as every bounce in the muddy road sent more howls into the air. William kept his eyes on Henry for as long as he could as he carried on trudging through muddy fields. It was bad luck for Henry to catch a bit from a shell, but he would by no means be the only one. The ensuing onslaught going on at this time would be much more tragic for many people. This little annoyance would be nothing compared with what might be coming their way.

William thought of the silver linings of clouds again and looked up. It was grey and the rain was incessant. In the end the rain would help diffuse the explosions of many artillery shells and it was the perfect weather to retire from the battlefield. But William was on his own amidst a small sea of retiring soldiers. His mind therefore wandered to what on earth was going on to the south, and hoping for the best, hoping that this offensive would fizzle out like all of the other offensives of the war, and it would keep itself away from him.

Chapter 2

"And if I catch you with this again, I will shoot you right where you stand" shouted the lieutenant at a cowering soldier. Such anger and ruthlessness were commonplace in the French army and to many a soldier this was one of many such threats issued to the lower ranks on a daily basis. It served to further annoy anyone around but by now even the threats lost their sting. Threatening a man condemned to die in battle to death was not as scary as it might have seemed in better times.

The French 41st division had spent many months defending Rheims further south but the sudden German spring offensive which had begun over a month ago had forced a sudden redeployment of men and material further north, almost defending the roads to Paris. The division was also very battle-hardened; their four-week stint fighting in Verdun in 1916 had made them all very aware of what real fighting was like. The problem with many in the 41st division was that they were all exhausted to a man, and the 'sacred union' binding the 'poilu' soldier to all other social strata of the army and nation was hardly holding strong in the minds of the common man at the front.

Moral was the key issue in the French army and no more was this more obvious than the 41st division. It was nearing the end of May and already over twenty men had been executed for desertion and sedition in the division alone. So, when that lieutenant shouted at the top of his lungs at the cowering soldier on the floor of the trench many thought that it might be another chalking up of executions for the month. To the surprise of a few that soldier got off with a last warning.

The men in the division had been retreating for what seemed like several miles now. The advance of the Germans in the first drive over the Somme River had frightened many thinking that it would threaten to split the British and French armies. To their relief the fighting largely subsided but at the cost of miles and miles of land. Amiens held which was a sign that things would not be so bad. The second offensive in Belgium threatened Ypres but it held. The key areas would be held, and Soissons would be the key area they would hold this day. Retreat did not seem so bad, but it was not good for many who could not help but see that victory now seemed further and further away.

One such soldier who did not see the optimism of a few of his comrades was private Maurice Renaudin. He was a copywriter in Sedan before the war and had made a modest but unremarkable living trying to flog his books of medieval tales onto passers-by in the town. Neighbours used to smirk as he walked by, whispering about how his house was more like a library than anything else because it housed so many unsold copies of 'Chevalier de Esprit', his first book which cost him more to print than to sell. A bitter man, he was always thin and detested the fashion of French style. He wore a long coat even when it was warm and though he was in his early thirties people used to guess how long he had until his 60th birthday. He kept to himself, shaking his fist at frivolity and waste though secretly he was jealous. He wanted to be the knight astride a mighty castle in his books but had to settle for mediocrity in a cul-de-sac by the Meuse River. He had visited the Argonne woods to the south many times to get away from the silently jeering public. He would often spend so long there that people would be shocked of his return. It was believed that at some point he would be accepted by wood nymphs and taken to his paradise underneath the trees where no one could hear him.

His parents fared no better with him. His father, Leon Renaudin, was a tough disciplinarian and fiercely patriotic. He was young when the Prussians came and defeated the French forces and from then on believed that France should have sought revenge at the next opportunity. Then again, Leon was just a magistrate and hardly in any position to see his desires through. Maurice's ambivalence towards France even from an early age greatly annoyed his father. Leon did not last long in Sedan and left home when Maurice was fifteen to work in Paris. Seeing his father leave was the last time Maurice ever saw him. His mother on the other hand was kind and caring, but she too was a French patriot. She raised Maurice to respect and marvel at nature, a lesson he would never forget. She too saw in her only son the mark of a dreamer and a man without substance, but she persisted in teaching him the good of life before and now. He had respected his mother, but he never believed her. When the war began, she stayed in Sedan and since spent the last few years living under German occupation. He had not heard a word from her since he left home to join the army. He was family-less and friendless at the beginning of the war.

It took the war to occur for him to find any sense of friends and he found them in the army. He was never one to jump to the aid of his nation but when the Germans bore down on Sedan, he had little choice but to fight to get it back. He even found love whilst on leave in Epernay. She was a tall dark-haired Parisian who had moved to the town to help serve food to soldiers on leave. He had never talked to her, he loved her from afar. She fitted beautifully into his story, as if she had been the inspiration for the love interests in his book all this time. On leave he would always go to the same place and ask for the same food and drink, hoping she would remember him. She never did, but he thought it would happen the next time. Her laugh was like a violin, but she laughed with others and not him. His jealousy always took the better of him which convinced him that he was not in the right mind to talk to her. This repeated over and over again.

He had no such trouble with talking with fellow soldiers in the front line. Finally, he was surrounded by people going through the same experiences as him. Finally, he could talk about things that others could relate to and found that he was often describing the problems and issues people around him agreed with. He found he could tell them what to think because he related to their minds better than any officer or newspaper could. They listened to him, and he spoke. He was articulate, occasionally stopping himself from letting his emotions lead him to tear up whilst talking. He would get into trouble occasionally for voicing his grumbling so vociferously, but he found a way of staying silent long enough to let the issue dissipate. Like clockwork, he would begin waxing lyrical about the trials of the average soldier again.

This little gift of speech was only drowned out by major developments in the fighting. In Verdun he hardly made a sound, saving it for the long journey back on the 'Sacred Way' road from the sieged citadel to Bar Le Duc. In Rheims he made a name for himself as 'Renaudin, the Goat of Rheims' for his stubborn feelings on everything wrong with the military and social situations. But he was respected for his fighting and earned a few ribbons for his trouble, though he was never promoted due to his infamous views on military hierarchy. Officers would shrug when they were questioned over their refusal to promote him, replying with thinly veiled contempt "Well, it's what he would have wanted".

Maurice and the men around him had found themselves far from Rheims with the Germans not far away. They had all witnessed the new German soldiers with orders to simply jump into French trenches without warning, without heavy packs or materials, and to cause havoc, clearing a way for the great military machine to follow behind. There were rumours that the new enemy were ghosts of dead Germans from the eastern front coming to the aid of their live comrades in the west. Maurice laughed off the idea in public, but in private he too tried to come to terms with the idea of ghosts coming for him.

"Crown Prince Wilhelm is coming!" shouted a sentry on top of the fire step looking out into the wasteland. Maurice and a few others poked their heads out. It was dusk, but there seemed to be shining glints of light coming from the darkness. An officer ran over, weaving around the many soldiers in the hastily dug trench, barely held up with slats of sodden wood. The officer jumped up onto the fire step as the soldiers around stared up in fear and anxiety at what might be coming.

The officer peaked over for a few seconds, knelt down and punched the sentry in the stomach. "There's nothing coming! That's just your eyes playing tricks on you again." He barked. He went to step back down and noticed the eyes of dozens of soldiers looking at him. He stared back at them, taking in the sight of worried eyes watching his every move. "You're tired. We're all tired" he orated. "But here is where we will make our stand. We go no further back and when they realise that they will go away and we will be able to sleep again!" He stepped back down and moved amongst the silent soldiers back up the line.

Maurice looked round to see that the officer had gone. He noticed that the officer was a Major. It was odd for a Major to be this close to the front line, and this fact only served to make the soldiers more worried. The only reason for a Major to be here was if the situation was so bad that the high command was now sending spare people to the front. He leant over to nearby soldiers standing next to him and whispered, "I thought he said that we go no further back, but he is making his way to the rear trenches".

"One rule for one, one rule for another" a soldier whispered back. A muffled hum of agreement followed. Generally, there was silence amongst the soldiers. The next battle was only a matter of time, no matter how many times officers might reassure them that nothing was happening.

They took turns standing on the fire step looking over the battlefield waiting for any sign of an attack. Each man would take their twenty minutes and then rotate, and this would repeat itself down the line. Maurice took his turn and looked over. Nothing was moving in his view, but he knew that behind the darkness thousands of German soldiers were taking their positions for the next attack. He strained his vision, thinking to himself that it might be a good idea to invest in some spectacles when he could. Abandoned carts and farmhouses were all he could see. He wandered if a German or two might be hiding behind one, or a sniper. They could easily see his helmet and aim a bit below it. Maurice took off his helmet.

Dusk gave way to night and the morning sun was widely expected at any minute. No one fell asleep but yawns could be heard in ten second intervals. Many soldiers had slumped to the ground trying at least to take the weight off their feet. Some were hauled up by a passing officer but doing that for everyone seemed like a fruitless task. Still, there was no sign of a fight about to start. The only thing concerning most soldiers at this time was the fact that most had used up their stash of cigarettes during the retreat and subsequent hasty digging of the trenches they were now sitting in.

Maurice looked up into the slowly brightening sky. He was convinced a bird was flying overhead and, in his mind, he thought that little bird was flying away because it was startled by sudden movements, probably by some Germans. Little did he know, he was right. From the corner of his eye, he saw the sentry at the time jolt his head back, his arms flying into the air straight after. The man careered back into the trench, falling on two others. He was shot clean through the left eye. He was still. One man shrieked as he looked at the wound "That's a short-range shot!" He then clambered up to the fire step himself and looked out. He too was shot, almost instantly and fell back into the trench. The attack was coming.

All down the line, whistles could be heard. "Allemande!" "Germans!" They are coming!" Shouts rang around the entire line, men jumped up to fire steps and shallow parts of the trenches lining their rifles up, some with bayonets and some without. Men jumped up and fell down in almost perfect synchronisation. It was clear; the Germans were much closer than many were expecting.

Maurice swung his rife from his shoulder to his hands, shaking which was customary for anyone sleep-deprived in battle, and took his turn to jump into a space on the fire step recently vacated by a soldier who was now writhing in agony clutching his shoulder nearby. He popped his head over the parapet and saw grey helmets bobbing up and down in shell holes and craters all over the place. He tried to take aim at a German soldier running sideways but had no time to react as the grey figure instantly dropped to safety into a shell hole. They were coming towards them quickly, moving so quickly most shots fired by Maurice's comrades were harmlessly nestling into the mud.

He swung his rifle to the left, then the right, trying to find a better target but there were too many to choose from and too little time to zone in on them. He knelt back down and fixed his bayonet to his rifle and then leapt straight back up. As he did, he noticed dead in front of him not twenty feet away was a German soldier, his helmet masking his eyes from the pale light of flares shooting up from the French rear. Maurice could even see the man smirking. Why was he smirking; Maurice thought. He saw why. The man was holding a steel grenade. Maurice tried to shoot the grenade from his hand. He missed. He reloaded. Again, a miss. He made three attempts, but it was in vain. The German solider threw the grenade and it soared towards Renaudin's friends. Maurice stumbled back, falling back into the trench onto a passing soldier. As he looked up, he saw the explosion. The grenade fell just in front of the parapet, sending the soldiers to the left and right of his now vacated space on the fire step all over the place. One or two soldiers jumped to fill in the gap.

Maurice was hauled to his feet by a passing officer. It was the Major again. His face was red, and he was bleeding from his left ear. His Adrian helmet had black streaks around it and his tunic was singed around the shoulders. The Major barked almost inaudible orders to him and flung him back towards the fire step. Maurice looked around again and noticed that some men were no longer falling back into the trench with wounds or

22

injuries. Some were jumping back, front first, in perfect condition. They were running.

Maurice gestured to jump back onto the fire step. By now explosions could be heard. The French artillery had finally woken up and were trying to help defend the sector. It was now totally inaudible, but Maurice's ears were never good at hearing anyway. He tried to jump up but slipped and fell back into the trench. He went to try again but looked up to one of the soldiers gesturing towards him, wagging his finger as if to tell him to stop. The man was subsequently hit by a bullet in their helmet and fell down himself, but he was alright. Maurice darted his eyes around. He looked left and through the melee of men shooting, he saw the flash of grey between figures of blue. It was unmistakeable. The Germans had made it to the trench.

He gazed over to the left, then to the right. Steadily, blue colours were being interwoven with grey ones. Grey tunics were becoming more and more obvious inside the long trench itself. Maurice looked up once again and this time jumped right back up onto the fire step which was now much less populated with shuddering men. He looked over and saw hundreds of German soldiers running towards him. He ducked down and looked left and right again. He made a rough mathematical calculation; he saw more German soldiers than he did French right now. French soldiers were already breaking and more would soon. German soldiers were already inside the trenches, so they were now largely safe from French machine guns that by now were firing intermittently as if the gunners themselves were unsure whether to stay or to go.

Maurice made up his mind. The matter was hopeless. The line was breaking. The Germans were coming. He jumped down from the fire step for the last time and made a left towards the nearest path to the rear. He stumbled over dead and dying men falling back from the fire step. He turned the corner and tripped over a dying man on the ground blocking his path. He shunted the man onto his side, facing his back against the wall of the connecting trench. It was the Major. He was motioning with his mouth to say something, but nothing was coming out. The man's final order would not be heard by Maurice or anyone.

Maurice ran as fast as he could, clutching his rifle to the rear. By now he was joined by dozens and dozens of other like-minded soldiers retreating in full flight, running as fast as was possible. He ducked and weaved as artillery shells were now firing on the French front line. It was as if the artillery men had realised that the game was up and firing on their own lines would be the best course of action. He felt that if he wasn't going to be shot by a German he would be finished by a Frenchman. He allowed that single thought to pass through his mind as he made for the rear.

He ran past a hastily made aid station now hastily making its way back. It was largely empty because the attack had come so soon and there was no point hauling out anyone of the trenches; they were in German hands now. Maurice looked around and noticed hundreds of soldiers running, some with and some without rifles, for the next line of defences they hope they would come across. Officers were desperately trying to round up retreating soldiers to get them to help with yet another rear-guard fight. Few were listening.

Maurice saw as a poilu punched an officer shouting at him to return to the battle. He looked around and saw sedition on a monumental scale, as men ran, some running over officers shouting and waving pistols in the air. He thought what he would do if an officer got in the way of his running. He thought that it would be a good idea to retain his rifle, so it did not look like he was deserting. He found a few other soldiers running together and ran with them. If he was in a retreating pack, it would be much harder to stop them with a single officer.

They ran away until the battle sounds became duller and soldiers around them started to walk fast. It was difficult to run with heavy weights on one's shoulders, but panic does strange things to ones' strength. Maurice thought himself so lucky. The battle was not long. It felt like it went by in a flash. One of his little pack of soldiers mentioned that the battle lasted for around half an hour before most turned tail and ran. He found that he was walking along with men from his own battalion and felt better.

"Look, it's the Goat!" pointed out one soldier of the group. They all looked around at Maurice and sniggered. "I bet you have many things to say about this now!"

"The same thing I said Rheims", Maurice retorted. "We break, we fall back, we think again. For the generals at the back, they have yet to start thinking". There was a small, muffled chuckle.

"Look." Another one exclaimed. "This is bad. I've never seen so many retreat like this before. We broke too easily this time".

It was true. Though the French army was low on morale it would fight long enough to slow the Germans down. This time it seemed as if the whole division was retreating 'en masse'. The French army was breaking and all around them was the evidence. No stomach to fight, a fear of the enemy and a lack of trust in the high command were all contributing to this and everyone around trudging back to a safer line were feeling it. It seemed as if the end would finally come, not with a great final battle, but with a French whimper.

"Where is Commander Foch now?" smirked another soldier. Maurice looked around and thought to himself that the Commander-in-Chief was probably still asleep in his bed.

A solider came up to Maurice and put his arm round his shoulder. He looked to see who it was. It was the soldier who was being shouted at by the officer last night. Maurice thought that this man was dead anyway as soon as an officer found him again. The soldier unbuttoned the middle of his tunic and brought out something; it was the something he was being shouted at for having by the officer. He pressed it into Maurice's free hand. He looked down.

It was a little red book.

Chapter 3

The shell of a town called Peronne stood smouldering by the banks of the remains of the Somme River. Its low medieval castle was all that people could recognise to discern that this town used to be called Peronne. The cobbled streets twisted in agony like the thorns on a rose. The evidence of a town fought over repeatedly could be seen around it with temporary gravesites for both sides scattered around it.

The town had been recaptured in the first German drive of the offensive dubbed the 'Ludendorff Offensive' by some, or the 'Kaiser's Battle' by others depending on who they believed was really in charge. The front which used to just envelop the town was now miles away. Even Albert, a town well to the west and mostly held by the British army, was in German hands from the beginning of April. Though one could hear the boom of artillery not far away, the town itself was granted an eerie silence that it had not heard for years.

One such place where noises could still be heard was in the ruins of the medieval castle itself. A temporary aid station had been set up a week after the town itself had been taken and it had grown to accommodate just over a thousand casualties. There were groans and moans as German soldiers clung to their wooden beds or stretchers begging for the agony to stop, even if it meant a short and sharp end. There were more minor injuries being treated than serious ones, but as the fourth offensive began it was difficult to choose who to treat and who not to treat.

There was one such patient, resting within the ruined medieval walls, who made no sound at all from the moment he was delivered. He had participated in the third German offensive at Soissons and received a painful shrapnel wound to the right side of his head. This wound would have been avoided with a helmet and he did indeed have one on at the time. An artillery shell had burst in front of him, breaking his helmet strap and flinging it backwards. Another shell burst nearby and that was when he was wounded. It was the kind of experience that would make anyone lose any faith in leather straps or the idea that there was only really one bullet for everyone. He had received two.

He had been bandaged up well. The wound was light, mostly only skin deep, but the wound was so long that the bandage had to cover a lot of the right side of his face, including his right eye which survived the ordeal but had left him with blurred sight in that eye. The bandage looked like an oversized eye patch. He had refused opiates to numb the pain, insisting that the medicine in short supply should go to more worthy injuries. He was receiving preferential treatment and despised it.

This was because his name was Captain Fritz Georg von Falkenhayn, the 28-year-old son of the discredited General Erich von Falkenhayn. His father was chief of the German general staff from 1914 to 1916 and was the commander for the ill-fated Verdun offensive. Erich had been replaced by Paul von Hindenburg and his quartermaster Erich Ludendorff, both of whom had masterminded the offensive occurring at the time.

Nonetheless, the 'von Falkenhayn' name was still respected, and this was extended to the son and daughter. This was more of a burden than a help to the son who felt the great weight of expectation on him both to do his militaristic father proud, but also to do right by the family name in the field of battle at least. But there he was, as the crucial period of the offensive was taking place, looking up to the sky outside in the light recovery area, cursing his bad luck.

Fritz was a young member of the Prussian aristocracy. Marshalled from a young age to be a worthy successor to his father's estate, titles and reputation, he excelled in his studies and his work. This was in part due to Fritz's devotion to his parents. He had been incredibly aware of his privileged upbringing and had sought to devote his life to finding a way of modernising that privilege to positively affect those he came into contact with and to find a way of bringing the ancient Prussian heritage into a new world, especially if it was peaceful. The war put an indefinite halt to that.

Fritz had been in the army and rose to the rank of captain in a mere two years. He never truly knew if his rapid rise in the ranks was due to his tenacity or due to his name. He had dreamed of following his father's footsteps serving the army in Asia, but the Great War shackled him to the European adventure alone. His rapid rise through the army impressed many back at home and his star rose in the upper circles of the Prussian aristocracy.

Nowhere was this more evident than in the mind of one Johanna von Kasamerik, one of the most beautiful young women in Prussia. Her family resided in castles around Germany and so she was often described as a princess without a kingdom. The only kingdom she wanted was one with Fritz in it and he duly reciprocated. They were due to be married in the late autumn of 1914, but events took shape and such a happy occasion seemed like a terrible thing to occur on the eve of war. This was especially true as the wedding venue was too close to the Russian invasion in 1914. The young couple would have to wait.

The reason why these two were to be married was, to the public, due to a long-standing love affair that would inevitably blossom into a dynasty bringing two great Prussian families together. The real reason was because Johanna had become with child with Fritz. In order to see that disgrace would not fall upon them due to the strict matters of children born out of wedlock, the two felt compelled to marry. Though the two were and always had been in love, the marriage itself had always felt slightly forced on the couple. As time passed, Johanna had her child in secret, and it would remain so until a marriage could go ahead and perhaps one or two papers could be filled in differently to the truth.

Perhaps it was due to this ordeal that Fritz in wartime was not as faithful as his soon-to-be-wife had expected. The inevitable 'forced' marriage had weighed heavily on Fritz's mind and war does strange things to people's minds anyway. This potent combination meant that his behaviour was not in line with his behaviour in peace. He frequented the delicacies of the conquered lands in Russia, France and Belgium and though this behaviour went largely unnoticed, to Fritz it was a constant source of regret and shame. It was a shame he would not so easily forget. He had decided that should he live to see it; he would leave it until peace had been found to deal with his behaviour then. He was not so sure if he would admit enjoying the pleasures of other women to his adoring Johanna or if he would simply keep it buried deep down as he had been doing for years already.

Perhaps it was for this reason that he lay still and silent in the cot in the aid station in Peronne. Perhaps he refused the opiates in order to let the pain from his wound keep him distracted from the regret and shame he had been feeling for so long now. Whatever it was, he would remain tight lipped even to his friends. He would only need to remind himself that he had no picture of his love from home anywhere in his officer's tunic. He did not want to be reminded of her in case he gave in to his base desires once again.

He had been in the aid station for just over a week, the entirety of June so far, and was starting to let the screams of agony inside the aid tents get to him. He tried to use his pillow to cover his ears whenever the cries got too much, but this was in vain. He longed for the night sky which was why he was outside most of the time so that he could distract himself further by counting as many stars in the sky that he could. He remembered as a child his mother holding him on her knee pointing up to the sky whispering "Up there is where your family is. The brighter stars are the ones who are waving back at you. When we all go, we become one of those stars and we will shine for whoever we are waving to. It will be an amazing view from up there, and they all talk to themselves about us down here. I hope you will wave to me, for I will be the shiniest star in the night sky for you". He looked for the shiniest star in the sky as he stared up from his bed in Peronne. He hoped it was not mother waving back to him. He was sure she was still alive. He had no reason to think she wasn't.

His ear pricked up as he heard shouting going on inside the aid station tent. He heard hushes and then someone giving a speech. He rolled his eyes, thinking that it was just some morale officer telling them once again to not lose hope and that the Kaiser was wishing them all a swift recovery. He had heard it before in aid stations in Russia, Belgium and France. Why would today be any different? He shuffled onto his side, giving up with looking at the stars. He did not want to think that his mother was up there. He would try to count sheep instead.

The speech did not subside. Fritz raised his head a bit and saw other men around him start to get up to go into the tent. Only one or two went in but he remained. Maybe these men hadn't heard the speech before. Maybe they wanted to hear the hearty thanks their commanding officers offered to them for their sacrifice. Fritz had been injured before, again lightly, and that coloured his mind about the note of thanks and sacrifice. He had only sacrificed smooth skin on his right leg and perhaps a nice facial feature this time. It was nothing for him to feel good about; others had sacrificed much more. He rolled on his back. The sheep had not helped.

His attempts to try to find peace in his bed were interrupted by an officer, clad in bits of mud. He burst through the opening in the tent. He was out of breath from orating inside. He looked like he had been running all the way from Berlin. It was the turn of Fritz and his compatriots outside in the recovery area to hear what this man had to say. Fritz closed his unbandaged eye in a vain effort to ignore what was about to be said.

"Brothers!" The officer shouted with passion. "The war is nearly over. We have nearly won! The French army is routed and what remains is making its final stand at Chantilly. We have taken Compiegne, Chateaux Thierry and Meaux is about to fall! The Americans have fallen back West of the Seine! The British are isolated at Amiens. We are a few miles from Paris!"

Some men raised their heads in sceptical disbelief. The men around this officer were not so easily fooled. They had heard this all before, but the officer carried on. "The final push is about to begin. We need every man who can carry a rifle and shoot with us at the front. This is it! We are about to win! Who is with me?!"

There was a long and awkward pause. Eyes darted around the officer as each man, some holding their injuries close to them, looked at each other. Was this man telling the truth? Was he just delirious? If this was true, why were there still streams of new intakes of injured soldiers still coming? They wanted to see proof, even Fritz, who by now was looking directly into the officer's eyes. They seemed genuine, if not slightly fanatical. After four years of war, what would possess a man to scream such untruths?

"Crown Prince Wilhelm is asking for one final push!" The officer continued. "One final push and it will all be over. I have just come from the front. You can see the Eiffel tower! I use my binoculars and I can see it. Come and see it!"

"Why should we believe you?" Squeaked one of the injured, his shoulder wrapped in pale red bandages. "Most of us came from Soissons and we did not get far."

"The French army is no more! The British are overstretched, and the Americans are falling back too far. Come, see for yourself". These were the last words the officer announced before rushing away as fast as he came to carry on spreading the news. Few were moved, and even fewer moved at all. Two men got up and walked out but Fritz was not sure if they just wanted to ask for help or if they truly believed the man.

Fritz laid back on his bed, unconvinced. He was sceptical also, as he was more hopeless than hopeful. Was this because of the anxiety and regret he felt, for the idea of the war coming to an end meant that soon he would have to pay the piper and come to terms with his infidelity to his darling Johanna. He tried to count the stars again.

An hour went by. Fritz was no closer to going to sleep than before. He was starting to feel his wound a lot more, but no nurse had been in sight for some time. He was tapped on the shoulder and thinking it was a nurse he murmured "it's hurting again".

A voice responded, "then come with us and make it hurt less". He recognised the voice, but it was not a doctor he knew. He turned round and noticed it was a solider, in full gear and helmet, towering over him. It was First Lieutenant Norman Gisevius, an officer who has been under Fritz's command for over two years. The men were kindred spirits on all things political, military styles and women. If Fritz had a brother, then Gisevius would be that brother. They had fought together and though Gisevius was a much worse shot than Fritz would have liked he was nonetheless a good man to have by anyone's side. He was as loyal as a man's dog and as such Gisevius was at his master's bed. Fritz looked at him with his eye and smiled, patting the man on the arm.

"You have a cheek coming here. You don't look injured." jokingly accused Fritz.

"Well, I have been looking for a doctor to cure me, for my feelings have been hurt. You are not with me to see the final battle!" Norman chuckled. "Are you just going to lie there and miss history being made?"

Fritz frowned; his puzzled face betrayed his scepticism. "After everything, you seriously don't believe it's all going to end soon?"

"Maybe, but it's easier to see that happening when you are marching under the Arc de Triumph." Norman retorted.

The scepticism turned to excitement. Fritz had last felt this before when Johanna first kissed him for the first time. From thinking it would never happen to suddenly believing it was happening, Fritz let out a loud laugh. He laughed just the same after Johanna kissed him. He believed and realised how his scepticism made him feel so silly. Laughing off the silliness was the best medicine for him. He bolted up right and went to get up from his bed, but he lost his balance and it took the ever-resourceful Gisevius to keep him from falling.

"It is good to see you haven't lost your sense of direction" joked Norman. "And look, you have no tunic on. Boots and uniform on and come meet me in the truck. We are heading off now and we have carriages to take us there".

"But Norman, I can't see" pointed out Fritz.

"Yes, I can see that, but God graced you with another. Use that one" confidently replied Norman as he unhooked the rifle he had on his back and leant it against the bed. "Hurry, hurry. There're only a few spaces left. You'll have to walk and if you do, you'll miss out on all the fun". And just like that, Norman was gone, leaving Fritz with the task of catching him up.

Fritz looked around for his tunic and boots which were neatly hanging by the foot of his cot. He had noticed that he wasn't feeling any pain anymore, but that thought alone brought back a painful throb or two. That would teach him to think. He dressed appropriately and made to leave, noticing that other people were watching him. As he moved for the rifle, he noticed other people getting up and dressing for battle. A wave of similar-minded actions was occurring.

One man shouted, "For Ludendorff!" Another shouted the same. Fritz was annoyed by this, for he believed that they were fighting for the Kaiser. He shouted, "For the Kaiser!" as if to remind them of the real leader.

Fritz ran out himself, leaving at least thirty other men to chase after him in a similar fashion as he was chasing after Norman. As Fritz passed by the tent, doing his best to avoid eye contact with men with more troubling injuries, he noticed his battered helmet on a shelf, burn marks faintly obvious from the last time it saw action. Next to it was an officer's cap, cleaner and in far better shape than its metal counterpart. He noticed that the strap to the steel helmet had been repaired. He decided which hat he would use. He decided to make amends with his old friend and took the steel helmet. If he could forgive the leather strap for letting him down, maybe Johanna could forgive him for letting her down.

Fritz boarded a truck, noticing that Gisevius was not there. He had taken a different truck. He looked out behind the truck itself as it started chuntering its way to the front line. He saw Peronne shrink into the distance, his little bed now just a memory. The night sky became darker and darker as smoke clouds began obscuring the stars. Fritz made a feeble wave towards the sky to say goodbye to the star that was shining at him the most, thanking it for thinking of him, just in case it was his mother. The stars blinked towards him for the last time before they were all obscured by the clouds of death.

As the truck got closer, Fritz noticed walking soldiers mentioning similar phrases in a sense of excitement. "Battle of Paris!" exclaimed one private of the 33rd Division. "Waterloo!" shouted another. There seemed to be an increased swell of excitement around, not seen since the early days of the war in 1914. There were confused faces in Fritz's truck. Most were unaware still of what was going on. One man shouted out to ask what was going on.

"The French have no more stomach for fighting. It's the end" one walking soldier shouted back. It all seemed vague and anything vague felt unreal to seasoned fighters and Fritz was one of them. He had heard enough empty optimism to disbelieve it for the rest of his life. It felt strange, as if he was in a dream. It felt as if he was being transported back in time and he would start to see the spiked helmets return to soldier's heads. Where were they being taken to? When were they being taken to? It all felt too strange.

The truck came to a juddering halt. The noise of artillery shells had been growing more and more deafening indicating that they had pretty much arrived. Soldiers in the truck began wringing their hands around their rifle shafts. One or two threw up as they contemplated entering battle again. Fritz held on to his dinner. The back plate fell down and two soldiers beckoned them to leave. They clambered out and down onto muddy ground. Boots clattered the mud over and over again as the men poured out of the truck.

It was Fritz's turn next. A solider barked for him to hurry up but noticed his rank insignia and instantly apologised and helped him down. Fritz got out, slamming his boots on the mud, and turned around. The sight he saw was nothing like he had ever thought he would ever see. The familiar battlefield was not much different to what he had seen before. Hastily erected trenches and defences were scattered all over the place. The ground itself was slightly flat, sloping downwards away from him. The view of the horizon was what was unexpected; he could see the gilded rooftops of Paris. In the distance, its top obscured by low level cloud, was the Eiffel tower. The officer at Peronne said he could only see it with his binoculars but now, even with his one eye, he could see the discernible steel struts meshing their way around each other to form the iconic symbol of France. It was more than within eyesight, it was within touching distance. Flames and flashing lights illuminated the French capital as short-range artillery peppered the outskirts. Notre Dame, the tower itself, seemed unharmed for the moment.

"Captain Falkenhayn! Glad you could join us" shouted a voice from behind. Fritz turned away from the spectacle. Otto von Below, General of the 17th Army, was sauntering his way towards him, flanked by bespectacled majors, colonels and captains alike. He seemed in a good mood. "Have you been enjoying the view?"

"I had no idea we were this close", Fritz replied, pointing back towards the amazing skyline.

"Yes, she is beautiful. About eight miles away now. Not that taking the city is our primary goal, you understand?" Below scoffed. He stood by Fritz and peered into his polished binoculars. He chuckled a bit and punched his fist in front of him. "Yes! Another strong point breached!".

"What is the goal, General?" Fritz asked, raising his voice over the sudden boom of artillery pieces making themselves heard not far away.

"This is but one of two main thrusts of attack. Here, at the foot of the capital, and Amiens. We take either of those and we will score a fatal blow. I reckon it will exhaust the enemy into peace." Below swung his arms out. "And it will be here where we will make the blow".

"What if we fail?" Fritz interjected, his scepticism putting off the General's optimism for a brief second.

"Then we will have sucked enough time and effort out of the enemy for Amiens to fall. Two divided armies will make for divided minds and that will win us the day!" the General retorted. He took off his cap exposing his bald head and scratched it. His optimism was getting the best of him and even at this historic moment he had to check his own emotions.

Fritz was startled by the rumbling of Tanks, twelve of them passing by the other side of the truck Fritz had just jumped out of. He noticed that they were clean and whirring without much difficulty. "Where did they come from?" he asked the General who was being prodded by one of his aids.

"Oh those? Ludendorff finally gave me what I asked for. These Panzers will form the spearhead of the final assault!" Below looked proudly on the metal beasts as if they were his children. His eyes were by now glaring as if he could finally see the end in sight. After all these years he was finally looking like a man who could see the end, the lines on his forehead betraying the face of a man constantly furrowing his brow in frustration before. Fritz had seen him a year or two ago looking much older. Today it was if he too had gone back in time to earlier days. He was reinvigorated. He kept clutching at his pistol in his pocket as if he was about to run towards the battle, waving it in the air, caring little for his own safety. The aids around him suitably restrained his arm so he could further concentrate on his role as decision-maker from afar.

"The final assault on Chantilly?" Fritz asked. He was still not entirely sure of his exact whereabouts.

"Chantilly? Chantilly?!" Below exclaimed with a sense of manic laughter interspersing with his words. He began walking off, his aids in hot pursuit, following the path of the tanks. "We've passed Chantilly! This is the final assault for the capital!"

The delirious general vanished into the dirt-ridden fog the tanks were ripping up into the air. Fritz was stunned. He had no idea the attack had been so successful. He was reinvigorated himself. His wound had stopped throbbing in pain and his rifle no longer felt heavy, a key symptom of a fatigued soldier. He too rushed forward, entering the shallow winding trenches, marked with hastily drawn signs, dodging the odd groaning soldier. He noticed that as he was rushing forwards, the groaning soldier on the ground rather than shouting in German started shouting in French. He was close, very close.

Fritz wound around the trenches, artillery shells whistling past him, explosions so frequent that he had thought that the day had begun because of the constant flashes. He fell onto his stomach against the front wall of a trench and poked his head up. He saw hundreds and hundreds of German soldiers, some from different regiments, all mixed together, running almost at full pelt, dodging rifle shots as if possessed by demons. They had no fear. Those who were hit seemed to keep going where once they would crumble to the ground. The occasional shouts of encouragement could be heard from all around. Fritz was just behind the wave going ahead of him. There was no organisation at this point. No officer was bunching up soldiers in a line. There were no obvious waves appearing. It was a free-for-all with only one way. He, as an officer, was not even given a hint of orders from the General. He remembered his training. In the absence of orders, go forward.

Fritz felt someone bang on top of his helmet. He looked up. "What regiment are you from?" the figure screamed at him. He was a lieutenant, his rifle pointing up.

"43rd!" Fritz screamed back.

"What the hell are you doing here? You're supposed to be on the right-hand side!" the lieutenant shouted back. He too seemed delirious, but it looked like was trying to get some sense of order. He was about to say something else, but he stopped as he noticed Fritz's bandage covering his eye. "Oh! Medical replacements?! Good! Come with me!" He banged on Fritz's helmet and ran forwards.

Fritz watched him and climbed out of the shallow trench. He bobbed up and down himself, jumping in and out of shell hole craters, passing by soldiers pointing their rifles ahead. He stopped, knelt down and took aim, and fired into the space in front of him. Too his astonishment, he found he had shot a French soldier in the back. They were running. He noticed the lieutenant he was following vanish into the ground. He got up and followed and saw that they had reached a French trench. It was similar to the one he was lying in beforehand. He realised that they had reached the rear trenches of the French final line. He poked his head out of the other side to see. There were perhaps only a few lightly defended lines between them and the open ground to the city. It didn't feel real. None of this felt real. Was he dreaming? Did he manage to get to sleep in his bed after all?

He was given his answer when the same lieutenant banged the top of his helmet again. "Good shot, I saw that! Sorry, you are more senior to me, sir. I cannot see so well!" he shouted to Fritz. It seemed strange to apologise in the middle of a battle. Fritz surmised that there was a feeling that this wall about to be over. "I will follow you this time!"

"Follow me!" Fritz shouted back. He banged on the man's helmet as if to get his own back and clambered out of the trench. They both ran together, other German soldiers rushing beside them. Some clattered to the floor as machine gun bullets peppered the vicinity. But for Fritz and his lieutenant they would be spared the same fate. Again, another trench was found. Fritz slid down, pointing his rifle either side, felling two French soldiers on his left who had not seen him coming, and one on his right who failed to swing his own rifle round in time.

Again, a bang hit the top of his helmet. The lieutenant really did have a knack for getting his attention that way. A good way, Fritz thought. It got your attention quickly. He looked round but could not see the lieutenant at all. Perhaps that was a tap goodbye, he pondered. He swung round to try to help clear the trench more but immediately fell over a body. He looked back and saw that the lieutenant had indeed banged Fritz's helmet goodbye. There he was, lifeless, on the ground having fallen in, hitting

Fritz's helmet in the process. Fritz looked to see what his name was. His name was Felix Hoffmann from Wurzburg. He was 20 years old.

Fritz picked himself up and carried on down the trench, rifle pointed out with his eye firmly peeled on any sudden movements. He could hear men cheering between artillery shell explosions. He saw someone move and raised his rifle but stopped as he saw the grey of a German tunic come into view. The two soldiers had just clambered into the trench and as quickly as they entered, they left via the other side. He carried on down the trench and came across two kneeling French soldiers, their hands behind their heads with their helmets off with a single German soldier loosely holding his rifle in their direction. He carried on down the line once more but stopped as the cheering started to drown out the now-fading sound of the artillery. Slowly it became apparent that all he could hear was cheering.

Confused about the reason for the jubilant noise, he clambered out of the trench with a degree of hesitancy and looked around. German soldiers were still running but they had smiles on their faces. Smiles, again and again and again, smiles past him by. He stopped one and asked what was going on. "Foch has surrendered! He is here and he has surrendered! Look" The private pointed. Fritz looked around.

There he was. The French commander was standing there, like a captain on the bow of his ship, his arms in his pockets, flanked by what seemed to be an entire line of unarmed French soldiers and officers. Some had their hands up; the odd helmet being held in the air. They were some way off, Fritz had to strain his one good eye to see the figures clearly, but the enemy general could be made out well. His white lapel and flat officer's hat were unmistakable. Crude white flags were being waved from sporadic areas and the German soldiers were running to line up to cheer and witness the historic moment. Under closer inspection Fritz noticed that it wasn't Foch, but a high ranking French general no less. It was a scalp that signalled the dire situation the French army was in. The fact that a French general was there giving himself up proved to all around that the end seemed like it was coming.

Fritz himself, never one to miss a party, ran over with delirium to witness the unique and incredible sight. German soldiers were stripping French soldiers of their rifles and packs whilst others were simply waving.

The cheering subsided slightly as exhaustion caught up with the victors as well as the vanquished. Discipline returned slowly to the German soldiers as officers ran to bark orders for the men to walk towards the enemy to accept the surrender.

Fritz could still see some French soldiers running back into the city and there were many. It reminded him that the war was not technically over, but with the surrender of so many French soldiers as well as their great commander it seemed like the blow von Bulow wanted had come to pass. He was grateful to have been there to see it, even if he did not see the exact moment it had happened. He was there, they were all there, to see perhaps the final scenes of this long and terrible war. They had come this far, and they were about to see the end.

For all who were there, this was no defining victory, but a moment of proof that peace would now most certainly be on German terms. The next few days and weeks would determine just how much of a say Germany would have. For Fritz von Falkenhayn this was not the end. He did not cheer as loudly as those around him. He found his loyal man, Norman Gisevius, in the delirious mob allowing for a much louder display of joy. Fritz did not share his doubts or concerns to Norman, nor did he attempt to. He simply took in the view and the sight of a battle won, at the cost of so much, and contemplated to himself the battles yet to come.

Chapter 4

The silence was deafening in the command tent just outside of Ypres. It was silent inside and for the first time in a long time it was largely silent outside. Troop transports and walking soldiers passed by the entrance to the tent where William Steele was standing, taking in the very silence that was overwhelming the officers inside. The ruined town was still smouldering from the last enemy bombardment that occurred the previous day. Only the march of soldiers, metal objects clattering together as they dangled down from tunics and trucks alike, the trucks themselves, were the only sources of noise. Very few were talking, aside from the same question bubbling up, why the silence?

In some way, most were grateful for the silence. It didn't quite feel like death was imminent and it allowed a few people to breathe a bit easier. Dust wasn't being thrown up into the air, so the sun was a lot more visible. It was warm so silence made the heat more noticeable. There was no wind that day and the late June sun was beating down. July was a couple of days away and summer was well and truly in full flight. The longest day had come and gone, though every day seemed long in the salient.

William gazed at the ruined town, the broken towers of the church and the cloth hall were still visible. He had never seen the town beforehand and judged from the ruins that it had been a beautiful medieval settlement. He hoped he might see it again in a better light and that it might be restored to its former glory. He even flirted with the idea of coming back during peace time as a pilgrimage when the war was over. Ypres had not quite instilled a mental feeling of horror and fear that it had somewhat given to many soldiers who were stationed there. Once again, Ypres distracted him from the problems at home, so it was a blessing in disguise. The picture in his breast pocket began to feel heavier.

The tent entrance was whisked open, and William passed through it to return to the silent tableau. Officers with heads in hands, watches being checked, maps being unravelled to be studied and ravelled back up again, anxious eyes, dotted around the place. The tension was palpable because every new update revealed a new setback. There had been no official update for almost a week and the commanding officer had not been seen in almost a week as well. There was talk that Field Marshall Haig would drop by for a visit, so the tent was clean. There had been, up until then, no such visit.

General Plumer had been put in charge of the Second Army that had been mostly settled in Ypres. Plumer himself had been withdrawn from the Italian theatre during the German fourth push towards Paris as he was seen as the best man for the job of administering the area. Initially he would spend hours and hours conversing with officers and soldiers alike and would often spring up without warning by deep-lying strong points along the line surrounding the battered town to conduct random inspections as well as asking for ordinary soldier opinions about what was going on. He was very much admired for his methods both at home and abroad. Ordinary soldiers still held him in highest regard for his actions during the Third Battle of Ypres. His breakthroughs were considered vital, and squandered by General Gough, who seemed like the Mr. Hyde to the Dr Jekyll that was Herbert Plumer.

One of the officers, a Colonel, unravelled the big map and studied it for the third time that hour. His left hand was visibly shaking, and he smelt like he had been smoking a cigarette every minute. William stood by his side and tried to follow the colonel's gaze. As if by clockwork, the colonel repeated the same words he had done many times before. "Paris isn't in enemy hands. This is good. It's deliberate. Amiens, we don't need. We can go around. The Germans are probably held up in the city and we can encircle them and cut them off. Why don't we do that? It's not bad at all. The line has held from Rheims to Belfort. Where are the Americans?"

Where indeed, William thought to himself, for the third time in an hour. The Americans had not been heard from in a long time. Word had it that they had fallen back thinking that the French would fight to the bitter end. The naivety of the yanks was cursed regularly by officers and men in the salient alike. Even at this time of uncertainty there was a search for scapegoats in the face of a colossal military disaster.

A colossal military disaster was looking back at William as he stared down at the maps. The German army had driven a wedge straight into the most vulnerable part of the Western front from Amiens to Provins. The front was now just a mile from the outskirts of Paris but for the British army in the north they were all but cut off. Losing Amiens was the greatest blow to the British and French forces because it left so much of the British army in dire straits. Amiens was the lynch pin and the German seizure of the town in mid-June had the force of a sucker-punch to the abdomen. The Seine had not been crossed but it was clear to the officers in the room that the Germans didn't have to. They were deep enough to cause the question to be asked; will the joint command of Britain and France have the stomach to carry on? The answer was not clear.

The map itself indicated the emotional distress that it caused for those in the know of the terrible disaster that had occurred. Circles in red pen were drawn with exclamation marks drawn next to them, the more exclamation marks that were next to the circle the more devastating the issue was that the Germans held that piece of land. The maximum amount of exclamation marks next to the circles was twelve, circling the land just outside of Paris. The circle drawn around Amiens itself had only three exclamation marks as it simply read 'No! No! No!'

The entrance to the tent was whisked open with purpose and the officers jumped up as if the headmaster was coming, military medals clinking together as if applauding. The entrant was just another colonel from another tent. The standing officers let loose a sigh of disapproval and returned their heads to their open hands.

An hour would fly by but to those in the tent it seemed like a day had passed. Perhaps they were all suffering from a dose of scepticism, and this was the symptom? They had every right to be, as the unravelled maps would vindicate the feeling that was not long ago akin to sedition and desertion. Where was the commanding officer? Where was Haig? A good half of the room were incredulous with rage restrained within their minds that the top brass had remained silent when there should have been decisive talk, but most importantly action.

Late into the evening as the summer sun was beginning to dip towards the battered horizon the entrance to the tent was whisked open. Once again, the jack-in-the-box officers stood expectantly to attention, though one or two laboured their way to their feet in a display of trepidation. In strode the be-meddled General Plumer, resplendent in his old cavalry uniform. He surprised some officers with the fact that he was so unusually well dressed. The field uniform that he usually donned was not to be seen. He looked as if he was going on parade, sword dangling by his side, his hair beautifully cleaned and his moustache handsomely groomed. The rings around his eyes betrayed a distressed man attempting to hide behind his station and accomplishments. He strode into the centre of the room.

Officers and men alike stood to attention, some pursing their lips with negative anticipation. Eyes darted around the room as if men were attempting to communicate telepathically with each other. Something was wrong and they were trying to guess. Why was the General so well-dressed? What was going on? William was one such officer. Still acting in his role, he shared the same concern, and furrowed brows littered the room.

General Plumer breathed in deep, his chest expanded at the cost of strength in his arms which dropped harmlessly either side. He regained his strength and raised them in front of him, grasping each other and folding. His head dropped slightly as he looked to the floor as if to gain some inspiration. He looked up at the officers as he read the room. To all but a fool it was obvious that optimism and hope was scarce. He lifted his eyebrows as if they were the cause of some terrible weight and began to orate. "Men, it has been a difficult period. There's no beating about the bush with this one. It's big and we are supremely aware of its ramifications. I have been in constant contact with the high command and have been kept abreast of the developments." He looked around and saw unease creep ever higher within the minds of the men.

He gestured with his head, silently pleading for the audience to sit. They obliged and he carried on. "The losses we have incurred in men and material have been exponential and at a greater level than the enemy. Worse still are the losses in territory both of strategic and political significance. The fact of the matter is that the Germans caught us all by surprise and we were too slow to react. A key error the high command made was their refusal to remove key pieces of infrastructure like train tracks and maintained roads which fell to the enemy allowing them greater mobility of arms, supplies and men. The timing of their attacks could not have been better, and we have suffered greatly with a reduction in men and morale. I don't have to tell you just how damaging that is especially after fighting for so long. Lord knows that the longer this damned war goes on for the more significant any losses are. Now, we have been resilient here. The German drive in our sector could not penetrate and seize Ypres and that is a testament to us all. Here in Belgium, we are the perfect definition of the British fighting spirit." He unhooked his arms and placed them purposefully on his hips. "But the same cannot be said for elsewhere".

He looked around for a place to sit himself, obviously burdened with the information he had and the duty he had to explain it. A colonel grabbed a free chair and placed it beside the rapidly tiring General. He took a moment to think but then waved it away. "The combined forces had been, as we know, ready for such a push to occur and it has always been my sincere belief that we were able to weather any storm that might come against us. Defence in depth has always been our strong point and that is what the Americans have been preparing for".

Mention of the Americans had always been a matter of tutting and thinly veiled barbs and this moment would be no different. The only difference was that such disapproval was done with supreme mastery in its subtlety and silence. Plumer himself shared the sentiment but chose to power through. "We must remember that we are a combined force. If one section breaks down, then it drags the rest down and as unfair and unjust as it may seem that is precisely what has happened. Our forces have had to move all over the front to front the gaps that were created due to German breakthroughs and French retirements; many French retirements".

At this point Plumer's face began to turn bright red. Anger was building and it was evident in the wobbling voice which had been otherwise stoic to this point. "Such action has put into question other areas of the line which had otherwise been steadfastly defended year after year. Amiens could have been held had it not been for our hand being forced, but forced it was."

He took a moment. He closed his eyes, rubbed his forehead and breathed in again, returning his hands to his hips. "The reason I have been silent for the past few days is because I had been ordered by Field Marshall

Haig to send as many men as I could to assist in a counterattack towards Amiens with the aim of retaking the town. The idea was suicide both for the attack and for the defence of Ypres itself. I therefore made myself unavailable to all in order to delay with a plan to have this order rescinded. I know this will no doubt make me the subject of a court martial, but I am not about to put the defence of Ypres in any jeopardy in order to bail out the incompetence of Haig, Fayolle and Foch."

With a stroke he had reminded all in the room of the humanity and bravery of the well-respected General. He had been a hero at the battle of Messines and now he was the hero of the battle of the high command. To most in the room he could say that he had personally kissed the foot of the Kaiser and they would all respect him no less. He continued. "I did not have to wait long. The order has been rescinded. In fact -"

He stopped himself as emotion bubbled up so much within the timbre of his voice he seemed as if he was on the verge of tears. Normally someone would have stood to ask if the man was alright, but all were rooted where they sat or stood, hanging on his every word. He continued, braving what was coming next. "In fact, all orders of attacks are rescinded. Marshal Foch, commander of the combined forces, has requested an armistice with the German high command with the permission of the French President and the British Prime Minister. As of eleven o'clock tomorrow morning the guns will go silent."

And with that, all were silent, both physically and mentally. Not a word was said in response, though Plumer himself was expecting something. There wasn't even a sound coming from outside as it had seemed that soldiers passing through had taken the time to pause their own manoeuvres. Only facial expressions could determine what the members of the audience were feeling. There were puzzled looks on some, shocked looks on others, insincere grins under furrowed brows on a few and blank expressions adorned the rest. They simply could not believe it.

One major stood up slowly, seeking clarification. "Is it all over then?"

"In a way, yes." Replied the equally shocked General, reminded of his own reaction to the news by the silent display of the room. "Terms will be given and likely accepted. Cessation of hostilities will begin, and we will see where it will go from there."

Plumer nervously toyed with the handle of his sword. He still seemed tense, but it was obvious that he had unburdened himself with the worst of the news. He spoke quicker, as if to wrap up an awkward dinner party speech. "You are to go and tell the men immediately. I will relay further orders as soon as they arrive. Dismissed."

General Plumer ended his speech but didn't turn round to leave immediately. He still expected outrage and shouting to spill from some of the officers. None were forthcoming, as if everyone was expecting someone else to start it off, and thus no one spoke. They simply stared back. Plumer was no coward and gave anyone the time and the chance to express their distaste. The distaste was palpable, but no one took the initiative. He went to speak as if off the record but by now even he was unable to express anything. Perhaps he too was waiting hopefully for someone to speak up in anger so he too could join them. He too said nothing. He turned around after a minute of unfathomable silence and left the officers to their staring. His every step was watched right until he was no longer in view.

William had watched every move and every twitch of the general. His first thought was wandering what it was that the general wanted to say at the end, but couldn't. He was no mind reader, but William thought the words that would have come out would have been 'I'm sorry'. He wasn't sure, but he thought he could sense it.

One by one, the various officers in the room left in stunned silence to go about what seemed like their final duties. The odd hushed conversation could be heard but it was largely inaudible to William. None made for him for comment or conversation because of his reputation as 'not one of them' and even at this period of heightened tension and unbelievability his stature with them was maintained. Then again, what conversations would be had? What was said had been said, there was nothing else to say. Best, he thought, to get to it and to spread the word.

The walk to the front lines was still very quiet. The evening sun was further giving way and thus it was the last time the sun would go down in wartime. William took in the view briefly, glancing to the horizon every five minutes or so. The broken roads twisted their way towards the burnt town and as he passed through the ruined houses, he thought to himself of the terrible waste that it all was. All of this resistance over so many years would be for nothing and though he had not been there for the entirety of the war it had still felt like a part of him was now a part of this place too. In the end he had to come to terms with the fact they he and the men around him had been defeated despite never losing the town itself. Battle wasn't necessary in order to lose; it was a decision made further away in better-lit rooms.

The cloth hall he had spied beforehand looked more depressed than before. Knowing of the impending armistice seemed to darken the rubble scattered around the foundations of where the old building used to be. The town square, infamous for the number of times it was shelled by the enemy, seemed to lift a haze above itself as the sun's light left the ground, obscured by the ridges around the town. William decided to walk straight through it, to the consternation of a sergeant who was lying down around the pounded rubble of what used to be a rather large house. "Get away! Do you want Jerry to shell us?!" he shouted. William gave him the curtesy of his gaze but not his words. The man didn't know yet that the game was up, but he thought he would give the sergeant a bit more time thinking that there was still something worth fighting for.

The trenches seemed less frightening; they were now just long holes in the ground with bits of wood in them with smelly men playing games of soldiers. That's all it was and that's all it would be now. How odd it felt, to William, that he knew something that the men all around him didn't, which made him feel more detached than he had already felt. Too his surprise, Corporal Jeffreys even seemed different, even though the soldier hadn't lost his simple charm at all. He thought he'd tell his adjutant before he made the general announcement but thought a good night's sleep was what he deserved. It would be asleep that would be largely guaranteed peace. The Germans wouldn't start anything now that the end was almost in sight.

Tiredness had been slowly taking over William's mind and body and it started to take its toll. As he got closer and closer to the front lines where a majority of his men were huddled together either as sentries or as sleeping bumps in the ground the tiredness increased. The tension of war had been on his shoulders for so long that it would eventually take its toll, but it would not make itself known until he was in some way safe from harm. This would happen every time he was on leave, but this was the first time such great fatigue was hitting him as he was walking around the hardened mud of the trenches. Every step seemed to become a greater and greater labour and eventually William sought the help of the trench walls to keep himself upright. Was it some sort of new gas that made one fall asleep? What a time to introduce it, if it was.

Eventually the ordeal took its toll and sleep was inevitable. William thought he could walk on with his eyes closed but that idea was put, quite literally, to bed. He slumped to the side and slid down to his knees, falling face first to the ground. He remained undisturbed in a dreamless sleep for a good long while, and it was a feeling most beautiful to him. The ground was warm, and his eyelids felt like great boulders that had rolled themselves in front of caves barring any light from coming through. It was not a welcome sleep, but it was sleep, nonetheless. The fact that it was dreamless spared him from the nightmares of home and the possible awful scenarios of matters with his love, Emmanuelle. That would be for another day.

It would be an earthquake on his back that would stir him back to consciousness. It was no natural earthquake that woke him, but the hand rumbling of a private from his battalion. "Sir! Are you alright? Are you hit?" the private intimately asked, genuine concern emitting from his eyes. The groggy Major rubbed his eyes, brown residue sticking to his right cheek as he raised his heavy head. His officer's cap had fallen out in front of him and to all but himself it would have seemed as if he had been in some way shot in the front. He revealed to the soldier that he was unharmed but well slept and he was helped to his feet.

"You're lucky. If I were a general, I'd have you for sleeping at your post." The soldier said with a smart grin on his face. His expression changed. "Heard there's some defeatist talk going around. Word of surrendering to the Germans. Didn't believe a word of it, of course. But, you know, is it true?"

Good lord, he'd slept right through the night! He checked his watch and saw that it was twelve past seven in the morning. The eleven o'clock deadline hadn't come but he was late in carrying out Plumer's orders. The morning sun was beating down and there was the sound of movement and life in the trenches once again. All seemed normal in acting Major Steele's section of the line. He knew he wouldn't be in too much trouble for his lateness. After all, the war was pretty much over at this point.

He thanked the private for the impromptu wakeup call and gathered his hat and his slowly waking brain and made for the front line. He started calling out for all who could hear him to follow him to a wide section of the trench so as many soldiers as possible could crowd round him. One after another, men started to follow his track to the large rectangle-shaped open square which had a high wall of sandbags on top of it. It had been used many times as a mortar post, but it was vacant at this point save the odd soldier trying to eek in a few more minutes of precious sleep.

About one-hundred and fifty-five men, William estimated, had managed to get in and around the large clearing. The company he was leading had largely adhered to his voice which meant that the rumours the private had mentioned had been widely circulated. They wanted to know what was going on. "I won't be long." William began, abruptly. "I have just been informed by General Plumer that from eleven o'clock today the armistice asked for by the high command will come into effect. We have been ordered to wait for further instructions past that time and when anything comes you will be the first to know about it. Please relay this news to anyone who is not here. The war's over, men. We're going home."

It was a short speech. William didn't want to mince his words. He wanted to get straight to the point. But this was not enough for most of the men who only lent a few seconds of silence before the shouting began. This was a very different reaction to the officers in the tent. Soldiers fumed and shouted their anger. The rumours they had heard were true; surrender to the Germans seemed to be about to happen. Shouts of 'never!' could be heard. Some even shouted 'Traitor!' directing the barbs at the high command where this order came from. The feeling of anger and distress was threatening to boil over, though William himself remained still and stoic. He remained standing where he was as the huddled soldiers began swaying around in fits of fury and anger. Few took the information in gracefully, fewer accepted the terms and walked away. Nothing William could have said would have made the situation any better. He wasn't in that sort of position nor was he afforded the ability to due to his relationship to the men. He was just a bystander, and though more than one or two soldiers shook their fists at him the anger was mainly directed at those who were not there.

Men stormed off, some chucking their helmets over the front lines where the odd stray bullet could be heard flying past from an obviously confused German sniper or sentry. Soldiers paced up and down the trenches trying to make sense of things and trying to understand why it was happening and what they could do to stop it or to resist the order. A few more eventually shrugged their shoulders and went about their way but this happened in very small drips. Acting Major Steele had lost control and discipline of his company.

A couple of hours went by. William remained in the place where he orated the news, still surrounded by incredulous soldiers, slowly contemplating peace. Perhaps the thought of peace had softened the hearts of some men. The problem was that most soldiers in his company had lost someone they knew; friends, relations, the lot. The idea that they had died for nothing poisoned the mind and rage was the symptom. For many that would never go away, even the thought that oneself was safe was not enough. Anger gave way to vengeance and that was starting to effervesce on the lips of one or two inconsolable souls.

The minutes began to tick by slowly. Ten-thirty. Ten-forty-five. Ten-fifty. Ten-fifty-three. Ten-fifty-five. The minute hand on millions and millions of men's' watches and clocks ticked to the central point. The hour hand nestled its way into the eleventh position.

The Great War was over.

Not a sound, not a whisper, emanated from the trenches or from behind. The sound of a slow and gentle breeze whistling through whatever it could find could be heard as heads looked up to see the sun beating down, its warm rays lighting up men's' faces and bouncing off shining metal dotted around the littered battlefield. No cheers from either side could be heard, though some were expected from the German side. They remained silent, maybe out of respect, maybe because the cheering could wait until later. It felt weird, but it felt easier to breathe.

For William's sector of the line the silence did not pass by with much of a second thought, aside from a collective sigh. The sentries did not stand down, they kept looking over the battlefield just in case it was all a great trick. It didn't seem like this was the case. Even at this point, though, no one was taking any chances.

"Something's going on!" shouted a sentry near William. He was leaning on the wall of the back of the same area he had been in for the last couple of hours and raised his head as he heard the shout. Not only he, but around half of the company heard the call and rushed to the parapets, rifles in hand. It was as if the war had not ended and to many this was perhaps the evidence they needed that this was all a great lie.

Something was stirring from across the battlefield. Figures could be seen moving and they were discernible as the enemy from their grey tunics and helmets with the sun's light bouncing off them. William could see this all happening with his very eyes. The Germans were coming out of their trenches, and they were walking towards the British front line. They were walking, in lines of about two or three men deep. Some were holding rifles raised to the sky, many were unusually unarmed, showing their empty hands not in a manner of surrender but as if they were about to embrace a friend or acquaintance. They were walking slowly, creating an unusual sight befitting of the unusual silence that surrounded everyone. The noise of the trudging of boots on hard mud could be heard getting louder and louder.

"What do we do sir?" angrily questioned a few soldiers around the anxious acting Major. William unbuttoned the leather cover of his pistol holster but allowed his fingers to play with the cover only. He knew that this was not a trick from what he had learned last evening. It was still no less bizarre. There must have been hundreds coming their way. He looked left and right seeing that he was by no means in the minority with his concern. Hundreds of men around him were similarly bracing for a fight, and not all from his own company. No other major could be seen in sight, in fact few officers could be seen either. It seemed as if the high-ranking officers had all retired, awaiting the end from their bunks at the rear. Acting Major Steele seemed to be the highest-ranking officer at the time. The eyes of hundreds were watching him.

He stayed motionless but with his eyes firmly fixed on the display. Men twitched and that twitched turned into a haphazard presenting of arms. Rifles were aimed at the advancing Germans. William felt dutybound to order the men to withdraw or at least to shoulder arms. The words did not leave his mouth. He was just transfixed at the spectacle. He hoped that the Germans would see the rifles being pointed at them and return. It was only an armistice, surely. He had been given no warning of a provocative action like this. He remained silent.

It wasn't clear exactly what happened next. No one knows who fired the first shot. Perhaps it was an accident, but it began a series of similar accidents. The crack of rifle shots filled the air, felling dozens and dozens of Germans who had reached but thirty yards from the front line in most places. German soldiers hit the floor, some in pain and others in self-defence. William was stunned at the counter-display of the men around him and still remained silent.

The Germans did not fire back after this first staggered volley of fire. After a few seconds some got back up and carried on walking towards them. They were followed by more who were either spared the volley or who were hit lightly. This second walk towards the British front line seemed to have convinced the men around William once and for all that the end had come.

Some British soldiers threw down their rifles and walked away. Most had realised that they had shot men in peace time and tried to erase the memory by throwing down their guns and walking away. William went the opposite way. He climbed out of the trench and walked towards the German soldiers now in a much messier line. He made his way around the shallow barbed wire, finding numerous gaps and picking one. He was followed by a few other like-minded soldiers, not all of whom had fired their rifles. As he walked towards them, he noted that they had blank expressions on their faces. He noticed one or two of them were staring at his pistol. He unbuttoned the holster to the vague wincing of a few German soldiers and tossed it on the ground.

He stretched his arm out, his hand levitating in the air expecting either a slap with a rifle or a handshake. Luckily, he was greeted to the latter, a private in the German army. There was no smile from the German soldier looking back at him, though William acknowledged that the man in the grey tunic had much more to smile about than him. The fact that even at this point there was not even a hint of gloating from the German soldier showed a mark of great respect. It did not take William aback, knowing full well that the propaganda of the 'evil Jerry' thrust down the throats of millions of people was just a ruse to maintain war support. The man in front of him was a human being just like anyone else, and despite everything was shaking his hand.

Not one to forget an incident, William pushed past the German soldiers and walked to see what the accidental volley of fire had done. He counted thirty men dead or wounded on the ground. He cursed himself for not giving any orders and felt the weight of anxiety and regret fill his mind. It was a feeling similar to the thought of the issues back at home, but now he was face to face with what was making him feel these awful feelings. Kneeling by one such man, he tried to say sorry but felt the same issue as General Plumer had, so no words came out of his mouth. The soldier turned out to be an officer, the clue given away by the red insignia on his tunic.

The German officer on the ground was clutching his shin. William applied a bandage to it and pressed down on the wound. The soldier looked up at him and nodded, grimacing in a bit of pain. William noticed that the man had a bandage over one eye. The acting Major raised his hand and looked at the man's hand too. They shook hands together briefly and then returned to the wound at hand. William looked down at the injured shin and without looking at the man he said "William Steele".

The German replied "Fritz".

Chapter 5

November was wet and cold. Even sleet and snow were making their first appearances as the last autumnal days waned into a more wintery feel. The trees which had the best part of three months to regrow leaves were discarding them as fast as they could. Even the birds, welcomed back for their song by all who ventured outside, were already making for warmer parts of the world. Haze and dew emanating from morning's embrace soaked the new grass which had been drowning under the weight of a deluge of rain from the last couple of months. Winter felt as if it would be very harsh.

For the world, harshness would be a largely indoor affair. The peace of Europe, guaranteed by both sides of a conflict now largely in the past, would be discussed in ways that would make the great storms of the past quiver in their respective rain clouds. Winning the war was one thing, winning the peace would be the other. Both sides had set about trying to achieve just such a victory though the definition of victory was different depending on what side of the room one was on.

The rooms in question were the stately rooms with high ceilings and large mirrors of the palace of Versailles. Its resplendent features had been somewhat dimmed by the relentless weather, though its insides were meticulously cleaned and beautified to the best possible standards. The interior of the palace was fit for a king, or a president, or a Kaiser. They had been packed full of dignitaries, diplomats and armies of clerks and representatives as far as the eye could see. The scene displayed that of a veritable beehive, only wasps and tarantulas had also been invited as well, and all were keeping their distance from each other as they decided which side should be the best insect. Talking was the weapon of choice, the tables formed the trenches, the beady eyes would form the bullets, the pens would be the bayonets. Occasionally artillery in the form of crumpled up pieces of paper would be thrown around, but this would be largely reserved for one side who used the levity of such actions to diffuse tensions as well as a way of getting one's attention in a loud and crowded room.

The Versailles Palace had been chosen as the venue for the peace talks and subsequent agreements for the very historic reason that it was here where the German nation was proclaimed all those years ago in the 1870s. The German high command had designated this place as the perfect venue as a diplomatic insult to the French who had considered that historic moment and the one being played out in 1918 as national humiliations. The Kaiser and his aids wanted to twist the knife just that bit further.

Through the months leading up to this meeting inside the palace of mirrors, the general feeling of unease allowed for blank continuity to occur within the societies of the respective nations. The French Third Republic carried on as it always had, seemingly attempting to live in some form of denial, thinking that this day might not happen if people chose to simply forget. The British similarly tried to keep their society moving forward but for both nations an armistice without a treaty simply meant that the war was being paused for the time being. This leant the defeated powers the time to gather their collective thoughts to pursue talks with all they had; trying to present a somewhat united front. Their delegates were eagerly talking, whispering and scheming depending on how well the talks were going. Though their armies largely remained at their posts, expecting anything and nothing at the same time, the politicians and diplomats were doing battle this time.

For the victors, there had not been a week going by without some sort of magnificent military display within the German nation. Though they too left a significant military presence in Belgium and France they had taken the opportunity to unite the German people under the militaristic applause that drowned out the peaceful atmosphere of Europe. The Kaiser himself had been seen either at the head of a parade or taking the salute as largely reserve brigades marched by his podium. There was no hiding the fact that not several months ago the fabric of the nation was fast unravelling, but it was a wonder for all to see what 'victory' had done to the spirit of the German people. This was by no means replicated within the minds and actions of the German delegates at the peace conference, though it was noted that they were always seen walking with confidence and their strides were much longer than their French and British counterparts.

The same could not be said for Germany's allies. The Austro-Hungarian delegation certainly mirrored a very surreal experience the ageing European empire was going through. Though it had been on the 'winning' side, its population was far less united than its Germanic neighbours and various different peoples within the empire were pushing against the ever-straining seams of the Empire itself. Emperor Karl, who was present at the peace conference looked strained himself as if he had not slept in years. He looked more like a defeated leader than a victorious one. He sneered with venomous disgust whenever an Italian member of the delegation passed nearby, showing his obvious contempt for those who had successfully undermined the foundations of the empire he was sure would crumble soon.

The same could also be said for the very small delegation from the Ottoman Empire. They had largely been beaten during the final months of the Great War and they too were fast watching their empire crumble. Their authority over the long-conquered peoples of Africa and the Middle East had all but waned and once again this was evident in the mannerisms of its delegates and politicians. The Sultan, Mehmed, did not even attend the conference, having instead to stay at home desperately attempting to assert his control over the flailing empire since the death of the previous Sultan in July. Though peace would have to be agreed by all in some way, for the victorious side, Germany stood head and shoulders above her allies.

The notable absences of any sizeable delegation were those of the Italians and Americans. In the minds of both nations, they had not been defeated in any defining capacity. Italian forces were still stationed on Austrian soil and had not moved an inch. The Americans on the other hand had left Europe much quicker than when they had entered. The American President, Woodrow Wilson, had declared in no uncertain terms that he would not allow the United States to sanction any such peace that was dictated by the German Empire. America's long period of international isolation would be the only course of action.

Other delegations from smaller countries played their part too but they were not afforded their own rooms to discuss their own matters, nor were they given time to speak at any great length during open discussions with all parties in the great hall. All though were generating their own noise, the different languages spoken over each other were enough to make a sensitive onlooker queasy just by trying to listen to the chorus of voices coming from each corner of the magnificent palace. The rain tapping furiously on the windows was a better sound to hear for most, and most took the opportunity to do so, even if that meant being soaked to the bone in the process.

Fritz Von Falkenhayn, freshly discharged from hospital in Aachen, was one such man peering into all of these different delegation rooms and groups. Dressed in a clean officer's uniform, still with a bandage on his head, he wandered through the corridors of power. When asked by the odd official for the purpose of his being there he reiterated that his invitation had come from his father who had been asked to attend with the German delegation. Fritz was afforded the luxury of watching on as the world talked endlessly about what the future would be. Providing balance within his own mind, it was not the greatest of postings he had ever received. By this time, he still had not returned home to his darling Johanna. He had made up his mind to confront his feelings and though he would not divulge the extent of his fidelity to his soon-to-be-wife, he would make up for it by throwing himself whole-heartedly into marriage, a family life and doing right by the woman who had stood by him during the entirety of the war. Her faith and loyalty needed to be rewarded and he thought his future actions could do that, rather than admitting the failures of his past.

"Your father is here?!" exclaimed a German politician. Fritz recognised him by the sight of him rather than his voice. Georg von Hertling, chancellor of Germany, had noticed the wandering captain and had shuffled from one side of the room to the other. Though it was a quieter area of the largest room housing the German delegation, it seemed to onlookers of a chess move where the bishop makes straight for a pawn nearing the end of the chess board. "I have not seen him in a long time, and I was certainly not expecting him to be here of all places" the 74-year-old uttered. He spoke slowly, mumbling in places and Fritz saw that his eyes were failing him behind well-worn glasses. Though this man held one of the greatest offices of the German state, second perhaps only to the Kaiser, he was not a great man. His eyes seemed to float away from whoever he was talking to. His unusual ability to make for Fritz unaided but also with a clear vision was a sight that caused a raised eyebrow from the odd member of the German delegation.

"He is with the Kaiser at the moment" explained Fritz, towering over the old chancellor. "Would you like me to introduce you?" This small insult went over the head of the little spectacled man who should have been part of the inner circle of the delegation which included the German leader. He had been, instead, relegated to the scrum of the giant German delegation room.

"Your father is back. This is most interesting. Most interesting. Georg mumbled to himself, thinking with no hint of speed. Fritz waited with a degree of patience as he expected some sort of elaboration. It came but at the cost of several minutes of Fritz's life. "He is not a man I would have expected Hindenburg or Ludendorff to want to have around at this time. This is a sign of change. I had thought this might happen but not so soon. It is a power play, a very interesting power play." The little chancellor looked up at Fritz, to which still one eye was staring back. "Be careful, boy. Your father is being used for something much bigger and you best not get used yourself. Mark my words; his presence here is noted and noted well. There will be another battle". Georg repeated to himself the words he had told Fritz to mark. "Noted well. Another battle" he would repeat over and over again. Fritz had no idea what the man was talking about specifically but the fact that it was the German chancellor who was warning him of something was enough for him to raise a few hairs on his back, albeit unintendedly.

All in the German delegation room were talking but in truth they were all waiting for the doors to the adjacent room to swing open, whereby the Kaiser and his aids would stride forth announcing their plans and intentions and what would, most likely, be the resulting agreement of the peace conference that was in its late stages at this point. The role of these delegates was less to make decisions and more to find out how to practically carry out the wishes of the leaders. Fritz was just a bystander, but he did want to see if he could coax out a piece of information from his father who was in that room. He was not allowed in, despite asking a couple of times if he could. The situation demanded the highest degree of security and secrecy and even the son of Erich von Falkenhayn was not permitted to violate that secrecy. He would have to wait with bated breath, along with the rest of the world.

Fritz moved to the window overlook the rear grounds of the palace. The rain was incessant, but somehow it seemed different from the rain he had come to know and hate whilst in the trenches. Perhaps watching the rain fall in front of you from inside rather than on top of you from a hole in the ground granted a man a different perspective of rain. Could the same be said of peace and what would happen next? He looked down and noticed a few delegates of different countries take in the air, escaping from the chorus of voices emanating from the building. They were soaked to the bone, but their ears were no doubt relieved from the pressure. He noticed two delegates start to argue amongst each other. Interested to see what was going on, he creaked the window open, hoping to hear what was going on. He discerned that one man was French and the other British. He could not make out what they were saying as he was not quite the linguist he was trying to be, but he saw that they were not happy with each other. How things change in peace.

He leant a bit further out and tried to make out the odd word, as the noise from the room he was in was masking the voices, still quite far away from the window he was looking out for. They seemed to be arguing about winning and losing about national shame, but those words were all Fritz could make out. The Frenchman suddenly pushed the Englishman which sent him to the wet concrete ground. This was accompanied by a spit and the Frenchman vanished back into the palace, leaving his English compatriot to pick himself up, aided at the last second by another man who Fritz made out was Bulgarian. Though Fritz had no idea what happened or transpired, to him it signalled the fractious nature of these talks. Members from the same side no longer agreed with each other. This would not be a straightforward peace, but it would make Germany's ability to pick off enemy nations one by one much easier. He was no diplomatic tactician, but Fritz could sense something coming. He only hoped that it would lead to a long-lasting peace. As he reminded himself that part of the delegation were the militaristic dictators of Hindenburg and Ludendorff who had run Germany like a dictatorship since the beginning of the year, he doubted peace was the defining motive of the conference.

The tiny melee was enough to distract Fritz from the doors to the adjacent room opening to reveal the small procession of leaders and royalty from their meeting room to the grand hall. Fritz's father formed part of the procession, flanking the Kaiser's left-hand side along with Hindenburg, Ludendorff, Crown Prince Ruprecht and King Ludwig of Bavaria scattered around the proud Wilhelm, his left arm tied to his sword dangling by his waist. The party made for the great hall where the main leaders of the various other national delegations began hurrying their way to the hall and the viewing galleries. Fritz and other German dignitaries did likewise. Fritz himself tried to get his father's attention but it was in vain. His father was not long back from his post in Lithuania and had seemed invigorated as well. His star had unexpectedly risen, and it was indeed a shock that he was included within the inner circle of the Kaiser at this, the defining moment of the 20th century so far. Fritz jostled his way to the front corner of a viewing gallery as the conference reached its most dramatic moment. Days, weeks of talks had come down to this moment. It had been long in coming but the future was about to be set down here.

The Kaiser took his place seated at a large round table and was joined on either side by Hindenburg and Erich von Falkenhayn, the latter given the solemn task of revealing to the nervous onlookers the terms of the peace. Pages were thrust into the view of the delegations of France, Britain, Italy and Belgium, translated for each party. The reactions were mixed, with the most vociferous anger coming naturally from the French. Falkenhayn nodded and allowed printed copies to be distributed to certain onlookers and extended members of other delegations. Fritz was able to get a good glimpse of the proposed treaty and read as fast as he could so he could not miss the sight of what happened in the middle of the great hall.

The terms were vast and wide-ranging, taking into consideration all elements of global affairs. It was a play at German domination of world affairs, meeting out punishments to some and affording leniency to others. There were obvious signs of contributions from the other victorious powers, but these were negligible in comparison to the obvious German dominance. Gasps could be heard around the great hall, one coming from Fritz himself on seeing the contents of the proposed treaty.

Germany would be afforded the entire overseas territories of France, including French North Africa, Central Africa and Madagascar. Even the Belgian Congo was to be transferred. The Portuguese colonies were largely ignored, instead favouring an economic partnership with Portugal which seemed generous to the Iberian state. Spain would also be granted an economic partnership in return for Ceuta but nothing else. The German Pacific islands still under the control of Japanese forces were to be retained, French Indochina would be handed over for German protection and Papua New Guinea was to be handed in its entirety to German control. The Ottoman Empire would regain its control in Egypt, but Germany would be the singular owner of the Suez Canal shares. Germany was to be given a greater empire to administer but it knew its limits and had acted accordingly.

The British were to be treated rather lightly. This was a gambit by the German delegation to divide the vanquished nations from each other. Britain had been offered a relatively easy ride in exchange for their agreement in order to isolate the French and it was evident in the proposed treaty. Britain would lose a few imperial possessions, but it would retain most of the empire including its hold on Canada, South Africa, Australia and New Zealand. Britain would be forced to pay reparations and an agreement on fleet size ratios would be agreed at a later date and its interest in European affairs would have to be curtailed but in terms of imperial prestige Britain had much less to grumble about than her French counterpart.

The real hammer blow was reserved for Belgium and France. Belgium would lose all of her Imperial possessions, but she would also lose her autonomy as a nation. She would be absorbed into a close political and economic union with Germany, essentially turning her into a puppet state, abolishing the monarchy and eradicating any trace of a Belgian military. France would be hit most of all. The entire provinces of Lorraine and the Franche-Comte were to be annexed outright and the Nord Pas de Calais was to be put under the protectorate of the German Empire with a review of that protectorate status conducted every five years, essentially placing it under perpetual German supervision. France was to pay Germany and her allies the eye-watering sum of 140 billion Francs in reparations, its standing army was to be reduced to a mere 150,000 men and it would enter into an agreement to align itself economically with the Germans, essentially absorbing the French economy into a German-dominated political and economic union, in which the new Eastern nations extracted from the old Russian empire were already a part of. This would be a long transition, but France was to accept a binding commitment to this new economic union with Germany at the head.

There was little in the treaty for Germany's allies. The Austro-Hungarian Empire was to receive fifteen percent of French and British reparations, the Ottomans an even smaller sum. Italy was forced to cede Veneto to the aged Austro-Hungarians and Italy herself was to hand over a small sum in reparations to them also. Serbia was to be incorporated into the empire and Greece was to lose her autonomy through the enforced appointment of a pro-Austrian government. In the room some expected the delegations from Germany's allies to complain that they had not received much in the way of reward, but they stayed silent in their chairs.

Fritz believed that such a treaty would not be signed. France would lose too much; accepting the treaty would most likely topple the government and plunge the nation into internal chaos. The French delegation indeed expressed their outrage, with the French Prime Minister, Georges Clemenceau, practically falling out of his chair in anger. He was respectfully restrained by other French delegates and after a brief shouting display from the comfort of his chair he stormed out of the chamber declaring that France would not sign the paper even in death. His empty chair was filled by Stephen Pichon, the French Minister of Foreign affairs who assured the room that he had the authority from the French President to commit France to the proposed treaty.

As it was made clear that the delegations had completed their perusals of the vast and harsh document the Kaiser returned to his feet and bowed. He left the room as the noise of talking grew louder and louder. Fritz escorted himself out of the room leaving behind the view of furrowed brows and contemplating looks to see if he could finally meet with his father. He made his way down a flight of stairs, feeling pain seeping out of his shin, and tried to intercept the leaving party. He went to the very same doors he had tried on a couple of occasions to pass through and waited there. The small procession of conquering men swaggered their way in poise and grace to the same room. Fritz waved from his position on the left-hand side of the door towards his dour-looking father. Fritz recognised the face, remember how it always appeared whenever his father was contemplating a move in a game of bridge. To Fritz's brief joy his father glanced back as father and son shared a few seconds of eye-contact. Fritz wanted to shout something, but he could not find the words. He simply stared and smiled. To Fritz's astonishment his father smiled back as if his father had pulled back the curtain of seriousness for just a moment to reveal his human side. The curtain was closed and his father broke eye contact. For Fritz it was more than enough for now. Such a moment was to be treasured always within a high Prussian family. Fritz had that moment right there. He might write the moment down and share it with his sister.

The party passed through the doors and once again they closed, the entrance to the room housing the most powerful men in the world shut. Fritz would have to be content with doing what everyone else in the building was doing; waiting to see if the vanquished enemies would sign. For it was no certain thing that they would do so. Perhaps, he thought, that peace would be refused, and the fighting would start again. The thought was enticing. It was not as if the British and French couldn't start again. Germany was just as desperate as the others to seek a peace. It was why they were trying to divide the British and French from each other wish vastly different conditions for peace. Germany was playing a risky game, but they were doing it well.

Developments did not take long to come. It was a mere few hours before a note signalling agreement had been sent to the German delegation. Romania, though she had not been talked about in any great detail in this proposed treaty, had accepted to peace negotiations based on the German timetable. It was small but it showed that the treaty was starting to see shape. Fritz waited by the doors to watch any more notes of acceptance coming in. Luxembourg was next to send its note of agreement, agreeing to join in the new economic and political union with Germany. The biggest nation yet, Japan, sent its note of acceptance to relinquish its occupation of German pacific islands. Greece, far from happy with her fate despite holding out for so long during the way, sent her note of acceptance. The acceptance notes then dried up.

The German delegation would have to wait for a further three days before the next note came in. It was no insignificant country at all as well.

Fritz was grateful that he had remained in the room with quite a few others who elected to not sleep night and day, waiting instead for any more notes of acceptance to come through. Fritz saw the next note come in and saw the expressions of joy come from those around. In a mildly exhausted state, he approached the small scrum around the man holding the note. Even Georg von Hertling, the little old chancellor had sprung out of nowhere to approach and leave grasping his hands in delight. Fritz caught a glimpse of the note. It read; 'Britain accepts'. The British had agreed, and this was no small thing. The British Empire had for around a-hundred years been the greatest power in the world. In accepting the German treaty, she had agreed to hand that mantle to the German Empire. Though Britain would hold on to many Imperial possessions she had committed herself to accepting the German Empire as the dominant force in global politics. It was not evident from what the treaty stipulated in cold hard evidence but to all of those in the room it was clear that Germany was now becoming top of the pile in the mess that was planet earth.

On the same day but several hours after the morning that revealed the British acceptance of the treaty, the Belgian delegation had sent in their note of acceptance. This was not unexpected, nor was it met with any sense of shock or joy, but it was a grave thing to accept the near eradication of one's nation. The Belgians had done just that. The note was greeted with soft nods and softly spoken blurting of "good" coming from a few men.

Fritz looked out from the same window as he had done before when he witnessed the altercation between the two men in the rain. He looked out over the plains, picking out the faint outline of the city of Paris not far away. He thought to himself what might be going on there in the halls of power. He thought he might see a car with the French note of acceptance coming towards the palace but unusually there were no vehicles on the road. It would be a slow day. Britain and Belgium would be the sole sources of post today. He decided to finally leave for his tent and slept soundly, dreaming once again of Johanna and the child he had met only twice for a brief time. He smiled, imagining her warm embrace as he fell into a deep and dreamy sleep.

Two further days passed before another note of acceptance was handed in. By this time the Kaiser had left Versailles to return to Germany whilst Erich von Falkenhayn, Crown Prince Ruprecht and Ludendorff remained from the inner circle in the palace of mirrors. Paul von Hindenburg had also left due to ill health, suffering from a stomach upset. Some thought he had contracted an illness that seemed to be quite prevalent in France, but it was later declared that he only had a slight fever. The next note to be handed in was from Italy. They had taken a while before deciding, issuing also a diplomatic protest and declaring their strong reservations to the treaty. One diplomat laughed when they read this stating to whoever was around him that "If the Italians want to issue a protest, then they shouldn't accept it at the same time! It wreaks of indecision." It did, but the note was there. Still, there was no word from the French; most of the delegation by this time had long returned to their homes. Only Pichon remained with a skeleton crew of other French diplomats and politicians. Little seemed to be moving from their end. The Serbian delegation had sent in their note of acceptance to the Austro-Hungarian delegation and so the Germans learnt of this development through their note of acceptance. The focus was still on what the French would do. There was great uncertainty and a bit of anxiety.

That anxiety would remain for another two days. Fritz would have his little wish granted. He did indeed witness a car coming, and it carried inside the French President Raymond Poincare, seated next to the now-ailing French commander Ferdinand Foch. The car stopped outside of the palace and the President, resplendent in the uniform of his office, stepped out tentatively as if onto a patch of ice. Foch did not leave the car, electing instead to allow himself to be driven off into the distance. The President trundled in and made immediately for the room housing the French delegation. An hour later a man arrived and handed a member of the German delegation a note.

The Third Republic of France, the final major power, had accepted the treaty thus to be infamously named; the Treaty of Versailles. Wild cheers greeted the news. Men hugged each other all over the room. Hats, if they were nearby, were flung into the air. One or two men started singing the German national anthem. Fritz on the other hand, stared out of the grand window once again, a smile creeping its way across his face. He started to believe, for the first time, that the war was actually over.

Little did he and many others know, the days of the Third French Republic were soon to be over as well.

Chapter 6

"You cannot expect my daughter to wait around for your return that might not come! Unburden her with emotion and let her go about her life in peace!" shouted Emmanuelle's father, Charles Melton, at the startled William Steele. He had barely informed Emmanuelle that he was due to be posted in Belgium with the Second Army. He had served in quieter areas of the front before, enjoying for a brief time working as a desk captain for General Ironside. His proficiency with the French language made him an invaluable asset to the locals in France and communicating with the allies further down the line. His orders had changed, and he was to be posted miles away from his old desk to the front line in Ypres, no doubt to be a part of the upcoming offensive planned for the end of July, 1917. The news was not welcome in the stately house of the Meltons.

William saw that his news was not only unwelcome to the father, but it would be also a terrible blow to the emotions of the daughter. Emmanuelle sat mournfully in her chair by the piano room window. She had not said a great deal for the entire time that William was there, but now her silence was deafening. She had defended William on occasion from the angry barbs directed towards him by her father, but this was not going to be one of those times. She seemed to find it difficult to even look at the man who had adored her for three years. He noticed this; he noticed many things.

"It isn't my fault!" pleaded Captain Steele, attempting in vain to appeal to good nature to absolve him of this news. "I have tried to keep myself out of harm's way, but this is war. I don't get to pick and choose my battles, nor whether I am to participate in those battles!"

"Then maybe my daughter should spend her time with someone who can choose!" It was a good retort; Charles had clearly found a good point. Emmanuelle heard this and agreed in unmoving silence, her gaze retreating further and further from William giving her feelings away. "You don't take my daughter's feelings into consideration and that is because, as you say, you can't. You don't have control over what you do or what happens to you. This is why we have the system we have in this country, boy. You can't escape your station; it's just not done. And you attempt to bring down my daughter's station in the most callous of ways. You are incessant". Charles was taking the initiative, almost beating William into a corner with his words.

"The feelings we have for each other transcend any station that might try to divide us!" William countered back with. His own emotions were bubbling up as it became clearer and clearer that he would have to do the fighting himself, certainly the fighting of saving the relationship he had so meticulously tried to help blossom and grow. "Emmanuelle is not someone who can be told what to do, she is her own woman! She can choose for herself!" He thought he could reintroduce Emmanuelle into the argument, but it backfired. She rose from her veritable viewing gallery and made for the door. It was clear that she wanted to have no part in this.

"How dare you tell me how my own daughter thinks and acts. Do you seriously think that you know her better than I?!" The tactic had backfired magnificently. Only the chime of a bell interjected at this time as William searched frantically within his own mind for anything to fight back. Nothing was forthcoming. He remained steadfast but he was now very much on his own. "I have been patient with you. I have let you have your little fun with my daughter and for that I am dreadfully ashamed. I knew from the first moment I saw you that this, fling, that you two have would not last. Now, I did not want that to be evident in your death or your maiming but my point still stands. Even if you were to live, boy, then you would not be fit, no matter the manner of your return, for my daughter who expected better before she met you and she reminds me constantly that she still does".

How could William argue against that major blow? Charles was bringing up information that he could not so easily refute. What was Emmanuelle saying about him when he was not around? It was not clear and Henry Forbes, who remained in constant contact with the Melton family, had relayed to William on occasion the mixed messages of attitudes the family had towards him. William was not on solid ground, and this became more and more evident as time passed. Certainly, William and Emmanuelle had started their relationship as close as anyone could be. They were hardly seen in public without holding hands or in each other's arms. But time had let that relationship decay as a disapproving father and mother, until her passing a year before, simply let time aid their erosion of a relationship they had never quite come to peace with.

William's own mind had been beaten up by this point. His anxiety had grown as the months went by and the war made it no better. Perhaps it was the time away which had helped to decay what was originally a blossoming couple. Had there been no war and no distance between the two it could be argued, certainly by the idealistic William, that they could even be married by now. He had in fact asked, purely unofficially in order to gauge the idea which, to his astonishment, Emmanuelle had in part agreed to. Though it was never official, and Emmanuelle's parents saw to that, the two were engaged to be married. William's entering the army in 1916 put pay to that notion in the short term, and perhaps the long term. William was too much of an idealist to let it slip away. She was the happily-ever-after he had been waiting for and he would do anything to keep it that way. This only made the anxiety even worse.

"Do yourself a favour and make this as painless as possible." Charles began to reason to the slightly shaken captain. "Don't you think she deserves it?" He had won the battle of wits, but it would take more than that to extinguish emotion. William was not so easily swayed. He stared back at the father, finally feeling able to do so.

"Only if Emmanuelle says so, and I know how she feels about me, so that will never happen." It was the last throw of the dice. If Charles could use information William couldn't disprove then so would he. It had a desired effect. Charles broke off his attempt to reason with the love-struck Steele and turned around. His own mind was whirring about what to say next but he was interrupted by the door opening. Emmanuelle was standing with a very well-dressed Henry Forbes in a dinner suit. He had just arrived unannounced and had decided to visit on his way to a dinner in the nearby town. William's eyes opened slightly, enjoying the view of a friend.

"I hope you don't mind me dropping in without notice. I do not mean to stay long. I have been making good time to my next appointment so I decided to tell the driver to make a little detour" announced Henry. He noticed the room seemed tense and tried to change the subject, whatever the subject was. William noticed with a hint of anxiety that Emmanuelle's hand was resting on his arm and her face so sullen before was now much lighter, though she herself was not exactly smiling. William forgave his anxiety for making him feel as if something was going on. He was just happy that he was not in the room alone with the angry Charles anymore.

"Isn't it wonderful, William? Your friend is here. And do you wonder if there is a space for you at this dinner you are going to?" Emmanuelle asked with intention, joining Henry in trying to change the subject.

William was irked. He did not like to leave so many things up in the air. "But I haven't anything to wear to it." He replied, perplexed as to why Emmanuelle thought it was a good idea to let this argument go by unresolved. His anxiety was surely getting the better of him. "Also, I'm just a captain. The function is for the Majors and Colonels."

"Oh, stop making excuses. It might be fun!" exclaimed a confident Henry Forbes. Henry's connections had afforded him the immediate rank of Major, yet he would never wear his uniform at home. He thought that it was a frightful thing to remind people at home that a war was going on. He believed that at home one must try to escape the grim realities of battle that was happening over the channel. The dinner itself seemed rather bizarre seeing as the entire nation was struggling to feed itself adequately. William was more than aware of this. The farm his parents owned back down in Devon was struggling to keep up with demand. Had he not joined the army he would have been sucked back home to help. He really did feel powerless.

"You can borrow a suit from daddy." suggested William's unofficial fiancé. The idea tasted fowl in the minds of both William and Charles; the first time they had passively agreed about anything. "You can be both off together and look after each other."

Emmanuelle's father relented, seeing sense in being generous as it would rid him of William's unwelcome company. He gestured his restrained approval and Emmanuelle rushed off to find suitable attire for William who by this time was fully aware of just how powerless he was around everyone there. Not Henry, nor Emmanuelle, nor Charles would listen to a word he would say, and he had never felt more unwanted. Even Henry's own invitation, more at the behest of Emmanuelle than him, felt insincere and restrained. William left the room, treading lightly as if not wanting to wake up a half-asleep wolf in a cave. He was licking his own mental wounds, knowing full well that he was still bleeding.

The suit was unfitting and unflattering. Emmanuelle did not seem to mind. She never did seem to mind whenever William looked silly beforehand. Sometimes she would even adjust her own self to make William feel less conscious. They were like a couple who were incapable of wearing clothes that fitted or looked good and they would laugh about it. They would laugh with the whole world. But whilst she laughed then, she did not laugh now. Where once she gazed, looking at each specific problem with William's attire and laughing every time, this time she simply gazed at the whole unfit ensemble and sighed. William's anxiety was starting to hit into overdrive.

"Come on now, William. I only meant to stay here for a short time. Wrap your clothes together and haul them into the car." Henry was impatient and his tone seemed cold.

"I thought I might leave my clothes here. I can pick them up later" William meekly replied.

"No, take them with you. You don't want to lose them before your deployment" Emmanuelle coldly reminded him. William was not due to journey back to France for three more days and had hoped to see Emmanuelle one more time. Leaving his clothes there would have at least given him a decent excuse to see her again, perhaps for the last time if her father was indeed right and he was destined to die. Emmanuelle did not even give him that small satisfaction. He did not query her and obeyed the orders of both Henry and William.

He bundled the clothes in to the waiting car and turned to embrace his love one more time. They did embrace, and it was warm. William noted that her grasp was not as tight as he remembered. He knew that his mind was now too anxious to see sense and thought nothing of it. He kissed her cheek and then her forehead. She looked up at him with bright eyes and her hair, straight and shining in the sun, her turned up nose pointing towards him, and he allowed himself to smile. He reminded her gently "I will always have your picture with me".

A gentle breeze blew from behind Emmanuelle. The ends of her shining hair blew towards William embracing his cheeks. "I hope you do" she replied. Finally, to his fragile and beaten mind she had given him cause to smile and to hope. It was small, but in dark times there would always be call for small mercies. It was a lesson William had learned from his own mother whom he had not seen, prioritising instead the company of his love over his parents. He turned away and made for the car. He jumped in, and gazed at her from the window.

Henry came by soon after. He also embraced Emmanuelle. It was a different embrace; Henry was taller and so required a change in tactic, as she wrapped her arms around his waist. She had embraced William around the shoulders. William cursed his anxiety for once again getting the better of him and looked away. Henry gracefully took his seat in the car. They waved as the car sped off to the next destination. William looked back as he could see her wave them off. Who was she waving to?

William rubbed his head, his anxiety unrelenting and reminded himself of the final words she said to her. "I hope you do". They were sweet words, with a tone so light it was almost as if she had sung them to him. He would treasure with his whole heart her picture, but he would treasure even more those four words. They would echo into his mind until he would next see her.

Henry leant over, noticing William was in a bit of distress. "Take your mind off it" Henry suggested. "It's a stuffy place anyway. Women are complicated and they are very unpredictable. It all seems too complicated to me. Maybe one day I'll understand what it is you like about this whole thing. Love, it always seems so messy". They were hardly reassuring words, but William listened all the same, desperate to find something else to think about aside from the ordeal he had been subjected to. So many things left unsorted, he thought. If he thought he was powerless then, he would be even more so in Belgium in the middle of war.

He assured himself that when he returned, he would make to see for her again, gaze into those beautiful eyes again, be softly embraced by the tips of her hair in the wind again, and hear her voice sing to him again.

Chapter 7

Buckinghamshire had changed very little since William last visited the county. It had seemed to lag behind its neighbours in bringing about its own natural Christmas spirit. The festive times were fast approaching and yet the odd leaf could still be seen hanging desperately onto its home tree for dear life. The grass around Whiteleaf Hill was glowing green despite the rain that had dulled the colours of nature's pallet around the rest of the country. Little decorations were sprinkled round the odd house and dwelling but that was all that reminded any onlooker that Christmas was coming and the new year was also fast approaching.

William Steele hadn't taken the train to Buckinghamshire much before whilst he was living in London. He had always been taken there by his love, Emmanuelle, who often rode in the car that she sent to pick up the love-struck man from Devon. It was not as if he disliked public transport, but the journey was expensive and the wages of officers and men in the British Army, at the time in a state of major flux and uncertainty, was not exactly great. It was also doing no good to his anxious heart that after such a long period of time away his love would not have made the same journey. Times were still tough and the cost to run cars these days was great, even for the upper classes. The view from the train was good and that made up slightly for the lonely journey William was taking.

He had forgone his officer's uniform both of his own volition and obeying the orders of the high command which had specifically requested its enlisted officers and men to remain inconspicuous in the public domain. There had been a lot of hearsay about what might happen in Britain following the signing of the Treaty of Versailles. The tale of the defeated foe would not end simply at the singing of a treaty and all over the land there was an air of uncertainty over what would happen next, certainly with the army but also with the powers that had governed the land up until that point. William had done his best to avoid newspapers and idle talk about this; he had little stomach for developing anxiety about what would come next for him when he had been living with a monkey of anxiety on his back for so long already. He thought he would try to spare himself from a double case of uncertainty, at least until he had settled his mind over the case of his love for his sweetheart.

As William looked around the carriage, briefly gazing over the view of reunited families travelling around the country once again to take in views and visit loved ones for the festive season, he noticed how women held their partners. The arm, so often shouldering rifles, straining under the weight of stretchers or holding one up against the wall of a trench, was now being tenderly grasped by women in such elegant ways. William felt his own lonely arm twitch every now and again in passive jealousy of other men's' arms carefully caressed by significant others. He longed for such a feeling and felt comfort in the fact that he was on his way to feel such a feeling himself. The train journey started to feel like it was dragging on.

A child that must have been no older than fourteen was walking up and down the isle of the carriage wishing people a good morning for no obvious reason other than he was happy that he finally had a reunited family and took his joy out on the other passengers in the train. He was greeted with cursory nods and the odd penny flung his way. When it was William's turn the boy, well dressed in a tweed hat and buttoned up shirt, wished William a good morning. The boy noticed William, hunched slightly and leaning against the window, and paused for a moment, waiting for William to reach his gaze. William did so slowly, unsure as to what to do with the presence of a human being trying to make his day just a bit nicer. He had saved this expectation for when he saw Emmanuelle. He turned and nodded to the child and whispered, "thank you". The boy looked concerned as if he was not convinced that William was indeed having a good morning. He reached inside his pocket and pulled out a penny. It had been given to him by a kind stranger who had repaid the boy's unprompted kindness with money. The boy placed it on the vacant seat next to William.

"Here. It's lucky!" the boy announced. He waited patiently for William to acknowledge the presence of this little coin which he, in turn, did. He picked the coin up, inspected it with his eyes which had barely left the horizon during the whole journey and put it in his pocket. It was enough to satisfy the boy who then made for the rest of the carriage to carry on spreading his innocent joy to others. William felt jealous that he no longer had that child-like optimism. He was 35 years old, but he still felt a longing for easier times. They seemed like a long time ago and war ages people; anxiety does too. But small gestures of kindness, one such gesture nestling comfortably in his left pocket, were things he had learnt with time and age to appreciate much more. Perhaps being older was not all bad.

The train made its juddering halt at William's stop near his destination. Turville was a sleepy village and just outside it lay his destination; the stately abode of the Meltons. He walked through the village as it was stirring in the midday cloud that was quite low that day. A few eyes followed him but he was not so much of an unknown. He was an old acquaintance to some in the village who remembered him and his love walking by their cottages in years past. He was not afforded any warm greetings but nor was he afforded any cold looks. He was simply a man given the mid-range form of greeting; nothing special. He had always been a man caught in the middle and this occasion would be no different.

The manor house lay just ahead. As he reached the stately home, he noticed it was looking brighter than he last remembered. His memory had been clouded by anxiety-induced thoughts and he noted that it had blurred his memory of colour. The manor was colourful and welcoming. The sight alone was delightful, but the occasion did not merit delightful emotions. William had still yet to see his love for the first time in over a year. He had in his other pocket, vacant of any lucky penny, the last letter he had received from her dated four months ago informing him of her good health and invitation to Buckinghamshire. The invitation itself was vague but it was all William had to go by to assure himself that he would be in some way still welcome; if only by Emmanuelle rather than the father who, to his annoyance, was also in good health.

He made for the gate which was unlocked and unguarded by any member of the household and entered the grounds. A couple of cars were parked outside. William thought that a very small party was going on inside for the windows were slightly steamed up around the right-hand side of the manor. The candles must have been lit. The end of the war allowed for lights to brighten up homes for the first time in a long time, but it was the middle of the day. A good occasion must be going on inside, William thought. He believed his luck was changing as he had timed his visit well. Perhaps Emmanuelle's father would not go too hard on him. Maybe the war's end and William's good health would prompt a change of heart. He would roll the dice no matter what in order to see his love again.

He climbed the stairs to the main door, hoping that they would fling open to reveal his long-lost love but had to settle for a loud bang on the newly polished brass on the door. The wait became excruciating for William. He had invested so much mental strength into this moment, and it had finally come. The vice had been twisting in his mind and now it was time to let it unravel. For a moment he rested his hand on his breast feeling an earthquake of a heartbeat occurring within his chest. This was the moment that he could finally breathe again himself and he would savour every breath.

The door creaked open. Whoever polished up the brass on the door clearly had forgotten to oil the hinges. To William's regret the moment was not yet over as the Melton's butler, Herbert Rolles, was standing at the door expectantly. "William Steele? You are here to visit Miss Melton, I assume". William was filled with relief that he was not forgotten, certainly by the mildly crusty butler. He had earned this familiarity from his frequent visits and noted the continuity in the butler's tone of voice. William smiled and the long-suffering butler turned and gestured for William to enter, which he did.

The view was glorious. He had not remembered its interior so well, only the angry father strutting within it. The ill-fitting clothing he was wearing as he left the manor for the final time also dominated his memory before rather than the interior decoration. Beautifully hand-crafted wooden frames surrounded elegant wallpaper and paintings to match. The landscape watercolour was a favourite medium shared by the entire Melton family and William had come to admiring the style himself. The ceilings were high allowing for the largest of paintings to be hung, made especially beautiful by the light that cascaded through the clear windows that seemed to stretch from corner to corner in endlessly connected rooms. This really was a palace to William and though Emmanuelle had always played the beauty of it down to him, this would be a marvellous place he would always hold in his heart as a little slice of high society paradise.

He perched himself on a seat in the front room, his hands locked into each other attempting to hide his nerves. He was never one for obscuring his emotions and today would be no different. He tried to distract himself whilst he waited by traversing his gaze over and around wooden leaves etched into panels in the walls, their curved edges creating a little shadow from the light from the midday sun. Noises of laughter could be heard from the rooms engaged with the voices of a few people. He heard Herbert Rolles enter that very room to inform the inhabitants of William's arrival. The heart pulsed quicker. He squeezed his index finger with his hand. The voices quietened and doors opened and closed.

After what seemed like a lifetime waiting, William was finally given what he had waited for, Emmanuelle. Her figure brightened his eyes and though his heart would remain at the same quickening pace he would afford himself the biggest smile he could muster. His hands, battered from the ordeal they subjected each other to in anxiety, opened up and strode purposefully to the woman who had dominated his dreams for so long. Her nose was unchanged, her hair was even brighter, and she greeted William with the voice he had fallen in love with.

He embraced her the same way the ocean embraces the sand. It was an embrace he had always rehearsed in his mind over and over again and now he was putting it into action. His chin nestled into her neck. His arms squeezed gently like a giant would gently squeeze a flower in order to pick it up to admire its beauty. To William, this was heaven. He was back. The world seemed, for him at least, at peace.

That was, until he noticed the embrace he was receiving in return. It was not a tight squeeze he had always remembered. She had always tightly squeezed him, often jokingly as a pretext to telling him she wanted to make she he was real. Instead, her hand gracefully touched his waist as if he was a vase she was passively inspecting. The balance of passion was falling far too greatly on his side and so his vigour for embracing her began to rapidly diminish. He retreated, feeling as if he was in no man's land again. What was going on?

He spoke, trying to make sense of things in his mind once again. "Emmanuelle. I love you. I have so missed saying it to you. But now I am back it is something I wish to say to you again and again and again". Though this was true his motive was to see what she would say back.

"I have always treasured my love for you. You are wonderful, William. Truly wonderful." Her voice seemed slower, but its song-like quality was undiminished. William's smile was reinvigorated, if not slightly hesitant. "I am glad that you are here. Your friend is here too."

She indicated for William to follow her deeper into the manor. The decoration in every single room seemed to improve though the colour seemed to be going a bit duller. Was William's eyesight going or did the light seem duller? He could not be sure, but he was still in a mild state of delirium that he was with his love again. He would follow her into the depths of Hell so long as she was there in front of him. He remained slightly on the defensive within his own mind but put it once again down to anxiety for his overthinking about their embrace.

They had passed three whole rooms before the destination had been reached. William expected to run into Emmanuelle's father who would no doubt be furious to see his return, but no such angry man was in sight. Instead, the door was open to reveal a man in bed, a few old bandages poking their way out of an ornate jar by the bedside. The man was seated, a glass of red summer wine, half-drunk was nestled in his hand. What looked to be Emmanuelle's glass was perched on the mantel piece of what seemed to be a living room that had been turned into a bedroom. The bed itself was large and there was a light wooden table with a couple of chairs either side. It had obviously been used frequently for meals as it was already laid for lunch for two. Long-burnt candles decorated the middle of the table. The figure on the bed put aside his drink and stood up with relatively little difficulty. It was Henry Forbes.

"William. It's you." Henry spoke up with slight astonishment. William had not seen Henry since he was wounded in Belgium during the German spring offensive. "I was going to write to you today". Henry indicated towards a desk that attracted little light from the smaller windows. It was bare.

"Henry. It's so good to see you. I tried to find you in the military hospitals around London. I thought you'd be there. How did you get here?" William asked.

"I was indeed there, William until the early summer. I couldn't stay of course. I had been discharged with honours from the army. I was going to make my way back to my estate, but darling Emmanuelle offered to assist with my recovery here. She's been an absolute darling and has nursed me almost back to full health. My leg should be as right as rain by the new year". Emmanuelle blushed at the compliment and walked to him, holding his arm.

"He has mentioned you a few times, especially when he told me about how he was injured in the first place." Emmanuelle informed William. "I'm so glad you were there when he was hit. I'm sure you did all you could to help."

"You were discharged from the army?" William asked with confusion. It had made no sense to him at all.

"Yes, did you not hear? Almost all the officers from the rank of Major and up have had their service reviewed. It all happened after the armistice. It's been kept under wraps for a while but it's starting to surface in the newspapers recently. Haven't you heard about it? I suppose they haven't reviewed you yet." Henry asked for a copy of today's newspaper. Emmanuelle nodded and rushed out of the room to get one.

"I don't know anything. I was only an acting Major after all." William replied. His anxiety was now growing because of the one thing he was seeking to avoid until he had seen Emmanuelle. To his inner consternation he was still anxious about it all and now he was being overwhelmed again.

"Doesn't matter, I don't think. It's all for show though, to make it appear to people that they are doing something about the whole peace deal" reassured Henry. He stood in front of William, slightly towering over him though his hobbling had brought his height down a little. "Maybe if you haven't heard anything it might be alright for you".

"Are you alright?" William asked, feeling concern for his friend.

"Oh, I'll be fine, Will. I have more than enough to fall back on. Emmanuelle has been looking after me well, Will. It's good to see you." He seemed awkward, not quite his ever-confident self. Perhaps it was his injury that had taken some of the wind out of his sails. William thought little of it, but he thought about it.

Emmanuelle re-entered the room and placed a newspaper on the table, moving cutlery and a plate for William to inspect the contents. William looked over with reluctance at the display. Indeed, the main headlines confirmed Henry's news. The British army was undergoing an apparent 'restructuring' as it pinned the blame of military defeat on seditious officers and incompetent defeatists. William read further as story after story described the more public inquiries into some of the senior men in the army. Generals and officers alike were being put on trial for their apparent disloyalty and their records were spuriously criticised. Public trials were described as Generals were judged and unceremoniously discharged without honours from the army. Some had been arrested and jailed as well. News articles had been explaining how each individual top-ranking officer had been personally involved in the debacle that was the Great War. Politicians and ministers were coming out of the woodwork to allegedly profess their long-standing suspicion with the army officers and led the charge for bringing those responsible to justice.

William read on, finding lists of names of those who had been discharged or imprisoned or worse. He was saddened to read that General Herbert Plumer, long-admired by many in the army, was not spared in the long-reaching 'review of the army' which resembled more of a purge than anything else. He had faced a public jury as if he was a war criminal and had been found guilty of all charges made against him. The general had been stripped of his medals and titles and was forced to serve ten years in prison. A footnote had even been unjustly dedicated to Major Rupert Haines; the Major William had replaced in 1917. The little paragraph declared that he had been discharged without honours and had been sentenced to two years in prison.

The worst was reserved for Field Marshall Sir Douglas Haig whose name was splashed on the headline of The Times newspaper William was inspecting. 'Haig Handed the King's Hammer' read the headline as the leading editorial described the man's fate. The old head of the British Expeditionary Force in France had been found guilty of gross negligence, murder, sedition and treason. He had been held in a symbolic manner in the Tower of London where baying crowds had gathered outside for his head. He had been turned into the great clown of the United Kingdom as he had been paraded in chains reminiscing the old medieval style of humiliating a vanquished enemy. William reeled to himself at how the article described the crowds, obviously whipped up into a fervour by the politicians and press who had led the charge for this man to be castigated as the main reason for Britain's 'defeat'. His sentence was not to be death as the last public execution had been in 1868. He had been found guilty of all counts and was sentenced to life in prison, exiled to an unknown corner of the empire where he would 'rot until death with the countless lives of dead men forever weighing down his guilty conscience'. The trial had lasted for a week and not one word was given in his defence. William witnessed the awesome power of manipulation in front of him and it was enough for him to look away in sadness feeling a bit nauseous at the same time.

"It's a bloodbath." Henry uttered. There had been no mention of Henry Forbes as far as William read, nor was there any word of William. There had been some small blessings and William felt that maybe he would publicly escape the lynching going on in the country. "I've been hiding here as much as anything. I'm surprised you have been able to go about your way so easily. You haven't been accosted by anyone, have you?"

William could feel the indent of that lucky penny the boy on the train had given to him. "No, I've been alright. Acting Majors seem to be exempt for now".

"For now, yes." Henry uttered ominously. "This won't be the end of things. The people will blame anyone, even if it's not true. In the end all that angry people want is someone to blame. It makes them feel better or less scared, I'm not sure which. They'll be pushed to be angry by whatever the newspapers or politicians tell them. If it isn't enough then they'll go for some other group and on and on until there's nothing left but the ideology that really has underpinned this whole thing. I'm worried, William. And I think you should be too. They won't stop until whatever wants to come next either forces its way into power or is stopped dead in its tracks. The clever thing is that they are currently going for those who would have the power to stop whatever wants to seize power first. Then when it's all over there won't be anything to stop them from getting what they want". Henry walked over to the table, hobbling slightly. He approached William. "This is what happens when anger takes over. They will topple our whole system. They need to be stopped."

William turned, with a sorrowful yet purposeful look. "These people are just trying to replace one dogmatic system with another. The old system wasn't perfect and whatever wants to come next won't be either. The real worry isn't the anger but the lack of a fair voice. There hasn't been one before, so why would it come now?"

Henry looked back with mild incredulity. "You surely don't take their side, do you?"

"it's not about taking sides, it's about what's right and wrong, true and untrue. We would rather lie than face the truth. We've been doing it for years."

Henry looked into William's eyes which were sad but somehow did not emanate any zeal or passion. He smiled and patted William's back. "You always were an idealist".

"I am, but unlike most, I did not let it give way to dogma and that's why I'm not a fanatic" William said confidently. He had forgotten where was; he had never seemed so confident with his own words before. He watched as Henry smiled and hobbled back to the bed. William's confidence was sapped as Emmanuelle rushed to Henry's side and helped him back to bed. It was not the gesture that William noticed, but the way Emmanuelle held Henry's hand. William recognised it; the same way the wives on the train had held the arm of their husbands. William remembered where he was again. He returned to his shattered mind, forgetting the confidence he was emitting to Henry just a moment ago.

"You still are an idealist. A dreamer!" Henry exclaimed as he sat back on his bed. Emmanuelle stood by him and looked down. "You really do spoil me; you know that?"

"I know I do" she replied. William felt a tingle down his spine. He felt like he was watching a couple, and he was the unwelcome guest. His throat went dry and his legs began to shake a bit.

"Emmanuelle" William uttered, hoping the girl of his dreams would turn round and tell him not to worry, and that she was simply a caring human looking after a broken soul. William would not be so reassured. Emmanuelle did not turn around.

"William. You are lucky to have such a good friend. I have enjoyed his company greatly and he has in turn given me such great company too" she uttered, facing Henry. She took his hand and raised it to her cheek. William looked on, his heart rapidly sinking as she did. "These past few months have been the happiest of my life and I would not trade that for the world".

William could not stand. He was witnessing his own little world collapsing. The tenderness he had long yearned for and dreamt of, waiting impatiently for, was now being felt by someone else. He tried to speak but no words could come out. He thought to protest but all he could do was watch as his heart unravelled in front of him.

"I have long wanted stability and confidence in my life. Since my mother's death I have been longing for that help that I thought could happen with you, William. I didn't know what I wanted but in these last few months I think I do." She turned to William who sat upright but was white as a sheet. "Henry and I have been good friends for a long time. We spent a good amount of time growing up together and since he has been here it has reminded me of those old and special times. Nursing him in my home has reminded me of all the feelings I had for him when I was young when we used to play games together. I loved you, but I love him. He can give me what I want, and right now I think that is what I need. This isn't easy for me and I'm truly sorry, I really am. I wanted to tell you in a better way or at a better time, but I think it would have been worse if I let you go on thinking of me when I can no longer think of you." She was still singing; her voice was as angelic as ever. It was light and every word seemed to hang in the air. But these words hung around and clung to William like weights pulling him down into the depths of an ocean. With every breath she made he felt like he was sinking more and more.

"But I've come back. I'm here now" William gasped as if he was gasping for air, trying desperately to change the fate that he had been so desperate to avoid.

"It's not like that, William. I love Henry and I always will. Please understand. In another time, in another world, maybe things might be

82

different but with the world as it is right now, please know that I am Henry's now. I'm sure you can understand".

William's hand fell on the table, using the open newspaper as a bed. He gazed over to it again as if he was attempting to get lost in its words again. His brain would not let him. His anxiety would not let him. It had won. "I don't understand. I love you." The words seemed so hollow to say. They were simple leaves in the wind by now. He looked to Henry who he thought might save him or say something that might save the day. He remained silent and could not even look at William, preferring to gaze at Emmanuelle waiting to see if she needed some loving support. She did indeed and he hobbled up to her and put his hand on her shoulder. She placed her delicate hand on his and looked at William, tears lining her eyes ready to fall down her cheek.

There was nothing left to say. Henry and Emmanuelle had an unwelcome guest in the house, and they had given their news for William to digest. William's eyes looked to the window as the condensation on the glass revealed more than they should have to his broken mind. He was sitting in a room where he had been stabbed in the back by his love and his friend to whom he still owed a lot to. William considered the debt repaid and stood up. He made for the door to the room but turned back, his own eyes fogging up with tears as he desperately tried to find the words to say something. None were forthcoming. What could he say? Emmanuelle stared at him, the tears finally cascading down her face.

He longed to wipe away those tears. He longed to hold her once more. He longed to hear her musical voice once more. He longed to tease her about her nose once more. He could not do this anymore. He simply stared at her, his breath speeding up as it started to work in time with his beating heart as it broke with every thump. He took one last look at her, thinking that it will be like the final goodbye from the greatest dream in the world that had turned into a nightmare at the last second. She was still so beautiful though her colour seemed diminished in his eyes. Her blue and green winter dress was catching the timid draft that was coming through the open-door William was holding. He thought he might smile his last smile to her, but the figure of Henry standing behind her made that impossible. He grasped the door handle and opened it further and stood in the doorway, ready to close it again.

"C'est la vie" he whispered, practically choking the words out through his dry throat and destructive inner emotions. He looked one more time into her eyes as he closed the door. As he did, he could hear the sound of his one-time unofficial fiancé bursting into tears. In years gone by he would break down the door and come to her aid. He simply looked at the door this time and sighed, letting his own tears dance their sombre way down his cheeks.

He noticed a stiff-looking man in the same room. Rolles was standing nonchalantly. He bowed and passively directed William to the front door. As he escorted the broken man to the exit, he lightly patted William's back. It was a small gesture, but now more than ever, William appreciated the little things. For now, it was all he had left.

As quickly as the door opened to greet him, it closed again. William could have sworn that he had seen the butler looking a tad more saddened than before, but he was not sure. There was no point in wondering. William could not escape the overwhelming feeling that was overtaking every sense in his body. The world seemed duller. His anxiety, temporarily standing down due to the concluded nature of its previous origins, quietly shuffled its way to the back of William's mind as it basked in the uncertainty of the national lynching of army officers.

William trudged down Turville village once more, waving a mental goodbye to the little place he had hoped he would move to with his love and spend the rest of their life in. He wanted to live near Emmanuelle's manor so she would not feel like she was too far away from her home. These were just dreams now, never to become a reality.

As he trudged to the train station, not knowing when the next train would be, he noticed a horse-drawn carriage pass him by. Not wanting to get in the way of anyone else, he darted quickly out of the road he was walking down. It slowly passed by him. He glanced to see that Charles Melton was inside and the two locked eyes. Even in victory, Charles would not even lend a passing cursory gesture of respect to the broken man. The carriage simply moved on past and William found himself feeling even more lonely.

He would have to go back to London and think about what to do in a house owned by the man who had stolen the love of his life, hoping to

God that the mob would not soon come after him. He was not even so sure that he could get his old job back at the French embassy. He was powerless once again, feeling like a leaf being dragged down the current of a stream. He dreaded what might await him at the end of the stream.

William sat alone and dejected on the train station platform. There was no news about when the next train to London would be. Hours went by. The cold afternoon moulded into the cold evening and the chill finally entered William's bones. He began to shiver, contemplating letting the cold air do its best to take its toll on him. After all, heaven would be a greater place to be than in an area which still harboured so many treasured memories. Even the train station itself glistened with the memories of yester-year. He was sitting on the same bench he sat on with Emmanuelle when they were both eagerly dreading the arrival of the train to take William back to London. They had both counted the minutes they still had left with each other, choosing sometimes to laugh the time away, and sometimes to sit together in silence in each other's arms. This was the first time William had longed for a train to come.

The next thing William knew he was waking from a nap. He had dozed off for an unknown time and had found his head slightly creased from the hard wooden pillow he had unexpectedly fashioned. He had not woken though, of his own volition as two figures seemed to be standing close nearby. His groggy eyes slowly started to recalibrate their vision again and he noticed two men in tweed hats and uniforms with green insignias on their tunics. William thought to himself that it was a brave thing for men to be seen in public in officers' clothing.

He swung himself round and sat up-right. The men approached him, and one took a seat on the bench next to him. The standing man then took his place opposite the bench and seemed to be looking side to side. The seated man leaned over to William and in a hushed voice asked "William Steele?"

"Yes" William replied. His anxiety returned with a vengeance thinking that it was his time to be arrested.

"You used to work at the French embassy?" the man asked, continuing to speak silently despite the train station being quite deserted.

"Yes, not for a long time" William admitted, confused at the line of questioning.

The two mysterious men looked at each other, nodding in unison. The man returned to look at William. He paused before asking "Would you like to witness the ending of the French Republic?"

Chapter 8

The old restaurant basement was still cold from February's harsh winter days. A couple of fur coats draped over a chair in the corner of the damp room available to anyone who had let the cold get the better of them. The atmosphere was also cold, with people seated around a long and wide table. Papers and pamphlets littered the tabletop in a random mess. The vague smell of sweat clung in the air which distracted those who breathed through their nose from the noises coming from the small street window at the top of a wall. It was a windy day but down in the basement most were safe from the draft though the window threatened to allow late winter's frost to enter the room. A warm orange glow bloomed at random intervals against the small windowpane. Paris was alight.

A couple of men in the room were wearing tattered old French army uniforms with the added decoration of a red arm band tied to the left arm sleeve. Two women in self-fashioned military regalia sat patiently but mirrored the attitude of the men inside; tired, exhausted even; but unable to close their eyes. They were all seated around the table with no intention of listening to anyone. It was a meeting with no one prepared to bring their own attention to it. It seemed better just to remain still and wait for energy to return. Hanging over them was a French tricolour flag with a red star crudely painted in the middle. A few more such flags were draped over vacant chairs with one big one sprawled on the table obscured by the pamphlets and letters.

Sitting at the assumed head of the table was the tall and thin figure of Maurice Renaudin, perhaps the most exhausted of them all. He had finally decided to grow a moustache with attached beard but his progress had been slow and so it was not quite as impressive as some that were on display in the room and around Paris itself. He had long disposed of his military uniform, choosing instead to don the clothes he wore when he last left his home in Sedan; a battered old suit and tie. His head was falling down the back of the chair with his legs desiring to hop onto the table to form a more horizontal pose. Perhaps that would help him relax. His voice was hoarse, so he had wrapped a scarf around his neck attempting to keep it warm in a bid to help it recover. Even though the odd man or woman would occasionally enter or leave the dingy cellar, barely lit by oil lamps, it would not stir him from his waking sleep. He might be approached once or twice by someone but even that would not elicit a movement of any limb. He simply refused, at this time, to expel any more energy for the time being.

Maurice Renaudin was indeed a sought-after man, but this was of his own volition. He had been very busy since the war's end and his talents which had made him a pariah within the French army had made him a local celebrity. His reputation as a belligerent, free to speak his mind, had earned him a small podium in the local barracks. He was listened to intently and he spoke with passion, railing against the elites for selling the French people down the river to the German aristocracy. As it became more and more evident that France was going to sign the treaty that would bury it as a proud nation more and more flocked to listen to what they believed was a man possessed to tell them what to do next. He would attract crowds of hundreds of men and his perorations would be retold in far less eloquent ways to more and more in the French army. He had become a cult hero within the ranks of the division.

When France signed the Versailles Treaty in November 1918 it agreed to break up the army. This initially threated to rob Maurice of his podium, but in fact it had unleashed him to the rest of the nation. He was quick to find himself a new way of speaking and he did so, unleashing his talents that he had masterfully hidden during four years of war. He began to write but not before he had finished reading. He had been given a little red book and he had kept it close to him ever since. He initially thought that it might be useful if a bullet came for his breast as it would probably be stopped by the thick pages. But then he buried his nose in its contents and found it to be more useful than a bullet shied. The Communist Manifesto, signed by Vladimir Lenin himself, greeted the impressionistic firebrand. He read its contents, feeling that he finally had an ideological ally. All he had spoken about seemed to be underpinned by political and sociological science that had been set down by Karl Marx and Friedrich Engels. All the ills of the world that he and many of his fellow countrymen were feeling had finally been explained. Though Maurice had mentioned many of these things already, finally he had something to link his ideas together.

Not only did the book inform him of why things were going so wrong for him, but what he could do to change it; revolution. It had occurred with such success in Russia and there was no reason to see from his point of view why it could not happen here. Was France not the centre of revolution for the world anyway? Did the French Revolution show that it was to be here that the great social and political experiments would bubble here and show them for their greatness? Maurice saw France's destiny under the red banner and had orated this as such to all who were willing to hear. He had used the anger of many to make them see the light.

France was indeed angry. The Versailles Treaty was widely seen as unjust and unfair. France had not lost the war, and this was reason enough for many to denounce the treaty as a dictated peace. The President and his government had painted themselves as traitors to France. What angered the people further was the government's reluctance to follow a similar course to Britain by conducting a harsh review of the French army; notably a harsh review into the officers and Generals. The French Government had instead opted to attempt to seek assistance from the army in order to keep order in France, as well as asking for assistance from the Germans to help stop the nation from falling in on itself. The army, now drastically smaller in size, was now the only source of authority within France. The 'sacred union' which had kept the nation going in wartime had completely evaporated, and thus the French army itself was secretly in open revolt with factions already bidding for its soldiers and authority. Factions began carving their own unofficial borders as the republic looked on in powerless incredulity.

The greatest mistake the French government made was when it decided to 'renovate' the Palais Bourbon which had suffered minor structural damage during the latter stages of the war. These damages were negligible at best, but it served as an excuse for the French parliament to gather everything it had and leave to set up a temporary home in Bordeaux. The French parliament, government and President had effectively fled the capital. The power vacuum left was not just in Paris itself but in all the major French regions which saw the move as part of the final death throes of the French Third Republic.

To the West of the country, the tricolour was hardly on display; instead, the white shield with black markings could be seen marking the identity of those living in Brittany. To the south the red flag with a yellow cross was waved in major cities along with other similar-coloured banners. And in Paris itself the blazoned tricolour with a star in the middle accompanied flag poles with the hammer and sickle waving to the side dotted the streets of the old capital. Nothing held the country together save the final symbols of authority that barely made a sound as justice was served by bands of roving citizens. Outdoor courts conducting make-shift trials and meeting out punishments became commonplace in major cities where people took matters of vengeance into their own hands. Throughout the land to varying degrees of regularity people with public ties to the officer corps or the republic were publicly tried and sentenced for their crimes and treachery. The very thing the republican government wanted to avoid was occurring anyway yet still they could not guarantee to themselves the full support of the army.

Nowhere else was the people's anger more obvious than within Paris itself. Only there was the old and infamous guillotine wheeled out in one or two instances and put to rare but public use. The favoured punishments of these flying people's courts was execution and death by shooting was the preferred method. They seemed to pop up quickly and they could be found in many of the city's open spaces. Some were more feared by others and few were safe. The more a Parisian had moulded him or herself into the angry crowd the less likely he or she was to be accused of being a traitor. This was because the choice of victims in Paris was largely arbitrary where a single display of any sort of meaningful wealth was treated as clear evidence of war profiteering and benefiting from 'German blood money'. Many valuables had been dumped into the river in an attempt by some to save their own lives, but sentries managed to not let these people get through the net.

Maurice Renaudin held an impromptu court which was found at the foot of the Eiffel Tower. There unlike other makeshift open-air court rooms he orated speeches in between sentences doing his best to allay the doubts and guilty consciences of anyone in the growing crowds. The long days and nights of his courts had earned his square greater publicity and it would only be a couple of months before his stall had been elevated by a

90

wooden structure. After a couple of months, it would take a guilty man or woman forty-five steps to get to the top of the wooden structure to be on full display whilst Maurice sat behind his even higher platform to pass judgement. He was starting to symbolise the law within the city and other open court areas started to write down his words and his sentences in accordance with the crimes of the accused. Maurice had developed a book of his own; the book of laws for the Parisian revolution. Most crimes merited the death penalty but it made for good propaganda and the book was put into bloody print in late February.

The man, whose own star was rising within the minds of more and more Parisians, was finally resting in the basement of a long-closed restaurant. It had been the first time in over three months that he had taken a breather from his speeches and his court sessions. He was wielding power though it was by no means permanent or protected. He was enjoying his time in the sun but he knew more than anyone that he was threatened with the end of the bloody party he had invested so much energy in maintaining. It was in this dingy basement that he had been discussing with members of a small and impromptu 'inner circle' about the possibility of forming a political party.

2 days prior to Maurice's waking slumber in a Parisian basement he had been contacted by members of the Bolshevik Party in Russia. The Soviet Revolution had been in full swing and it was clear that very prominent members of the Russian Communists had seen in Maurice a keen ally and kindred spirit. They had offered money and, more importantly, weapons in order to assist with his growing popularity and quest for 'influence'. The seed planted within the feverish mind of this fanatic was the idea of a political party. He was given the idea of using the old republic to further his own long-term gains which he had though, yet to set down. It would be the best way, informed the Russians who had contacted him, to spread support throughout the rest of the country. Only then would France be able to rise up against the oppressors.

This was the reason for the meeting in the basement that had ended up becoming a meeting of sleep. The meeting itself had started several hours ago but Maurice was in no fit state to orate his plans, nor would he countenance another to do it for him. His fanaticism had inflated his own ego and thus he was unable to let anyone else dictate the most important of plans. Maurice was under no illusions that he had to solidify himself as the leader of this new movement starting in the basement of a disused restaurant.

It would fall to the next day when the self-proclaimed leader would finally muster up the strength to dictate his plans. He did not stand, electing instead to sit and allow himself the comfort of sitting down whilst he expelled what energy he could muster into outlining in full his plans to his inner circle of ex-soldiers, guerrilla fighters and confidants. Maurice had few friends to call upon so these would have to do. He would not despise these people, but he would always keep them at an arm's length. He orated his desires allowing for others to write them down.

"I have decided that the French people need to realise their destiny. The upcoming elections to the French assembly are vital. I know I have originally said that we should boycott them but in fact it is the perfect time for us to use the old and decaying structures of the state to impose our new state from within. The trouble with the state now is that it is fractured and that will do us no good. We will suffer greatly as people if we do not keep together the French nation. Therefore, we cannot wait. We must begin with great haste to spread our message and develop our brand. We have two months, but it is possible. We must use the apparatus of the capital, seize the assets of those we judge rather than burning them to the ground. We must steal to win. We must reverse the separatist trend for then and only then can we even begin to rally against the evil of the Versailles Treaty and the evil bourgeoise capitalism that fuels it. It is the destiny of France and we must be there to guide France towards it".

He listed off the initial points and outlined the programme of the new party, calling for the mass nationalisation of all French assets and services, tying the French nation to the new and developing International of workers and to eradicate, by any means, any resistance that might come against the new party. He stated that he would develop more principles of the party in time as he himself admitted that he was still waiting for guidance from the Russians who were much more advanced in their Communist revolution and were showing them the way. The people around him were encouraged to spread the word, began printing and distributing with an eye to seizing the initiative before anyone else tried to do something similar. Maurice and his band would have the upper hand being the most influential revolutionary group in the capital, but the rest of the decaying nation needed to be seized as well.

Renaudin's revolutionaries began to be discussed even if they were not fully understood in town after town after town. The Parisian printing areas were so well-used that Renaudin was fast becoming infamous within the heart of the French nation. The newly created 'Patriotic Communist Party of France' or the PCPF had been formed; the star that had been crudely drawn on the tricolour flag was adopted as the emblem and Maurice Renaudin was made the party leader and secretary. The PCPF was very soon officially allowed to be in the running for the upcoming French elections on the 1st May.

Maurice carried on purging Paris of anyone that dared to speak out for the republic or against the new authority that was fast seizing control of the city. The republican government from Bordeaux would occasionally threaten to send in the military to attempt to wrestle control of the city back and on two occasions they did so. Maurice and his followers simply hid in the shadows, employing an old tactic Maurice used when he had to avoid punishment in the army. As soon as the military left the capital would once again fall in all but name to the Patriotic Communists. There was talk of assassinating the mayor of Paris but Maurice quelled any talk of such a move, fearing the threat of alienating potential voters. This was after all perhaps the last chance the nation would vote in a national election; the threat of a breakup of the French nation was real. Maurice could not antagonise moderates who by now were beginning to listen to his propaganda outside of Paris, outside of the control of the flying courts that were ruling Paris with fear. In other cities the PCPF was seen as a potential uniting force by some that could possibly reform some sense of national order.

The nominal head of the fastest-growing political party in France was soon able to rule and dictate without being present in day-to-day meetings. Many within the inner circle had heard enough of his orations to assume what he wanted done without him actually saying anything and they were largely correct. Few times did Maurice have to check the actions of his cronies, of whom remained largely unchanged for the whole election period.

That would all change with just a week to go before voters went to the polls to determine the future of the French Republic after the Great War. This would be the first time the nation would get to voice their opinion on the war, the treaty and the nation. Much was riding on this and many opposing voices knew so much was riding on this. This was why with just under seven days before the polls opened Maurice received a letter from an unlikely source, the old lion of Verdun.

Philippe Petain had been known as a war hero with the victorious battle of Verdun masterminded by him. He was still a Marshall in the army and had still commanded great respect with many soldiers both in the army and those who had been discharged. After the war he had fled to the south where he had developed the myth of an army that had been stabbed in the back. He had become an outspoken critic of the French republic and after the war declared that the war could have been won had it not been for the armistice that was sought after by a desperate French government. He was right in many ways, though he failed to disclose to those who adored him that he was just as much a defeatist as his government was in 1918. But the wily old lion was too much of a war hero to ever let the defeatism define his reputation. He was a hero and he used that to his advantage after the war. He had remained in Marseille for a long time, developing his own patriotic movement which gained widespread support in the Occitan region of southern France. His own new party 'The Popular People's Party of France', or the PPPF, had gathered so much support that it was beginning to make serious inroads in the west of France as well, previously seen as an area of separatist support. Even in Bordeaux where the old French republic has set up its final stand the hooked cross of Petain's party could be seen dangling out of the windows.

Many ex-soldiers flocked to the south to become a part of the movement, helping him develop the most powerful paramilitary organisation in France. He was barely threatened by the French republic and military. He ruled by decree in many southern French cities. Only Toulon proved to be a bit more difficult for him to gain support. A sizeable majority of the city favoured instead Renaudin's Patriotic Communist party over Petain. It was this and the meteoric rise of Renaudin's own profile that prompted Petain to send a message to the tall thin man in the old capital city now seen as perpetually on fire.

The contents of the latter astounded those who read it, making sure to read it before it was handed over to the self-appointed leader who only a year ago was a lowly private in the French army. When it finally reached Maurice, the letter itself creased with dirty thumb prints, the contents forced the tired leader to his feet and forced himself to pace the room deep in thought. The letter indicated that Petain was offering a partnership with Renaudin. The two parties could at the last moment form an anti-republic league, uniting the two parties under one banner. Therefore, whilst it was no certainty that either party could form a majority big enough to end the republic from within, it was almost a complete certainty that if they worked together the same goal could be achieved. It was an electoral pact that tantalised and agonised the leader into giving it a lot of thought.

Maurice's inner circle could not find a consensus. Some argued for the party to fight on its own merit rather than selling out the party. Others saw the pragmatism and urged Maurice to take the offer seriously and to give it the affirmative if the primary goal was to end the republic once and for all. Maurice, for one of the few moments of his life, was unsure as to what to do next. It was not clear, and he was torn. Petain was playing a good game. Maurice had the numbers and Petain had the means and the military. The two combined would be unstoppable. But what would it cost? What would happen next? Maurice would have to really do his best to come out on top afterwards, but would he not have to do that anyway? His party was still young, and it could not hope to compete with an established figure at this early stage.

Maurice overruled those who disagreed him, allowing them to leave the room and inner circle, and he stated to those who remained what his reply would be. "Tell the Lion of Verdun that we accept".

Chapter 9

The invitation had been burning on William's dresser in his little apartment in London for a long time. It lay there in full display which was quite against the intentions of the mysterious strangers who had sword William to utter secrecy. He had let it prop up against an empty picture frame where a photograph had once nestled inside. That photo had long since been disposed of but not without a large glass of something strong. The letter was something different to gaze at from his bed. He had dreamt of what the letter meant and what exactly was waiting for him. He had not received such a gilded and mysterious invitation. Perhaps he was the only one in the whole of London to receive such a letter. Maybe the next-door neighbour also had one. He didn't know. He was given orders to be tight lipped about the whole affair.

The letter specifically asked the recipient of the letter to be at Paddington station at a six-thirty in the morning on Friday the 18th April. The recipient was to take nothing with them and to wear plain clothes. No one, not even the recipient's family were to be aware of the note, the date or the destination. The letter was not signed, only the initials I.W.G.C. was engraved at the top. The initials were not known to William who simply treated the whole affair with scepticism. His mind had been soured still by the affair with Emmanuelle and he had since fallen into a deep depression. Life after war was hard enough, especially with such uncertainty all around.

William had tried to re-enter the office of his old job at the French embassy, but he had been politely refused; the situation in France was too volatile to keep the embassy open at that time. It was his only possible means of returning in any quick way to a normal life. He thus entered the same long line of returning soldiers waiting for a job to appear or hoping for a new life somewhere else. William briefly fantasised with going abroad to find his fortune somewhere in the empire but his ability to fund such a venture was too low for any guarantee of a journey back. He would not take such a risk.

He had also flirted with the idea of returning home to his parents in Devon. They had kept him in the loop on a bi-monthly basis about their comings and goings. They had decided to move to Exeter, choosing instead to hire some ex-soldiers to work on the farm. In the city itself they had funded the opening of a small accountancy firm where they had made a good profit. Their stock had risen once again as William's had somewhat fallen, though he was still a commissioned officer in the British army and had still somehow avoided the purge of British officers, which by now was running out of steam. The idea to return to the family home was very tempting but it seemed like too much of a backward step for a thirty-three-year-old man who was still trying to make something of himself like his father, who had built his way up from a lowly farmer to the owner of large tracts of land in south Devon. Returning home would be a supreme admission of failure and William knew there was little chance he would ever venture out from home as he did before, again.

He would meet his fate in London either to the end or as part of a springboard to the next great opportunity. That was why the letter had secretly meant so much to him; it was his only way forward. He had no idea whether it was just a hoax or a great prank. Perhaps as a final insult, his ex-friend Henry has treated him to a final hilarious stitch-up. Perhaps it was the best thing that could ever happen to him. He had no idea and the conversation with the two mysterious men on the train platform in Buckinghamshire was too short for him to have any idea about what was coming. He would make the journey, but he would take his revolver with him, just in case.

For that was what his life so far had made him. Where once he was care-free he had become cautious. Where he was once trusting he had become suspicious. Where he was once excited, he had become apprehensive. The William before the war, before the ordeal with Emmanuelle, was more content and naïve but with hope for the future. Perhaps this metamorphosis was being experienced with hundreds of thousands of men up and down the country as they slowly returned to a former life with a very different perspective of the world. A couple of men from his company had reportedly suffered from some sort of delayed shellshock and couldn't work the fields anymore. He had not quite succumbed to that fate but he too noticed the great change that had occurred within him.

All these thoughts were commonplace at night to William who had little else to think about. He was out of work and the clock was ticking on his financial ability to remain in the house still owned by the family of the man who he believed would be marrying Emmanuelle by the end of the year. The ordeal sickened him and he became more and more alone with the sickening thoughts. Sleep became impossible, sitting still became impossible and even walking around a changing London that had seen riots and demonstrations in infrequent regularity and size would not help sedate his whirling mind. He had taken to drawing in his room with whatever he could afford. He had painted the same views from his two windows again and again. The paintings would not get any better but they served their purpose for a brief time.

The night before the letter's date arrived William had customarily not slept for a minute. Was it excitement or anxiety that overflowed within him? It was a similar feeling had felt the first time he was involved in a battle during the war. He had no idea what battle would be like aside from the odd comment in the training grounds in Kent and Northern France. He had chosen not to believe the odd scare story and would instead go on his own instincts and experience. Though he would be given a rude lesson in the realities of war he did nonetheless feel mixes of excitement before zero hour. On that night, especially an hour before go-time, he felt once again as if he was holding his watch to his eyes, his whistle to his mouth, waiting for the signal to go. Paddington would be his battlefield that day.

Paddington station was one of the few sights he saw that looked similar before and after war. It had extended its size a bit and trains seemed more readily available to come and go but in terms of its structure, its delightful clock and its smell it had remained largely unchanged to William's delight. It did not need to change so why would it? Structural continuity made William smile and he allowed himself to do so for a moment. It was not a busy morning though the sun was just about to slide its spherical structure over the soot-covered roofs of Central London. The hustle and bustle of the day would not commence for a while longer and only two trains were waiting in the station that morning. They both looked like they had been sleeping there overnight, resting their tired wheels before they would expel clouds of smoke making their way all over the western parts of the country.

The last time William was here he had returned from Buckinghamshire and so he was desperate to create better and nicer memories here. He walked slowly past the places he once stood and sat at as his younger self in past times seemed to materialise in those places. The past self would wait here at the train station to await the train that would take him to see his darling Emmanuelle. The trains from this platform also took him to and from his home and this gave him a warm feeling of safety. He was much younger then and still he could see his twelve-year-old self hanging desperately to the arm of his mother as the family were rushing desperately for the train back home. His parents were always sticklers for getting to places on time so he could see his younger self waiting patiently and impatiently on the station seats. One such seat was still after so many years missing an arm rest which had enabled an eight-year-old William to rest horizontally on the chair. If he was asleep, he would only be woken by his mother when the train was but five minutes from leaving. The small mercies from parents were things William believed he would never forget, and this meant that he could still see them being acted out in front of him as he passed the very place that they happened.

Once again, though to his slight confusion, he had found himself waiting on the station platform, though there was no hint of a soul moving to greet him. Perhaps he was on the wrong side of the station? He did not exactly know where to stand so he had made himself as conspicuous as possible. Six-thirty passed and still there was no sign. William thought that the funny joke had begun and thought about leaving. He watched the station clock, making a pact with himself that as soon as fifteen minutes passed, he would leave. As fifteen minutes passed, he made the same pact again. He knew that leaving would condemn him to lose the only thing he was hoping would help him get a life again.

The clock elegantly slid its hands into the seven-thirty position. Little had stirred for an entire hour and commuters were beginning their daily dances to work. William thought to himself that he got the date wrong. He had brought the letter with him as it was the only bit of proof that he had to show to whoever was meeting him. It was the only bit of proof to William to show that he might still matter. He took out the letter and checked the contents for the hundredth time. He was right and spot on. The time had come and gone. Whoever they were, they were either late or not real. William cursed his luck in his mind and stood up to walk out.

No sooner had he stood up when a stranger from a group of people walking past him thrust his hand into William's dangling counterpart. "There you are! Great to see you. It's been too long. Come with me! The car's waiting. Blimey, you're late. Two sugars in your tea as usual, squire? You always were a two-lumper!" The man seemed to be rushing through some incoherent one-way conversation that had left William speechless. William did indeed take two sugars in his tea but he had not made this known to anyone but himself and a couple of men in his company. The man hadn't let go of William's hand yet he was already moving with William closely following him as if guiding him away like his mother. William looked back at the station where had been sitting for over an hour and noticed the apparitions of his younger self melt away.

The car was black, the windows so thick you couldn't really see. The man who had accosted him laughed and opened the door practically throwing the startled William in. He fell onto the leather seats within and felt the car spinning into gear and driving along at a speed faster than he had ever felt a car go. He sat upright and saw two men staring back at him with expressions that resembled the contortions of a face that had just bitten into a lemon. They seemed unwilling to talk and they spread that feeling towards William who likewise didn't feel like talking. He just wanted to see what would happen. A more vocal William would have asked questions and demanded answers. But by now he was just happy to be doing something different to staring out of his window barely able to paint the tops of the houses he was looking out on. They could be driving to the seaside to give William a nice day on the beach and he would not mind. He was just happy to be out of London and not at home. He occasionally blurted out the odd "hello" but he would not get anything back other than a cursory nod, but that could have been as a result of a bump in the road.

Though the journey itself was long it had seemed like a moment for the startled William Steele. He was back out in the countryside though he had not expected his destination to be what it was. The giant structure revealed itself slowly after numerous mysterious checkpoints on a long country road in the middle of nowhere. From the undergrowth of William's view from the car arose the mighty walls of Blenheim Palace. It was gigantic with marvellously well-kept gardens littered around the baroque masterpiece. William noticed the large amount of human presence around the palace which resembled more of a military complex than a large palatial house that it had been for many years.

The car rolled into the courtyard and William was ushered out of his motor-carriage as quickly as he had entered it. He was rushed through the magnificent entrance doors, briefly taking in the view of the glorious stone columns that flanked the entrance. He was taken through, flanked by the two men who had stared at him the entire journey, to a large smoke-filled room. There were a few people huddled around the desk on the other side of the room but because of its size William could be forgiven for thinking that his entrance and presence on the other side might go unobserved. He took in the corners of the room, thinking that it was more of a painting in itself. It was beautiful and would be so much better presented if it had more access to natural light. This room was clearly located more in the centre of the palace itself, for the only natural light came from a small glass dome in the ceiling. The room itself was gas lit though these were being extinguished on William's entry.

"Major Steele!" boomed a voice from the other side of the room. The voice sounded familiar to William's ears, but he could not be sure. The figures on the other side of the room seemed to have noticed his presence after all, but not after a good minute or two of awkward shuffling on William's part in his very comfortable armchair he had found himself in. After noticing his surname echoing about the room, he had spied a bottle of whiskey near him with two empty glasses. He fancied a look at the bottle to inspect the quality but immediately thought it better to remain seated and still. The two men were by the door William had entered and though they were not looking directly at him he knew that he was in the corner of their eye. Any sudden movements might prompt them to action. He sat still.

The figures on the other side of the room stirred towards William. Two of them were in distinguishable officers' uniform and another two were in similar looking uniforms but rather than the red lapels and insignias they were green. One other man was wearing a suit similar to

William's attire. They were all making for his chair. "Well, are you Major Steele or not?" cried the voice again.

"Well, acting- "William replied hesitantly.

"Acting what?" came the voice again. He began to see where it was coming from. Field Marshall Edmund Ironside and General Plumer were walking towards him. He had read that they had both been condemned to prison and yet they were making their way towards him. William had remembered Ironside's voice from when he used to work for the Field Marshall back in 1917. The small party made their way to William who was about to stand to attention when he was waved to remain seated by Herbert Plumer.

"He was never promoted to Major, Edmund. He holds the rank of captain" one of the officers with green insignias stated from behind the two commanders.

"Oh, does he?" No wonder it was easy to keep him under wraps!" the chuckling Field Marshall retorted. "Yes, I've always liked him, you know. Good desk man. Good to have a metal in your surname too! Iron and steel! We've got the right man" exclaimed Edmund Ironside. He seemed rather chipper for a man who according to the newspapers would be a few months into his long prison sentence.

"Right, Captain Steele. Let's get this over with, shall we?" Herbert Plumer, four months into his apparent prison service, stated. "You were working for the French embassy before the war, is this correct?" William nodded. "That means you are well known to the French diplomatic service, correct?" He had been well known for his work at the embassy, having mastered the French language better than many of his colleagues. He had long discussions with the French ambassador, Pierre-Paul Cambon, about the long-desired alliance between Britain and France having seemingly foretold of the coming war months before it began.

"I remember interesting conversations I had with some of the French diplomats, yes" William humbly replied.

"Enough for them to remember you, it seems!" Ironside interjected.

Plumer carried on informing William of what was going on. "How aware are you of the state of internal politics of the French state, Captain Steele?"

"I don't know much. There's an election coming" William admitted. He had not kept abreast of what was going on in Europe, taking the popular view that affairs on the continent were assumed to be the express interest of Germany who was seen to be in charge of everything over the channel.

Plumer sighed slowly. "You have much to catch up on. The important thing is that we don't have, currently, many ears to the ground in France right now. It's not the best place currently for an Englishman to find himself in now. France is experiencing political upheaval, and most worryingly one such new development is the rise in French Communism. It's proving very popular and it looks like they will establish some sort of foothold in French politics when the elections come along in a week or two's time. We're worried that something similar might happen here, and the Prime Minister is waiting until after the French elections and for enough information on the rise of this political ulcer to be collected, whereby he will then call for an election here. We don't want the Labour Party or some other ghastly organisation to have any similar toehold here. We need spies, on the inside, to help us understand just what is going on, how support for this movement is taking hold and how best we can stop such an awful revolution from occurring here, alright?"

William was startled by the news. He took in the information, trying his best to contemplate and understand what was being told. "Why do we have to resort to spying?"

"Intentions must be kept secret. Officially the army is more interested in sorting out the troubles in Ireland, but the Prime Minister is much more worried about the fate of the French Republic." Plumer gestured one of the officers forward. "Officially, Edmund and I are serving out our prison sentences. Luckily the government has seen sense to put us to good use by giving us this important task of political observation of a foreign power. We would like you to join a small group of people who will infiltrate France and report back on what exactly is going on over there so we can avoid any catastrophe here. Do you understand?" William nodded, he had little to say. He was overwhelmed.

"Officially you will be sent not as a representative of the British army but as a representative of the new Imperial War Graves Commission." Edmund Ironside explained, indicating the reason behind the green-coloured lapels on the officer's uniforms. "The organisation has been officially set up to coordinate the building of war cemeteries around the old battlefields. We will use the organisation to funnel operatives such as yourself into France."

William, seemingly adding layers of overwhelmed emotion to his already-overloaded mind, allowed his eyes to wander to the suited man who had remained quiet the whole time. General Plumer follow his gaze and grinned. "Of course, Britain isn't the only country interested in the goings-on in France".

The man, tight-lipped, young and well-dressed stepped forward. He had a swagger that seemed out of place in Britain. As he spoke, he gave away the reason why he looked so different. His American accent betrayed his mysterious background. "John Edgar Hoover. I represent United States interests abroad. Your information would be most useful to the American administration. Pleasure to meet you, by the way". The man extended his hand, something that had not been done by the British top-brass. William, eyes wide open trying to take information in, extended his own and their hands shook. "Good, firm handshake. I trust a man who can do that".

The seat William had found himself in had gradually become less and less comfortable. He was sitting in the resplendent nerve centre of an organization that was secretly sending out spies. He realised the magnitude of the situation as it dawned on him that he was forced to know information that could get him into trouble if he spoke about this experience to anyone. He was still not sure if refusing this post was going to do him any favours too. "Why have you chosen me?"

"You're known to some of the important people within the administration of the French Republic. You can speak French well, you have military training, you're a serving officer, you don't have any important ties to this country, certainly not after your meeting with Miss Emmanuelle Melton". Plumer listed. Mentioning of Emmanuelle sent the coldest of shivers up William's spine, not just because he was surprisingly reminded of her, but because they had known about it in the first place. They had revealed, possibly on purpose, that they knew much more about him then he had thought. Plumer removed all doubt; "And you haven't met with your friend Henry in a while. You're the perfect candidate, aren't you?" Plumer turned his back on William to ask one of the officers for a piece of paper. Plumer turned back around. "We've saved you from the angry mob but we wouldn't be able to save you if you got into any trouble in France. You'd be on your own over there, but this is a simple reconnaissance exercise. It shouldn't be so difficult."

"How long would I have to be in France?"

"At least until the end of the year. The details will be made obvious to you when you arrive." Edmund Ironside replied.

"Do I have to decide now?"

The American agent piped up again. "Well, you can wait. But you don't exactly have much to go back to, now do you? Just go for it. No need to paint from your window anymore. You can do some actual work for your country." It weas clear that he had been watched and his information had been given to the Americans too.

"I guess I don't have much of a choice." William resigned himself to saying. Agent Hoover slapped him on the back hard.

"Good man" Plumer quietly exclaimed. He nodded to the two men who had been waiting by the door, signalling that they had finished their business with the startled Captain.

William saw that his time was up and stood up. He made to turn away but thought about this moment and took the opportunity to ask; "Marshall Ironside, sir. Why did we lose the war?"

The question seemed to visually irritate the Field Marshall who had by now turned around to walk away. The question seemed to hit the back of his head with a great thump that it had forced him to come to a juddering halt.

"We didn't lose, the French just gave up."

The party disappeared making a slight murmur to themselves. They were probably talking about the arrival of the next spy to be recruited to the Imperial War Graves Commission. For William, his time in the nerve centre of Blenheim Palace was up. For now, William's time back in Britain would soon be up. The chaos and coming maelstrom that was soon to engulf the whole of the French state was in full flow and William Steele was going to have a front row seat.

Chapter 10

Graudenz had experienced a great heatwave in June in 1919. The grass around the town was turning brown and the trees were slightly wilting from the heat. The town itself was quieter than usual during the day, mostly because the inhabitants did not fancy going out into the sun too much as it was almost too hot to enjoy the summer sun. The rainy season of the earlier part of the year seemed more appetising and many yearned for cooler days even if it meant getting soaked to the bone; it was better than sweating to the bone. The monastery was busier than usual because its cold walls and colder interior provided much needed respite from the heat from the summer sun. On Sundays during mass people would huddle in from outside just to enjoy a few holy moments of cold enjoyment, cursing those who would open the door to enter or leave as hot air rushed through wanting to enjoy the same effect as the people inside.

July had barely begun but it was not exactly greeted with much enthusiasm as the Prussian citizens knew that the real heat was still to come. But there was reason to celebrate on one of the hottest days of the year so far. For on this Wednesday, 2nd July, 1919 was the first-year anniversary of the ending of the Great War. It was marked with no joy or fun but with commemorations of respect and military parades. Lines of people filled the streets of many towns and cities across the German lands watching the pageantry of military marches and military bands striking up many different tunes to such masterful timing. The Kaiser himself was standing outside of the Bellevue Palace as an entire division marched through the Tiergarten in Berlin where hundreds of thousands had arrived to witness the spectacle. The warm occasion provided for a sweaty affair with soldiers and onlookers doing their best to not succumb to the heat. To those who wore full military gear, including Kaiser Wilhelm, it was an even more difficult ordeal as collars were pulled and water discreetly passed between dignitaries.

The Unter den Linden Road which prostrated itself in front of the Brandenburg Gate was similarly filled with people and marching bands alike. The Kaiser had promised the greatest peacetime military display and parade the nation had ever seen and he did not disappoint. Imperial German flags lined the street, were draped out of windows, were flown by proud onlookers and it was a great success. The heat merely provided the glisten on the helmets and medals of all who were there, though the odd fainting did occur. A few people joked that those who fainted were really fainting with national pride rather than the heat. When fainting men and women recovered, they would say something similar.

Scenes like the one in Berlin were recreated in every major city and even small towns attempted their own forms of pride. However, it had been agreed that a minute's silence would be held at eleven o'clock to remember the countless dead of the Great War. This mark of remembrance had been agreed by all nations on either side of the war and in their respective time zones the minute's silence was marked. In Britain thousands of people gathered around a newly created cenotaph in London to mark the minute's silence. In France the inner turmoil meant that people simply held the minute's silence wherever they were standing at the time. It seemed like an odd pause in between the celebrations in Germany where national pride seemed to effervesce from so many people that holding silence for a minute seemed difficult, but it was done.

A parade was also occurring in Graudenz which experienced a bigger turnout than the size of the town perhaps merited. The reason for a larger than expected turnout was because the salute was being taken by the reinstated Chief of the German General Staff, Erich von Falkenhayn who was flanked on his podium by the esteemed Field Marshall August von Mackensen and the 'Lion of Africa' that was General Paul von Lettow-Vorbeck. In only a few cities did such a collection of German generals and military leaders rival the prestige and fame of these three that were accepting the salute in Graudenz. Men, women and children arrived from all over West Prussia and beyond to witness the parade itself with these three heroes of the war and they did not disappoint the crowds as they stayed longer out in the heat with their incredible military regalia than was expected of them. All three of them had decided to stay and accept the salute until the last row of soldiers and well-wishers passed them by. They themselves had not expected such a turnout of people and army personnel including many wounded veterans and so afterwards they could be found lying down in a dark basement recovering from the warm ordeal.

Graudenz was not a special town by any means. It did not merit the great turnout of people and dignitaries at all. Graudenz was the town hosting, on that day in the afternoon heat, the great wedding of Fritz von Falkenhayn and Johanna von Kasamerik. It was an overdue wedding, but the big day had finally arrived. The couple hadn't exactly wanted the big day to fall on the anniversary of the armistice, fearing with some justification that the anniversary would upstage the wedding event. The trade-off was that the wedding would be attended by great dignitaries and Fritz's father seemed insistent on the matter. The fact that the couple could not choose exactly when to get married had annoyed the young groom, but this was supposed to be the happiest day of his and his soon-to-be-wife's life. They would both make sure that this came to pass whatever the circumstances.

The wedding itself took place within the ruins of Graudenz castle. The venue itself seemed like an odd decision but its history and beauty had seemed irresistible to the couple who had first fallen in love there. No expense was spared in turning the ruins into a glorious outdoor wedding venue and Fritz's father did not disappoint. With his new role as Chief of the German General Staff Erich von Falkenhayn had access to much of the royal purse and with the Kaiser's permission funds were directed towards a great and pleasant union. This fact was not greeted with great happiness among some, especially with the Polish people living in the area, most of whom did not line the streets to join in with the celebrations.

The wedding itself went by in typical Prussian fashion. Fritz had not wanted to attend his own wedding in military uniform, favouring a slightly less harsh attire, perhaps one that was not so well insulated on such a hot day. But, once again, his father insisted on adhering to all of Prussian tradition. Johanna's blonde hair beautifully cascaded down her back as she walked down the aisle, not a single strand touched her bare shoulders. Her dress was long and beautifully elegant. She was indeed the Princess without a kingdom, and it seemed apt that they would be married in a ruined castle; to many these two would build back up such a castle and turn it into something magnificent. This was indeed a desire shared by the couple and they would come to personify such a desire to re-build the old with a splash of the new. They were the perfect couple on display during a perfect ceremony.

Fritz could not keep his eyes off his bride, even when they were expected to face the front to allow the abbot of Graudenz monastery to follow through with the Christian ritual of binding two souls together. She could let her eyes leave Fritz, but it was only due to her desire to do things right that allowed her to look away. She too was in love with her knight in field grey armour and only relief would share space within her mind, relief that the marriage had finally happened. Though it was only the two of them amongst the hundreds of attending well-wishers who knew about the child secretly kept away from the public, it seemed that the relief of marriage could keep the anxiety at bay. Soon they would be able to raise their child, who was barely five years old, with the proper love and affection that he so truly deserved.

The afternoon heat was taking its toll on the entire wedding party and as the abbot droned on about the wonders of God's love certain members of the congregation casually gestured that the holy perorations should come to a swift conclusion. Only one well-wisher had to be taken away to recover before the happy couple made their way back down the aisle having kissed for the first time as husband and wife. The applause that followed the couple as well as cheers and whistles were loud and as warm as the day was hot. The couple greeted all who passed them as they all individually expressed their hopes and aspirations for the newly wedded pair. To Fritz's delight Norman Gisevius had managed to come to the wedding and the two shook hands as if they had not seen each other in years. It had only been a year since they last shared a conversation with each other. Handshakes and hugs were sweaty and sticky, but Fritz noticed that Johanna didn't mind in the slightest. She would greet anyone no matter the state of their perspiration and, not to be outdone, Fritz would do the same. One after the other, they would wish their best and the couple would repeat the same phrase of "we are grateful". Indeed, they were, especially to the father of the groom who had bankrolled the entire event, and yet chose not to bring that fact up at all. He wanted the event to be glorious. Expense was also not spared for the following wedding meal.

All were invited, including some well-wishers from outside of the wedding party. As a gesture of good-will Fritz's father had organized for a random selection of locals to share in the spoils of peace by providing them with a table from which they could enjoy the hearty feast. Johanna had changed into an equally beautiful evening dress and Fritz had loosened a couple of buttons at the top of his tunic. It had been the part of the wedding that many were looking forward to; not only because it was the part of the event where food was served, but also because the day was finally becoming cooler and slightly more bearable. The happy couple took their places at the head to the table and found themselves seated between the military dignitaries who partially upstaged their presence.

The heat had caused a lot of the well-wishers to reach frantically for any form of liquid and so the wine and alcohol flowed in alarming rates. If it wasn't the heat that had made people unable to stay still in their chairs it would be the large quantity of alcohol which would do it. Despite this, the party was also a great success and laughs could be heard emanating from every corner of the venue. Erich von Falkenhayn did not disappoint.

The speeches were brief, to the relief of many, and even the famous General and Field Marshall, the alternative stars of the party, made speeches publicly declaring their feelings about the joyous occasion. Johanna's father made the funniest speech of the evening, but it was Fritz's father, Erich, who made the most interesting one. "It is not us who will say what the future may hold for these two, they will make their own futures. But they will do so within the world of the Kaiser and a restored Germany that threatened to destroy itself from within as well as from outside. They will be masters of their own destiny, just like their beloved fatherland. That is my guarantee." It sounded more political than anything, and it prompted Fritz to casually ask for clarification as the speech came to its conclusion.

Fritz leaned over after the applause for his father's speech had died down. "Thank you for your kind words, father. Johanna and I do so appreciate everything you have said. But what do you mean by 'threats from within'?"

Erich, who by this time had thrown back quite a few glasses of wine and was slightly less stiff and tight-lipped than his sober self was, leant in his chair for the entire head table to hear. "The inner enemy, son. We all have one. It is the inner being that wishes to dictate and shout at the expense of logic and reason. When we are threatened with great stress, we can either

111

learn or we can start shouting and flailing our arms about. We can keep pursuing a destructive course or we can lose a battle to win a war. The inner enemy is that enemy which seeks to dictate and be destructive. And why? Because it is easier. It is the mark of intelligence that makes one step back before making a step forward. We must be wary of the enemy within. That is why we have a brilliant Kaiser, hmm? He sees this and he has done the intelligent thing; he has won the war of within, himself and the nation. That is why he weas chosen by God to lead the German people." Fritz remained confused as August von Mackensen and Paul von Lettow-Vorbeck lent forward in silent agreement. "This country was threatened from within by the very people who wanted to dictate and rule without reason or logic. We could have given in to them, but it is this year that it has changed. We here, are the evidence of that change."

Erich had reminded all of those who were listening of the great changes that were going on within the halls of power in Germany. Paul von Hindenburg and Erich Ludendorff, the two men who had masterminded the final years of the war, had begun to rule Germany by decree, frequently side-lining the Kaiser both on military matters and domestic matters. National resources and people were used like pawns in their game, and they had used their unprecedented powers to great lengths. It was widely expected that peace would provide them with the international stability needed to further consolidate the power they had over the German nation. The fightback against the growing power of the two men who were considered dictators of Germany had to begin in haste or they would gain perpetual dictatorial power. The fightback had to come from somewhere and to the relief of many from within and outside of the German Parliament it would come from Kaiser Wilhelm himself.

It was not an accident that Erich von Falkenhayn had been included in the inner circle of the German delegation during the peace talks in Versailles. Fritz had learned little of its significance and during the wedding dinner Erich, aided by the two other famous dignitaries, outlined the significance of the previous months within Germany. The wine probably made them all far more talkative which is why Fritz would learn all about these events now, but it was the wine that made him, and to his surprise his new wife, more than willing to listen.

For it was the inclusion of Erich von Falkenhayn at Versailles that had first indicated the fightback against the dominance of Marshall Hindenburg and General Ludendorff within the halls of power. Erich symbolised the Kaiser's power challenge and this first showed itself in the peace treaty demands. Erich divulged that it was the express desire of Hindenburg that the demands should be harsh on all defeated enemies, including demanding the breakup of the French nation itself. Britain was to lose all its colonies and a puppet government was to be imposed in many other countries if the self-appointed dictator of Germany got his way. It was von Falkenhayn and the Kaiser who had softened the peace demands.

August von Mackensen chimed in with information of his own. It was his discussions with the Kaiser that influenced the battling king to re-appoint Theobald von Bethmann-Hollweg as Chancellor of Germany following the passing of the previous Chancellor Georg von Hertling, the old be-spectacled man who noticed Fritz's presence at the Versailles peace conference. Georg was seen as a puppet Chancellor of the two dictators and so it was crucial that this was reversed. The reappointment of Theobald, who had declared his unrestrained support to the Hohenzollern monarchy, to the position of chancellor was a crucial step on the road to reasserting the constitutional monarchy that was threatening to break down during the war. The Kaiser had apparently leapt at the idea and the tall and brilliantly moustached veteran had been placed back in his office of state under the nose of Paul von Hindenburg. Erich von Falkenhayn did not personally like the man and as von Mackensen mentioned his name the father of the groom stood up and excused himself for a minute or two.

Lettow-Vorbeck, silently listening with the bride, the groom and the bride's wide-eyed parents listening in to this information for the first time, took over from von Mackensen. He divulged to the table that the final insult to date involved the father of the groom himself. Erich von Falkenhayn was reinstated in April at the express request of Kaiser Wilhelm, to replace Paul von Hindenburg as Chief of the German General Staff. The move essentially cut the authority of the would-be dictator and his lacky, Ludendorff, from under their feet. Since then, the two men had not been seen in Berlin 'strutting around like peacocks' the General put it and had presumed to be powerlessly scheming somewhere in Bavaria, though the Bavarian King himself had already personally expressed his support for the reinstatement of a constitutional monarchy and had personally vowed to keep their eyes out for the jilted men.

It was Fritz who, on conclusion of the story of political intrigue, expressed concern that the two men were still held in very high regard as the key reasons for the eventual winning of the Great War. The General, famous himself for masterminding the famous battles in Africa against the British during the war, gestured towards Graudenz and stated "why do you think the celebrations are so great? It is the attempt to associate victory with the Kaiser."

"What if it doesn't work?" asked Johanna, having listened just as intently as her husband.

"It will, and we will have won the peace." August von Mackensen assured. The Field Marshall seemed to exude an aura of certainty with his station and his age that gave his words the needed authority to reassure those who had leaned forward in their seats in wander and such reassurance allowed most to recline back into their seats.

The discussion seemed to have made some forget about the real purpose of the afternoon, but it had already been upstaged by the anniversary of the armistice. To the growing consternation of Fritz, the wedding itself have been overshadowed by the appearance of these two heroes of Germany. The event was clearly being used as an overt display of strength and consolidation by them and though for the happy couple it didn't matter so long as they were together, the fact would linger at the back of Fritz's mind, sitting in alongside Fritz's guilt of his war-time impropriety. Yet, one look at his bride was enough for him to forget everything, even the surrounding wedding event that was still in full swing, and the two would know that all they needed was each other. Their hands clasped together as if to validate the same thought in their minds. All they needed was each other; the rest was simply window dressing.

Music had begun to play as the band, fresh from their warm-up as part of the parade in the town in the morning, started to play medleys of military tunes as well as old classical music like Mozart on various brass instruments. Well-wishers alike tapped their feet to the tunes. Fritz's own mother who had frequently excused herself to greet every guest, finally took her place at the head of the table. She herself knew that her husband

Erich was going to talk at length about things she found dull or distressing so she had masterfully played the part of chief hostess. She had used the hum of the music to let her son know that she quietly shed a happy tear during the service. She did not want anyone to know of her emotions leaking out in such an undignified fashion, but she would not forgive herself if she did not tell her darling son that she was so happy and so proud.

Fritz's sister, Erika, a few years younger than Fritz, had not exactly taken to her role as deputy-hostess very well. She had always been a bit more of a rebel within the fiercely conservative family and she remained true to form as she dressed in bright colours, made smart comments towards guests and had drunk more than most, giving her the unusual confidence needed to 'sing along' with music that did not quite meet the necessary musical requirement for vocal accompaniment. She occasionally hugged her big brother, also declaring her happiness for him, but this was much more short-lived. She retired from the party early and was last seen singing as she was escorted back home. Despite this, Fritz was grateful for her coming. Fritz knew that when it came to marriage, she was beautiful and her time would come, just not today.

As the sun died down, giving more and more people a bit of respite from the hot July day, Fritz and Johanna privately whisked themselves away from the roar of the party as more and more people reached an inebriated state of even greater euphoria, whipped up by the band who started to increase the tempo of their music. They crept into some of the darker corners of the ruined castle, stepped over large rocks and old bricks strewn across the ground and sat together in the darkened shade of one of the ruined towers. Fritz pointed up into the sky, telling Johanna of the story his mother told him; that the stars were all the souls of departed loved ones and the shiniest of all were those who were sending their love the most. They both pointed out which stars shone brighter and guessed who they might be. Johanna had one or two family members which she believed were up there watching. Fritz thought of many of his friends who died during the war who would have loved to have come to the wedding. There were a few instances of some, who had died, who had pleaded with Fritz to give them an invitation to the wedding once the war was over. He had consoled himself with the feeling that they had the best view; from up high.

Fritz consoled his mind which begged him to come clean about his affairs with women during the Great War by revealing that such a perfect night could not be ruined with such a confession. The day might come but it would not come now. Fritz could, for the first time in a long time, be at peace with large parts of his mind. The two simply sat and eventually laid against each other as the stars danced in random formations around the night's sky. The occasional cry for one or both could be heard from the party but just for a brief moment they would enjoy the evening together, alone. They kissed, and they could not help but smile at the same time as they did. The world, for all its troubles and woes, was all right for now with them.

The moment was somewhat ruined by a more urgent shout that had followed what sounded like a scuffle some way in the distance. The two rolled their eyes, assuming a traditional Prussian bar fight had begun and laughed together as they tried to guess who was involved. Fritz thought that Norman Gisevius had finally done what he had always said he would do and try to kiss a lady at a wedding, hoping that it was good luck, and would have probably been slapped by the poor woman's husband. Johanna thought it might be someone arguing with the band about what music to play next.

Neither of them was correct. The scuffle was much more serious than had been hoped. The party had been interrupted by an assailant who had infiltrated the party. He had not been seen at the wedding himself, not even during the toasts and dinner. He had been thought to be one of the waiters but his outfit suggested otherwise. He was being held down on the ground by the time Fritz and Johanna arrived. Johanna's mother rushed to the couple, thanking her lucky stars that they were both unhurt.

"What is going on?" asked Fritz, confused about why the music had stopped. It took Fritz's mother to indicate to the band that they should carry on playing music which they obliged with doing as the crowd murmured. One or two men rushed by Fritz as he looked puzzled at the assailant who was dragged from the floor at a quieter place within the ruins of the castle.

"Your father has been hurt." Fritz's mother told him quietly. "Come with me. He is alright." Fritz followed his mother, asking Johanna to try to

116

keep people entertained. She obliged as Fritz rushed to see the assailant on his knees, a police officer standing over him whilst a slumped Erich von Falkenhayn sat up against a table that had some of the leftovers from the dinner on top of it. The father of the groom had been stabbed, though the injury was not fatal. He seemed furious which was a good sign to those tending to his wound.

On closer inspection, Erich had been wounded with a knife in the shoulder, just a few inches above his heart. The assassin had not done his job well. "Thank God you've had enough to drink" Fritz noted, "otherwise that might really hurt".

"I will be fine. It is not serious. But I was worried this might happen." Erich said angrily, directing his ire at the assassin. "I should have seen him coming. Next time they will not even be able to draw their knife before I have them on the floor like that." Erich looked up at his son. "Now don't let this ruin your special day. We must keep up appearances. People are watching!"

Fritz knew he had a duty to his father as well as his wife. This occasion had two purposes and though he wished it was just one he knew he had to play the part. He nodded, choosing against his better instinct to hug his father who, for a moment, he feared might be mortally wounded. He was just about to make his way back to the party, with the duty and desire to keep the happy occasion going despite the attempted assassination, when he stopped. His mother begged him to go but he instead made for the assassin.

"Please, your wife is waiting. Just go and enjoy your night. We will just say that your father had a disagreement with a drunk guest and will return later. We will bandage his shoulder and he will have one or two glasses of wine to mask the pain. We will deal with this later" Fritz's mother said, taking impressive charge of the situation.

Fritz nodded but he still wanted to ask just one question to the assassin who was cowering silently in the corner. He knelt in front of the man and asked his one question before he would act as if this never happened; "Who sent you?"

The assassin raised his head. He did not look at all familiar, but he stared back at Fritz with an uncomfortable amount of confidence and replied; "Hindenburg".

Chapter 11

The French elections had settled everything and at the same time had settled nothing. The nation was still fractured into pieces, the Republic was on its last legs, extreme politics was on the rise, yet in the autumn of 1919 it still remained. The elections on the 1st of May had seen unprecedented rises and falls of political parties and notable politicians. Yet somehow, despite everything, the pro-republic faction which had banded together moderate parties for the election had returned a sizeable selection of MPs and the new President Paul Deschanel was chosen take over from Poincare as President. He, by no means, had a majority within the French assembly or Senate, as the anti-republic league had gathered enough support to return Assembly members in numbers capable enough to fundamentally disrupt French politics. But for all who read the results of the election in newspapers up and down the land the result had been a stalemate, with the republic able to limp on for just a bit longer.

For the alliance of Renaudin and Petain the election was a debacle. Their messages were often conflicting, the league couldn't decide publicly or privately who would take the reins of president in the wake of an election victory and there was another anti-republican party which seemed to benefit greatly from the mixed messages of the Communists and Petain's Patriotic party. To make matters worse, as Renaudin toured France trying to drum up support within the inner cities of France, the republic had taken its own steps to wrestle back real control over Paris. After the results of the election were established, the old republic limped its way back into the Palais Bourbon to claim back the symbolic capital of the nation. Though the majority of republican support remained in and around the west and south-west the seizure of Paris was a masterstroke, even if it did not exactly guarantee the survival of the Third Republic.

For Renaudin and Petain, the two becoming closer and closer partners in the weeks leading up to the election, the real enemy was the new 'party' that had stolen the thunder from both of their support bases. The real 'winner' of the French election of 1919 were the Bonapartists. Prince

Victor Napoleon, Napoleon V to his supporters and the press, had come out of seemingly nowhere to storm to first place in terms of single party sizes. In terms of numbers in the assembly he had amassed 31% of the total seats, compared with the republican alliance that amounted to 35% and Renaudin and Petain's alliance which amounted to 34%. Though Deschanel was narrowly elected as President, Napoleon V came in a very close second leaving Renaudin and Petain flailing behind. The Bonapartists had appealed well to the workers with their roots in Marxism and to the autocrats with their history and centralist policies. They were outspent by their political rivals but had managed to garner support in areas that had expected to vote for separatist parties. Brittany, Normandy, the Loire, Limousin, Picardy and even large sections of the Rhone area had seen a large groundswell of support for Napoleon. Even the Nord Pas de Calais, able to participate in the election despite being under perpetual military occupation by the Germans, largely expressed their support for a Bonapartist restoration.

Thus, in a dimly-lit room in the city hall of Toulon, Renaudin found himself sitting dejected surrounded by a thinning inner circle. He had been blamed for the election debacle for allying himself with Petain and had lost many of the acolytes who had initially joined him back in Paris during the early days after the end of the war. He had acquired new allies including the influential Ludovic-Oscar Frossard who had previously been a member of socialist groups in France and was instrumental in developing relations between Renaudin's Communists and the Bolshevik Russians. Thanks to Frossard, Renaudin was able to acquire weapons for his own paramilitary force so they could effectively protect Communist rallies and break up opposition rallies. Almost all of the other parties during the election were doing the same thing and thanks to Frossard, Renaudin was able to exercise some muscle of his own.

Phillipe Petain had met with Renaudin frequently both during and after the election to consider their strategy. They had both agreed that with the drastic fall in support for the republic it could be assumed that remaining support for the republic might drop to its lowest point in either 1920 or 1921. They both agreed that should nothing come of the surge of anti-republican support however, the survival of the republic might see a renaissance of the Bordeaux faction. The real enemy though were the

Bonapartists. Whilst together, the anti-republican parties were in total control of Parliament including the Senate, and could achieve the threshold of 60% votes needed to change the constitution. But the Bonapartists had signalled that they had no intention of working with Petain and Renaudin citing their extremism being too great and their messages being too contrasting for trust to ever be created. In fact, the Bonapartists had expressed their support for a retention of some sort of Parliament, only that its power should be drastically reduced and handing power to the President. Renaudin and Petain wanted a wholesale abolition. Republican sceptics had a political home with Napoleon V.

The grand strategy of the two men was mixed but they had found a cordial liking of each other. The Field Marshall and the private had become a dynamic duo who made up for each other's weaknesses and benefited from each other's strengths. They would even go over the heads of their respective inner circles when they consulted each other and an unlikely friendship brewed as both men resisted calls from their own factions to disassociate themselves with the other. The bond lasted and, thus, contributed to Renaudin sitting in a much quieter room in the late August of 1919.

Travelling around the country had not tired the thin and tall man, who by now had achieved a beard that was prominent if not long. Frossard was by his side and was able to take command of the party in Maurice's absence, which occurred a lot from August. In fact, Maurice only surfaced in public once during the whole of September. He had kept to himself for a while, and could be heard cursing in his little flat on the south of Toulon, overlooking the Mediterranean Sea. He had become more bitter and twisted in his own company and with a few of his old friends. Only with Petain did he seem sanguine enough to have a prolonged conversation with.

He had good reason to be angry with the world. He had believed with religious zeal that the Communist ideal would take hold in a post-war France and believed that his time had come and gone. He had lost his chance and cursed the fact that he was the junior partner with Petain. Though Renaudin's Communist Party received more votes, Petain's paramilitary had been so impressive compared to Maurice's rag-tag band of ill-dressed 'freedom fighters' that the fall-back position of armed insurrection would only hand Petain the whip hand in such a situation. The Russians were slowly redressing the balance but their input had slightly dried up of late as it became more and more clear that Russia was heading for an almighty civil war and the Bolsheviks would need every rifle they could make. Maurice was soon to lose his most powerful lifeline.

On top of this, Maurice had found that his own parents had not even voted for his party. They had sent a letter each to him expressing their deep disgust and anger. They were ashamed that it was their son that was trying to bring about a 'silly little red rebellion' to France and it had prompted them to disown him. This letter had been used as useful election material by the Bonapartists and the Republicans. Maurice found himself surprisingly heartbroken at the news, especially as he had longed to see his mother again, though she had long since been out of his life for a while. Some of his inner circle would say in hushed tones to one another than Maurice's contracting of the Spanish Flu in late September was a curse sent by his parents. Though he made a full recovery in October, he vowed to himself and those who could hear from the adjacent rooms that he would settle the score with his parents once and for all.

As the October winds began to lose their warm, autumnal feel, Maurice made for Paris, doing his best to remain inconspicuous, to see the old city once again. He had enjoyed the days when he had 'ruled by decree' there and longed for them again. He walked round, slightly out of breath due to the weakness he was still feeling as he recovered from the Spanish Flu, to see the great buildings he once strode in pretending to be an emperor. They had been emptied during his time as dictator of Paris, yet barely touched due to the lingering reverence many people still had for the historic buildings. He felt an overwhelming sense of loneliness. He wishes silently to himself that he could go back in time and use his few months of fame to find real people who might be his friends, and perhaps find a girl with whom he could fall back to if and when things got hard. The last few months would have been an ideal time for him to fall into the arms of a woman and fall asleep, ready for when he would next try to seize power. He thought he might try in Toulon where he was still a reputable figure but he was no longer the celebrity he once was. Whilst his Paris was a sea of destructive chaos, Toulon was doing its best to get back on its feet. No one set fire to anything and no flying courts were needed to meet out punishments. Thus, no one needed to hear Maurice's speeches to any degree. Maurice felt his throat, missing the hoarse feeling that occurred whenever he had spoken for too long.

He made for the large wooden stage that had been created for him so he could be seen by thousands of people as he made his speeches and doled out deadly punishments to his victims. To his great sadness he noticed small remnants of the once-famous stage scattered all around the foot of the Eiffel Tower. Clearly a bonfire had been made with the express purpose of condemning Maurice's stage to oblivion. To him, it signed a warning shot; if you do nothing, or if you lose, you will be forgotten. An all-too familiar chill went up Maurice's spine. The excursion to Paris had given him the impetus to fight again.

Before Maurice made his return journey to Toulon he detoured to Epernay. He wanted to see the cemeteries that were being built around there. He made the journey and saw the construction of military cemeteries. They were being constructed out of white stone and the crosses had been chiselled magnificently. Through gritted teeth, he acknowledged that the republic was doing a good job in building places to commemorate the fallen of the Great War. He asked one or two of the builders where the big cemeteries would be. He was informed that Artois and Verdun would see the biggest ones. He pledged to himself that he would see them as soon as they were complete.

Also, in Epernay he wanted to see the girl he had fallen for but never spoken to during the war. He had hoped that the woman had not returned to Paris and had instead stayed here in a much purer part of France where the countryside rivalled the old battered walls of the capital. He thought that with his new stature he could finally sum up the courage to talk to her. He did not even know her name; he would have to just go on the sight alone. To his delight she had remained and had somehow looked even more beautiful than before. Her café was much quieter and she seemed far less-rushed off her feet. He asked a nearby stranger what her name was. He finally managed to find out the name of the love of his life; Cecile.

Armed with this new information, he thought he could finally speak to her. She was not busy; she was not surrounded by far more impressive soldiers than him. He had a name that many across France had heard of. It seemed like it had meant to be. No sooner had he made a slightly confident step towards her when a man in a uniform with green lapels and a strange accent had walked up to her and given her a kiss on the cheek. He was not French as his accent was not discernible and he wore a uniform that seemed more at home in Britain. He watched as the two conversed and she laughed in the same manner that she did when she was talking to the soldiers during the war. Once again, she seemed unassailable to Maurice. Though it was only one man, his mannerism alone was far too overpowering for Maurice to compete with. He simply looked on as the two walked together back into the café and seemingly out of Maurice's life. He turned away, but instead of allowing pure defeatism to once again dominate his mind he made a similar vow that with Cecile he would settle some accounts.

The un-triumphant return of the Communist leader to Toulon was met with a small conciliatory wave from the odd passer-by but with little else by most people. It was a depressing sight but for Maurice the sight looked even more depressing than usual. The docks were not teaming with life and commerce and the restaurants did not have many occupied seats. Maurice sat down outside one and was almost instantly joined by a nervous waiter. He asked for a coffee and was told that the price had doubled. The weak Maurice looked up and asked why. "Times are difficult. I am the only waiter in this restaurant now". Maurice declined and stood up to walk away, prompting the waiter to cover his head in his hands in great distress. Maurice was not sure what was going on.

It took the unusually happy Ludovic Frossard to help Maurice understand what was going on. As he took his familiar seat in the main room in the city hall, still looking dejected which was slowly becoming an oft-seen 'Maurice Renaudin look', his well-connected lieutenant bounced in clutching his little notebook that was open at a page with hastily drawn numbers and charts. He seemed glad for Maurice's arrival and sat down eagerly by his side, showing the open pages in his notebook. "Look, look, look!" he said as he pointed to incomprehensive gibberish to Renaudin.

"You're going to have to explain this to me, and slowly." Maurice meekly replied, clutching his forehead as he felt a headache coming on.

"They've been printing and printing and they've only made things worse. It's the scandal of the century!"

Maurice sighed, understanding even less than before. "What are they printing?"

"Money, man. Money. Millions of Francs have been printed to try to pay the Germans and settle war debts to America. Everything until now has been sold off and now they are just printing money!" Frossard dived inside Maurice's pocket and took out his very thin wallet. He emptied it out onto the table. "This money is worth half what it did last week! Have you not noticed?"

Maurice hadn't noticed any changes as he had been making his own way travelling around France. For the past week and a half, he had been on the road hitching rides from any passer-by with two wheels going south with a space for a passenger. He had noticed that the brows on people were becoming more and more pronounced but he thought that was because the days were getting colder. "What is happening?" he asked.

"Inflation. Massive inflation. Today's money is worthless and it will only get worse. I've been looking at the trend and, in a few months, the whole economic structure will collapse. This is wonderful news! The people will soon lose all trust and hope with the republic and they will come to us!"

Maurice knew Frossard was on to something. His own party had stood fast on the question of economics during the election and they had staked much of their reputation on a coming economic depression. They had railed against capitalism, something that Petain had not done with much enthusiasm himself, and though it had not been a great vote winner it was something that could benefit only Renaudin's Communists. Support for his movement would swell and momentum would be his once again. The news seemed to stir energy from within him that had not been seen since March and April and he grasped at Frossard's jacket lapels. "This is it!" He exclaimed. "This is what we have been waiting for!"

The two embraced enthusiastically and Maurice made for Petain's residence in Marseille. Though the dwindling members of the inner circle begged Maurice to use this coming development to the Communists own

125

ends, Maurice and Frossard argued to the contrary. Petain was to be informed and a strategy was to be built around it. They seemed excited and Frossard was instructed to recommence fresh communication with the Bolsheviks in Russia and was told to await further instructions. A new lease of life had taken a hold of Maurice and his inner circle as the makeshift headquarters of the party started to hum once again. Communication was re-established with other party buildings in other cities as soon the next step was about to be decided and quick action was to be imperative. The party was set as Maurice and Petain were due to make a fateful meeting.

Marseille was similarly desolate with depression seemingly hanging on the lampposts on every street corner. It was a larger city than Toulon, with a grand cathedral and grand streets that stretched wide and long, but it suffered from the same malaise as Toulon and other towns and cities across the whole of France at this point. Soldiers in military regalia littered the streets as Petain's centre of paramilitary activity was still resting, awaiting their next move. The military presence was once again breath-taking to Maurice, teaming with jealousy that he did not have at his disposal such a vast and professional array of soldiers.

The Lion of Verdun had been eagerly awaiting his new friend's arrival. He too had heard the news about rising inflation, though he did not see it in the same positive light as the tall and thin communist who had taken his seat in front of the smart and well-kept desk of the old Field Marshall who was still a commissioned officer in the French Army. He was still being paid by the state and other than using the funds to undermine with a view to destroying the state he had spent vast sums on sprucing up his adopted palace in the centre of Marseille.

"The last thing we want to do is let this coming event pass us by. We must be ready" Maurice initially outlined, cordially refusing the invitation of introductory small talk offered by the Field Marshall. "As the trust in the republic falls ours will rise and it is that trajectory that we must exploit".

"Your trajectory." Petain retorted. He was not to be out-witted by Renaudin who was going to attempt to paint the coming economic catastrophe as a win for both of them. "Why should I be so happy to see this coming? I have to pay for my men".

"Your men would believe firmly in the cause we both have. It is not as if they can turn against you now that they have nothing to go back to".

"It is true. Restlessness to act has caused a fluctuation in our numbers." Petain had been surprisingly candid about revealing the issues he was having. It served as a reminder to Maurice that they were still good friends, even though they were ideological opposites. "But what do you suppose will happen? There is no election coming. The republic could easily ride it out and take the credit for the inevitable recovery. There is an event but there is no opportunity."

"Then we must create our own opportunity" Maurice replied ominously. The Field Marshall raised one of his bushy eyebrows, his adjutant guarding the door of the room leant forward slightly himself.

"Our own opportunity, Renaudin? What do you mean?"

Maurice smiled, the invisible ominous clouds seemingly circling around him in Petain's eyes. "We failed to finish the republic by democratic means, but we were never supporters of democracy in the first place. Maybe instead of knocking on the door we should break it down."

"Break it down?!" Petain exclaimed, betraying his interest in the subtext by refusing to lean back into his chair.

"We never had the means to win an election, but together we have the means to win something much more straight forward. With ruin on its way we can draw millions to our banner and with a rifle in their hands we can take power by force, but better by intimidation. With your army and with my growing ranks of the people we would easily outnumber the dwindling supporters of the republic. We cannot let this opportunity pass us by so is it not the right thing to do?"

"What of the Bonapartists?"

"They are a party without an army. They are not worth talking about" Maurice dismissed with a swish of his arm.

Petain seemed ready to counteract the scheming privately but his mind seemed to keep his body at bay enough for him to listen. He leant back into his chair not in protest, but in thought. "You think we can win?"

Maurice smiled, knowing he had his man. "In a few months we will have all we need to win."

Chapter 12

The change of scenery did wonders for William Steele. He had a plan and he felt like he mattered. He did not expect nor plan for this to happen; his original idea was to chase down the titans of industry in London. But with everything he had once lost of his old life it had made it easier for him to adapt to this new life. He had a better reason for being that had been handed to him and he had chosen to seize it greatly. Emmanuelle did not figure in his mind in the slightest. His old role in the army was one of the reasons for him being selected for this special task. He did not miss his old friend Henry and he no longer felt that he had to retreat to the sanctity of Exeter with his parents. For the first time in a while, he was feeling free.

The task at hand had not been so simple to understand in the initial stages. He had arrived back in France as a coordinator for the Imperial War Graves Commission but secretly, he was to research and report back on his findings about the French republic and the rise of extremism, notably the rise in Communism. It was never going to be a straightforward task, but he was quickly introduced to high-ranking politicians of the republic as he frequently travelled between Paris and Bordeaux, occasionally visiting the old front line to keep up appearances but also to revisit the old scenes of war.

William also did get involved in a couple of cemetery building projects of his own volition. One such site he was interested in was in the largest British war cemetery outside of the long-destroyed village of Passchendaele. He had helped deliver materials to the site which would be called 'Tyne Cot' and for over a week he stayed in a tent to help wherever he could with the site construction. He had been rudely reminded of his primary role in a coded message sent to him, which prompted his return to Abbeville where the Commission's headquarters in France was located.

He was ordered to submit reports bi-weekly, or monthly at the latest. He would receive whatever funds he needed for his travels and lodging and to reward him for accepting this drastic anonymity he was paid handsomely for his work. After just four months he had amassed enough money to buy his own place in the English countryside, though this had to be done through someone else. In fact, William had never even seen the place he had bought, only in pictures. He had fallen in love with the place because of its large field and though the cottage was small, it was homely enough to call home. The interior was more modern than the 18th century exterior, complete with a thatched roof and three chimneys. Though it was still modest, it was something he could go back to when his mission was complete.

He had learned a lot on his journey from city to city, talking to people from politician to farmer about what they thought. After the French elections in May it had become much easier for him to target specific areas of the country from which he would extract the best information. He reported back about the mutilated peace people were grumbling about. He had found that Communism was a way for people to vent their anger and it had proven to be a decent protest that had political and philosophical roots in more ancient struggles. But he too noted that some people had fallen out of love with the idea of these extremist ideas because they had found that once they had stopped thinking in groups and started thinking individually, a trait that found an impressive home in France, the politics of social groups and social divisions seemed ridiculous. He found that those who had the means to make their lives better, and this seemed to exist with farmers a lot, fell out of love quickly with extremist messages quicker than others. In the space of a few months William had identified the reasons behind this new extremism; defeat in war, shortages of necessities, class struggle. In the space of a couple more months he had identified the reasons for defeating extremism: individual strength, ability and time.

His report was read eagerly back in London. He was sent notes of congratulations and thanks. Even the American agent had personally sent over a note of thanks. He had been told that, with the aid of his and many other people's work, the coalition government in Britain would feel much safer to begin plans for a new general election. William never knew just how much his work agreed with others, nor did he know if what he found was in fact correct. He was never sent any corrections of his findings, nor was he allowed to know the identities of other people with similar missions to him. He would have to hope that his findings were enough.

He had met with many people up and down the land, including the new French President Deschanel, and even had an audience with Princess Clementine of Belgium, daughter of the deposed King Leopold of Belgium and wife of the self-styled Napoleon V. His reputation which had been sewn by the French ambassador to Britain had granted him privileges of audiences that were sure to be the envy of many at home. Though he always managed to maintain that his work was purely for the benefit of the Imperial War Graves Commission he never once failed to ask the important questions. His ability to speak improved. His last conversation with his friend Henry at the Melton's house reminded him of his ability to ask for the right questions.

And, as the winter winds set in blowing from the Atlantic Ocean over the French nation, William was able to recline in his chair in Abbeville knowing that his six-month mission was almost complete. He could soon return home and finally enjoy his new little estate. But to his astonishment he had felt a bit of dread at the prospect of returning. He had found a new lease of life and it would be foolish to think that such a lease of life could be easily replicated back at home. He still had nothing of substance to return to. He could use his new talents to pursue a career with a newspaper but such an opportunity didn't exist. He would lose his treasured status of a man who mattered and the prospect weighed heavy on his mind.

He had also come to enjoy the company of some people and places around France. He had enjoyed the walks along the coast of Bordeaux; a place he frequently visited and enjoyed. The bastion of the republic seemed to have awarded that part of the country with a serene and ethereal beauty, that made nature's colours dance in sunlight or moonlight. The roving plains of the centre of the country made one feel as if civilisation was so far away and William was at one with nature. The fields and forests seemed barely untouched by human hands. Paris, once it had been liberated by the republic's army, seemed bustling like it had always been. Food tasted better and wine felt stronger to drink.

One place stood out in the mind of William most of all. The little town of Epernay seemed so quiet and peaceful that he had considered building a house of his own here. Though it held little special meaning for him for his work, it was home to a beautiful woman he had long conversations with; Cecile Huget. She was beautiful with chestnut brown hair and eyes that were so beautifully blue and green that looking into them reminded one of the deep waters of the ocean. The two had struck up a conversation because she had been known to be constantly conversing with soldiers during the war. She was thin and always wore an apron. She was always working because she was a single mother trying to raise her child whom she had with a soldier who died in Rheims in 1917. She felt it was her duty to raise him to be as good as his father and William provided a little to help her. Though she was grateful it did not define their relationship which grew with every visit William made to the sleepy little town. She came to like the Englishman, but though William played with the idea of a relationship with her he never acted upon it. It only made her want him more, though she did not have the time to act upon her desires.

Abbeville was not so beautiful to William, but it was a good base of operations for the Commission. From the tallest buildings in the city, one could see over to the occupied region of the Pas-de-Calais. William had noted the heavy German military presence, but it was not as obvious as was first thought. There were far fewer French flags flying in the region, but the Germans kept their presence as scarce as possible. William never stayed in the Calais region long, preferring instead the free and beautiful lands of the west, centre and east of France.

In his little apartment in the south of Abbeville, William had been waiting with a significant amount of trepidation for a letter informing him of his passage back to Britain. He would be notified of the date and time of the departure of his ferry across the channel. He looked forward to returning to speaking in his mother tongue and he looked forward to seeing his parents, especially as a month ago he had been informed of the ill health of his father to the flu. His first port of call would be to see his parents and to enjoy his time with them before finally arriving in the cottage that he had never seen before. Despite the things he would leave behind there was something to go back to.

He thought long about Cecile and on occasion rued his decision not to express his feelings to her; but he believed that the time might come, just not yet. He had reason enough to return and should he be able to then it would be the first place he would visit. He did not have a picture of her, but she gave to him a little rolled up piece of newspaper that she had fashioned into a feather. She had torn bits out of the side to give it the shape and she had given it to William the last time they saw each other. The reason was sentimental. He had asked her about more help he could do for her as she told him about her son and her financial situation. He indicated that he would be happy to send money back to her as best he could.

She had refused his offer, telling him of a little tale about a sparrow with a broken wing. "The sparrow", she said, "had broken his wing because of a tussle with a cat. This was not the first cat the sparrow had escaped from but the last cat had managed to break his wing, meaning the little sparrow had to hop away to safety. A little girl had found the sparrow tweeting in pain and hopping around in circles. The little girl took pity on the sparrow and tried to look at the wing, but the sparrow jumped away. The girl did not understand why the sparrow did not accept her help. The little girl gave up trying to look at the wing and lay on the ground on her side, resting her head on her outstretched arm. She looked at the sparrow making his painful dance. She opened her hand as if to wave at the sparrow, but the little bird did not think she was waving. He hopped to her hand and fell into it, falling still for the first time ever. She had feared that it had died in her hand. She opened it and saw the sparrow sleeping in her hand. She saw that all the sparrow wanted was to not be hunted anymore and to feel a loving embrace. The sparrow's wing was healed, and he flew away. Though the girl missed seeing the sparrow go he always reminded her that he was always close to her. He left on her windowsill once a week two little wooden sticks in the shape of a cross to say thank you. She could always hear him sing every morning". All that Cecile wanted was love, not money, and though she never said it in so many words the little tale alone made William understand that she wanted something he would not give her. The little feather made of newspaper would be a reminder of that story and of her. It became one of his most treasured possessions.

William had just about finished his little sandwich lunch in his room by the time a rather loud tap came from his apartment door. He had been used to a more relaxed tone of getting his attention, but this seemed a bit more forced. He opened the door to see Charlotte Dornier, an administrator with the Commission who liaised with William whenever he had a report to deliver or had a letter to receive. She had begun their professional relationship in a gruff and no-nonsense manner but as the months passed by, she had softened her treatment of 'agent' William Steele. She was a hard-nosed woman but she was often respected for her straight-talking behaviour. She seemed more annoyed than usual that day and William feared that his months of hard work getting into her good books had all come undone somehow. He prepared himself.

"Charlie. It's been too long" he said, trying in some way to rescue the friendly relationship they had built up.

"Steele, this is an awkward time so I would rather suspend the pleasantries today." She replied, refusing friendly talk. William dreaded what was coming next.

"I do have some leftover sandwich if you like. The boulangerie was especially generous with my helping of meat in bread. It'll warm you up as well. You seem frosty." William joked. Charlotte did not even crack a smile.

"There's a letter here. No, it's not what you were waiting for. It's serious and it's awkward for me to read to you." She handed him the letter. He took it, noticing that it had already been opened. Charlotte was always nosy. He wondered what it might be. He had been doing a good job, he had been earning well. He thought that maybe it might be bad news about his father but the last he heard he was getting better. As he opened the letter, he did not recognise the header. It had been sent to him via the German embassy in London. He searched his memory for whatever it could be. He spared himself the useless seconds of inner turmoil and speculation and dragged out the contents of the letter. Charlotte found it difficult to look at William as he read the letter.

The letter read "To the British representative. The German government wishes to request the urgent attendance of Major William Steele of the South Essex Regiment. Following investigations into the conduct of forces during and after the signing of the Versailles Peace Accords 1918 it has come to the attention of the authorities that Major Steele was involved in a massacre of German soldiers at approximately nine past eleven o'clock on the morning of July 2nd, 1918 around the town of Ypres in Belgium. Major Steele has been identified as the commanding officer in the sector of the battlefield where the incident occurred. The Major has therefore been requested to stand trial for the murder of twenty-three soldiers of the German army. The trial will occur in Berlin on March 20th, 1920 where Major William Steele is to be present at the initial hearing. He will be granted a council and the right to waive his attendance should it not be possible to have his attendance. We will expect a reply within the week." The letter had been signed by the German consulate and bore the German Imperial seal.

William sat down, unable to catch his breath as air in his lungs suddenly deserted him. He looked at the note, thinking that it might all just be a dream and he might wake up but it was no use. Charlotte simply muttered "you should reply soon".

"Surely the British government will protect me? Or the commission?" William pleaded with Charlotte who remained stoic.

"Look, the commission don't want to risk anything being uncovered so they have ejected you. The British government probably don't want to risk anything either, so they've accepted handing you over to the Germans already. There's no going home ferry for you for now. I'm sorry." Charlotte entered into the apartment, a stunned William still trying to get some air to refill his spasming lungs and patted him on the back. "Best not to think too much about it until the trial" she said, the hollow words bouncing in and out of William's ears. She left the room, as William let the letter fall out of his hand. His muscles ceased up, his mouth dried out as the air that managed to seep its way back into his lungs provided no respite from his shock and horror.

The Imperial War Graves Commission had abandoned him. The British government had abandoned him. The Germans were coming for him and he could almost imagine the military car coming from Calais to pick him up. He looked at the window contemplating whether he should run or stand trial. Every sinew of his being told him to run but he just sat there, his new lease of life trumping the old instinct to run and hide, perhaps like he did when Emmanuelle had broken his heart.

He decided to sit and wait. He decided to accept his fate.

Chapter 13

The youthful spring air swept through the wet cobble stones of the streets of Graudenz. The air smelt of the evaporating dew of the spring showers washing away the last of the frost of the winter. Flowers were making their early start towards the heavens but timidly waiting for the right time to bloom. Winter had been unusually kind to the citizens and to nature which had only to wait until late January to be released from a thin blanket of snow. The town itself, however, had lost its sheen because the snow was not there to help retain its famed colour on the roofs and steeples. The rain seemed to have dampened the spectacle of the old town and all inhabitants were hoping for sun to be well on the way to returning to them.

But it was not the dull colour of the town that was seemingly sucking out the joy of the town itself. Black sheets and white sheets dulled black or grey were dangling from window panes. Townsfolk had replaced curtains with black material. The spring wind had to dance its way through and around the dark waving fabric dangling from homes and buildings all over the place. The town was quiet. The quiet that surrounded the town like a thick haze was at its most deafening in the estate that overlooked the town itself.

She was an understated woman compared to her other half, but she was by no means silent, and found fame locally rather than the more national variety attributed to her husband. Her name was said politely and with grace between townsfolk. She was a local celebrity and this suited her to the ground. She was by no means revered as a saint, or war hero, or entrepreneur, or any other title that was more commonplace during this time. She was simply a compassionate woman who saw to her duty in a modest and with dignified grace that refused public accolades of gratitude. It was as she had desired.

The life of Ida Selkmann was that of the old school. She was a traditionalist but she was also an individual with headstrong beliefs symptomatic of female Prussian aristocracy. A woman with no desire for rank or title, her marriage to a man of rank and title led some to believe that she had changed her mind on the idea of fame and adulation. They were soon to be proved wrong as she did not follow her husband into the same light. The wife of Erich von Falkenhayn was not to be the ever-present idol of the officer class, nor would she let her name be mentioned when Erich himself went to Berlin or to the house of the king. She was simply to remain as a supportive wife in the minds of those who mattered in Imperial Germany.

This modest desire had its boundaries, and those boundaries reached all across the globe, but the boundary stopped around the town of Graduenz. In her adopted town she decided that it was there that she would best exercise her individuality and headstrong nature. Graudenz would be her pride and joy and her actions and efforts to make the town as good as she could make it were deafening displays of care and attention to a town which deserved no special attention. It was not a town that was highlighted on any map, save Ida's own.

Ida von Falkenhayn was devoted to her faith. She insisted on attending the church services every Sunday, sometimes at the exasperated expense of her more agnostic husband and antagonistic children. She insisted that she be accompanied by her family and when she failed to convince them to accompany her, she would soldier out on her own all the same. Her regular appearances at the church services came to be a highlight of many a local townsfolk's week. She always sat and knelt at the front, singing softly and sitting quietly before the service would begin in silent contemplation. She was at her most approachable and most visible during and indeed after the services to the local population. To the consternation of the priest, after each service most of the leaving congregation would make for Ida to shake her hand and wish her well for the day instead of the head of the church in Graudenz. She would sheepishly accept the attention, and silently revelled in it. She would occasionally throw a little smile towards the lonely priest at the doors of the church, cheekily acknowledging her winning the popularity contest each week.

The reasons for this adulation came from her tireless work to increase spending from the Prussian local and regional governments in the town itself. Through connections but mostly through her unwillingness to accept

137

a rejection letter, the town itself benefited from restoration work to medieval buildings, the repair and reconstruction of throughways and roads and the extension of the town with more and better houses skimming round the edges of the town. But best of all was to come.

The very church Ida could be seen in every week was her greatest achievement. It was an understated building which saw little love given to it for over two hundred years. Its steeple had been requisitioned as a hotel for bats, birds, and other wild animals. Its roof had hardly kept the rain out and the heat in and it was not uncommon for the attending congregation to be asked to relight the candles that had been blown out from passing wind outside. The church had been unloved for so long not for want of trying but because it seemed like a needless expense when there were other more pressing concerns that were of a great priority.

Those priorities had been dealt with successfully by Ida and so the final and most important project for her was not only the restoration of the town church but a push to increase its size possibly into a cathedral mirroring the great gothic structures dotted around Germany at the time. She had visited the great cathedral in Bamberg as a young girl many times and had been spellbound by the Gothic architecture that made it one of the wonders of Bavaria. From a young age her mission was to bring the great spellbinding feeling to her town. Graudenz would be the town she would attempt to grace with such a masterpiece.

Ida wrote tirelessly to the local and national authorities making passionate pleas for the money and the resources to renovate the tired little church. The exhausted regional government decided that, after over twenty letters previously informing her of the impossibility of such a venture, they would release the funds necessary for the church to be refitted. The cathedral would have to wait. When she received the letter informing her of the change of policy towards her desired outcome, she smiled in a way that had been rarely seen in the Falkenhayn household in many years.

Her family did not see the individualistic side of Ida. Her gracious and well-known manner was displayed in her actions to make the town better. Her own mannerism hardly ever changed and meeting her in occasional parties with the well-to-do of Imperial Germany one would get the impression of a cold and isolating woman. Though in reality she was anything but this, her behaviour towards her own husband and her children did not display the warmth typical of a loving mother. She was indeed good, and warm-hearted, but she could not lose her Prussian upbringing that demanded respect and tradition to be the order of the day. She was stiff, quiet and resolute with her family and her consistency in this behaviour was a marvel that matched her desire for a better Graudenz.

Such emotionless behaviour was fit for a Prussian husband who showed similarly little emotion in return, but to children who desired more emotion she could not do more. She was brought up by her mother who showed slight elements of warmth and care, but when it came to her passing Ida was broken. All she could think of was the warmth of her mother and the awful truth that it was gone. Her solemn vow to herself was inscribed on her heart; that such warmth would not be on display to her children so that in the event of her passing such pain would not be experienced again. She lived by that vow and though it left a bitter taste in her mouth when her children cried out for her motherly warmth, she knew that it was for their own good.

Her approach to motherhood was not exactly appreciated, especially because she did not explain her methods. Her vow simply became a part of her character and thus it needed no explanation. Her son, Fritz, had desired his mother's warmth and love greatly until his military training was drilled into him at the age of 12. It became a source of great sadness that Fritz was not afforded the necessary love of a tender and caring mother, and soon after his fourteenth birthday he no longer asked how his mother was, nor did he have his arms out stretched for a hug as night time demanded his sleep. Erika, the younger sister of Fritz, accepted her mother's coldness much earlier, however though Fritz learned to accept coldness, Erika decided to make such emotionless behaviour a part of herself as well, if only without any rhyme or reason. It came to be the reason why she did not leave the nest of the family house to make her own way in life. She would remain with her mother and so further soaked up the behaviour of emotionless contentedness with the world.

They were all aware, however, of her tireless dedication to her adopted town. They celebrated warmly with her when she was greeted with the news of the impending news of the church's rebirth. Her smile was not seen in such a warm state of elation before and for a soft and brief moment the whole family shared in the delight together. The church was to be revived and so indeed Ida was to be revived in some emotional form. Perhaps she might turn her emotions towards her family once her work on Graduenz was nearing completion in her eyes. Perhaps with the final push to her dreams for the town coming true she might be liberated from what left her quiet and cold to her family.

The news would not be greeted with action, certainly not for the foreseeable future. A few months after they had received the news of the redevelopment of Graudenz church, Germany had made the irrevocable decision to go to war. Graudenz would have to wait. Ida would have to wait. Her husband was whisked away to the military high command and was rarely seen back home for the duration of the war. Fritz was swept off to fight a year later. Only Erika was left with her mother and she began to accompany Ida to church services to pray for the safety of Erich and Fritz.

The war did not diminish Ida's spirt or determination to carry on her work. She scaled her ambitions down, asking for much less from the regional governments who had their own priorities to look to. She won little battles of her own and this was of great comfort to her. Though the war would be fought and won by men she had her own battles to win and this gave her the individual identity she had held on to from such a young age. Houses were not built but made safer, warmer and higher. Roads were not repaired but instead maintained. Holes in the church itself were plugged up and the bats, rats and birds were successfully evicted from the impromptu steeple hotel. And all the while Ida remained at the front of the church congregation week after week as the world tore itself apart. She repaired her own little paradise whilst all over Europe great armies were pulling paradises down.

Her sightings at Sunday church services became slightly less frequent during the latter part of the 1916. As her husband was busily orchestrating the Verdun offensive Ida had noticeably missed one Sunday service every now and again. As 1917 rolled in she began to miss a couple more services in a row. On her return from a couple of weeks absence she would be greeted with more vigour from townsfolk. The priest rather enjoyed the absence of Ida on occasion as it meant he would be greeted more often by his flock. Though as the absences became more and more frequent, even he forgot his playful jealousy and wandered what was going on.

Whenever Ida was asked about the reason for the absences, she would grace the inquisitors with responses all-too familiar to her family. They would be told nothing and so nothing what is what the congregation knew about what was going on. These instances were incredibly infrequent in 1916, slightly noticeable in 1917 but by 1918 there were occasions where she would miss almost two months' worth of Sunday services. Rumours circulated that Ida was ill or that the war has shaken her faith, or that she was making secretive journeys to Berlin to enquire as to the health of her husband and son.

The truth was hidden from all, even to Erika who was not aware enough to be able to find out for herself. After the war's conclusion Ida returned with more frequency to the church and she almost immediately resumed her previously successful campaign to fully renovate the church. She was informed after much delay that her request would have to remain pending until the national purse was rebalanced after the costly war. She received no word and though she kept writing to the various governments she began to receive nothing back.

Her absences at Sunday church services returned as 1919 let go of the summer breeze to let in the winter winds. This time she was becoming less and less conspicuous at home. Though Eric remained largely in Berlin as he took up his senior post in the military high command in peace time, he too was aware and concerned about the infrequent presence of his wife. Fritz and his new wife Johanna made infrequent trips to the family estate but they noticed that his mother was remaining in her room with greater frequency. Erika remained clueless but now more-so than usual. She mentioned to Fritz that she had turned away well-wishers from town with no news of the situation of Ida.

As time marched on the tireless builder of Graudenz and stoic mother of the Falkenhayn family retreated to her bedroom more and more often. On a couple of occasions Erika would knock with variations of force to enquire as to the health of her mother. She would receive the response that had become synonymous with Ida. Concern gave way to worry, which in turn gave way to anxiety. The door to Ida's bedroom remained locked even to her own husband. Fritz, Erich and Johanna started to make more frequent visits to the estate but time and time again were met with verbal and non-verbal exclamations of dismissal.

That was until March's thaw was well under way. Fritz had made a visit on his own to the estate as Johanna was attending a stately party in Konigsberg where Fritz was invited but turned down in order to be with his mother that day. Fritz arrived at the estate as dusk was starting to prepare the nights sky and was met by the housekeeper who informed him that she was still not allowed inside Ida's bedroom. Fritz made his way around the estate to the window. He had done this many times before and each time was greeted by closed faded purple curtains softly caressing the inner glass of the window. This time the curtains were open.

Fritz walked briskly through the main door. Erika was sprawled on the sofa fast asleep still wearing her walking clothes. He climbed the velvet-covered stairs and arrived at the door of her mother's bedroom. The door had been left slightly ajar. He walked through slowly and quietly. His mother's bed faced away from the door towards the large window. Dusk's light was streaming through the window panes. There she lay on the bed. Her skin was as white as fair snow and her strong brown hair had lost its shine and colour. She looked very tired. Her arms rested out of the duvet as she lay there. The room was immaculately tidy which had the hallmarks of a mother dedicated to a tidy home. It gave Fritz comfort to see the tidy nature of the room as it was a symbol that his mother was still very much herself.

As he entered softly, gazing at the room and then at his beloved mother, her eyes met his slowly but strongly. She smiled in a way that was reminiscent of the smile that adorned her face upon reading the letter telling her of her initial success to renovate the town church. Fritz looked back and responded in kind.

"Hello darling" she uttered softly. Her voice sounded forced which brought Fritz's initial assurances to a swift conclusion. "Thank you ever so much for coming. I've missed you".

"I've missed you too mother" Fritz replied awkwardly. He had not spoken to his mother face to face for months. The last time he did she could barely keep her eyes open at the dinner table. "I thought we could go to church this Sunday. I haven't been for a while because I've been saving myself for when I can go with you".

She smiled and looked away towards the window. "Could you close the window? I'm feeling a bit cold here."

"Well put your arms under the covers too. Save the warmth underneath, you'll feel better then". He went to the window but found that it was already closed. He furrowed his brow and turned around. She was gazing out of the window. He looked out and saw the stars just starting to come out to play in the darkening sky. He walked to the foot of the bed and took off his winter coat and draped it over the duvet that was covering his mother. He put her arms underneath the covers and then sat at the end of the bed.

Ida continued to look out as the stars began popping out all over the place. "Aren't they beautiful?" she whispered softly. Fritz looked out of the window and nodded his head.

"There aren't any clouds tonight. It's the first time that's happened for a week I should think" he said.

"Do you know what's up there, darling?"

"Stars, mother. Things in space that light up when the sun doesn't hide them" Fritz said, thinking this was one of his mother's little quizzes out of nowhere which was a traditional way Ida thought about education.

"What are they really?" She asked, slightly pushing more with the volume of her voice.

"I don't know what you mean" Fritz said, looking back at her. She looked into his eyes, blinked slowly, and gestured with her head back towards the window. He looked back as more stars came out to play with the others. He stared silently for a time. He was just happy that he was finally talking to his mother again and in her presence. He wanted this moment to last. It felt to him as if he was young again and finally getting the attention, he had desired when he was young. He wasn't going to waste a second.

Eventually, Fritz replied "I don't know. What are they?"

"Love, darling. Each star up there is a life that has loved. And when you look up at the stars you see all of the stars up there are those who are no longer with us who love you. The brighter the star the more that life loves you. They look down on you and wish the world for you. My mother told me this and her mother told her the same thing". Ida began to lose her breath a bit. She remained silent to gather up more strength.

"Which the brightest star for you, mother?" Fritz asked, taken away with the beauty and mysticism of his mother's words.

"My mother up there. I can see the brightest star up there. I stare at it every occasion I can. She watches over me. Love watches over all of us by those who care for us the most" Ida's voice began to shake a bit.

Fritz looked up into the night's sky from the foot of the bed. He looked around to see which was the brightest star to him. His eyes were fixed on the growing night's sky. He felt like a child again, looking desperately to find something perhaps before his mother did. He noticed a star up towards the north. "I can see the brightest star!" Fritz softly exclaimed. "It is getting brighter. Is that someone up there who loves me?"

He looked back inquisitively hoping to find an answer but received none. He looked back to see his mother's eyes closed and her left arm which had wriggled free from beneath the duvet. Her arm was outstretched towards him, her fingers pointing towards him, reaching towards him. He looked at his mother and immediately his eyes darted to signs that she was breathing. He was awarded no signs. She was gone.

His own breath left him as his heart stopped in his chest. He looked on, hoping beyond hope for a sign but he knew she had gone. He looked down at her outstretched hand. She was trying to reach him to hold his hand. Softly and timidly, he placed his hand in her outstretched one, hoping that it would satisfy her final unspoken wish. Her hand was cold but he grasped it, like a child would grasp its mother's hand whilst crossing a busy road.

His eyes returned to her peaceful face that was facing his. His emotions got the better of him and he looked away. He found brief comfort in looking back at the night's sky. He easily found that brightest star in the sky. It twinkled with unspoken wonder towards him. He knew it was his mother. He gazed at it and squeezed his mother's hand one more time. As he did the star seemed to twinkle. Tears streamed down his eyes as he remained grasping the hand of his departed mother.

He had held the hands of dying soldiers in the war before as they slipped away. Over the years he had begun to feel little when it happened. This was unlike anything he had experienced before.

Fritz remained staring at the brightest star as it was accompanied by many more less bright companions in the night sky. The love he had always wanted for his entire life from his mother was now entering his heart all at once. It would be a while longer before he would let go of his mother's hand for the last time.

As the blackened sheets and cloths daubed the front of most houses the congregation of mourners passed through the streets of the town Ida had done so much to create. The understated coffin rested upon a more lavish horse-drawn carriage. Townspeople lined the streets or stared outside open windows to watch the quiet procession pass by. Fritz, Erika, Johanna and Erich marched in slow time behind.

As they walked along there were huddled whispers about what happened to Ida. Still, no one really knew what caused the death. The official cause was pneumonia, but it hadn't been accepted as truth. As Fritz processed down the road to the church, he overheard people speculating. Some thought it was an illness, some thought she had died from the flu sweeping through Europe. One note of speculation irked Fritz at first but as he heard it twice and then three times more, he began to hear it again in his mind. He put it to the back of his mind, but it remained. The speculation was that she was poisoned and that the culprit could have been Hindenburg or maybe even a British or French assassin. Such speculation would have seemed wild and unnecessary, but Fritz absorbed it in his emotionally scrambled mind. He walked on past the rumour but it clung to his uniform.

The procession reached the church that Ida had loved so much. The service commemorating her life was as dignified and as understated as she lived, and the priest vowed that as long as he lived, he would carry on fighting for Ida's final dream to be realised. The church would become what Ida dreamed of.

The congregation left soon after, allowing for Ida's resting place to lie beneath the church she loved so much. Everyone, save Fritz and Johanna, made their way to the massed citizens of Graudenz waiting outside to pass along their wishes of condolence to the family where they shook hands and accepted flowers. None hid their emotions well and a vow was made that no one would sit in Ida's place in the church until it was rebuilt according to her desires.

Remaining inside for a while longer, Fritz knelt in front of Ida's coffin awaiting its burial beneath the church. He rested his hand on the lid and allowed for his head to fall. His officer's hat fell to the floor as he wept softly. Johanna, standing beside him gently placed her gloved hand on her shoulder. He recalled the rumours and felt a twisting in his heart. The feeling was painful in thinking that his beloved mother's death could have been avoided. He felt compelled to ask the question in his own mind and the absence of any sure answer further twisted the handles of the vice firmly gripping his heart and his mind.

The thought's flames were fanned by the impending trial he was due to attend concerning the trial of British and French officers for their part in the killing of German soldiers after the end of the Great War. Perhaps the rumours were true, and this thought twisted his mind to the point that his head twitched as he knelt at the foot of his mother's coffin.

Johanna's hand gently squeezed Fritz's shoulder. "Stay here a while longer" she suggested. "Let the feelings and the memory rest. I will go to Berlin and see what I can learn about the trial you will go to. Stay here, and when you are ready, I will be waiting for you. It will be alright".

After a few moments Fritz nodded and Johanna's hand slowly left his shoulder. She could see that pain and grief were playing havoc in his mind. She briefly crouched down and placed her arms round him and gave him a swift hug. She stood up and walked away slowly, leaving Fritz alone for the last time with a mother he loved so deeply. His mind was awash with sadness but also with growing hatred for an answer he could not find. He swore to himself that if justice needed to be found he would find it in the trial that was soon to come to pass.

Chapter 14

Munich seemed like another world entirely, especially a world that was largely exhausted by war and aggression. The city seemed alive from dawn to dusk with celebrations and parties reminiscent of the pagan rituals of old. Lit braziers seemed to be dotted all over the city as masses of people sang and cheered around them at night. During the day the main attractions were the marching soldiers making their way through the streets like clockwork figurines making their pre-determined rounds on an unseen mechanism. The whole city buzzed and hummed with energy in a manner that could make a neutral onlooker believe that this was the current centre of the world.

If the city did not convince one that world events were taking place right here then one would have but to wander towards the great Nymphenburg Palace. The regal building was the nexus of the city's energy and buzzing. Crowds of people emanated towards the location of the palace. It's once luscious and ornamental gardens had been trampled over by people eager to get as close as they could to the building itself. The local police force had initially attempted to hold people back and away from the well-kept flower beds and neatly trimmed lawns but such an endeavour was bound to fail.

The city earned its status as the world's most energetic city in that time due to it hosting the infamous international trials of national enemies. These trials were due to take place in Berlin but a change of mind from the organisers led to Munich becoming the new venue. Nymphenburg Palace, loved by the Wittelsbach monarchy as a summer residence, had been totally requisitioned for the occasion; no doubt to put in to the shade anything Berlin was planning to do to host the event. The palace rooms accommodated for as many dignitaries to visit and to watch the trials as possible. After the first few days of the trials commencing a decision was made for extra seats, standing room and the construction of hastily-erected viewing galleries for as many of the public as was possible.

William Steele had found himself adjacent to the very centre of the energetic throng of the city. He had been held in what used to be a rather beautiful hotel that had been stripped bare for the purpose of housing those awaiting trial. The Hotel Laimer Hof was made the impromptu prison for those awaiting the judgement of the baying mobs. This was in part due to the proximity of the hotel to the palace, but the main reason was that it was easily accessible to the crowds who frequently gathered round the building to shout and curse the inhabitants. William could hear and see it all.

His repurposed hotel room had been stripped of any semblance of comfort or colour. The window had been awarded with extra metal bars and the bare necessities remained. His window looked directly onto the street below. Little else to do in his temporary jail cell, he frequently watched from the window in mild horror as he witnessed the sort of militarism that would have been more commonplace in ancient Rome or in the era of Napoleon. Military songs were sung, flags were waving and the ever-present German marching battalion of soldiers seemed to increase in frequency as the crowds grew. He struggled to stay at the window as crowds decided to once again begin their shouts and screams by the hotel, favouring instead to wait until they had subsided before reappearing to carry on watching the ritualistic spectacle.

William had been locked up in the building for over a week. He seemed to be waiting an age. He still had no idea what was going on nor how things were being conducted in the palatial court house nearby. He attempted on occasion to acquire intelligence from similarly locked up neighbours in adjacent rooms. Little could be garnered because sentenced people were being taken away elsewhere. From what he could find out, he learned that the trials were to last a few weeks and that the entire nation's newspaper writers and journalists were in attendance. There was even talk of recordings of the trials making their way to radio broadcasts. The entirety of Germany was listening in to what was going on.

He also noted that his neighbours who came and went were all military officers and soldiers who were on the front lines of the front at the war's end. British, French, and Australian soldiers along with one Canadian and one Algerian occupied nearby jail cell rooms to him. Each one as oblivious as the next as to the reason this was all happening.

"Whatever happens, be safe and strong" William would say to them as they were taken away. Each time they were escorted to the palace they were surrounded by angry citizens cursing them as they were escorted by a large presence of police officers. This would drag many of the angry mob away from the hotel, allowing William to make his way to the window to watch the palace light up once more. Cries of joy would emanate not too long afterwards, which meant that a judgement had just been passed.

Though William remained he was hardly daunted by the wait. Though his nerves were initially raised his prolonged stay had given him time to process the scene and thus time to digest things. He was very doubtful that guilty men were being sentenced to death. His worries settled just on the desire to see his parents and Cecile again. He could live with anything so long as he was able to go back to them at some point.

Occasionally when a jailor came into present William with his food for the day, he would ask the man about when his time was to come. "It has been delayed because a witness has not yet arrived". That was all William would ever get as an explanation. He would have to be content with staying alone with his thoughts.

He thought more of Cecile and her golden hair. Her child to whom he had grown slightly fond of, began to appear more alongside her in his mind. Was this a sign that he was ready to be a family with them? He thought it might but paused to once again think of what Cecile said to him soon before he left her for the final time. The story of the sparrow reminded him of the little feather made out of newspaper which remained tightly tucked into his inside jacket pocket. He thought about the story and how he was unable to see what it was that Cecile really wanted. The story of the sparrow was one of knowing what people actually needed, rather than what it seemed to be. He had seen things too literally and thus the underlying emotions were often missed. Had he noticed it more might he have seen the writing on the wall with Emmanuelle? Such thoughts annoyed him as he once thought he was more aware about things than most people. Perhaps Cecile was helping him see what he once could not and with that he would be able to understand more of the world, and even himself. Perhaps he could soon stop trying to love with his brain, and start loving with his heart. He felt within him a small spark igniting. He began to understand.

The trials were ending their second of three weeks and William had remained for each day. As night grew and the braziers began to light once more a new neighbour could be heard being unceremoniously thrown into the left-hand cell. William, ever eager to help the hours go by with talk sat up against the left wall and knocked on the hollow wooden carvings adorning the sides. "Are you alright there? Have you been, or are you yet to go?"

"I've been" the voice spoke back after a few seconds. The voice seemed to carry a familiar tone in the air. William had not heard a familiar voice for a long while, save the familiar voices of the hecklers below who had begun to make their way from the hotel to their beds to recharge for the next day's berating.

"You've been? We haven't had people who've been come back here before" William exclaimed. He was excited. Perhaps he could garner more information than ever before with this new voice.

"Hang on a tick, who are you?" the voice enquired.

"William Steele, British army. Well, sort of. You?"

"William? Good lord, William? It's me! Henry, it's Henry!"

William's excitement was checked. The voice of one who he had wished never to be near again had been hauled into the next cell. He cursed his luck and pursed his lips. "Henry. I'm sorry you're here" he said, allowing for diplomacy to rule the day.

"It's a relief to hear your voice, Will. It feels like coming home." William rolled his eyes in disdain. "How long have you been here?"

"Couple of weeks now. They just say my trial is being delayed."

"Sorry to hear that, friend. It's sheer madness in there" Henry uttered, his voice wobbling a bit betraying mental exhaustion.

William was reminded of the useful intelligence Henry could give him. "What happens in there? What is going on? I've been stuck here guessing".

"It's a mad house over there, William. There're hundreds of them with their burning eyes looking at you. The judges have already made their

151

mind up long before you even enter the hall. No bloody 'innocent until proven guilty' thing going on in there. More of an interrogation than anything anyway. And they don't really listen to you, it's a show trial, a bloody show trial". William could hear Henry slump down to the floor, sitting on the other side of the wall William was propped up against himself.

To anyone else, William would have asked if the man was alright. The memory of Henry in Emmanuelle's bedroom still hung over him too much to extend such polite and caring conversation, or even the phrases. "Is there anything I should know, Henry?"

"You'll be approached by your legal representative. Don't be fooled, he isn't on your side. Oh god, I'm still shaking." He took a breath. "He'll offer you a deal. If you plead guilty then the worst sentence you will get is being sent home in disgrace to deal with the consequences from your own government. If you plead not guilty then you could be locked up for months whilst they think about reconvening subsequent hearings. Basically, you'll be locked up for many months to come".

"But wouldn't our government come to one's aid?" William asked with perplexity.

Henry replied with exasperated incredulity "Good lord no. They've wiped their hands publicly of their responsibilities to us. No doubt to save face as best they can. Bloody shirkers".

William thought of the choice soon to be given to him. It seemed hardly much to sacrifice one's honour for expediency and being sent back home would let him achieve his desire to see his parents and possibly Cecile again. The newspaper feather in his pocket, however, began to feel weighty. Was he thinking with his head or with his heart? He became unsure so he asked, "So what did you decide to do?"

"I took the deal! Of course, I did. I don't want to be hauled away to the dingy prison in the middle of nowhere waiting for a date for a trial that might not come for months. Besides, I've got things to come back to". That really annoyed William, even if Henry didn't mean to indirectly mention Emmanuelle. "I advise you do the same, William. No sense in sacrificing your freedom for your pride. It might get beaten out of you anyway. Take the deal."

William fell silent in contemplation, ending the conversation there. He looked out of the window as the question of taking the deal or not began to dominate his mind along with the knowledge that next door housed a man who had fallen from grace in his mind so much that it had led him into a life of mental isolation. But in that very thought William found the proof he needed that Cecile was right; he was thinking too much with his head and not enough with his heart or anything else. William had until today been trapped very much within his own mind which had dictated so much. If he was to find liberation it would be by setting himself free from what was holding him back. Might that begin with forgiving his old friend, he thought. Seeing as he was about to attend a vicious and angry trial, he thought that this moment was not exactly the best time to let bygones be bygones.

Instead, the two men sat on the floor on each side of the walls in silence. The silence seemed to last a while. William thought that he could steal a few little hours of sleep as the dark night sky began crawling over the city, but his mind was whirling with fantasies about what might happen at this trial. He had done this before, but he had new information. His fantasy seemed more sophisticated this time and it kept him awake.

The silence was broken a few hours later as the city bells chimed for the last time before their own bedtime. Henry was obviously in no mood for sleeping himself as he awaited his extradition back to England. "It's really going crazy back home" he uttered. "Liberals are getting a kicking. Doubt they'll last much longer. Old Welshie is looking like he's on his way out. That stuff really interested you, didn't it? Political things?" William rolled his eyes again and did not give Henry the curtesy of a response. "Then again, I suppose all you can think of right now is the trial".

Another silence followed but was interrupted again by Henry. William sensed that Henry didn't want to be left alone quietly with his thoughts and wanted to use him as a distraction.

"I'm really sorry, you know". William's eyes lit up. Was this an admission of guilt? William, who had slumped his upper body to the floor sat back up slowly but with purpose. He stayed silent allowing for Henry to elaborate, and wanting him to elaborate too. "Such a beastly thing to happen." William allowed himself a slight nod. "How are you holding up?" Such a question left William lost for words. What could he reply with? Again, this wasn't exactly the time to have a questioning of such fundamentals that had dogged him for so long. He elected to stay silent again.

After a pregnant pause Henry carried on the seemingly one-way conversation. "No, of course it's not something you probably want to talk about. But I'm here for you and so is..." He stopped himself to William's relief.

"Don't you think you've done enough?!" William quietly mentioned with thinly veiled contempt. He cursed himself for allowing emotion to leak out. He vowed he would not that again.

"No, I'm sorry. It was just all so sudden. When did you find out?"

William furrowed his brow. What was Henry going on about? He knew very well. He was there. The stupidity of the question only riled up William further but he restrained himself before he made his emotions known. He took a deep breath and looked out of the window again.

"William? Are you ok?" Henry asked, inquisitive that he did not get a response.

"I'm fine. I forgive you. Now can we please stop talking about it" William shortly interjected. He didn't forgive Henry, but saying it might just shut him up. It failed.

"I'm here for you, William. And when you come back, we'll go and..."

"-Would you stop it!" William interrupted with a raised voice. He stood up quickly trying to mentally shake the heartless questions out of his mind. "Stop talking about it. The last thing I want to do is revisit that painful, painful memory. William's vow to withhold his emotions had been firmly broken. Emmanuelle's voice was ringing louder than ever before in his head; those dreaded words informing him of his unwelcome presence in her house and heart. "I don't want to hear about you and her ever again!"

"William? What are you talking about?" Henry replied in genuine bemusement.

"The thing, the thing. I don't want to hear any more!"

"Oh god, William. You, you don't know, do you. You've been here two weeks so you can't have known. Oh god, oh god". Henry's tone worried William further. It did well to break him of the voices of the past in his brain but it was anxiety that took its place.

"What, what on earth do you mean?"

"Oh god not like this. This isn't how anyone should be told." Henry paused briefly before he spoke. "It's your father. I'm so sorry, William. Your father passed away last week Monday. The flu, the one from Spain. It took him, quickly. He wasn't in pain, I promise. William. I'm so sorry. William."

The news hit William like a cargo train. His brain felt like it was swimming, his vision began to blur. He stumbled round the blank room unable to catch his breath or steady his body.

"William? William!" Henry shouted, but his voice became hard and forceful. It knocked William off his feet and as he tumbled to the ground, he could hear the sound of waves crashing against rocks. His dizziness had finally reached its peak and as his body and his head hit the floor his eyes closed as his brain put itself to sleep amidst the overwhelming force that it had been subjected to in the last hour, day, week and month.

Chapter 15

"Not yet, not yet!" Frossard exclaimed to the impatient Renaudin. The two men were pacing around and around the dimly lit main room of the city hall of Toulon. Hesitance, doubt and pessimism had swept over the entire city like a tidal wave. "The conditions are not correct. We must not ruin our once chance of success with irrational moves. We must not be impatient.

"But we are not expecting resistance! The whole point of this was to provide a show of force that no one would resist" Renaudin pleaded. His words portrayed him as a man ready but he most of all was not privately ready to take the plunge. He was racked with doubt, unsure as if plagued by his formative years as a younger man failing at many things in the past. He had no idea when 'the right time' was. He was simply hoping that someone else would know, and he would try to take the credit. "Any word from Petain?"

Frossard balked at notion of Petain pulling their chestnuts out of the fire. "He is waiting for a time that suits him, not us."

"It is both of us, Ludovic. We are committed to this. He will do what is right when the time is right. He knows most of all. He is a general!"

"And we are the people!" Frossard barked back. His importance and high standing to the party and the cause were reinforced in the steel of his voice. "We have the guns. We have the men. We have the presence all over France. It is we who make the decision. Besides, we cannot wait long. Fewer and fewer guns are coming from Russia due to the civil war. We cannot rely on waiting any more. We are stockpiled." Frossard tried to calm himself down with talk of strength but he failed to try to sit down.

Another man was also present in the room at the time, but he neglected to join in the pacing circus. His name was Boris Souvarine, a Ukrainian-born Jew, had fought in the war and his experiences had scarred him permanently. Talk of armed insurrection seemed to mentally pluck at his waning sanity at times. He had worked his way up the party as a keen journalist and writer. He had written many articles for Frossard's newspaper 'LHumanite' many times and was seen as a useful ally in the fight for hearts and minds of the French people. He too was well connected to the Bolsheviks but his use remained in the print of newspapers. He was known as Varine to all and in recent weeks had become an infamous name associated with the Communists. Some in the country believed that he was now running the Communist party, though that might have also been down to the unflattering characterisation of Renaudin in many other publications. Varine was seen as a more romantic and attractive leader. But he remained loyal to the hierarchy and he was too valuable to be seen as any sort of threat.

Varine chimed in with a few details of his own; "The other question, whose answer would help us know when the time is right, is what is the strength of the opposition? Surely, we need only display a show of strength that is significantly greater than those who oppose us. There need be no actual fighting". Varine's words seemed relaxed but a sense of a plea for peace laid underneath his words as subtext. "And from what I know I doubt there will be much zeal from opposing sources that matter."

"And what makes you sure? How can you be so sure?" Frossard asked, waving his hands about.

"Because soldiers of the republic keep buying and reading our newspapers. Hardly the actions of those who would vehemently oppose us." Varine's serenity and calmness further unnerved the pacing duo.

"He speaks nonsense. Soldiers buy newspapers so they can wrap their food in it" Frossard dismissed with increasing displays of hand gesturing.

"And what of the economic state? I thought that was giving us the way in?" Renaudin asked. His simplistic view on economics continued to hamstring his ability to grasp the current situation.

Frossard sighed. "It was not as bad as first feared. The worst came in February, but just one month on it is slightly better than it used to be. It's still bad, but it is better and that is not good. People are angry and it is still favourable to us. Confidence in the Franc and the republic is extremely low, but I estimated that the worst was still yet to come in terms of inflation. It is stable and if it continues to remain stable then it will improve. That is how the market works. Time isn't on our side. We must do something soon, but not yet". Frossard seemed muddled, caught between two houses.

Maurice stopped pacing, standing behind his chair. His hands firmly grasped the top rim of the frayed leather upholstery. Frossard was only making things harder for him to understand. How he longed for Petain to march in declaring that hostilities had begun. He was saddened that he could not walk in the same footsteps as generals, or even Vladimir Lenin whom he idolised. He could not bring himself to be the decisive leader even though he was the nominal head of the party. He began to question his very role. Was it not the duty of a leader to make the toughest of decisions? Were people not looking to him? He privately faced some hard truths of himself. He had risen to the top not because he was better than others but because there was no leader in the first place. He thought of his time in Paris during the early months. He only led because no one else wanted to. He showed no skill, no decisiveness. He simply sat in the right chair at the right time. People had crowned him leader because he was there, not because he earned the right. The thought stung his mind and his head collapsed onto the rim of the chair. He breathed heavily, unaware of the slight spectacle he was making to the other two men. Frossard stopped pacing as if realising that he was making things worse. The tall and thin man, bent over a chair in obvious distress was distraction enough for Frossard and Varine to pause for a moment.

"Is our army ready?" Maurice asked meekly, his forehead remained resting on the rim of the chair's back rest.

The two men looked at each other, hoping one had more definitive things to report. Varine spoke out first, slightly unsure of the validity of his words; "We believe so. The sense of injustice, the need for something different and the desire to get it are still ever-present. I suppose we won't know the true extent of our capabilities and size until we give out the call." Frossard nodded in approval to Varine's words.

Maurice slowly raised his head. "The whole world is not watching us at the moment. These trials in Germany have attracted all of the attention. I don't think this is good for us. It is a distraction. Russia's civil war is also a distraction. Whether people are angry or not because of their worthless money is irrelevant. They are angry now. We must remember that France is exhausted by war, or rather, those who still belong to the republic are. This does not go away in a matter of a couple of years. It will stay for a while and so long as we have a greater desire to change this country than they have of defending it then we will always have the upper hand. If what you say is correct, Frossard, then we will wait for our perfect time. If what you say is true, Varine, then our men will continue to wait".

Frossard listened but was unsatisfied with the words. "We are going round in circles! We know this. We have said this over and over again. We are very good at talking. You most of all, my friend. But we need to think of conditions for success. Right now, we are guessing, and we do so because we are not in control. Your flirtation with the lion of Verdun have simply made you more confused and we are less likely to make a decision than before. You have given him the whip hand!"

"That is enough" Maurice said softly, silently hoping that saying it might egg Frossard on.

"No, it isn't enough. The fact of the matter is that whoever decides to call for action first will be the nominal leader of the insurrection. In the end you are both pulling different ways. At the end of this when we succeed..."

"Not if?" Maurice toyed.

"When we succeed" Frossard continued, ignoring Renaudin's interruption. "When we succeed there will be only one chair and we must make sure it is you sitting on it."

That, Maurice thought, was all he was good at. Sitting on chairs. He felt like a puppet king every time he was mentioned. His own eloquence was what fuelled him and what got him to where he was in the first place but now his speech was being put into question. It shook the fundamentals of his whole reason for being. What was worse was that now there was another man who was not eloquent in speech but with the pen and that seemed mightier at the moment. Varine's penmanship certainly had more energy than Maurice's public speaking. He elected to walk to the door.

"Where are you going?" Frossard asked with vague incredulity.

"To speak to the people" Maurice replied as if in a dream. He felt compelled by his own body to remind himself of just what he was good at. He swung open the double doors and made for the upper levels of the city hall. Frossard's voice could be heard in the background pleading for him to return and make a decision. Bystanders masquerading as party elites around the building looked around as to what the commotion was about. If Maurice walked by, they would nod in his direction. They were not exactly willing to get involved, simply to understand what was going on before they slumped back into whatever was dulling their boredom at the time.

Toulon's centre of government, occupied by Renaudin's Communists, was a tall but unattractive building, especially to those who favoured the more medieval setting that was on display in most French towns untouched by the Great War. Its size had been inflated similarly to the city itself which had sacrificed culture for size, sacrificing beauty for expediency. No such city best summarised the public perception of Renaudin's party and supporters. The city hall itself was tall and the tallest part had no balcony but a large bay window facing west.

Renaudin made his way to the bay window at the top of the building and once he had made it, he attempted to open it. The key to open the window belonged to the real owners of the government building but they had been long chased out of the city. Maurice resorted to kicking his tattered boot against the hinges to try to break the lock. Instead, the window's hinges, rusted due to a prolonged period of neglect, gave way and the windowpane fell to the ground with an almighty crash.

The crash served its impromptu purpose of garnering attention around the area. Renaudin stood sheepish at the windowpane's old home. He looked out of the window as a few men with rifles rushed to see what was going on. They looked up and saw their awkward leader. Their eyes were joined by a small gathering of passers-by similarly bored with nothing happening. A little gathering of fifteen or so waited to see what was going on. Renaudin looked out of the window and was disappointed by the turnout. But that would not stop him.

Maurice approached and placed one of his feet on the old windowsill. It moved uneasily so he thought against placing the other foot on it, electing instead to pose. He took a deep breath and closed his eyes in an attempt to summon his powers of eloquence again. He opened his eyes and began to shout.

"Men and women of France. Your dedication to the cause has not gone unnoticed. Every day I see symbols of resilience from each and every one of you and I am grateful. No one can doubt the unbending spirit of the worker who is free and who is ready. For that, I thank you. But we must be in no doubt that the struggle has yet to begin. This city is just the first step in a long walk to Paris and the whole of France! We have been biding our time so that others may realise that our cause is the right one and when the time is right, we will use the force of the people to bring those in our way to heel. They cannot and will not stand in our way as the inevitable march of the worker is brought to France and the world. We must not let our convictions be shaken by doubt, or by anxiety or uneasiness. We must not allow ourselves to succumb to doubting that can come with time. After all, that is exactly what the oppressors are hoping for. They wish to wait it out to see if you will crumble. Little do they know that they are walking into our trap. The longer we wait the surer we are of success and victory. Each day more flock to our banner. Each day more wake up to the injustices of the old world. Each day our ranks grow bigger, and our victory is made more sure and more swift. I can assure you that when final victory is achieved you will look back on these days as the days that won us that victory. I thank you all from my heart and I will eagerly greet you all on the day when we can say that the French people are finally free!"

Renaudin's short and sharp speech was met with faint applause. He didn't take the applause and walked away from the window. He did not get the adulation he desired. He did not get the crowds he wanted. But in that short time, he had found his voice again. He walked back down the hall and this time the wandering people inside the building who had managed to hear his words through the walls began patting him on the back. Other people elected to make muffled gestures of applause as he walked past them. He was satisfied.

For three more weeks, Maurice made daily appearances from the window to make speeches to whoever wanted to listen and each day more

161

and more people appeared at the foot of the building to listen. At its peak, Maurice's speeches achieved a few hundred to appear to listen to him. It seemed to give him a new lease of life as it reminded him of what it was that he was good at. He might not be the great general that made decisions but he was a man who could speak and speak he would. The crowds applauded and as Frossard and Varine looked on they couldn't help but forget for a time the plague of indecision rife in the upper echelons of the party. For a brief time, each day they could all forget the shortcomings of the day and simply listen to someone speaking well.

It distracted them all, for a time. Eventually, however, the same tableau reared its head; pacing around a dimly lit room returned. At the end of March Maurice sat whilst Frossard paced on his own. He had quite changed his mind this time.

"We must do it now, Renaudin!" Frossard exclaimed, his gesticulating arms making their whirlwind appearance again. "The Bolsheviks call for it. The people call for it. The time is now. There has never been enough support for us than this. The Franc is unstable again and the republic is teetering on the brink of disaster. Even Petain has been seen striding about Marseille with marching bands and the like. He is clearly preparing for something." Frossard seemed energetic to the point of driving himself around the room like a motor car.

"I have to say, the winds do seem in our favour at this time" Varine chimed in, sitting down in his usually unnervingly calm fashion.

"We don't even have to fight. We just have to send the call to all of the cities in France. It is time. The part representative in Tours agrees, so do the representatives in Clermont, Toulouse, Lyon, Biarritz, Limoges. Do I need continue?" Frossard asked, expecting just one answer to come from Renaudin.

Renaudin was, however, in a slightly more self-confident mood. He had been revelling in the adulation from his speeches. He felt more assured of himself again and thus was less inclined to listen to his cronies as much as he used to. "Has Petain mentioned that the time is right, right now?" he asked with a hint of sarcasm as if knowing the answer already.

Frossard looked at Varine in exasperation; something that was becoming all-too-familiar to the two men. "No, but this is not just about him and his fascists. This is about us."

"Have we heard from him?" Renaudin asked again.

Varine replied "No."

Renaudin looked anywhere but into the faces of the two men waiting with slightly incredulous expressions on their faces. "Then we wait."

"We cannot wait! We must send out the call now!" Frossard said, raising his voice, insisting that he be listened to.

"Not yet", Maurice said, like a parent talking to an impatient child. "Not yet."

Chapter 16

Eyes were staring from every direction in a room where William stood alone. The eyes belonged to the ornate decorative paintings and ceiling art which surrounded him in an adjoining room to the great hall of Nymphenburg Palace. The room looked full of a most recent renaissance of life. The sign of cobwebs beautifully lit by new and perhaps temporary lighting brought the old underused quality of the palace with the new purpose of the building itself for the time being. The eyes, long dimmed by years of underuse and underappreciation seemed brighter than ever. The dusters did their work well.

William was not in chains. Nor was he in any major discomfort. He felt in the lap of luxury, having spent only one other time in a palace when he was last in England. Here the baroque element seemed to impress him greatly and he had wished similar architecture remained in England. The eyes staring at him seemed to glare less and to find understanding more. The ladies, the gentlemen, the cherubs and other animals seemed to share some sympathy to William, or so he thought. He was just glad to no longer be staring at four very boring walls back at the deconstructed hotel. He did miss the view from the window. There were no windows in this room, only candles and lights. Four upholstered sofas faced each other from each wall and a low table anchored the room in the middle. Papers of unknown entities were strewn across the table. William had tried to make sense of them but his broken understanding of German made his ability to translate the contents impossible.

He had spent a couple of hours inside after a brief journey from the hotel he had been shacked up in for over two weeks. By the time it was his turn the crowds outside had peaked in their energetic zeal already so the abuse directed towards him seemed to have little sway. He considered himself one of the lucky ones and thus felt slightly lucky that his soul had not been shattered on the little journey to the palace unlike others he had witnessed. Perhaps, he thought, that the reason Henry was so broken as to confess his guilt to a crime he probably knew nothing about was in no small part down to the torrent of abuse he received on his way to the palace. William was lucky.

His mind seemed to wander between many things in his mind. Aside from the obvious consideration of the treatment he was about to receive in the coming minutes, he thought about his father. The passing of his father seemed such a shock at first. In a way, however, the news seemed to not find much room in his already full mind. The trial, Cecile, Emmanuelle, Henry, they all had managed to reserve their spaces in his mind and the news of the passing of his father would have to wait patiently outside. There was no doubt, however, that the news would find its way inside sooner or later. For now, he was in the eye of the storm of his mind at this point. It was a temporary state but it had left his mind, for the moment, in a state of perfect balance.

There was a particular painting that was hanging on the south wall that seemed to peak William's interest. It was a watercolour painting of eagles circling over a wintery mountain peak. The imagery seemed typically Bavarian with symbols and depictions so obvious to most. The painting left little to interpretation. Such a painting was, to the consideration of William Steele, indicative of the German condition. Overt symbols of pride, honour and discipline seemed to be commonplace in Germany and during his brief stay in Germany for the first time he noted that to the common German citizen the concept of subtlety and nuance was perhaps an alien concept. It is easier to see what is in front of your face than wondering what its purpose is or what it all meant. That, William thought, was what the painting symbolised and what appealed most to Germans.

Such considerations were interrupted by the door to William's room in the palace opening. Two men and one woman walked in; one in a soldier's uniforms one in a suit and tie looking nowhere near as smart as his military adjutant and a woman in a dull suit carrying some clothes under her arm. She laid out the clothing on a sofa closest to the door and stood waiting for the nod from the man in the suit who, William noted, seemed to be the most senior of the trio. The woman received what she had been waiting for and, after a cursory glance towards the Englishman betraying a hint of contempt, left the room. The soldier stood by the door watching William with eyes that would have seemed out of place amongst the more sympathetic ones dotted around the room. The man in the suit, whose briefcase looked like it had seen better days, approached William. He seemed exhausted and sweaty.

"You are Herr Steele, yes?" the man asked.

William looked around the room. "Could it be anyone else?" he joked, finding levity in the bizarre question. He expected a handshake but before he could reach his hand out the man turned and pointed towards the clothes on the sofa.

"You are to put these on now, OK?" The man seemed like he was going through the motions. William approached the sofa. What lay before him was a military uniform, well preserved as if it had just been made. British army, not from his old regiment but it was close enough. 'Yorks and Lancs' read the shoulder straps.

"Why do I have to wear this?" William asked, perplexed that he was expected to dress up for a trial.

"I am your legal representative, Christoph" the man said. Finally, he had a name. "I am to be assisting you in the trial and I will be translating where appropriate". Christoph laid his briefcase out on the low table and opened it as similar papers seemed to cascade out.

"Where are you from, Christoph?" asked William, curious that this man did not sound similar to the Munich citizens.

"Germany".

"No, where in Germany?"

"Frankfurt. It is where I was born." William felt relieved. This man displayed the attributes of a German, but he did not seem angry like the citizens. He seemed more tired, anxious, and not as polished as his southern brethren.

William picked up the uniform. "Why do I have to wear this?"

Christoph ignored William's question and proceeded to recite something that seemed like he had done it before. "The trial is to...ascertain... as to your movements on the days after the cessation of hostilities of the war. You will be directed to answer the charges of your motivations. Here I am authorised to ask in advance how you would answer the charge put before you."

William would finally receive the clarity he had been dying to know from the moment he received the letter informing him of the trial. "What is the charge?"

Christoph took a breath. "You are being charged with deliberately killing German soldiers in peace time because you disagreed with the outcome of the war. You are being charged with holding an irrevocably hostile attitude towards Germany. That is the charge."

It all finally made sense. These were trials of vengeance, of pitting nation against nation in peace time and keeping the fires of animosity burning. This, William thought, was the true notion of a German peace. No coming together of nations and people, but a fundamental redrawing of national lines. Not content with winning the war, Germany now wanted to win the peace and through acts of vengeance over single individuals and, by association, nations Germany could defeat what she could not fight on the battlefield. William was in a war zone once more.

"Well, I refuse to accept the charge" William stated with a degree of defiance.

Making overt signs of ignoring William, Christoph carried on; "You are to decide if you wish to plead guilty or not guilty. If you plead guilty your trial will last but a short time, an hour maybe. If you wish to plead not guilty then there is no guarantee when the trial will finish, or indeed where. If you wish to see your loved ones again, I will advise you to plead guilty. It is no bad thing. It is a bigger matter that does not concern you." No hint of emotion, no understanding of the preposterous nature of the charge, not even the less-Teutonic-minded Christoph paused to acknowledge the slight absurdity of his words. "You would like time to think it over, yes? The trial can be delayed for only half an hour so I recommend..."

"Not guilty". Christoph seemed to expect a much longer period of contemplation, but William had thought about this already. Though Henry Forbes's presence was unwelcome, he had given William the time to consider what to do. William had railed against the vengeful nature of disgruntled people in Britain. To go against his principles in a place where the whole world seemed to be watching would be the height of iniquity. Besides, for the time being a prolonged period of time away from home might give William the time to come to terms with the death of his father better. The idea of going back to a fatherless home was a worse alternative to a German prison. Perhaps this was hyperbolic, but to William at this point it seemed extremely logical to choose a far less pleasant approach if only to hide away once again, and this time from something truly devastating.

"You might want to take some time..."

"Not guilty. I plead not guilty" William said, interrupting Christoph's genuine offer of time. Christoph's eyes darted to the soldier at the door. He shook his head slightly. The soldier tutted and put his hands to his face, wiping his skin down and groaning into his hands. He trudged off slowly, closing the door behind him.

"Well, you see, it is highly unusual to do this. Don't you want to go home?" Christoph asked. The sincerity of his question seemed to warm to William, but by now William was starting to feel adrenaline course around his body. He had made the decision and immediately his mind was asking, or even screaming, if what he had just done was right.

"The matter is settled, Christoph. I assume you will be helping me with my case."

Christoph seemed to look more exhausted and sweatier than before. "It is not something I am used to. I am here on orders of the imperial crown. I am here to assist only". He made for the door himself, scratching his head and undoing his tie slightly. "I will return when the magistrate is ready and when the crowd is seated. Good luck". Christoph left the room, leaving William alone once again to gaze into the eyes of those looking back at him. Their previously sympathetic quality seemed to have evaporated.

There was little choice in wearing the costume laid out for him. He proceeded to dress for the part he was to play in a show he knew little about. The garment was long, it did not fit him well. A deliberate ploy, he considered, to present him as a dishevelled Englishman to the people. At least it had been cleaned from the last time it was used by the last poor unfortunate soul. A little blessing, William considered, amongst a sea of impending fate washing round his ankles. The eyes of the paintings and wall decorations around the room seemed to exude angry stares towards him now. The feeling was palpable, and it raised his heart rate another notch. His calm and collected demeanour that accompanied the whirlwind in his mind was evaporating as the drums sounded in his mind and, as if by some dark magic, from a nearby room.

His time had come.

A knock on the door broke William's staring at himself in a glorious and small mirror. He had lost himself for a second contemplating his attire. He felt like he was a soldier again and at the same time not. He felt like a British representative and at the same time himself. He felt like a criminal and at the same time an innocent human being. The knock on the door repeated itself at a louder pitch. "Alright!" William shouted in a monosyllabic acceptance. The door swung open revealing William's Frankfurt acquaintance and two soldiers accompanying him.

"Herr Steele. You are not changing your mind at all?" the similarly dishevelled lawyer asked, his sweat betraying his hidden fear.

"I have nothing to change my mind about. I am ready" William said, hoping his quickening heart rate would not be given away, but the tone of his voice was beginning to shake. He resorted to movements on the heads from then on, hoping a moment's respite of the mouth might give him time to recover.

The lawyer turned round beckoning William follow. The guards gave the moment a douse of urgency and William duly followed. He was led down ornate corridors of exquisite decorations. Paintings from better years before greeted him over and over again. Great water colours barely covering magnificent wall ornaments. Suh majesty that has been built up over hundreds of years in the royal Bavarian palace. Art and culture seemed to burst out of every nook and cranny of each corridor. William desired ever so much to take in the unique view.

With every step, however, the beauty around him was being obscured by the sound of louder snare drums. He felt as if he was being led to an execution hall, a noose waiting to be hung around his neck. The lights felt as if they were fading from clean electric light into a more pagan colour of flame. The sound of crowds murmuring and quietening down every so often provided the undertone to the drums. Even William's own footsteps, loud as they were on the marble floors, now were silent. Beauty, light and now sound had gone. He was close.

The mini procession stopped at great and tall doors. They were made of a well-treated oak with brass adorning the rims and handles. Two soldiers were waiting and on seeing the procession proceeded like the changing of the guard at Buckingham Palace to swing into a form of pagan pageantry. They unshouldered their arms together at the same time and began to open the doors. The drums stopped their military beats. The creaking of the doors quietened the crowd. William was pushed forward first. A guard behind him dug the butt of his rifle into the small of William's back. The pain surged him forward and in a mere four steps he had arrived. The daggers of a thousand eyes could be felt on him as he looked up and around. Hundreds seemed to have been crammed in, a second gallery on top had been reserved for dignitaries and reports to get a better view. It looked like a theatre made of wood and adorned with soldiers and fire around the rims. To his left, he saw the myriad of supporting cast; the three judges waiting to cast judgement. An empty box and chair were waiting for William, where no one was pointing to him to go towards. He hesitated and heard the crowd murmuring softly as he waited there, assuming someone was to take him to where he needed to be.

Instead, William's little lawyer scurried over to the theatre floor and up to the plinth of the right-hand judge. He leaned over whispering something inaudibly to the judge who listened and then grunted in unbridled annoyance. William hesitated yet still, and the murmuring of the crowd grew. A man stood up from the gallery and shouted at him, presumably to move, and William obeyed. He shuffled, taking a moment to hold up his trousers which were beginning to lose their rigidity around his waist. A stifled chuckle could be heard. He took his place and sat in his seat. He saw his lawyer look over and point him to stand quickly. William, like a marionet, stood up to attention.

A soldier in steel helmet and no weapon strode forward. The congregation also stood up. He proceeded to recite something from memory. William's lawyer scurried over to him and whispered in his ear that the Kaiser oath was being read out. William nodded and waited. As the main finished the congregation shouted in unison "Ja!" and then sat back down.

The left-hand judge then stood up and proceeded to read out the charges. The lawyer translated as fast as he could for William who did not take his eyes off of the speaker as he had the English version dripped into his ear.

"This court has been summoned to do its duty in the cause of dispensing justice for Imperial Germany. In the chair is Chief Justice Holler, Deputy Chief Justice Rehnquist and Deputy Chief Justice Hammerman presiding. In the absence of his majesty Emperor Wilhelm, Chief Justice Holler will assume the duties and roles as laid out in the Imperial German constitution. The case before the imperial court is as follows. The state of Imperial Germany tries Mr William Steele, captain in the British imperial army, accused of wilful murder of twenty-three German soldiers after the agreed cessation of hostilities between the Central Powers and the Triple Alliance. The charge is murder in the first degree with intent. For the benefit of the court the defendant has been given leave to plead howsoever he chooses. The return statement was that the defence would like to answer the charge with 'not guilty'".

At the very moment 'not guilty' was mentioned the tension was raised to an almost uncontainable anger. The congregation seemed to sway an inconsolable annoyance. Even the judges seemed to move awkwardly in their resplendent thrones. The pressure of anger with no ally in the room seemed to mentally push William through some sort of vice. He winced a bit and tried to ride out the collective annoyance shared in the room. He sought solace in the now-stoic seeming lawyer who moved unflinchingly during the minor ordeal. The lawyer waited diligently for the judge to continue.

The judge continued; "Due to the sensitivity of the charge at hand the court has decided to act with as great a swiftness as possible. We shall hand judgement based on the cases before us. The defendant's case handler will also act as interpreter for the benefit of the assembled national and

171

international reporters. Would the prosecution please commence with the charge?"

William had barely noticed the desk on the other side of the temporary theatre. There, a large man who had benefited from a great availability of food had been sitting compiling few notes and taking a moment ever now and again to study the contents of the British officer in the overgrown uniform. He seemed rather jolly, and his nose and ears glowed a hazy red indicating his penchant for alcohol. He stood from his desk and the crowd seemed to lean in to hear his peroration. He left a moment's pause to collect the respective attention of the room.

"Gentlemen. Ladies. My lords." His voice boomed across the hall, the raised platform seemed to shake with every vowel and consonant echoed. William knew why this man had been chosen for such a task. "I implore you to gaze for a moment to mine own self. I do not speak for my own sake but for the sake of our beloved fatherland. Not since the days of its inception has this great country awoken to its purpose, its role in the world and its destiny. Our great kings remind us of our duty and we are grateful. We play our part for its glory and its survival. Survival, ladies and gentlemen. Has not that not been our rallying call? Are we not here today because of our collective awareness of the great burden we must all carry for the sake of our survival? Well now we are allotted to thrive!" As he spoke those words, he raised his arms, and a great applause brimmed the air. Finally, the audience seemed to have their champion win the room. "But", he continued, "in order to thrive we must do right by the justice of the new world we lead. Justice that, if adhered to, will ensure our continued survival and ability to thrive. Without adherence to justice, we would have the rug swept from under us. We would fall and right when we are about to find out who the culprit is a dagger is lodged into our backs. The very people we had hoped would join us in this new peace are the very people who would seek to undermine it. They would prefer to break us and we shall not let it stand. And..." He swivelled to stand and gesture towards William "Standing before you is the symbol of those very people. Far from moving into the new world with justice and fairness they seek to undermine us and drag us back into the very fight for our existence that ripped people apart in a long and ungodly war. Here is the proof that while

172

we talk of peace there will always people that whisper and scheme about conflict."

The audience were being riled up into a quiet frenzy and only the large man's overwhelming voice was keeping them in check. As he made his speech his voice grew louder and louder until the very foundations of the palace seemed to sway with every word. Even the judges who had no doubt heard something similar for the last couple of weeks could not easily hide their glee on hearing words they no doubt agreed with wholeheartedly. But they like the rest of the audience had little time to collect themselves as the red-faced man moved swiftly on in his declaration.

"We shall make it plain to the world that not only is this man guilty of his crimes but that he also fits exactly the same profile as those we have seen before in this courtroom. The very same devils who wish to end us when peace has been achieved will have justice served upon them. We call for nothing less and nothing more. Justice for those who died. Justice for Germany!"

A standing ovation bubbled more and more until he finally stopped speaking and a chorus of cheers rang out around the room. Only the soldiers lining the backs of the hall remained still in any sort of meaningful way. The dignitaries on the top gallery cheered with their canes and hats, the lower gallery cheered with applause and whistles. Even the reporters took a moment from their busy scribblings to cheer with delight. The man had made a masterful performance, William thought, and he had only finished his opening lines.

The trial had begun.

Chapter 17

The opening salvos had been blasted around the courtroom, almost everything from the case for the prosecution. Documents were presented indicating William's presence in the area. Grieving family members of the deceased were quickly wheeled in to say their piece. Eye witnesses declared William to be at the scene and all that William's lawyer could do was state the same claim that William was not at fault due to the lack of evidence of intent. Though the argument seemed sound it paled into significance against the eloquence of the opposite side who snorted at the notion.

Yet in the opening hour, by which time it was becoming clear that this trial was seemingly lagging on for some reason to all, William had said nothing. He was still taking everything in. His mouth which had failed him when trying to hide his fear before the trial had been locked ever since. He sat when evidence was being shown to the court and the audience and stood when being talked about by witnesses and the prosecution.

The prosecution was indeed eloquent but it lacked the evidence to shut this case. The threat of banging William up in an unknown German prison for months seemed like it was coming to a head. Either this trial was to be wrapped up today or it would be consigned to a footnote in an afterthought later in the year if he was lucky. The last of the day's light was slipping away and the judges were looking at their watches impatiently. Something was missing.

"I heard a man shout fire and I instantly put my hand to my cheek as I felt a sharp pain like a needle passing through my skin to make a stitch" a witness said, finishing up his story. "I fell to the ground and in a matter of minutes I saw figures come from where the shots were fired. They were British, from the same regiment as the defendant. I saw him pass among us and as I was carried away, I saw him stop by one of our officers and he started speaking. That is all I saw."

"Thank you, grenadier Eckhart" judge Rehnquist uttered sharply and the plain clothed soldier shuffled off and he retook his seat at the front of the congregation.

"Would the prosecution care to introduce any more witnesses?" judge Hammerman enquired. The large man shook his head with a sigh. He instead leant over behind him and whispered something to one of the guards lining the stage. The guard walked out of the room in an orderly manner.

"As we continue to wait for further developments it might be prudent to hear something from the defence if they have anything further to add?" Rehnquist enquired. He briefly looked at William's lawyer before looking out of one of the high windows wistfully catching a last glimpse of the sun's light. The Frankfurt lawyer paused, went to say something but William put his hand on his arm which had been resting on the rim of William's box. He looked over inquisitively. William nodded to him and whispered;

"Alright. My turn".

"It would be advisable to let the process just carry on" his lawyer advised him. William's mind was made up and he stood up himself. His lawyer's eyes looked at him silently begging him to sit down.

"Translate." The lawyer nodded. William looked over and around the hall. The eyes were staring at him collectively again. Not since he entered the room had he commanded the attention of everyone. This attention was in stark contrast to that given to the prosecution. The judges all leant back.

"You have something to say?" Chief judge Holler asked in English, raising a grey eyebrow. A light snigger came from one of the dignitaries in the upper gallery.

William gripped the rim of his defendant box with his fingers. His nails dug slightly into the wood and he took a breath. His breathing seemed all over the place so he calmed himself by taking in a few deep breaths. He had done this before when aiming a rifle during a tense battle. He had done this before when a surgeon plucked at a piece of shrapnel in his shin in 1915. Like those times before his breathing slowed and he could think again. He took in one last breath and then spoke.

"Back home, after the war had ended, I went to see my sweetheart. It's all I had wanted to do, especially in the last months of the war. When I went home, I saw she had left me for a man I once called my best friend. All I wanted to do was punch him in the face. After the war ended my countrymen started fighting amongst themselves over who was to blame for losing the war. People I once looked up to were thrown into the street for the birds to eat. And, here today, I am blamed for the deaths of soldiers and for continuing the fight against this country. What links all of these instances together has got nothing to do with justice. It has nothing to do with fairness or with righting wrongs of the past. It is about revenge. Revenge is what drives men mad, drives them to overlook the basic parts of human decency and life. We can seek revenge in everything we do. You could seek revenge by punishing me for a crime you yourselves have declared must be answered for. The people of my country at home can and do seek revenge for losing the war by declaring those in the spotlight to have been guilty of the crime. I could seek revenge by punching the man who stole my love. But if we are forever consumed by revenge under the guise of justice and fairness then we will be forever consumed by it. Vengeance is a dragon that is consumed with eating his own tail. Why seek revenge when there are fundamentals of humanity we could instead turn to?"

William noticed his interpreter had stopped. William's breathing had steadied, his heart was still racing and so he took a moment to glare at the lawyer. He silently begged for him to continue. The lawyer, looking back at him paused, and then continued.

"Where there is hate, instead let there be understanding. Where there is anger, instead let there be peace. Where there is vengeance, let there be forgiveness. We don't have to do it but it is a far better alternative."

The chief judge leaned forward and waved his hand gesturing for the talking to end "I think we have heard enough of this." His interruption did little to deter William who moved his gaze onto the judges.

"Can you not see that you are consumed? Whilst I talk of the very things that defined humanity for centuries in our churches all I hear and see is a new religion sweeping this courtroom, this nation, all of Western Europe! It is a religion of hate, blame, anger and vengeance. They are now accepted behaviours of this new dogma you now call justice. Even if what you say and believe is not true it does not matter so long as it adheres to your religion of revenge. When will it end?"

"That is enough" interrupted Holler again. Again, he was ignored.

"When will it be enough?! When the executioner's axe is bloodied when will you say enough? When no one stands in your way? When the last vestiges of dissent are left hanging at the end of a rope?!"

The large prosecutor stood up and gesticulated towards the judges, who in turn gesticulated to the guards who looked at each other. William, sensing his time was coming to a swift and abrupt end took advantage of the final moments of freedom, even as people started banging their fists on whatever they could find.

"All you do here is break and break but you cannot rebuild! You cannot because you are consumed by your desire to sew division and hate. And when all is dust and ash who will thank you for standing up for your new religion of absurd justice?"

At that moment his interpreter stopped translating. A guard burst into the box behind William and dragged him off. As he was dragged away by his arms backwards through the door from whence he came he shouted one last time; "When will it be enough?!" The dignitaries were practically fainting with indignation. The lower gallery shouted German obscenities and as the large oak doors closed the whole fracas seemed to die down slowly as the sound dissipated throughout the palace. A chorus of wails and fury adorned the hall William had been dragged out of.

William was dragged unceremoniously through to a back door of the palace. He was whisked into the back of a truck, driven down a road of angry townsfolk and was hauled up the stairs of his old hotel and back to his old, gutted room. He was dumped on the floor, bruising his left cheek and squirmed a bit on the floor wincing in pain from the rough treatment he had just been subjected to.

The guards went to leave the room, but one turned back and punched William in the stomach, winding him with intense pressure. He curled up into a ball as the same guard kicked him a couple of times in sheer frustration and then left in a huff out of the room, slamming the door shut behind him.

William's mind was still whirling from the oration he gave. He was not one for speeches, let alone speaking in a hostile environment. He had never enjoyed giving such speeches to his men in the trenches during the war. He had shied away from public speaking whenever the opportunity presented itself. This time he was a man possessed. He gave himself a moment to see if the aftertaste was sweet. He felt his stomach creak in pain. It was not a sweet taste.

He looked up slightly to see the familiar nightly blanked descend over the rooftops of Munich. There were no stars tonight as the clouds had rolled in. He continued to lie there and after a while he sprawled himself over the floor as soon as his stomach allowed him. He lay there on his back and looked up to the ceiling.

Had he done the right thing? Or was it pig headed?

An hour went past before the door to William's cell opened once again. William, still lying on the floor, felt his stomach wince in pain in preparation for another assault. Instead, William felt someone grab him by the oversized lapels of his military garb which he was still wearing. He was hauled to an upright position sitting up against the left-handed wall. William was still dazed and still coming down from the mental high he had found himself in after the ordeal of the trial. A figure was standing in front of him, his fists seemingly clenched. The figure moved around the room looking at him. It paced around a bit finishing only to re-clench its fists around William's lapels.

"What the hell was that?!" the figure growled. It had a German accent. That didn't fill William with any hope. "What were you trying to do in there?"

William's gaze focused itself. It was a man in a field-grey trench coat. The face seemed familiar. He tried to make out who it might be.

"You could have gotten yourself killed in there. And for what?! All for your stupid little speech!" The figure seemed irate.

William responded meekly, the air from his lungs was still only slowly coming back. "I said what I had to say".

The figure let go of William again letting him slump down. He returned to his pacing. "Oh, sure. You had to. And look where it got you. Idiot!"

"Who...who are you? Do you know me?" William whispered. His strength was slowly coming back to him.

"Do you seriously not recognise me, Mr Steele? I'm the man you helped up on the battlefield. Fritz. Von Falkenhayn. Do you remember now?"

William's heart sunk. Of course, he thought. The expert witness was this man. He had given his hand out as a gesture of goodwill and it was coming back to bite him. "I remember" William said solemnly. "You are here to convict me?"

"I am here to do my duty" sharply corrected Fritz.

"And why are you here now?" meekly enquired William.

"To look into the eyes of a fool. What was all of that? What were you trying to do? Are you mad? Is that it? How can you say these things? You don't understand things, that is clear. Don't you understand that we need justice so that we can live in peace. Do you see? You are wrong. All of this must happen so that we can move on and build peace! If that justice is also seen as revenge, then so be it. And better that it happens now!"

"Is that what you think, sir?"

"It is the truth!"

"How, how are you so sure?"

"Because...because we are the victorious ones!"

William smiled softly. "There is the problem. This has everything to do with victory, not with peace".

Fritz scoffed at William's words. His overtly thin patience had been worn out long ago. William watched him put his head in his hands breathing through his fingers and trying to calm down. "Look. I am here only to do what I came to do and then I will return home. When this is all done, you will go home. Stop making this complicated".

William rolled his eyes. "You think it will end here? It will never end. Not until the war really ends. Not until everyone is eaten up in revenge".

Those words seemed to rile Fritz back into anger and he clenched his teeth. He approached William in an aggressive manner as if to assault him. William put his arms out in defence but found it a needless gesture. Fritz seemed to stop himself. Fritz chose a different tact and bent his knees to square his face up to William's. William stared back, watching Fritz's eyes dart to each of William's eyes again and again.

"We need justice. It's the only way we can move on and live in peace. There will be no more deaths if we achieve justice here. You are part of something bigger than yourself" Fritz said, doing his best to pronounce every letter to stress its importance.

William grinned slightly. "Not justice. Victory."

Fritz blew air out of his nose in utter frustration, closing his eyes briefly to compose himself. "I don't know who you are, or what you believe. But this is not the time for rambling prophets. Now, I know that this country is beset with problems and matters that have not been addressed since the war's end. I can see that very clearly." Fritz's words seemed to fill William with a vague sense of encouragement. Fritz noted this and deliberately changed his tone, pointing towards himself. "But it will be we Germans who will decide how best to protect and care for our people after the war. Not you."

Fritz expected a smart word or two to come out from William's mouth, but William remained silent. He simply stared back at the angry man. Fritz angrily got up and walked back towards the door, opening it fully and storming straight through. William watched him leave and noticed a figure staring back at him. She was dressed in black, and she had a concerned look on her face. She stared at William for a moment.

"Johanna!" Fritz shouted from down the hotel hall and the woman moved away slowly. William watched her go as the door remained ajar for a bit longer before a guard finally woke up and locked the door shut.

William stayed slumped on the floor, unwilling more than unable to move. But eventually he gave in to temptation and shuffled to the window. He noticed soldiers that had taken him in the truck were below and talking amongst themselves with the occasional pointing thrown in every few seconds. Cigarettes were being shared. William was in the mood for one himself. He tried to make do with inhaling at the same time as one of the men as they let smoke fill their lungs. It did not help.

After half an hour of waiting William noticed commotion in the street and the smoking soldiers seemed to have been egged into movement. They made for the hotel door. William felt his stomach wince in pain again. Perhaps they were coming back to finish the job?

5 minutes later the door to his makeshift cell was opened again. The same soldiers marched in and pulled William up to his feet. In stepped Christoph, the Frankfurt lawyer who walked up to William. "It seems that they do not wish to delay any further. You are going back" he said nervously, as if talking to a school bully. "You are not permitted to speak. But you must come."

William, feeling little alternative could be found with two big men holding him arm in arm disabling his ability to move independently. He bobbed his head and was carried back into the truck. For good measure, on approaching the same truck William was thrown into the back, banging his left cheek and causing a slight cut. Before he could collect himself the sound of the engine rattling could be heard.

Round two of the trial was about to begin.

Chapter 18

The makeshift upper gallery of the court room hall was beginning to creak under the relentless weight of its guests and their fineries. The stomping of feet and the slamming of walking cane ends had reduced the floor to a grey mess. But to the bespectacled well-to-dos of German society the quality of the floor paled into significance when such entertainment was occurring right in front of them.

The gallery was large. Its raked seating allowed for a great field of view and it could fit a good one hundred into it. A few Generals, politicians, rich businessmen and their better halves heaved around the treated wooden structure with relative ease, stopping only to have a polite conversation with acquaintances. The gallery had the benefit of back rests to their seats allowing for added comfort whilst the city folk milled around underneath amidst long lines of benches. The neutral observer it seemed as if a beer hall had been constructed below and a theatre-style auditorium had been constructed above. Barely a few metres separated them, but the craftsmanship was such that it suited both parties. So long as the entertainment continued no one grumbled about the severe lack of quality that in less feverish times one or two might want to point out.

Fritz von Falkenhayn and Johanna had retaken their seats at the top right of the gallery. Fritz had been afforded an easy exit point so he was ready to be called up to the witness stand. He had been slightly dreading making an appearance. The emotion of his mother's death had done anything but pass from his mind. Johanna knew this all too well but said nothing to address it in fear of riling up his mind further. She did nothing but hold Fritz's arm when she could. She felt reassurance, fleeting though it might be, enter his body when she held his elbow. They exchanged glances every so often as all were waiting for the resumption of festivities.

"I don't know why you suggested we see the man. He's worse than I thought" Fritz murmured.

"You need to know the man you intend to condemn. Is that not a decent thing to do?" Johanna replied. "The verdict would break him as it has broken others."

Fritz baulked at the notion. "They get what they deserve."

"Do they? How are you so sure?"

Fritz didn't respond and didn't even look at Johanna after that. He had nothing to reply with, content in the feeling that the court would have the final say to end the matter. He looked towards the stage as the judges were slowly filing their way back in. They were slow to retake their seats. Their seniority demanded aid and they were duly assisted back into their seats. Fritz looked over to the prosecution bench where he was to get the nod. He had not even met the head of the prosecution and had missed most of his opening speech. But he made eye contact all the same and the large man nodded and waved his hand indicating that the time was coming.

After several minutes of low murmuring and twiddling of thumbs the large oak doors on the left-hand side of the room swung open and the defendant and the little sweaty lawyer shuffled their way back in. The murmuring died down and a deafening silence hung over the hall. William was led back to his box and chief judge Holler proceeded to stand slowly. The growing age of the evening was taking its toll on him.

"After a brief pause, we have come to the decision to continue the trial. Owing to the recent availability of a key witness we will allow for the prosecution to continue with an eye to coming to a verdict. The defendant has agreed to conduct himself with greater respect in this court room. The defence council have apologised for the recent outburst and will endeavour to make sure that it won't happen again. Would the prosecution care to proceed?" The chief judge bowed and sat back down.

Fritz was given the nod and a squeeze on the elbow from Johanna. He went to move but found his elbow wasn't allowing him to continue. He looked and saw Johanna gripping his arm. She waved for him to lean his ear in. "Look" she whispered. "Ludendorff is over there" she gestured her head towards the upper corner of the hall.

Fritz's blood ran cold. He had remembered his wedding when someone attempted to kill his father. He remembered the idle talk of citizens in Graudenz as he walked behind his mother's coffin. Hindenburg and Ludendorff, the two men who had been surrounded in a veil of mystery and intrigue had barely been seen in public and suddenly Fritz had seen him. Why was he here? What was he doing in almost plain sight? The old General was doing his best to stay inconspicuous amongst the crowd, but little could get past the eagle-eyed sight of Johanna.

"What do you think he is doing?" Fritz whispered back.

"I don't know but I don't think it's good. Be careful. Something is up" Johanna warned. People were starting to look around towards Fritz who was holding up proceedings with the pause. Fritz looked on as the dignitaries started turning round towards him. The figure of Erich Ludendorff did not move. It was him.

Fritz made his way downstairs and like a bloodhound he began looking for clues on his way to the stage. He looked around and suddenly he began to notice things. As he walked through the lower part of the hall, he saw that there was not a single flag or emblem of the Kaiser hanging in any part of the room. Not even a flag or emblem of the Wittelsbach monarchy of Bavaria was on display. An odd thing to be missing in one of the great palaces of the great kings of old. The soldiers lining the hall were wearing different insignias on their tunics and helmets that he had not seen before. And why were there so many? Fritz had not been in the court hall long but he noticed a subtle and strange aura hanging around the place.

He was beckoned to the stage and he obliged, moving at a slower pace in confusion. The presence of Ludendorff was suspicious, and now he knew that the beady eyes of the right-hand man to the field marshal who wanted his parents dead was upon him. But so were the eyes of hundreds of people and perhaps the entire nation poised on his actions and his words. He was due to play his part but in whose performance was he a part of? Was it the performance of justice as he thought or was it something more sinister? He gazed over to the figure of the accused. The cut on his cheek was new and it had been barely treated.

Within Fritz's mind a torrent of thoughts whirled around. He held his head at one point to prevent the feeling of spinning from overtaking his natural rigid stature. He was approached by the leader of the prosecution. The room fell silent. "Captain Fritz von Falkenhayn. That is your name, correct?" asked deputy chief judge Rehnquist. Fritz nodded. "Case for the prosecution, your witness please."

"I would first like to apologise for forcing you to relive the terrible memories of that awful experience" the large man declared. This was a familiar trope he said before cross-examining a witness. It was always met with a chorus of sympathetic tutting and Fritz was awarded a similar response. "Were you the senior officer in the advanced sector of the front during the matter in question?" Fritz nodded. The large man seemed a bit irate. "For the benefit of the court would you please articulate your answers."

Fritz did not want to speak. He was still trying to make sense of things. "Yes" he blurted out, hoping no one would notice that his mind was elsewhere.

"You were wounded in the leg during the incident in question. Is that wound still visible?" Fritz nodded and raised his right trouser leg slightly to reveal a greyed scar. A gasp was heard from the upper gallery. "You received this wound from the matter in question?"

"Yes" Fritz replied.

"Do you recall seeing the defendant at the scene?"

"Yes".

"Do you recall seeing men lying dead on the ground around you?"

"Yes."

"As the senior officer at the scene do you believe that the wound you received and the men shot around you was a deliberate act by the defendant both on an individual level and an organisational level?"

At last, Fritz felt a spark go off in his mind and this question gave away the game. All this time, Fritz had believed that this trial the rest of the trials were a matter of achieving justice for the fallen on that day. This was seemingly made clear in the newspapers. But this question was asked, not in order to extract justice but to extract intent. The phrase 'organizational level' showed that this was not a question about assigning blame to a person but to an organization; the British army. That's why William was wearing a uniform; a fact that seemed odd to him when he first saw

William Steele in the defendant's box. Why wear it when the war was over and he had no need to? Because blame was being associated on the British themselves, not the person. Why were there no insignias of the Kaiser anywhere? Because it's the Kaiser who was advocating a policy of reconciliation which caused Hindenburg and Ludendorff to be thrown out of their positions as nominal dictators of Germany. Why was Ludendorff here? Because this whole trial was his making. The trial was a means to rile up antagonism and to reignite hatred and war-like sentiment against France, Britain and the other enemies during the war. This whole trial had nothing to do with justice and everything to do with scheming, revenge and war. Peace was never the answer.

Fritz looked over to the defendant with incredulity. He was right in part, only the culprit was instead sitting up in the gallery waiting for him to play his part. Accuse the defendant of a deliberate attempt to kill Germans in peace time. Accuse the British army of a conceited motivation to carry on the war. Accuse the enemy of still being the enemy and to pass judgement. And whilst the advocators of peace are shunned, thrown out into the streets for the last time the jackboots of the vindicated warlords stride back into the corridors of power.

"Captain von Falkenhayn. Do you believe it was deliberate?" the prosecutor asked again, his face seemed to wobble as the rest of his body remained still. Erich took a deep breath.

"No."

The crowd seemed to receive a jolt of electricity. One dignitary from the upper gallery stood up shouting "What?!" Fritz looked over to see if it was the wily Ludendorff but it wasn't. More people started to stand up shouting "Guilty! Guilty! Guilty!" The judges appealed for calm. The crowd were having none of it and after the ignominy of William's outburst earlier they were not willing to back down. Soldiers closed ranks in front of the stage as the crowds left their seats in order to attempt to mete out their own judgement on the defendant. "Hang the man!" some shouted. "The British want to kill us!" shouted another. "It's war they want!" others shouted. The soldiers pushed the crowd back again and again until an attending sergeant-at-arms shouted for unshouldering of rifles. The soldiers did as they were told and unshouldered their rifles using them to push the crowd back. After a few minutes the crowds began sitting back down, though some had seen enough and began filing out.

Deputy judge Hammerman appealed to calm by attempting to readjust proceedings. "Would the prosecution care to ask the question again. It may be that the witness did not understand the question properly".

The leader for the prosecution, who seemed to have gone as bright red as a cooked lobster during the ensuing fracas, approached Fritz's box yet again. His voice had become slightly hoarse. He certainly was not well equipped for the matter of things going unexpectedly for him. "Do you believe that what happened at your sector on the 2nd of July 1918 was a deliberate attempt to kill Germans by the defendant and the organization he represents?"

Fritz breathed in again. The judges seemed to lean in slightly as did a few onlookers. "No."

A few people stood up this team but the presence of the soldiers at the front of the stage deterred a similar stampede to occur. A collective groan could be heard. One be-spectacled gentleman in the upper gallery shouted "declare him guilty anyway!" A chorus of agreement could be heard. Not wishing for this to go unnoticed the leader of the prosecution nodded his head and appealed to the judges.

"The man is guilty anyway. We have enough to prove as such." It was all the large man could muster. The inability to land the killing blow with Fritz's testimony had taken the wind out of his sails and indeed out of his lungs.

"The witness is dismissed" judge Hammerman declared. Fritz was led out of the witness box and ushered away to the side door so that he could retake his seat. He walked back with an even greater whirlwind in his mind. Did he do the right thing? Or had he created an even greater target on his back? No greater a target than the one on his father's back, he thought. He took his seat next to Johanna who returned to squeezing his elbow.

"Well done" Johanna whispered as the judges talked amongst themselves for a verdict.

"Did Ludendorff react?" Fritz whispered back.

"He stormed off. Whatever you did he didn't like it."

Fritz leant back thinking that the next assassin was being primed to take him out. It was a sad and mildly scary feeling. He squeezed Johanna's arm back. She stared at him and smiled. "You did the right thing". Fritz seemed unmoved by the kind words.

"I don't know" he replied. She smiled back and rested her head on his shoulder. It was a small but lovely gesture. He felt reassured that she was with him and for the first time since his mother's death he stopped feeling alone for a moment. Perhaps what he did gave him some sort of freedom from the torrent going on in his mind. He did seem less dizzy.

The judges had been in conversation with each other for some time. People were getting agitated and some began fiddling with whatever they could fiddle with on their clothing. Buttons, jewels, medals, collars, the ends of dresses, all were being caressed by fingers as the judges took their time deliberating in public. Eventually they stood up and walked away and out of sight still in deep conversation. Their absence from the room started making people feel more uneasy. The soldiers stayed ram-rod in their places.

After ten minutes the judges re-emerged. They seemed a bit out of breath themselves. They took their places but did not sit down. Judge Rehnquist began to speak. "The court has deliberated the merits of this case and the evidence provided before it. Due to a lack of evidence of intent and the relevant authority at the time of the incident to establish intent the court has come to a decision. The decision is that this case is to be stripped from the records and the evidence of this case being conducted is deemed void and all relevant materials are to be seized and destroyed. The relevant reporters must submit their documents to the postmaster for inspection. Subsequent trials are to be suspended until further notice pending an investigation. This court session has concluded and has been declared as a public exercise. Court is adjourned". The judges then made a prompt and hasty move for the exit, leaving a stunned crowd rooted to their seats in disbelief.

After several minutes of confusion and hopes of clarification dashed people started awkwardly filing out. The anti-climactic end to the court session had sapped the life and energy out of the hall for the first time in 19 days. Like wandering sheep, the crowds in both sections started leaving the hall. Soft and overheard murmurings reinforced the confused and bewildering emotions that had left many dumbfounded into silence.

Fritz and Johanna silently inhaled together and waited a big for people to leave. Fritz was not exactly public enemy number one in the hall but the stares he was being awarded by passers-by from the gallery and from below seemed to indicate that he was very much public enemy number two.

As they both went to stand up an icy hand appeared from behind and pressed Fritz's shoulder down. The pair both looked back to see an unknown apparition in a black suit. The sight frightened Fritz more than ever since the war. The apparition spoke.

"General Ludendorff's compliments. He wishes to have moment with you. Would you care to stay a while longer?" The voice seemed soft yet menacing. Fritz nodded. The fact that it was just a hand and not a knife was already a blessing. The figure vanished into the moving crowd, leaving the pair rooted to the spot. Fritz's heart raced and all Johanna could do was hold on to dear life as her husband's body started turning ice cold.

After 15 minutes the hall was all but deserted save a few people left cleaning up the mess of chairs and benches. Polishers began their little rituals in preparation for the next day's events. They were joined by a familiar figure who made its way back to the couple rooted to their seats. "Herr Fritz" the figure spoke. "Please follow me. Madame von Falkenhayn. You will see your husband at the grand entrance momentarily".

They looked at each other in mild relief that they would see each other again. Johanna nodded and gave Fritz one more squeeze on his elbow and kissed his cheek. "I will see you very soon" she said reassuringly. Fritz was once again reminded of how lucky he was to have such a diligent and supportive wife. Though, had she not pointed out the presence of Ludendorff then maybe he might have been able to keep his head down. Was ignorance bliss? She made sure he was not given the option of being ignorant.

The figure beckoned Fritz out and up a small and winding staircase. Barely a moment seemed to pass before he was led to an insignificant door in a dimly lit part of the palace. The figure opened the door and obliged Fritz to pass through. Doing as he was told; Fritz entered a well-lit office room which looked like a temporary installation. In fact, Fritz saw a slight resemblance to a poorly made-dugout in a trench. Papers were stacked hap-hazardously around the place and a singular window with the curtain mostly drawn down adorned the wall at the end. Standing by the window was the man he was there to see.

"The tight-lipped man has arrived" the booming voice of Ludendorff said. He was looking out of the window at the people sprawling out of the palace into the night of the energetic city. "I am grateful for a moment of your time. Come in. Come in."

Fritz took a couple of steps into the office as the door was closed behind him. He did not hear the door lock and so felt slightly more reassured. He walked behind a chair and rested his hands on its back. "What do you want?" Fritz asked with unmasked trepidation.

The infamous General turned around. His scowl was barely masked by his moustache. He was wearing a plain suit which seemed to make him less of an imposing figure but to Fritz; a man who served in the very army under his command, he was still an imposing man. "I witnessed your little vow of silence in the court room just now. I have to ask." He paused a moment electing to remain standing. "Why?"

Fritz gripped the back of the chair for stability. "I disagreed with the question. That is the end of the matter." Ludendorff snorted audibly.

"I think it is not. Tell me, what was going through your head as you took the stand? You did not seem at your best." The wily General showed off his talent for spotting a weakness in men. It was what made him so imposing to all who knew him or knew about him. Fritz did well to reply with any words at all, let alone with any semblance of coherence.

"I'm not in the business of stoking any fires. I just want justice and peace. That's what I came here to help achieve. I will not see conflict desired because of me". Fritz looked down. Despite his forthright words he could not bring himself to look into the General's infamous glaring

190

eyes. He thought he was going to hear another snort of laughter. He didn't hear a thing, and it made him worry.

The General's words seemed longer and more drawn out, making them more weighted and deliberate in Fritz's ears. "Justice. Peace. They are meaningless words if they do not act for something. Isn't that right, Herr Falkenhayn? There must be thought and action behind it." The general took a step towards Fritz. "What do you think you have achieved here?"

Fritz searched his mind. He did not think that far ahead, and opted instead to think of what he had avoided. "I've stopped this, whatever it is. Whatever you intended to do with this court case." He looked up to see the General with a raised eyebrow. "You orchestrated this whole thing, didn't you? Why?"

Ludendorff's laugh confused Fritz's mind. "Yah, you are perceptive."

"You want to turn Germany away from peace by preparing her people for war."

"My my, the young protégé really has his ears to the ground. Your father has taught you well. I do hope his insufficiencies die with him." Fritz jerked his head up to meet the taller General's eyes. Those words seemed to hit him like daggers. Ludendorff, seeing that he was riling up his opponent, smiled and took his seat his desk. "You are not so well versed with the matters of state. You do not see threats where they really are, or indeed where they might soon be. Oh, don't worry about it, there are more senior men who share similar blind spots to you. The Prime Minister. Your father. Even the Kaiser cannot see. But to those who can, do not worry also. We might have been pushed to the wings but we will wait there until we are needed once again". The General seemed immensely confident, and that confidence irked the captain who was still reeling from the comment about his father.

"Your little court stunt has fallen flat. It will not be long until your cause falls flat too." Fritz said with defiance, hoping that his actions in the hall might be enough to hold himself up in the office.

Ludendorff snorted again and turned his head to the window. "The city has not fallen flat. It still teams with patriotic fervour." He turned his head back. "Yes, your little stunt might have been slightly annoying for getting the word out but we have enough to go on. 2 weeks' worth to be exact." He leant back in his chair in quiet contemplation. "And there is one thing you must know, my little rebel. Even if you did succeed, all I have to do is wait. There will come a time when the *peace* as you call it is threatened because of some incident somewhere nearby, sometime soon. Then, our corner will fight again and you will us back. I have time on my side, little Fritz. Just you wait and see".

Fritz had heard too much to argue against. He had finally run out of things to argue against. He had not the time nor the capacity to carry on the argument which the wily General was winning in that room at that time. He moved to the door. The general got up and leant over his desk.

"And when it does happen you will be thankful that we are coming to your aid!" the General said, raising his voice. Fritz made for the door, opening it and pushing past the figure guarding the door.

"Oh, and Fritz!" the general called out, stopping him in his tracks briefly. "I'm terribly sorry about your mother". An icy chill fell down his spine. The words seemed to sound deliberate, as if he was apologising for killing her. Fritz did not want clarification. He could not stomach the idea. Perhaps his mind was playing tricks on itself. He did not look back as he rushed out and sped to join his waiting wife.

As they left the palace he stopped and stared back and up the palace. The lights illuminating the palace walls were dramatic. He found the window of Ludendorff's temporary office. He saw a dark figure staring out and he knew that he was staring down at him. Fritz turned away.

"What happened?" Johanna asked. She had been in a worried state for a while.

"I will tell you about it in the car. We will set off tonight".

"You go ahead. I need to go somewhere first" Johanna said. "I will see you soon".

Fritz nodded, wanting to get as far away from the palace as possible. The car was situated in the southern part of the city with a driver awaiting them. Fritz kissed Johanna on the lips and then spirited himself away, fearing reprisals from people who had witnessed his court-room defiance. He looked back as he saw his wife escaping into the night through the streets. He did not know where she was going and in better times, he might have worried where she was going. He had too much on his mind. His mother, the trial, meeting the man who would make Germany a dictatorship, all too many things to allow his mind to make any further space for the concern over the whereabouts of his wife. He sped away himself into the night and into a long and twisted road to some sort of mental recovery.

Johanna made her way to the hotel where William Steele was being kept. She had hoped that he was still there. She made her way through the guards and asked if the defendant was being kept there. She was told that he was there, due to be shipped back to England in the coming days. She asked if she could see him. She was granted permission.

She opened the hotel room door and there he was, slumped on the ground, with another cut on his cheek. He seemed to have been given a bit of a rough ride back to his cell once again. She looked at him and pitied him. This man was a pawn in a big game and her heart sank. She did not see an enemy; she saw a big game of chess with little regard for its pieces. Her husband was one, and this was another. She noticed that he was seated, with tears running down his cheeks.

"Are you alright?" she asked in her not-so-fluent English.

"My father. He's dead." William replied. With the passing of the court case, he was allotted space in his mind to grieve for the first time. Johanna's heart grew for this man. She sat on the floor next to him. He was slightly shorter than her. She noticed that he couldn't keep his eyes open. The tears in his eyes were pulling down his eye lids. The man was visibly exhausted.

"Did you know your father well?" she asked. He nodded softly. She sighed and pointed to the night sky, indicating to William to look outside. He did so, and she began to tell him of the same story Fritz's mother told her son on her death bed. Johanna told William about the stars and who was now up there looking down on him. She pointed to the brightest star for William to find.

Chapter 19

Munich was a much quieter city a few weeks after the curtain came down on the final trial. The city seemed to soften though the odd band of roving townsfolk singing boisterous songs could be heard every other night. People seemed to go about their normal lives again. No more fire pits, no braziers lighting the sides of streets, no marching bands, the streets of the city turned into eery quiet. Perhaps people finally caught up with sleep or perhaps the hangovers started hitting badly. No one quite knew or cared to ask. There seemed to be a general acceptance among ordinary people that the fun was over and there was work to be done and lives to be led. An undertone of some residual fervour remained, especially if one visited Munich and compared it to other German cities. Flags still waved, soldiers could be seen every now and again. But the legacy of the trials seemed to have had their day; at least for now.

Even the great hub of excitement; the Nymphenburg Palace, seemed quiet. It had barely been cleared out in the three weeks since it had hosted its last performance. The gallery had been deconstructed but the stage had yet to be dismantled and the benches were still there, though in a disorganised manner. Many of the lights were off and the palace was itself deserted. Only one or two engineers popped in once or twice a day to take away another bench or twist out another piece of wood from the stage. The palace looked as tired as its people. Even the windows seemed to sag in the light, creating a tired-like persona to the great building.

The mid-April warmth caressed the flowers of the great palace gardens to begin their ethereal blossoming. The air seemed lighter and fresher than in years past. A light breeze rolled in from the south, bringing with them a light scent of the southern Bavarian mountains. The grass was healing well after weeks of being trampled over. The early birds nestled in, saving their spaces in the nooks and crannies of the gardens for the building of their nests in the coming days ready for summer. It would seem that the summer of 1920 would be a bright and warm one so many birds would make their way to these climbs in order to take advantage of the temperate weather.

Though the gardens themselves were not strictly for public usage more and more people wandered into the grounds to take in the renewed vigour of nature in the mid-spring air. Security seemed to be lapsing slightly around the palace but many attributed that to the general lethargy of the city itself. In fact, once or twice a wandering guard might find one or two people sleeping peacefully in the garden grounds underneath a still and stoic tree. Most guards would sweep these people off the gardens and back out into the city but the odd one would simply walk on by allowing a few minutes more napping to be had at least.

On a crisp Thursday afternoon as the sun temporarily nestled in behind a few scattered clouds one figure could be seen walking through the deeper gardens on his own. He was carrying a walking stick and twizzled the ends of his moustache with relative frequency. He did his best to avoid passers-by and when he sat on a garden bench his head was always lowered so as not to catch anyone in a brief eye contact. A tall and elderly gentleman he was, marvelling every so often at the diving flights of a thrush, a robin or a sparrow in and out of bushes and hedgerows that were neatly cared for. If anyone did catch a glimpse of his eyes when he was caught following the flight of a small bird on its journey to or from its new nest, they could see his mind was far away, as if flying with the very little winged creatures. When he sat down on a bench, he used his cane to toy and play with a squirrel that would perchance to cross his path. His smile at interacting with the very denizens of nature allowed him to eke out the odd chuckle to himself, especially when the animals playfully responded. And each time a squirrel or bird did him the honour of their presence he would doff his hat to them to thank them for taking time out of their day to bring joy to an old man.

He had a minder who would make sure he was alright but the old man was insistent that he stay out of the gardens. Having his minder around always seemed to remind him of his senior years and he resented it. Even his cane, though a useful stick to use to bring joy to squirrels and birds, served to remind him of his advanced years. In truth, the reason he visited these gardens was because it had reminded him of his youth. In days when he was younger, he would visit the well-kept gardens of his town and sit and talk to the trees, entertain similar woodland creatures, and chase them with no desire to catch them. He could do little now to chase a squirrel though once he allowed himself to try, only to be forced to give up the pursuit after a good ten seconds out of exhaustion.

Eventually the thoughts of the cane, of his minder waiting for him at the edge of the palace grounds and his inability to chase the woodland creatures brought him to a well-disguised emotion of sadness. He would sit and lower his head, cursing the cruelty of time. He often thought of time as an animal that robs people of gifts bestowed to them each year until the final thing robbed from a man was his life. He cared little for that gift for he thought that without other gifts then life seemed all-too-little to care about. If ever he felt overwhelmed by those thoughts, he would slam the butt of his cane down on the ground a few times. Vibrating his body out of a funk seemed to do the trick.

So, on that crisp Thursday he took his almost-daily walk around the palace grounds. He stopped by and doffed his cap to a stray thrush as it landed and hopped its way into a nearby bush. "Have a splendid day, sir" he said in a low and shaky voice as he walked past, donning his hat. His cane seemed a bit heavier today but luckily there were not a lot of people in the gardens on this day so he needed to do less weaving in and out in order to avoid their gaze. He was walking into a deep part of the grounds to one of his favourite benches. It was in a slightly sunken part of the gardens so it was not directly hit by wind. It was also directly under a large beech tree which allowed for shafts of sunlight to descend on the bench meaning that he was able to lean in one direction or another in order to be in or out of the sun. He reached the bench and sat down slowly, grasping his walking stick, waiting in hopeful anticipation for a squirrel to cross his path in order to play with it. Ten minutes went by and no such animal joined him that day. He tutted to himself and placed the cane in between his legs and held it at the middle. He sighed and contemplated life for a bit longer.

Something did then approach him but it was in no way connected to nature. It was a large and well-dressed figure with a bushy moustache. It approached the old man from the path behind the bench. The old man heard the figure approaching and leant back, exhaling in dissatisfaction that his natural sanctum was being disturbed. He did not give the figure the curtesy of moving his head, electing instead to carry on staring ahead at the open grassy ground in front of him. The figure approached the left-hand side of the bench and then said softly "Good afternoon, Paul. I thought I would find you still here. Are you sure it's wise to be out in plain sight?"

The old man huffed and didn't reply. He grasped his walking stick and rested it on his lap. He sat silently for a bit longer, hoping that the figure would go away, though he knew very well who it was.

"What would people say if they saw the great Marshall Hindenburg out and about amongst the people? They would say that you have given up on leading Germany. How the mighty have fallen. Is that what you want people to say?"

The old man lowered his head and took off his hat. He let out another great sigh, letting his large stomach raise and lower itself. "You were never one to mince your words, Erich Ludendorff". He spoke with great effort as his body contorted within itself from a relaxed state into something much worse. The figure of his old friend made a familiar chuckle and walked round the bench and faced the seated marshal.

"How long have you been staying in Munich?" asked a serene Ludendorff.

"2 weeks."

"How long do you intend to stay for?"

"I haven't decided yet." The old marshal looked up to the trees, inspecting the new leaves. "I hope until the blossom of the gardens is at its most beautiful." He saw his old friend turn away and take a couple of steps away from him. "Your little scheme was not a great success?" Hindenburg asked as he leant upright on the bench. Ludendorff stroked his head.

"There were a couple of complications that I did not see coming".

Hindenburg smiled wryly. "That's not like you, Erich. Not like you at all. What happened?"

Ludendorff turned around revealing a frown that betrayed his emotion. "We lost momentum in the last week. We have solidified our base but it is too local." His eyes darted around the sunken area of the garden, making sure no one was around to overhear their conversation.

"It is a start. A good foundation is what we need and thanks to you we have that. I am not worried".

Hindenburg's words seemed to do little to reassure his old friend. He sighed and sat on the bench. "Time is against us. Every day that passes our goal is made harder." He looked over hoping for acknowledgement of his worries. He received nothing.

"I take a different view of time" Hindenburg said, resenting Ludendorff's presence. No woodland creature would dare approach now. "There will be opportunities that come our way soon. I think, perhaps, that we should stop forcing opportunities from now on, don't you think?" He asked the question without even glancing over.

Ludendorff became agitated. "We cannot simply sit by and hope for the winds to change. We must blow them ourselves. If we are to dismantle and rebuild the country, we will need more than to simply wait!" Hindenburg finally glanced over but with a frown. He held the gaze for a moment before returning to gazing into the distance in front of him. Ludendorff realized his emotions were getting the better of him and collected himself. "Listen, Paul. We must act with lightning speed. Every day peace seems more likely the Kaiser will be seen as being right. Why should we stop creating the threat? I don't know where it will be otherwise."

Hindenburg looked up into the sky. This was a conversation he did not want to have at this time. He thought, however, that the desire to avoid this conversation was growing more and more frequent. He stayed his tongue, allowing for his junior to speak his peace.

"We can't awake the German people sitting from here" Ludendorff said, beginning to wave his arms around. "We need to be right there, in Berlin, leading them to their destiny. I'll do whatever it takes to shake the German people into the realization of their superiority if I have to."

Hindenburg glanced over again. He was concerned about the words his partner was saying. He had heard such perorations before but believed them to be destined only to be uttered from the lips of the inebriated in dingey beer halls. He grasped his walking stick. "Superiority?"

"Yes. You see it, do you not? Well, certainly not the modern Germans who shake hands with all alike. Certainly not the Germans who bow down to some God." Hindenburg twisted his hands over his cane growing more uncomfortable. Ludendorff turned to his friend and asked "When was the last time you listened to Wagner?"

"Oh", gasped Hindenburg, searching his memories. "Not since I was last in Bayreuth. Why do you ask?"

"Paul, the music. I attend the operas when I can. It is a magnificent display of ancient German glory, the likes of which that have not yet been seen in these lands for eons. And we were so close to getting there. But then the damned Kaiser went and sought for peace. Peace! When we were on the verge of victory. You agree with me?"

Hindenburg looked away. "What comes after victory for you, Erich?"

"The Volkisch state. One built on blood and iron, built on the backs of the ancient German heroes of old." Ludendorff had worked himself up into a fury. "And we aren't getting any closer to it by sitting here!"

Ludendorff rose to get up before he felt a harsh smack against his lower stomach pushing him back down. He looked down and saw Hindenburg's cane pushing him down. He stopped talking and looked over at the old marshal who pursed his lips and spoke. "I once heard about this idea of a 'Volkisch state' by cranks and ungodly fools. They spoke of a twisted utopia of fire and ash. An end to all that God has given us in favour of some Germanic paganism reminiscent of the dark ages. I did not think of any of it, believing the idea to be as a result of too many days alone in the darkness howling at the moon. I did not expect such words to be coming from your lips, old friend."

"Paul, listen. When you listen to Wagner- "

"-When I listen to Wagner, I listen to music. That is all. When I pray, I pray to God. When I serve Germany, I serve my Kaiser. The people who say what you say would listen to cranks, pray to a twisted cross and serve some godless fool. This, we are not here to do." He looked over, pressing his walking stick further into Ludendorff's lap. "You will follow my instructions and my instructions only. We are only to return to power with the Kaiser. When we are in power, we will win the war instead of coming to peace with it. We do so in order to achieve national survival and for the Kaiser, not for this ludicrous notion of a pagan ritual of fire and death. Do you understand me?" Hindenburg's dull and greying eyes, losing their sight ever so slowly were all at once ablaze to Ludendorff. "Do you understand me?" Hindenburg repeated. Ludendorff nodded. The walking stick was raised and Ludendorff sprung to his feet dusting himself off. "And that had better be the last time I hear of this 'Volkisch' nonsense".

Ludendorff nodded. He cleared his throat which had been building up with a sort of zeal that was threatening to bubble over. "So, what do we do now then? You are in command."

Hindenburg leant back, exhausted from speaking with such an irate nature. He sighed. "I am confident, old friend. Our opportunity will come, and it will come soon. In time I will tell you what I have been doing whilst you have been playing judge, jury and executioner. All I will say is that you will have to raise your vision outside of this country you seem to love too well.

Ludendorff raised his eyebrow, frowning in the knowledge that his friend and commander was keeping secrets from him. "Where should I set my sights on?"

Hindenburg turned his eyes to Ludendorff as he was about to walk away. He smiled softly, raising his right arm and pointing to the right, and said; "France". Ludendorff huffed and walked away, leaving Hindenburg alone again. He took his walking stick and tried once again to coax the squirrels and the birds into lending him their time to play.

Chapter 20

'They shall not pass', the phrase was etched into posters, paintings and even the door to the grand hall of the Lion of Verdun. The Longchamp palace, to some the jewel of southern France, was awash with the trinkets and statues of a bygone age. Flags flew from every direction from the old palace that looked like it had not quite understood that the Victorian era was over. Its marble edifice was splendid to look at and even more splendid to walk in to. It was, naturally, closed to public eyes but it remained a sight for those who wished to walk past its splendid grounds. Beautifully maintained as a grand work of art, it stood as the centre of energy for the wily leader of Petain's revolutionaries.

Battle-flags and emblems of dozens if not hundreds of old French army and navy regiments were on display around the grounds turning the great palace into the shape of a military complex, which in a way it had become. The palace was the nerve centre of Petain's popular movement, one of the many anti-republic political parties but one of the most popular in France. The palace became a pilgrimage for supporters all over the country to come and pay their respects to one of the most infamous generals of the great war. Pilgrims were invited to pay their respects in kind or in literal coin to the movement, and volunteers were attending in their hundreds to be foot-soldiers of the movement. Many of these had served in the French army before. The 'revolutionary poilu regiments' were organised from the palace and so lines of well-outfitted men littered the grounds, the nearby roads and streets and wandered haphazardly around the giant southern city. The city seemed absent of those trying to get on with their lives save the restaurants and farmers occasionally selling their wares to the city barracks, hungry for food and action.

"I will bet my share of ham for your share of bread for this week" declared volunteer private Villeneuve. "You are not so good at cards this time around."

"That is not true!" protested volunteer private Arundel. "Last week you were deprived of chicken for the second time. I know because it was me who took it from you!"

"You have this argument every time. Just show what it is you will risk and play!" exclaimed volunteer private Lorrens. He fumbled the cards in his hand and then dealt two each to the men. "If you keep arguing about who is better than who then I will take my cards and find other hungry soldiers to take food off of them.

The betting party were surrounded by around twenty other men in the street, licking their lips as the delicious items were produced on the tables. The game was played out slowly as the sun came out and its heat forced onlookers to remove their helmets. All seemed quiet save some murmurs at the back until private Villeneuve chuckled as he produced the winning move. He slammed down the card, trumping Arundel's gambit. The defeated private looked down in shock and then immediately grabbed Villeneuve's wrist. He jerked it towards him, and three cards fell from the sleeve.

"You fiend!" shouted Arundel and flipped the table as he got up, throwing private Lorrens and his cards onto the cobbled stone ground, the food falling to the ground as two of the onlookers took their chance and lurched for the chance to steal them. The card players took to each other instead, throwing wild punches at each other. Arundel took a few swipes at Villeneuve landing only one on his shoulder. Villeneuve staggered to the ground, reached for his nearby helmet and flung it at Arundel, landing a blow to the side of his head which caused him to stagger. Villeneuve kicked Arundel's standing leg from under him causing him to fall. Villeneuve pounced on him and attempted to strangle him until he was dragged from the flailing foe by members of the crowd. Those in the crowd who wished to see the fight continue then took to those trying to stop the fight and a small melee began, whilst the winners of the fracas made away with the bread and the ham.

The commotion garnered some attention from some passers-by, two in peaked caps and one without. They peered round to see the fight. The two men running away with food tightly protected in their arms ran past the onlookers. An arm shot out to stop one of the men who frantically searched for the face of the figure stopping him. The moustache adorning the face was mildly familiar. The famed General Louis Franchet d'Esperey's eyes stared back. "What is going on?" asked the General.

"Nothing, General" the man meekly replied before the arm of the General was slowly withdrawn. The man rushed away into the winding streets and out of sight. The small party of three watched him run away.

"It is worse than we thought" the hero of Salonika muttered disparagingly.

"We are almost out of time. We must act now" noted the other figure, that of adjutant Maxime Rolland. He turned to his commander, the third figure. The harvest is the poorest seen in an age. We cannot sustain this.

The third figure walked on ahead of them, tutting to himself and mumbling inaudibly. The two men walked quickly to catch up to him. "It is not a matter of if but when. Our potential strength falls by the day. Discipline and strategy count for nothing if morale falls. We cannot allow for this to happen" d'Esperay implored. The figure remained unmoved and carried on his hasty way. The two men looked at each other gesturing to each other a confusion of what to do. The figure huffed and puffed as he stormed off towards the palace.

"Your guest can wait a minute or two I am sure" Rolland said in an assuring tone, slightly out of breath running after the figure. "We need not make haste. You wanted to return via the sea did you not? I think, I think we are going the wrong way."

"Phillipe!" shouted d'Esperay. "Would you kindly return to a light walking pace!" Still, he was ignored. "Or are you trying to run away?"

The figure finally stopped in his tracks. As the other two were finally catching up the man turned round and pointed at the General. "I did not run at Verdun. I stood and I fought, and I won. I do not run away!" The gravelly voice of the Lion of Verdun shouted as if he was once again standing in the fields of the now-hallowed grounds. The Marshal waited to embrace the awkward silence. "I do not run away." He declared in a quieter tone as he lowered his arm.

The unmoved General replied "then tell me what it is you intend to do about the food shortages". He received no reply. "If the great Petain does not know then how are we to act? What do we tell the men?"

"Tell them nothing more than they will soon fight to liberate France from the enemies within. That should be enough food for any man or woman or child. If it is not then they are no longer welcome here." Petain waved his arms around alongside his declaration. He turned and carried on his walk alone. Rolland made to follow but he was held back by d'Esperay.

"Let him be. He must now meet with the reds. It is delicate enough and he always works better when he is alone" the general regretfully sighed. "Let us go another way and see if we are needed nearby. Are you hungry?" Rolland nodded. "Then that makes more than two of us".

The marshal made his way up the palace stairs. Soldiers stood to attention as he made his way past. He would usually signal his appreciation but on this day, he simply staggered on by. Doors were opened for him as he made his way through the halls of a time gone by and made for the room housing the distinguished guest. He breathed in and out a few times, composing himself before he entered the room. His confidence was great and his swagger mirrored that of a prowling lion as his namesake and reputation would have suggested. His resplendent marshal's uniform glowed in the light of the room with a wide round table. Sitting there was his guest that he was expecting, but though it was indeed a guest from Toulon it was not the man he had met many times before. Sitting in the chair was Boris Souvarine. He looked scruffy in his trench coat which seemed unusual in the heat of the time of year but he seemed undeterred.

"I was not expecting you. I was told that Mr Renaudin was to attend. Has he been detained by something?" the famous field marshal asked, taking his seat. He rested his arms on the chair's arm-rests whilst his guest had to slump on a chair that was barely enough to be called a stool. Petain was known for the subtle mind games.

"Sadly, Maurice has another engagement that he wishes to attend. At least, that is the official reason I am sure you would wish to give. My name is Boris Souvarine, but you may call me Varine."

"Yes, I have seen you before but I did not hear you before. So, you do have a voice. Do you also have authority to speak? I do not waste time with those who have little to do".

Varine seemed unphased by Petain's petty barbs. "I am constantly in the ear of Renaudin. He requires my council on a constant basis and so I am, if you would care to believe, the mind of the movement."

Petain leant forward. "So why are you here?"

"I am here because I am to speak on behalf of the good of the movement, even if that good runs counter to that of Renaudin".

Petain's wispy eyebrows raised up. "This is the first time I am hearing of a split in motivations."

"It is not a split" Varine brushed the thought aside, "It is a natural progression of ideas. Renaudin is a dreamer but dreams have many loose ends. This is evident because he still does not know what a France with you and him at the head entails. He simply looks only to the overthrowing of the dead system and no more. I am sure you have thought much of the day after?"

Petain nodded, though he kept his feelings on the matter a secret even to d'Esperay. Petain had no intention of letting anyone even remotely connected to the reds of Moscow anywhere near the levers of power. Petain had always planned on using the socialist hordes as fodder until they had ceased to be of use. He had always outwardly maintained a desire to work with the socialists. Only a couple of months ago had he and Renaudin famously agreed on the writing up of the accords of mutual cooperation, promising to consider a form of governance peacefully once the republic itself was overthrown. The finer details of what that meant had been deliberately left out by both sides. Petain secretly held no intention of involving Renaudin and maintained a great secrecy about his desire by any means to prevent the sharing of power.

"And I am sure that Marshal Petain is not willing to discuss the matter because his intentions are less than totally willing to talk about some form of power sharing. Am I right?" asked Varine. The question seemed to pierce Petain's mind like an arrow. It was as if Varine had peered into his very mind, even at that moment. It was the first time anyone from the red movement of Toulon had asked him that question, and he was thinking of his ultimate betrayal at that very moment. Had he said something out loud? He searched his immediate memory but found nothing. He went to speak but his mind and tongue failed him. "I would not presume, but I think I may be closer to the truth than I think."

Petain sighed to allow him the ability to speak. "So, what if that was the case? Would you go to Renaudin and convince him to end our partnership after so much has been agreed? You know very well that you need me and my armies."

"So, we do. But I want to be on the right side of history, and not dead by your hand. Anyone who does not see that you hold the whip hand in this partnership is a fool. Renaudin is one such fool. You and I, are not." Varine took out a piece of paper with some scribbles on it and slid it towards the wily field marshal who perused it slowly.

"What is this?" he asked, desiring not to read it.

"A possibility. A future French administration. You as its head, as president with far reaching powers. Myself as Prime Minister. It would placate the masses and allow for peaceful power sharing. None have to die save perhaps those who would do away with you should the possibility arise."

"You are willing to sell out Renaudin and the movement?" Petain asked, sceptical about the idea.

"I am sure there are things we can find agreement on. I am not so draconian in my beliefs of a socialist paradise. It is not as if things are going terribly well in Russia with the Bolsheviks. If we can find common ground now then we can make a nation of common ground." Varine appeared sincere in his thinking. Petain rolled his shoulders, indicating a warming to the idea.

"And what if I refuse? What if I retained the whip hand and used it to the full extent of its ability?" Petain pondered, though his decision rested on Varine's answer.

Varine shrugged his shoulders. "Then I would naturally attempt to use my position to convince Renaudin to break the partnership."

Petain laughed. "He wouldn't dare. It is impossible."

"Maybe it is impossible. But do you want to take the risk?"

Petain's face returned to its serious dour demeanour. He reclined in his arm chair. The door opened and d'Esperay and Rolland entered. Petain raised his arm and beckoned them to leave. They did so, closing the door slowly and quietly. "How can I trust you when you are attempting to double cross your own?"

Varine made a gun gesture with his hand and pointed it to his temple smiling, "Do I have a choice against the man with the whip hand?"

Petain nodded and took from his breast pocket of his tunic a silver pen. He looked at it and added his initials to the bottom and slid the paper back to the scruffy middle-aged man. "What will you do with Renaudin?"

"Whatever is necessary for the agreement to work" Varine reassured. He stood up but Petain begged him to wait.

"One more thing. On a point of order, please relay to Renaudin that we are to march very soon. I want his assurances that all is ready from the beginning of next month. We don't want to steal a march on you, especially when you've gone to all this trouble" he gestured to the piece of paper. Varine inclined his neck.

"I will relay this to Renaudin. Our forces will be more than prepared, should the need for it arise. Our combined approach will make armed resistance impossible. The republic will see little sense in asking for resistance when we both make our move."

"Quite right!" declared Petain. "I await to hear the agreed day". He inclined his head and Varine slunk to the door and vanished from Petain's eyes.

Petain reclined in his seat and looked up at the walls. He read his infamous inscription 'They shall not pass' on the walls and grinned as his mind became awash with fond memories of the glorious battle of Verdun. He could hear the wondrous huzzahs from his soldiers as he drove down the road of the sacred way. He closed his eyes as he visualised those memories. The hero of Verdun. The Lion of Verdun. The lion that was stabbed in the back by Foch and the British. The lion that did not lose as those around him lost their heads. He bit his lip in anger as the memories turned to ash and he gripped the ends of the arm rests with his hands.

The great marshal of France was freed from his inner turmoil by the door opening as d'Esperay and Rolland re-entered the room. They approached him, sitting either side. d'Esperay removed his peaked cap as did Rolland.

"So? What happened? We cannot starve for any longer. That was not Renaudin. Do we march?" d'Esperay asked frantically.

Petain opened his eyes and glared softly at his general. "We march".

Chapter 21

The waves lapped the sides of the transport boat gently. The breeze was calm though darker clouds could be soon on the far-off horizon but making steady pace. The steel plates of the R.M.S Carmania yawned quietly as the ship passed through the shallower waters of the North Sea. The laugh-like sounds of seagulls had not been heard for twenty minutes as the shores of Friesland began falling into the haze. The summer's day warmed the open metal pieces of the boat that made it almost too hot to touch, and though some on board chose to enjoy the rays of sunshine all they could on the odd deckchair, most stayed below deck to take a few minutes sleep due to the early start of the voyage from Wilhelmshaven to Folkstone. The ship's smoke columns billowed wistfully behind as it made good progress.

She was an experienced vessel. The R.M.S Carmania had been granted many transport duties during the Great War. Evidence of this was still fresh for all to see. Scratches on the deck from bored soldiers, an entire case of ship logs cataloguing every journey was stowed away and the quarters below deck still had not lost its rather odious smell.

Her commander, captain James Fitzroy, had hoped that the ship would return to more beautiful tours of the world, as the ship had originally been built to take people to see the world. Alas his fate was to steer her around the dull North Sea as the pride of the ferry service from Germany to England. He was grateful that the naval guns had been removed but the relegation of the ship to her present duties seemed to take what was left of the shine of the old ship presently of the Cunard Line. He was often seen prowling the decks greeting passengers who were either relieved to be leaving Germany or depressed at having to go. It was his unfortunate duty to lead the fleet of the ferry of the doomed.

One such passenger below deck had made quite a name for himself. The presence of a minor celebrity had mildly perked up the spirits of the doomed sea captain. He made his way, as did most of the passengers on board that day, to the second level deck in order to shake the hand of one who had only just been discovered in England's daily news outlets in paper form. His deeds were not great but it was the first piece of news that had somewhat ended the deluge of shame the British tabloid press had seen fit to report on a daily basis. Though he would not be famous on a nation-wide scale he would be known enough to those who had bothered to gaze at the third page of the Sunday Times newspaper the day before.

The man in question was none other than William Steele. His deeds in the Munich court room had, against the wishes of the German press, leaked out into the United Kingdom press corps. The story of a man who stood up to bullies had circulated to a modest degree. Strict instructions had been made to the journalists not to sensationalise the story for fear of national offence. But enough was written to make those who had read the articles interested and for the name of William Steele to be spoken about in well-to-do coffee shops in Westminster and beyond.

William himself was uncomfortable with the level of attention. His character did not lend itself to accepting lavish praise, but knowing that the story had leaked out put a target on his head. He would be no friend of the Germans anymore and to those who wished to see order prevail, and the memory of his confrontation with Fritz von Falkenhayn was still etched in his memory, he would be an enemy. He knew this very well. Still, hiding away in the back of his mind was a sense of pride which enabled him to shake the hands of those who would offer it.

His mind was distracted. He had been bundled into a car and taken straight to the coast and on to a ship bound for England. He had not been granted the ability to return to Epernay and Cecile. He had vowed to make it right to see her and to finally accept her advances but fate had once again pushed him away to England. He felt once again like a prisoner. He did not want to go back to England.

Certainly, he had not even considered how to approach the news of the passing of his father. His father, the great Benjamin Steele of Devon, known for his ability to tame land into farmland had been seen as an ever-present force to those who knew him. William could not conceive the idea that his father was in any way weak. Benjamin seemed full of energy on most days, refusing to give up when the family farm seemed unable to provide anything of substance to live on let alone sell at a profit. Benjamin had a never-say-die attitude that would most certainly have won him a medal or two if he had fought in the Great War. To the relief of his family and the farm he was refused active service and instead sent to the industrial centre of Bristol in the service of 'reserved occupation'. Though he was in his early sixties he had no desire to act his age and provided valuable work in munitions factories where he eventually trained women in the art of fitting and fixing aircraft with the parts and weapons needed to help with the air war. He had no preliminary training with aircraft but his history of mechanization of the farmland leant him the necessary expertise.

The farm could not kill him. The factories could not kill him. Even a bout of tuberculosis, caught early, could not kill him. He seemed destined to live forever and in the mind of his son, William, a life without his father around seemed impossible. Felled by the Spanish flu, the great Benjamin was to end his forceful sojourn in the world. William had known little about any other details but was determined to find out what was going on, when he was mentally ready.

He thought of his mother. Niamh was an able woman who had come from Ireland on the wishes of her father to marry and Englishman. She was a calm but small-tempered mother who taught William discipline enough to help him survive in the army and to the best of his knowledge she was not on the side of the rebels in the Easter rising in 1916, and was no ally to those determined to be granted a free Ireland. She had been an Irish national in her early years but time seemed to soften her beliefs until she naturalised to the English, or rather Devon-ish, ways. She provided needed comfort to William's father when things seemed desolate but she herself had not the ability nor the strength to assist with the maintenance of the farm. During the war when her husband was away, she did her best, but the farm fell into troubles. Though she was rescued by the returning husband who saw the farm back to within touching distance of her former glory she had always resented her inability to tend to the farm and Benjamin's ability to do so.

Now, with Benjamin gone and never to return, Niamh would be left in a more vulnerable and more worrying state. William knew this and so knew that his time to shape up and face the family home without a father was short. The thought made the journey seem much longer and a greater sense of dread hung in the air.

"How on earth did you manage to keep your cool?" asked an eager passenger. William had been lost in his mind thinking of the predicament of his mother seemingly without looking away from the eyes of the latest well-wisher. "Did you feel them all want to kill you?" William's eyes refocused on his current predicament.

"It was a nightmare" he replied. It was his go-to reply whenever people asked questions, he didn't have the answer for. He gazed around the re-carpeted cabin seeing two small children peering through the open cabin door at him. He looked over and one of them ducked their head away whilst the other waved. He waved back with a ginger grin.

"Bloody hero you are. Don't think I'd have the stomach for it. Sometimes when my missus is yelling at me the last thing I want to do is be in the same room!" the passenger stated. "I faced shelling in Arras and I would still prefer that over someone yelling my ear off".

"You served in Arras?" William asked, trying to change the subject.

"For a brief time. Communications unit. Didn't see much action apart from laying down wires. But blimey was I glad when it was over". The question seemed to work, derailing the conversation about William's story sufficiently for him to nod and excuse himself.

He walked up and outside, finally having enough of the stuffy air that seemed to hang around him. He took to the main deck and leant at the edge watching the water pass on by. The sea seemed to be chopping up a bit and William gripped the hot steel edges to keep him from swaying backwards. A larger jolt against the side of the boat took him off balance and his hands slipped off the side, he staggered back and just as he was about to fall, he felt a pair of hands grab his arms and he was pushed back onto his feet. He heard a chuckle behind him as he steadied himself.

"You may be a dab hand at the spoken word but it takes more than a few fancy phrases to be a dab hand at sea, sir!" The voice of captain Fitzroy greeted William's ears as he spun round. "But I'm grateful you are here all the same".

"Slightly rough waters, are they not?" William protested meekly.

"Yes, storm is coming. Unusual for a summer's day but there it is" he pointed over to the south-westerly area. "Probably been bouncing its way down the French coast. We'll make port before it becomes a problem, don't you worry". The captain seemed to be smiling more than usual as his face seemed like it had not seen a smile for a good while. "And it's not every day we have the man of the hour on board. Can't have him hurling up his guts on deck. Don't want that on tomorrow's headline. The man who stood up against the Kaiser fell down against the current. Doesn't sound like a good story to me".

"I am perfectly capable of holding my own, sir" William protested.

"So you say my boy." The captain patted William on the back spinning his eyes slightly. "So you say." Well, don't you worry. An hour to go and you'll be able to step on dry land I reckon. Now, I've been thinking about how you really got under the skin of those fancy judges." The captain's accent reminded William of home. "Is it true that one of them fainted after your speech?"

William regretfully searched his memory. Little could be found to corroborate the question. "Woozy maybe, but I don't think any of the judges fainted".

"Ah, must have been fainters in the crowd I reckon. No doubt they would be hurling their guts out over the side if they ever set foot on a ship in open water!" The hearty laugh of Captain Fitzroy boomed from bow to stern. "Can't wait to get home to tell the tale to all and sundry, eh?"

"Can't wait" William replied dishonestly.

"Well now, can't be here all day. I don't know if you've noticed but I've got a ship to run. You aren't the only important person on this craft!" The captain seemed to be suffering from a touch of jealousy. "Come up to the bridge sometime soon. Can't have you wasting away in steerage this whole time. Tell us all tales of your adventure. The first officer is particularly excited but, don't let him scare you off!" Another hearty laugh belted around the ships deck as another hard pat on William's back spun his eyes around again. The captain waddled off and out of sight. It would be the last William would see of him until disembarkation had commenced.

The arrival had been delayed by half an hour. The storm had changed its course and rather than passing by harmlessly behind the passage of the ship it had changed course northwards and forced the Carmania to slow its speed in order to wait for the storm to pass. Arrival in Folkstone was still choppy and eventually William did as the captain predicted. An ill-timed jolt of the ship coincided with a similarly ill-timed burp and William released the contents of his stomach over the gangway rope. A few chuckles could be heard including one from the onlooking captain standing at the side of the ship. Even one of the children William had noticed whilst he was talking to well-wishes in his cabin could be seen laughing his head off. William's pride took a knock and he hastily made his way on to dry land and safety.

The train bound for London was ready to depart sometime later and after a brief stint reacquainting himself with England he was spirited away to London. The country seemed very different, very hostile, very angry. Graffiti adorned many buildings, boarded up windows were a common sight around the streets and the infamous hammer and sickle emblem of the reds could be seen carved into stone or scrawled on street signs. The only thing more alien to William's eyes but more common a sight was the presence of policemen patrolling the streets. Even members of the armed forces were in plain sight as well. To William it looked as if the war was not yet over, though the enemy had certainly changed.

There was one place William was headed to before making for home. His old house in London he had stayed in before the war, owned by his once good friend Henry Forbes. Though his new cottage was all set up he wanted one last look at the old house. He had not returned since the war's end. He had entrusted a member of his old army regiment to collect his things from the house to take to his new place of residence. A corporal Cartwright, though no longer in the armed forces, had taken all he could into a car and driven to William's new estate. William wanted to be sure that all had been taken away.

The house itself was boarded up. Not a soul seemed to have entered the building in what seemed like years. The door seemed to be off one of its hinges. It seemed like a forced entry. William stepped into the building and noticed every piece of furniture covered in white sheets. Cobwebs adorned corners, walkways and corridors. Insects and mice were the new tenants of this once bright townhouse William and Henry used to call home.

William climbed the stairs to the second floor. His old floor. The door itself had suffered a similar fate to that of the front door. He peered inside, but the rooms were too dark. The blinds had been closed for some time as when he went to open them dust burst into the air flittering through the soft shards of grey light from the outside. He saw his room as he remembered it, just with no personal effects. Cartwright seemed to have done his job well.

He searched through the various places of storage, finding little of note and nothing worth taking with him. All that remained in the rooms were memories of a time long gone. Some papers from his old city work remained, resplendent in numbers that now made no sense to him. His bed, though with no mattress on top of it, remained fixed where it had always been. It seemed that his room had been ransacked of comfortable things as well, for Cartwright had no need to take a mattress himself. The thought spoiled William's mildly fond memories of this room. He pressed on the bedframe and noticed it had not been moved at all. The frame was made of a good oak and so was heavy to move itself. This fact aided William's little hiding spot, underneath one of the bed's legs. It was a stash of notes, money he had saved in better times. Emergency money should he ever return to London in trouble. It had been squashed down partly as a hiding space and partly to prevent the bed rocking due to one of the legs being shorter than the other. He raised the bed frame with slight difficulty. There, one thousand pounds, money he had earned in the city he had put away. A hefty sum it was, but William was never one to spend so much money. In truth, it was money he was saving to take back home to help his parents either with the farm or to move out of the farm. He pocketed the money, and though it was useful to have, it was less compared to the money he had earned whilst in service to the government during his time in France as an intelligence officer. It might go some way, he thought, to helping with the predicament his mother might be in after the passing of his father.

He went to the window to peer out at the familiar scene of south-central London. He noticed a figure in the street, too shrouded in shade to make out. He thought little of it and looked over the rather messy roads of London. The city seemed darker, even for a summer's day. The clouds seemed to have cobwebs dancing from them, as they looked as if they had not moved from their perch over the city that was once the capital of the world, the centre of the world. Berlin had that title now. London looked like an afterthought.

Nothing of note remained here. William left the room and the building for the last time. The front door's final hinge gave out as he left and the door came crashing to the ground. The figure William noticed in the corner of his eye rushed off at the sound. Time, William thought, to leave London so he might not have to see it again. To home, he thought. He knew he had to face the music, and so he would. Delaying the inevitable would be a fool's errand, and so he would not wait any longer. He had come to his old house to avoid the music, but now it was playing in his head too loudly now. He made for Paddington station.

He walked through the streets unaided, noises of either passers-by or policemen disturbed his thoughts and his serenity. Compared to the febrile atmosphere of Munich, London seemed to emulate a museum. In effect, it was a museum; a museum to an age that died after the war. The city resembled a monument to a glorious era that had come to a very abrupt end and its own fate had yet to be decided. Even though two years had passed since the wars end the city had yet to choose what to do next.

He passed by Hyde Park. He was not far from Paddington. Even the greenery of the city seemed dulled by its presence in the capital. The grass had been scorched by previous weeks of heat and the trees seemed to be wilting as well. There were walkers in the park making their way around making the most of the scenery and the summer day even though the sun was nowhere to be seen. There was no smell of summer. It was just a place to walk.

Suddenly, as William was walking through the park, a hand pressed against his chest. It was no male hand. It was soft, delicate, and its padding betrayed the presence of a soft white glove. He looked down and saw that it indeed belonged to a woman. He turned his head and gasped, unleashing all the air from his lungs. Standing beside him, arm in arm with a man in a rather run-down dressed suit was the fair Emmanuelle. Her golden hair, curled delightfully as it was in years past, barely covered one of her two sparkling eyes. Her dress a pleasant shade of baby blue and the thinnest of scarves draped over her neck contributed to the colours and thoughts rushing into William's eyes. Her brow was furrowed. She looked stern, as did the face of the man caressing her arm; Henry Forbes.

"William. Oh, thank God. Henry look; it's William. William. Oh William!" she exclaimed clutching his light jacket.

"Emmanuelle?"

"Oh, don't say my name as if I am a stranger. You were there in Munich with Henry. Gosh weren't you brave" she exclaimed. Henry seemed similarly pleased to see William.

"Yes, it was a nightmare" William said, trotting out the same old line.

"But, you two are such great friends, are you not?" Emmanuelle states with a degree of innocence, though William knew full well that she was aware that they had ended their relationship as friends long ago.

"William, thank goodness we found you. We knew you were arriving in England today and we had hoped to find you here." Henry seemed most grateful for seeing William and put his arm on William's elbow. William remained motionless, as if talking to ghosts.

"Why have you been looking for me?" William asked, his head spinning, perhaps still from the ordeal on the ship or perhaps from seeing these people again.

"We went to your new estate in Oxfordshire hoping we could find you but we only learned that you have just come back! They kept you a long time, didn't they?" Emmanuelle said, seemingly ignoring William's question.

"How did you know where I live?" he asked, dressing the question in quiet indignation.

"Who doesn't know where the man who stood up to the Kaiser lives!" Henry stated. "We've been searching for you."

"Why" William asked again, indignation reaching boiling point.

"Your dear friend, Henry, was pushed around terribly badly and returned in disgrace. His money is gone, his family have disowned him. He stays with me but in truth, my dear Will, we too are struggling. There are debts, from many places, that both Henry and I must pay off. It is a disgrace and we are finding ourselves on the edge of society. My own father must soon sell his estate as well as he is no longer able to work." She seemed to break down into tears, overcome with shame. Henry looked down and though attempting to console her found himself rooted to the spot.

"I took the deal, William. I caved. I am no man. But I did not know the consequences of my decision" Henry defended.

"We rarely ever do" William replied. He took Emmanuelle's hand, trying to steady her as her limbs began to shake.

"I am forever to live a shamed life for even asking for your help" she said, her voice trembling as she leant into the support of William. "We are in need of anything to keep us afloat. We are drowning in a sea of debt. I cannot even begin to say how much we are broken by this".

William felt broken inside. Though he could not bring his emotions to the surface for fear of falling for them again he put his arm on her shoulder, as Henry did the same. The uniting feeling restored a bit of her senses as she looked up into William's eyes. Her scarf fell to the ground as Henry went to pick it up. He noticed a couple of walkers were peering round to see what was going on. Emmanuelle, on realising that she was making a scene, collected herself and returned to Henry's arm.

"William, you are dear to me and this is why you are the only one we could come to. England is awash with debts herself yet you remain strong, defiant in the papers and our treasured companion. Could you find it on your heart to lend to us any possible chance of support and help?" Henry reached over with his free hand and patted William's arm again. A slight flash punctured William's eye as he did and William looked down at Henry's hand. Adorned on one of his thinner fingers was that of a slightly shiny ring. Henry noticed his gaze and retracted his hand slowly, looking down so as to avoid William's gaze which now forced itself onto Henry.

218

"You are married?" William asked in a sombre tone.

"A year now" Henry stated softly and ashamedly. He straightened his neck and looked down at William who he was still taller than, trying to retain some level of dignity.

"Another debt" Emmanuelle softly added.

"And you call me a good friend" William retorted in thinly veiled disgust. There was a slight pause as none knew what to say next. William was not sad, he noticed that he felt no remorse, only anger, but an anger tinged in wilful acceptance. Was this the feeling of one who was able to move on? Perhaps. He did not care to ask this time. His limbs started vibrating slightly as his anger took over his nervous system. He reached into his inner jacket pocket and took out the money he had retrieved from his old house and took the lion's share of it into one hand and pushed it into Henry's chest, pushing him back a bit.

"William..."

"Take it. Use it to salvage what little shred of dignity you two have left. You come to me begging for money as if what you two had done before wasn't enough. Go on. Spend my money. You aren't worth the scrap of paper it's written on anyway." William paused to turn to go away but turned once more to the distraught couple. "But promise me one thing. You never seek me out, you never speak to me ever again. Never look for me. Never stop me in the street. If you see me in the street you take a different one. You see me on the train, take the next one. You read about me in the paper, turn the damn page. It would make my life considerably better when you do. Do me that favour and you can have that money guilt free. Lord knows you have enough guilt to pay off already." And with those words, William left the couple standing there in Hyde Park, Emmanuelle clutching Henry in slight spasms of tears and Henry standing ram rod but broken.

William walked away taking one look back at them, watching Henry clutch at one of the bank notes as it slipped his grasp falling to the floor. He turned his back hoping beyond hope that that would be the last time he would ever see those two ever again. He felt his heart mending, and his mind slowly focusing. He left the park as the clouds seemed to finally rumble their way away perhaps one day to let in shards of light onto the desolate city.

The train bound for Exeter heaved its metallic body out of Paddington with William inside it. He looked pensively out of the carriage window as the sights of old London town started whirring faster and faster out of his view. The train made good time and after a nap or two William found himself back at home, with a waiting mother ready to join him in a long and solemn process of mourning the loss of a great farmer, a beloved husband, and a wonderful father

Chapter 22

A very shocking news story dominated the German newspapers. The headline of the 25th June 1920 edition of every daily newspaper in Germany and in other nearby countries, including in the nearby Austro-Hungarian empire which had been facing its own sets of internal crises that summer. One of the oldest dynasties in Europe, a central part of the German state and one of the most prestigious households, had fallen. Though that was what was stated in the newspapers the official line within the palaces of Berlin and those around the Reichstag went with the line that the household had simply vanished. Whatever the truth was the news was categorical in its reporting. With the official abdication of the last king, king Ludwig III, the Bavarian Wittelsbach monarchy had officially ended.

There was visual consternation at the revelation of this news. The German parliament, liberal in its nature and in its make-up, declared openly its united outrage at the news. The chancellor, Theobald von Bethmann Hollweg, gave a speech decrying the actions of "the cowardly actors who had given in to political pressures unnecessary to listen to and even more unnecessary to invite in." He was referring to the growing infamy of the one-time dictators of Imperial Germany who had been widely credited with the toppling of the Bavarian royal household. Even the Kaiser had exploded with rage on hearing this news. The whole nation seemed to be in a fit of fury and seemed to the rest of the world that it had wounded itself, directly putting into question the effective primacy of the German nation in European and, as was slowly being believed at the time, world affairs. How could a mighty nation even consider itself the greatest of all nations when it cannot even keep its own nation together.

Though the toppling, or the apparent disappearance, of the Bavarian monarchy did not seek to threaten the very fabric of the German nation it was nonetheless a humiliation that dwarfed the actions of a British acting major in a Munich court room a couple of months ago. Action on behalf of the German parliament was decisive; condemnation of the move and bringing those responsible, including Ludwig himself, to justice. An official court of enquiry was set up with the task of perusing the letter of abdication, defining its legal implications, and correcting them when necessary. The official order was that the Bavarian state would be absorbed in entirety, with the Kaiser given the title of King of Bavaria himself. The chancellor declared in his official statement to the Reichstag that Kaiser Wilhelm had agreed himself to the move and that it should commence as soon as possible.

This was to prove no easy task. Following on from the official letter of abdication a new 'provisional Bavarian government' was proclaimed headed up by notable allies of the one-time dictators of Germany. Otto von Lossow, previously a major general, but was drummed out by the Kaiser along with hundreds of other officers following the end of the war due to his close links with Hindenburg and Ludendorff, was proclaimed provisional president of the new government along with Ritter von Kahr as prime minister. The Bavarian parliament had seemingly sworn in the new administration, though it was widely reported that the Bavarian parliament would have voted for anything so long as it would take over quickly from the speedy departure of the king. In effect, Bavaria was in a state of limbo between stability and open political rebellion.

The whole event made little sense to the onlooker from afar or even to citizens in the north of Germany. But to those in the know, it was all the work of the one-time dictators who were attempting to return to power if only for now content to rule behind the scenes. "They have taken Bavaria from a king who was just waiting for an excuse to leave" the head of the German general staff, Erich von Falkenhayn grumbled to his son, Fritz who had taken his wife to decide on a house to buy in Berlin. "We cannot simply drag the German army down there. It would be an even greater disaster".

Fritz's father had never been quite the same since the passing of his devoted wife. He had buried his head in his work and was finding new ways to distract himself from his thoughts. He had spent practically most of the year deciding troop transfers from Germany to the occupied French areas and working on defensive systems around the borders of France. He had been due to journey to German Tanganyika to help make a decision on future deployments to German Africa. He had developed a noticeable tremor in his neck and his head never seemed to settle in place. He had brushed it off as simple nerves of the job but Fritz became ever so slightly concerned with the deterioration of his father into a shaking workaholic.

The wily General August von Mackensen, with his bristling moustache and fast-greying hair, cut a calmer demeanour, but brushing his hands through his hair several times in order to do something with the nerves he felt inside. "The last time I saw the old King he was in a state of near-exhaustion. We bled his kingdom dry for the war and victory only delayed the inevitable breakdown. I suppose we must take some responsibility for it. You certainly thrust many a Bavarian division to its death in Verdun". Erich snarled at the thought, though the accusation was true.

Paul von Lettow-Vorbeck, due to join Erich on his journey to Africa, agreed with General August. "The vacuum was created long ago. It was going to be filled eventually. Sadly, public enemy number one knew that too. Should we be so shocked?"

"In the eyes of the public we must" Erich stated, waving his hands. "Why in God's name did we do nothing about it for two whole years?!"

"Well, you can't blame yourself. It isn't your responsibility" August calmy reassured his friend. Erich collapsed into a chair.

"There's always something I can do. I can talk to the Kaiser. I could have sent a detachment down to pacify the region. I could have done something to prevent the hastiness."

General Paul spoke up. "It should have been handled by the chancellor. It's the whole reason why the Kaiser put him back there in the first place; to stop the bloody army having to do everything. Let's face it, gentlemen. The chancellor, the whole damn parliament, has been caught napping. Hindenburg has stolen a march on us and taken advantage against a slow, sleepy, cumbersome, bureaucratic and hubristic gaggle of politicians."

"That's the thing about the army" Erich said regretfully, rubbing his eyes with his hand. "They always act quick enough to get the best possible outcome. We're an army run by politicians now. We go slow too."

"Well maybe we should ask your son what to do next, hmm? Herr Fritz. Tell us. What should be our next move?" August turned and said with a wry smile. "Let's see if tactical nous is hereditary". Both August and Paul looked with a jovial expectancy at Fritz in the corner. He was the only one not in uniform but rather in a summer suit. He didn't even have a hat with him to rival the grand peaked caps of the generals in the room. He shook his head in silent protest but was encouraged nonetheless. "Come on, man. Insight. Insight!"

"Can you arrest the leaders and appoint a new government?" Fritz asked with little expectation. He was let down by tutting from his father.

"No, no, no. That makes us no better than the bloody men who put them there in the first place" his father sighed.

"The boy does, however, prove my point. Whatever we do we can't simply ignore the new president and prime minister. Even if they are tin pot puppets of a greater problem." August reasoned. "Someone is destined to go down there and quickly to talk sense into these people. The Bavarian government are just spooked by all of this. We need to provide our own stability, surely".

"If only it was that simple my dear friend" Erich said with his hand rubbing his closed eyes. "We have to think of what the gruesome two have up their sleeve. They'd be expecting us to do that. They must have a plan."

"Is it pressure or is it armed revolt?" asked General Paul.

"If we knew the answer to that then we would have a much greater chance of solving this issue" Fritz's father angrily stated. "No, regardless, one must go down and see to it."

"Who should go?" Fritz piped up. August and Paul looked over, aware that anyone but Fritz could be a good candidate. Erich seemed the logical choice as head of the German General Staff. August was a well-known general and could garner support due to his name. Paul was a similar well known general, known as the hero of the African campaign. A similar charm offensive in Bavaria would do a decent job. But the answer seemed most logical.

"It'll be me. I have a grand threat on my side in my post. Should I deem it necessary I could have the army down there in a matter of hours so they would have to listen to me. You can't send anyone else. I'm the most expendable of the most important army officers." Erich seemed at peace with the idea and the thought seemed to assist him. After all he was still looking for things to divert his mind from the unfinished grieving process for his late wife.

"I wouldn't consider it a major issue. You can only do what you can do there. If it takes the damned Kaiser to go down to settle the matter, we'll do that, but we'll only know if it's necessary if we start with you" Paul said. Erich looked at him in reluctant agreement.

"I've never liked Munich in summer. It's much better in the autumn. Maybe I can stop by the mountains on the way back. What say you, eh, son? Fancy a jaunt around the mountains with your old father? You could bring your charming wife with you" Erich said, determined to not be alone for this proposed trip.

"Sadly, I cannot. Johanna is with child and it would be a terrible burden on her to travel" Fritz replied. This was in fact a lie. Johanna was not pregnant, but the daughter born before they were married merited no more hiding. She was to turn six soon and she had been patient enough. The rouse was the only way to bring his daughter into the accepting arms of his father and the Prussian aristocracy.

"Oh, of course. Did you tell me before that she was pregnant? I confess that I have been far too engrossed in my work to remember these things" Erich said, pleading his innocence when in fact he had never been told before. His two friends rolled their eyes at each other, silently murmuring at the understatement Erich had just uttered. "Then it shall be a very brief journey for myself alone."

"Oh, for heaven's sake, we will all come with you, won't we?" August said, determined to not hear Erich's whining about being left alone. "I'll see to my dear friend Prince Max if he can put us up in one of his little suburban villas near the city and we will be ever present nearby. Oh, come on, Paul. Don't look so glum. No sense setting off for the African continent without Erich in pursuit? A few more days in sunny Bavaria can't hurt us. And you, Fritz. Care to see your father in action? It would be good to have you shadowing your father in order to learn a bit more of internal diplomacy?" Fritz nodded silently. "Good man! Paul?" Paul nodded nonchalantly. "There we are. It's settled." The general got up from his chair. "We will provide you with an escort, sir. Let us know the jump-off time and we will be there with you at zero hour. I am off to bed, packing my overnight bag for a jolly old trip, what? Good! That's settled. Germany can sleep easy. I bid you good day", and in a flash the general upped and left the room.

"He seems overly confident, doesn't he?" Paul retorted after witnessing the performance.

"It's how he became so famous" Erich quipped." And at any rate neither he nor I can think of a suitable alternative than me talking sense into the puppets. What if they don't change their minds? Then what?"

"You're the chief of the General Staff, you have other means. Even if it goes against the spirit of things, the army might need to step in."

"What, to try to take down the very heroes that won the war? Impossible. But I have no alternative. It is the way of the world." Erich put his head into both of his hands and groaned. "I always thought of Hindenburg as an idealist, not a schemer. His lacky Ludendorff, that's a man unhinged. A shame at that".

"I did meet Ludendorff after the meeting. He seemed to suggest a very radical new political approach. Something I did hear back before the war ended by a few officers. Very radical." Fritz included. Paul seemed impressed. "Though not someone I would like to have talked to anyway. Trying to spoil my wedding. Johanna will never forgive him". The thought produced a winced look on Erich's face, recalling the incident. "If you'll excuse me father, sir, I must see to the condition of my wife". He stood up as the others did bowing towards him.

"Please do send her my fondest wishes" Paul asked.

"And mine" Erich added. Fritz inclined his neck and left the room, and soon walked out of the door of the War Ministry, taking only a few moments to gaze at the heroic and archaic paintings lining the hallways. The depictions of battles of yester-year seemed to over-glorify the actual events to such a grotesque degree, certainly to Fritz. Such painting that is used as propaganda loses its charm and beauty, and Fritz could notice that in the frantic brush strokes of several of the supposed masterpieces.

One such painting, that of the great siege of Kolberg between the Prussians and Napoleon Bonaparte, managed to retain a certain degree of beauty. Though the flags were billowing and the fortress seemed to have a gothic-like quality the odd face could be made out in the painting. The faces were not smiling or etched with pride. There was a solemn beauty to the melancholy feel of the figures involved in the painting. It leant the smallest element of reality and to Fritz that allowed beauty to enter into the artwork. It was a small detail but it caught his eye as he passed it and gave a solitary minute of his attention before he moved to the exit.

Johanna, diligent as always in her mannerisms and her fashion, was busy discussing prices with a man who was willing to sell his house that was located very close to the Potsdamer street, one of the busiest streets in Berlin. It was a modest building, but it retained a remarkably quiet interior despite its proximity to the hustle and bustle of the city. Tucked away in a street lined with spruce trees and flanked by two larger dwellings the house was the perfect spot in terms of its location and in terms of its quiet demeanour. The current tenant, a Mr Theodore Krampmeiner, had just reached the age of sixty-three and had decided to move to the Pomeranian coast, by the Baltic Sea. He had become resentful of the city and was looking for an excuse to move. Johanna had little trouble in knocking down the price a few Marks before coming to a preliminary agreement with the Berliner.

"You make for ruthless bargainers in Prussia, do you? I know when I have been bested my dear".

"Even more ruthless with a sword or rifle if ever given the chance, Mr Krampmeiner" Johanna kindly retorted. "But you have kindly listened to me, and I am grateful that are understanding of our circumstances".

"It is easy to understand when your husband is the son of military royalty!" laughed the soon-to-be coastal resident.

Johanna replied quickly "I am able to act independently of my husband and still able to achieve great things." She had always resented the idea that she was trading off her husband's father's fame. At that moment Fritz turned the corner of the main street and could be seen coming down the street. He begged his forgiveness for the lateness which was given. He was told of the agreed price and agreed himself then and there. The deal was struck and by the end of the month the house would be filled with what was needed.

The couple, content with their relatively speedy house-hunting adventure, took to one of the tea rooms on the grand Potsdamer street. Johanna was informed of the deception about her child and that Fritz's father had bought the lie. Though regretful of the situation as she was, the same as when the incident first occurred, she too accepted the necessity of deception.

"I am also to go to Munich again. This whole Wittelsbach business requires my father to go to the city to talk some sense into the new government. Either that or threaten them. I'm pretty sure if he didn't offer himself for the task the Kaiser would have forced him too anyway."

"I am to come with you? You know that I must see to the new house. You know, the one we just bought?" Johanna replied with an irksome quality.

"I know, I know. It will not take long and I will help as soon as this task is complete".

Johanna folded her arms, hardly hiding her contempt. "Every time we are to do something, something else comes up. It is as if you are being sucked into the machine of state more and more. Before, we were to attend to my sister's own wedding, but you could not come due to manoeuvres in Posen. I waited for two hours to meet with you at Bayreuth for the arts festival before you turned up and excused yourself from practically everything there was to do there. Now, I know you were tired from your work, but your work is overtaking you. And you told me you were finished with the army, yet I see you, still with a uniform on."

Fritz returned Johanna's gaze with a more blank expression. "I am a mere administrator now, not a common foot-soldier anymore. You know this. I am doing my duty. It is what is expected of people like me."

"Do you only have one duty? Is your wife not a source of duty as well?"

"Of course, as well. But I must prioritise."

"You prioritise the army in a time of peace. How on God's green earth does that make sense?" Johanna raised her voice, attracting attention, but her stern attitude that was well known to Fritz allowed her the strength not be undeterred by the unwanted attention. Fritz was less able but continued the heated conversation.

"I must assist with order. It is my job. We need order. It is my duty to keep order. It is plain to see in Bavaria and all over the world. Do you not know that?" The words seemed to echo the same that were barked at William Steele in the jail cell in the hotel in Munich. Fritz noticed it himself and sank into his seat.

"You know, you did not used to talk like this. Ever since the terrible passing of your mother you have been obsessed with the word 'order'. It's as if you blame her death on the absence of it, and you are trying to make up for it now. I'm right, aren't I? You are not consumed with duty; you are consumed with revenge. It is eating you up and is dragging you away from me, it has dragged you away from your own son, and it is dragging you away from the world. You think you can use order to keep the world the way you want it but I don't think you realise just how powerless you really are." Johanna's words seemed to pass into Fritz's heart until he sat up straight and the words seemed to bounce off his breast.

"I am not powerless. I am Fritz von Falkenhayn! I command respect and authority. And therefore, I have a say in whether there is order or not. It is my duty." Fritz said sternly, though could not look Johanna in the eye. She stared into his eyes noticing eyes that looked fierce but under closer inspection seemed lost and untethered to any bedrock of safety.

"You are confused, darling. You are not seeing straight. Don't go to Munich. Your father does not require you. Stay." She reached her hand out to hold his that was resting on the table, offering a mental olive branch. But rather than allowing her hand to rest on top of his, he pulled it away and in doing so knocked a silver spoon off the table. As it pinged onto the wooden floor the noise seemed to disturb the fragile stability in Fritz's mind, and he stood up abruptly. He looked around, not quite understanding why he was stood up and eyes were staring at his. His mind whirred and all he wanted to do was leave the tearoom. He stormed out, looking and feeling perplexed as his body seemed to move him. He whisked away leaving his wife staring at the disappearing figure of her husband.

She looked around at the eyes of those who witnessed the scene and sighed. Her dignity allowed her to stay, and she finished the rest of her cake on her own as the eyes around her slowly moved away, one by one, to return to their own scenes.

Chapter 23

The stipulations of the peace accords of the Great War could not have come at a worse time for the rapidly deteriorating French Republic. The inflationary spike of the Franc had led to a major devaluing of the currency and thus the reparations owed to Germany had been substantially reduced. The decision to decide on the French currency as the benchmark for reparations had proved to be a disaster and thus the subsequent decision was made to speed up the economic union between the two countries. Plans were published to tie the value of the Franc with that of the German Mark with the view to eventually phasing out the French currency altogether. This would be in effect one final humiliation for the French state. There were also rumours that the Germans intended to unilaterally seize French ports all along the north and west coast in order to start to control international trade with the possibility of seizing goods in lieu of payment towards the war reparations.

To the slight surprise of the Germans the British had largely paid off their share, miniscule though it was in comparison with the French bill. British delegates in Germany had expressed their desire to continue working with the Germans for a more peaceful and collaborative future. The British were seemingly willing to overtly declare their intentions to leave the French diplomatically to their fate. This only served to condemn the French republic further into their own demise.

The final insult to the French republic was that of their own making. The slight economic upturn had proved to be short lived. The dreams of a republic carried along by its strong economic output turned out to be a chimera. The President of the republic Paul Louis Deschanel, providing the only miracle to the republic by managing to stay in power despite the turbulent merry-go-round of ministerial appointments, attempted to publicly assure the nation that the economic upturn was here to stay but a disorganised protest of factory workers in many western French cities including Bordeaux put a stop to any hopes of recovery. He looked more miserable by the day and in the fateful month of July 1920 in a final gamble he sent what was left of the French military into the factories and attempted to forcefully end the strikes. The gamble proved to be of little benefit, quashing the protests in Bordeaux and Brest but failing in almost every other instance. The stunt served more to benefit the anti-republic league, of which Maurice Renaudin and Phillipe Petain had been elevated to the head. 'The marshal and the boy' they were known as.

And so, the day republicans had feared, and the revolutionaries had looked forward to, had come. It came at the perfect moment. The annual national day of July 14th had arrived. It was known as the day of the republic in France, Bastille Day to those outside of France's territory. A day of honouring the revolution that brought about the French nation as it was known then, it should have been a day of solidarity for the republic. Instead, once again the fateful choice to cancel all planned events for the day forced the impetus of the day into the hands of the revolutionaries housed in Marseille and Toulon. In truth, the event had also been cancelled the year before but the proximity of that day to the end of the war allowed for national introspection rather than celebration. 1920 would be no such year for that.

The day had been agreed by both Renaudin and Petain as the day of action. Renaudin was to send out the call for the workers of France to rise up and declare the cities seized. Petain was to march is conventional army, hungry for battle and food though they were, to Bordeaux to march on the temporary buildings of the government to force the surrender of the president and cabinet. The grand show of force was deemed enough to not expect any resistance. No counter-push would occur if the initial gesture seemed too great to overcome. The die seemed to be cast for a short, sharp, transfer of power at which point the anti-republic league would agree on some sort of method of power sharing.

Phillipe Petain had already marched his army as inconspicuously as possible to the jump-off point. They were many in number, and though they did not outnumber the French army their concentration of numbers would overwhelm any resistance if it was offered. Maurice Renaudin waited in Toulon by the telegraph machine for the word to come out, at which point telephones would ring informing him and the men around him of the success. Ludovic-Oscar Frossard, the main link between Renaudin and the Bolsheviks, had since the turn of the year passed rifles and ammunition in the utmost secrecy to known allies in cities all over France in preparation for the armed uprising. The moment was perfect. The time had been agreed. As the dial hit nine-thirty the moment would arrive. The day seemed fair in the south of France. Reports of thunder and lightning arriving from the Atlantic had been passed to the planners but it seemed inconsequential to them.

The two men, leaders of their respective factions; though in truth Renaudin was communicating with a far greater number of 'similarly-ambitious' red leaders in other cities whereas Petain had no such problem, knew the time was right. News had been circulating for some time that the Germans were embroiled in internal turmoil over the Bavarian question. They knew the Germans would want little to do with such an insurrection whilst they had more important matters to turn to. Petain himself, giving way to delusions of grandeur, posited that were he a roman imperator and had asked the spirits for predictions they would all agree that he would undoubtably succeed in his venture. He was ready to lift the shame of being stabbed in the back. He was ready to right the wrongs of the past. Even General d'Esperay bristled with anticipation in the rear regiment of the army column. He looked around at the assembled forces and recalled easily the sights he saw in the Macedonian front during the great war. He too had the burgeoning feeling to avenge the stab in his back.

Maurice was more sanguine about the moment of action. He had boasted to many about his control of his movement but he was making a great gamble of his own. He needed to use this moment to show how in control of the movement he was. He refrained from actively taking to the barricades, choosing instead the safety of his makeshift bunker in Toulon for the time being. But he knew that soon he would have to be out in the front lines at least to be seen so that he would be seen as the logical leader of the French reds. The hammer and sickle blazoned on the tricolour banner would have to be flown by him atop the Lycée palace if he had to.

Not only did he have to prove his authority within the movement, he had to prove his authority against his ideological enemy but anti-republican ally, Marshall Petain. He needed to prove that he was just as much, if not more, in command of the situation as the Lion of Verdun. So, he decided, at nine o'clock, to seize the initiative. He sent the orders to rise up half an hour before Petain was due to march.

The telegrams were sent off. Phone calls were made where possible. Maurice, Frossard, Varine and about twenty other men and women waited in absolute nervous breakdowns for replies to come back. A mock-up map of France had been laid on a grand oak table waiting for red flags to be placed on areas where success had been found. Blue flags were awaiting any negative responses, and golden flags represented the apparent location of Petain's forces, which had split in two with the greater bulk south-east of Bordeaux, south-east of Toulouse and directly east of Montpellier with the aim to ensure success in the south. Renaudin was counted on for success in the north and so that was where the bulk of their hopes lay. And so, they waited.

They didn't have to wait long. After just ten minutes, responses came from all ends of France. Red revolutionaries had successfully risen up and seized key strategic administrative areas in Lyon, Clermont, Nice, Nantes, Paris and Rennes. In most of the cities declared they were more prepared than Renaudin could have hoped for. Even Montpellier, designated as a key target for Petain, had fallen to the revolutionaries without a shot being fired. There was still no response from many key northern cities including Brest, Rouen, Reims and the key target of Dijon still remained elusive in the first half an hour. But they were now committed. The revolution had begun, though in truth it was too early to say and none had the time to react. Renaudin now had much to lose, and still, he had yet to hear the reaction of his partner in Bordeaux.

Petain did not learn of the march stolen on him by his partner in this great gamble. Ever a stickler for military discipline he awaited the exact moment the clock struck nine-thirty before ordering his forces to advance on their respective targets. When the message returned to him that Montpellier was already under revolutionary control, he chalked it up to trigger-happy reds, but news slowly filtered that the ambitious Renaudin had sent out his orders already. Petain was furious. "How dare the insignificant little one-time foot soldier get the better of me!" he exclaimed. He snarled in his staff car as Bordeaux came into view. He folded his arms and looked to onlookers like a toddler having a tantrum. He was now chomping at the bit to get stuck in. "It's a race now for supremacy. We must win!"

Petain's unofficial army reached the barely defended city and the sight of his legions forced the local militia to surrender without a shot being fired. His car and personal guard sped through the streets to the government building. The stunned onlookers could barely believe what they were seeing. The hero of Verdun ahead of a large force of French irregular soldiers, looking like they were part of the army but were anything but, was just as bewildering by the hushed rumours of armed insurrection in cities around the whole of the country.

Petain's heart sank as they neared the governmental building near the sea. The building was emptied, important documents gone or partially burned and no sign of the president or his cabinet anywhere. "Where the hell are they?" he growled at his adjutant, Major Rolland. d'Esperay's arrival only soured his mood further. "Explain. This is not going to plan!"

The general was similarly incandescent with rage. "It's your bloody son of a whore partner, Renaudin! He's messed our whole operation up. The government must have taken flight at the first sign of trouble".

Petain made for the governmental communications array and ordered a broadcast of the signal that Bordeaux and thus the government was under the control of the revolutionaries. "And when you are able to, get me a direct line to that pip-squeak in Toulon. I want a word with him". The city was secured along with Toulouse and he hastily ordered the advance northwards towards Limoges and Poitiers. He wondered, without having the president or prime minister in his grasp, whether they would in fact face some resistance. There was no sign of the French army there too. Something seemed to not be going to plan and it was perhaps the most important thing, certainly in the mind of the cautious revolutionary marshal.

As he and Renaudin would come to discover only later in the day, the show of force was great but not great enough to force the present government to their knees. They had fled the city for the north as soon as they heard of the first signs of insurrection in Lyon where the revolutionaries were at the hastiest. They had gotten wind of the plans a few days ago and had redeployed the mass of the French army in the north. Their strategic success would be on display as Renaudin's map would house only two red flags in the central-north area of France. Paris and Rennes would be the only cities to have declared some form of revolutionary control, and Paris itself was set upon by a mass of French regular forces by the following day.

Both Renaudin and Petain were left perplexed. As Petain's forces marched on Limoges, taking the city without a fight on the 16th July it seemed that the North of France had somewhat solidified itself. When Petain finally did get hold of Renaudin he had exchanged his anger for confusion. "Where are your men in Amiens and Rouen?" he asked. Renaudin had no answer. He did not understand. The French government had fled but they were by no means a rallying source for the flailing republic.

The answer to the solidifying of the frontiers, proved with the suppression of the Parisian revolutionaries and stiff resistance at Poitiers and the northern part of the Auvergne region, would come on the 18th of July as Renaudin dithered and Petain paused his advance as his cautious nature overtook his willingness to win the revolutionary race. Few had expected what occurred to save the republic but a simple examination of political developments before would have proved useful in determining the success of the revolutionaries in the first few days of the insurrection.

President Deschancel, eager to prevent his country from falling into the hands of two extremists in the south, had met in secret with a distinguished figure in Orleans a week before the fateful day. The man in question was Victor Napoleon. The leader of the Bonapartists was seen as the least worst of those who wished to see the end of the republic. The president had made many mistakes but even he knew that his time was up. He convened a secret meeting with Victor in order to come to an agreement over the future of the republic. The republic could not defend itself against an insurgency. The stipulations of the German peace allowed only a small force that could not hope to stand up to both Petain's military movement and Renaudin's reds as a combined force. The army might not even want to fight for the republic anyway. Only Victor's Bonapartists commanded any sense of respect. A reactionary respect, it was agreed was not exactly a step forward, but it was enough for the fated president to offer the keys to the country. He entrusted Napoleon V with the keys to the nation if, and only if, France was subject to armed insurrection from her own people. The president pleaded that should the worst come to the worst that Victor would maintain the integrity of the old French ways and though he may mould a future Fourth Republic in his own image that the spirit of democracy would maintain itself. Victor agreed and the Orleans Accords were signed.

And thus, the president was not the real antagonist to Petain and Renaudin, but to Victor Napoleon. The army rallied to his banner; the tricolour of France with a golden eagle in its centre, and like-minded defenders of the republic and committed Bonapartists of which there were plenty in the north made themselves available for active service. All of this was conducted in similar secrecy to Frossard's arms smuggling to the revolutionaries. In parts, Frossard unwittingly armed members of the Bonapartist volunteers. When the time came for those volunteers to arise themselves, they did so in their thousands. Men and women who might have fought instead against the republic finally found a credible alternative.

Even Petain, who had relied in part to desertions in the armed forces to aid the anti-republican cause, had to settle for paltry numbers. Of the 150,000 active members of the French army only three thousand transferred themselves to his legions. Both he and Renaudin had been weakened by the success of the Orleans Accords, forcing a major re-think once the first few days of the insurrection had passed. Renaudin secretly wanted to retire and strongly considered fleeing to Russia. He regained his composure in the privacy of his own room in the make-shift Toulon bunker but his resolve had been shaken. Petain, resting somewhat on his previous fame in the Great War, believed that a resolute show of force in the coming days might change more minds and more might rally to his banner, but he decided to spirit himself away back to Marseille to convene an emergency meeting with his generals and Renaudin's representatives. He especially wanted another word with Varine, just to check that their previous agreement still stood despite the setbacks.

The meeting in Marseille two days later revealed little else but the one thing they had feared. The lines had been drawn. In certain areas soldiers were starting to dig fortifications, and even trenches were beginning to line parts of the new front lines of France. Barbed wire was being strung out and artillery pieces were reluctantly being pulled into position on both sides of the divide. There was no evidence that the Bonapartists nor the anti-republicans were contemplating surrender. Petain and Renaudin were far too deep in to the issue now. Neither Petain nor Renaudin thought that there might be another chance, especially with the Germans so embroiled in an internal matter of their own.

Announcements had been made in Paris that Napoleon, who had made himself supreme commander of the combined forces of the republic with Deschancel as the nominal president, that he would fight until the very end. His announcement had been seen as boisterous, charismatic and bold and perhaps tinged in a veil of over-confidence. But it had the desired effect, sending a message to the meeting in Marseille that there would be a fight for the very future of France. No one would submit peacefully.

The French Civil War had begun.

Chapter 24

The walls of the cottage were strong, re-built after careful consideration about the maintenance of the old-world charm. It's south-facing front looked down the shallow decline of the hill it was built on until it reached the next steeper hill. The estate itself was surrounded by trees in a horse-shoe shape allowing for the modest garden to be hidden from its neighbours. The beech trees bristled in the soft wind that rolled over the plains of Salisbury. Though cottages like this had been built all over the plains it was clear that this one was made with deference to the idea of solitude and calm.

The interior of the building was modest, a larger than usual fireplace provided the central masterpiece, with tiles of exquisite age surrounding its protective walls. The upstairs bedrooms, three in number, were not large but were enough for anyone wishing to live in content beauty and splendour. One or two large wooden beams rested on parts of the ceiling. And above the ceiling a downy brown thatch provided the metaphorical cherry on top. The curtains caressed the edges of each window in a sea of white and green colours. Most of the floors were covered in deep red carpets and all of the lights had their own small shades of red and white to make sure no harsh light ruined the quiet and humble demeanour of the contents inside.

Robins and sparrows loved the area. The wooded pasture north of the estate housed many creatures who often made their wild pilgrimage to the cottage's estate. Foxes dared not to join for fear of the groundsmen who patrolled the areas with their rifles. South of the estate farmland of every variety from wheat to livestock, cows a particular favourite, were found in ranks of five or six in a row. Thus, the cottage lay on the border of wildland and farmland, appreciative of the benefit of being amongst both. Rabbits were a common sight, thus, and though they had learned to easily escape the wicked bullets of the roving gangs of farm defenders they rarely ventured further than the estate as it was a beautiful spot to sit and hide from the shade of the summer sun. If one took a small stroll around the forty-acre space one might see a rabbit or another similarly fluffy creature taking a moment to sit and adore the spectacle of tamed and untamed nature whilst leaning backwards on a broad and welcoming tree.

Acquiring provisions for the cottage was a difficult undertaking, especially if the nearby farmers were not at their most generous or if business was slow. A car would be needed, and if no car was available than one would need a horse. The cottage itself contained a small stable area near the front area. The current occupant had no need for such a beast and thus the stable turned into a makeshift garage for the small yet necessary automobile. There was no village nearby, instead it would be a good twenty minutes down a long and windy road before one would find some form of adequate civilisation.

Finally, like the little signature on the very edge of a beautiful painting, inscribed on the lower corner of the right-most beam the architect had left his initials and the date of the completion of the building. "E.H., 1788". Edward Herbert had built many of the other cottages around the area but few had not been torn down and rebuilt again during the 1800s. Many had been repurposed for the new ages in order to house bigger and better tractors, livestock or technology. This cottage had been left in as original a state as possible as per the requests of its many owners, even the new one.

That newest owner, a Mr. W. Steele, had requested absolutely no altering to the design, interior or exterior. He had only seen pictures of the site and had fallen in love with it terribly quickly. He was granted custody of the house but had yet to visit it. The property had fallen prey to the less-wanted wild custodians for over a year so work had to be done on it to bring it back up to speed. And so, that is what he did on his arrival along with his mother. They arrived in the mid-July heat to attempt to bring the cottage back to its internal former glory, along with taming the estate's gardens which had taken it upon itself to outgrow its designated areas.

William's mother had agreed to sell the farm following her husband's passing. The job to maintain the farm in Devon was too great a task and memories had soured there too much to stay. Niamh decided to look after the cottage as best as she could and though William envisaged living there, he had his mind set on another place he might soon live, Epernay. The plan was for William to carry on paying for Niamh to stay here whilst he went and attempted to make a living in France with Cecile. That was, if Cecile would still accept him. He did not know if she would but he was willing to roll the dice. Money would then be sent back here until William's mother could find a way to sustain herself. Selling the farm would help for a year or two but no more.

William would not learn of the internal turmoil in France until July's end was drawing near. Often, when he had made the slightly arduous journey to Salisbury's urban area, he had the slight apprehension that he was being watched. The dark figure he noticed briefly whilst he was last in London had followed him to Salisbury and though he was curious he dared not ask for fear of what he might find out. But eventually, the figure found him. Once again, as it was at the station last year he was greeted with the usual bizarre, overly-familiar and rushed confrontation.

"William, awfully good to see you!" the man in a large hat said, ushering with force the confused William into his car, another man standing by the open door.

"Yes, ever so kind of you to let us drive you to your holiday destination!" the other figure cheerfully exclaimed for all to see.

"No, no, I insist you let me drive. I let you drive last time!" the voices continued; William resigned to the impossibility of an attempted escape. He was bundled into his own car and was driven off, another car following closely in tow all the way back to London. William looked out from the window at the sights he hoped he had left behind. It seemed the dark city was determined not to let him escape. London had always felt like a prison to him, even when he was working at the French embassy. The buildings seemed to tower over him, curling over him with their faceless grins and empty eyes. The people seemed no different. He had been out of London for barely more than a month and the city looked different due to the sun finally breaking through the clouds. The police and army personnel were still rigidly patrolling the streets but graffiti was a bit less easy to come by.

The car followed the more methodical driving lanes towards Whitehall. The car passed a series of military checkpoints lined with armed soldiers, some bearing machine guns and others housing a parked armoured car. William had not seen such militarization of London's streets before. Something was up. He was pushed out into the street and then pulled into the famous Downing Street and bundled into house number 11 where he was dressed down by a military adjutant and coerced into a room with a high ceiling and golden wallpaper that lit up the room. The curtains were drawn and William's eyes were set on the familiar face of one, General Plumer. Edmund Ironside, the other figure from the last time he was given this secret treatment, was not there this time, though the somehow more sinister presence of the American agent J. Edgar Hoover could be seen as well as a couple of new figures. These two men sat in chairs behind desks on either side of the room. They immediately sprang to their feet as William was guided to enter but no seat was available for him. So, he stood, still in his Sunday best, awaiting the reason for the hurried and slightly uncomfortable treatment he had been subject to.

The first figure, that of the Minister for Foreign Affairs, Arthur Balfour, spoke first. He announced himself and apologised for the nature of William's journey. "It is a most sensitive and indeed time sensitive matter" he assured William. "We would have preferred not to require you, yet, here we are." He gestured to the other new figure who introduced himself as Major Pearson.

"You may not have heard of me before" Major Pearson said advancing on William, his strong Scottish accent giving away his origin of birth in Edinburgh. "But I have heard of you. In fact, you've done me the honour of writing to me with excellent ability. Mark me- "he addressed Plumer, and Balfour "-I told ye he would be a fine man to choose. A fine man."

"I'm sorry but I don't have the honour" William mentioned confusingly.

"No, I suppose you wouldn't, but that would mean that I am very good at my job" Pearson chuckled, patting William's shoulder and turning away. "He's a strong lad. He'll do very nicely".

General Plumer spoke up. "Major Pearson plays a key role in heading up British intelligence in foreign countries. He has his ears to the ground in countries all over the world, though not perhaps in America, where our friend here assures us that what he knows is all we need to know". The sinister figure of special agent Hoover snorted quietly on his lit cigar.

Balfour looked on, seemingly losing his patience already which to William seemed a trifle harsh seeing as he had just arrived. "Now, see here, Steele. This is your next assignment- "

"Next assignment, sir?" William interjected. "The last time I heard from the likes of you I was being let go so I could be easily arrested by the German police. I protest at the idea that I am somehow still in your employ". He seemed indignant by the thought to all in the room.

"Come now, William. You must understand necessity? Circumstances you put yourself in forced our hand. And well done with dealing with it. Again, Herbert, a most commendable choice." Pearson seemed in a jolly mood.

"I was led to believe as I lay beaten and bruised on the hard floor of a jail cell in Munich that my usefulness, or my role with people like you was finished", William was raising his voice now, seemingly losing his own patience at being asked for yet another assignment.

"How's that, that new dwelling of yours, hmm?" Arthur Balfour asked with thinly veiled undertones of cynicism. "Paid for by the British taxpayer you know. Take the king's shilling then run away once you've had enough? Not the done thing, man!" William's words left his mouth, thinking of the one piece of stability he had only recently managed to establish himself with.

"Yes, we've let you go to your parents to conduct personal affairs, but times are changing again and we couldn't wait any longer" Plumer stated in a matter-of-fact tone. "Arthur, as you were saying".

The foreign secretary bowed his head and continued, sitting down and retreating behind his spectacles. "The thing is, France has fallen into chaos. Civil War; they love it the French. Seems that the parties that want the republic and the whole damn system done away with have had enough waiting. They've taken advantage of turmoil in Germany and, well let's face it here as well, and some unholy alliance has forcefully occupied most of the major cities in the southern areas. But, as if by some miracle, the republic or a form of it, still stands. President Deschancel has seemingly stepped down and in his place is one, and I can't believe I'm saying this, Victor Napoleon."

"I really thought that their little political stunt during the French elections was some sort of joke but some people really like him" Pearson interjected.

"It's a progressive shift away rather than revolutionary, but revolutionary all the same" Balfour elaborated. "A man for the moderates which brings with it a lot of money and followers who would rather avoid violent revolution through a military or communist dictatorship. At any rate, front lines are slowly being drawn with the revolutionaries of Phillipe Petain and Maurice Renaudin on one side in the south and Bonaparte and the republicans on the other side in the north. Now, we have no idea what the outcome might be, nor do we have any clue who it is we wouldn't mind seeing coming out victorious. Reason would suggest that we would want the republicans to win but the idea of a Bonaparte as president naturally proses some big problems. On the other hand, we simply have no idea what Petain's military junta and Renaudin's reds might do in a future victory. The main question for us is which party is more advantageous to us to support. Pearson's, shall we call them informants, are limited only by their connections. Otherwise, they are very good. We have informants in both camps, some closer to the top than you might consider but we have one gaping hole; an informant close to Victor Napoleon."

"I really did try to find someone else but none were available". Pearson's words seemed hollow and untrue.

"Your time previously in France yielded some useful information, some directly from the mouth of Victor Napoleon himself" Balfour said, leaning forward.

"His wife, sir." William corrected, maintaining an element of purposeful insolence.

"Dash it all, I don't care if you were talking to his damn parlour maid!" barked Arthur Balfour. "The fact is you spoke to a member of his household. You are to return to your post and give us as great a knowledge about the intentions and desires of the commander-in-chief of the Northern forces as well as accurate and up-to-date development on his side of the divide. Is that clear?"

"And what if I am unable to reacquaint myself with his household?" William asked, continuing his passive and quiet protest at the situation.

"Then don't come back to England" Balfour said, incurring the eyebrow raising of Plumer and Pearson. "We need to know as much as we can for the sake of these isles and you will be a part of that effort. There we are. If you'll excuse me, gentlemen, I have other matters to attend to." Balfour got up from his desk and locked his eyes on William until he opened the door.

"You're the best chance we have at getting an insight into one of the candidates to be the next leader of France" Plumer said, attempting to cut the tension. "We will ensure it is worth your time. An allowance will be sent to your mother and you will travel under the protection of the diplomatic service. No more hiding amongst the grave diggers this time, alright?"

The more conciliatory tone prompted William to remove the visible tension in his body and he thanked his old commander. "And may I say, you look well for a man who is serving his time in prison" William quipped. Pearson and Plumer laughed at the statement.

"You see? A sense of humour. Just the man, eh? Just the man" Pearson seemed to enjoy his grin. J. Edgar Hoover finally made his move to the door and, though saying nothing, gave William a smile that seemed as insincere as ever. As he left the door Major Pearson chuckled and, in his reassuring voice, said "pay no attention to him, laddie. He's a problem for someone else, not you."

"When am I to depart for my mission?" William asked.

"Yesterday, my dear lad. You left yesterday in order to attend the diplomatic conference in Canada with the imperial party. Your little excursion elsewhere is on the morrow but seeing as the morrow is in only several hours, I would suggest you make haste as soon as you leave. You know my address, make sure your kind letters reach me in good speed. My thanks. You're free to go." Pearson gestured to the door and William left, slightly feeling the ache in his leg from standing for as long as he did. He was gestured out of the building and back into his car which was now bereft of its driver and adjoining passenger. He sped away with lightning efficiency and made for the coast and the familiar sight of the R.M.S. Carmania.

Chapter 25

Epernay was always going to be William's first stop. He had felt the great desire to return there as soon as he left it in the first place. Going against his direct orders to make haste for the household of Victor Napoleon, he instead chose the household of Cecile as his first engagement. He had been shown preliminary maps of the supposed front lines and Epernay was safely nestled in the north. He had been told that British intelligence officers were finding it near impossible to travel south of the lines due to the open hostility they met. It seemed as though the revolutionaries were just as hateful against the British as well as the republicans and the Bonaparte loyalists. Only a few days had passed since he had been hauled into London against his will and already developments were taking place. Battles were about to be fought and tough skirmishes were taking place all around the front lines. The Auvergne region was now fully in revolutionary hands and there was a call of conscription in the northern territories. It seemed as if the civil war was escalating, sucking in more and more people to participate.

William was making his way down to Epernay, as far as he was aware miles away from the more intense fighting taking place to the West of the country where most of Marshall Petain, now formerly of the French Army after his official dismissal was announced by Commander Napoleon and his old commanding officer Ferdinand Foch, who had come out of retirement to lend his expertise to the republicans. Epernay would be spared the initial movements of front lines is the town lay over one hundred miles away from the fast-solidifying line. In fact, on William's arrival the town looked no different to when he left it earlier in the year.

There seemed little evidence of a civil war occurring bar the occasional recruitment poster for both sides. It seemed as though both camps were attempting to garner support as the civil war threatened to split family member from family member. That was the biggest change of all. People were hardly speaking to one another for fear of coming across a supporter of the other side. What were people to do? Doff their cap to them or attempt to do away with them for their cause? Thus, the sensible thing to do was to say nothing. A truce of sorts hung around not only Epernay but in every other city that William passed by. Conversations kept themselves to superficial topics like the weather or the time of the year, or how hungry they might be. The French people seemed to be in a dream-like state, not sure of what to do or what to say. A nation in a civil war was one thing, but a people not entirely sure what the future may hold was a sight William thought he would never see such a like again.

Arriving in Epernay was a relief. The wait was over. The town was quiet, but it always had been rather quiet. He walked, almost jogged his way to where he knew Cecile as and to his utter delight there she was, still running the little café from her own house, two regular patrons still sitting outside almost looking like they were about to expire. Nothing had changed and it made William smile. The house, a slim terraced building, looked as rigid as ever with its stone edifice jutting out unevenly but in a manner that made it pleasant to look like to the naked eye. He felt happy to be there. In a way, it felt like home. It felt safe which seemed ridiculous when a civil war was raging barely a hundred miles southwards. Yet, as William ran his fingers over the metal railings surrounding the edge of the street, he felt a slightly whimsical feeling as if in a childlike state of seeing your best friend, and indeed your love.

The thought did occur to him; what might she say or do on first seeing him? Would she still remember her feelings for him? It was not long since they parted but to William it had felt like an age. He crept over to the front of the café and looked over to Cecile who was busy tidying away one of many glasses of cloudy cider from an occupied table. He waved over gently towards her, apprehensive but excited. She looked over and saw him, initially mistaking him for a new patron, though he still might be. She smiled and waved gingerly back.

William remembered the one important object in his inner-jacket pocket. He still worse his jacket despite the time of the season demanding a lighter attire. He took out the feather made out of newspaper that she had given him when she told him of the story of the little injured bird. She smiled, with a slight chuckle. He smiled back and nodded. She approached him. He could see she was wearing an apron above a black knee-length skirt and a blue short-sleeved shirt with slight white lines cascading down. Her hair has been made more blonde by the light of the sun. she was happy to see him.

"I understand now." He said softly to her. "I understand". The story of the bird wanting to be loved, not to be helped, had been etched in his mind for so long. It gave him the impetus he needed to drop so much that had hurt him for so long. He was not consumed with the weight of the world; he could think and see what was in front of him rather than straining his eyes over the whole world. Now, here and there, he could finally see her. She was more beautiful than before. The practical and rational scales dropped from his eyes and he finally saw the Cecile who had begged for him to see clearly. He was ready to be with her, he was ready to love her.

"You are returning for a while?" she asked, her accent as soft and sweet as the summer breeze that had pushed William towards Epernay on his journey.

"If I could, I would stay here for a lifetime" he replied, looking deep into her shining blue eyes.

She smiled again, as her patrons in the café started clicking their fingers asking for her attention or assistance depending on their condition. After all, it was just her working there. But she ignored them, choosing instead to focus on a man she had thought of constantly a few months ago, frequently a couple of months ago and occasionally the last month. "You are here on business?" she asked again, noting William's diplomatic corps insignia on his jacket.

"Not here. I am here for you" he assured her. She smiled again. She beckoned him in and offered him a seat. He sat there and though she occasionally fashioned him with a glass of cider every now and again he simply sat there and waited until the last of the regulars staggered out, each one eyeing him up with suspicion as they passed him by. The café was then closed and there he still sat. She wanted to see if he stayed and he had lived up to her hopes if not quite her expectations. The long summer's day gave way to the long summer's evening and as soon as she drew her apron from her body she went over to where William was sitting and looked down at him.

"Are you open?" a staggering man passing by asked obnoxiously.

"No, go and find another place to fall into" she shouted in French. He waved his hand at her and staggered away.

The evening, the night belonged to them. And they intended to not waste a single moment. And that would carry on day after day after day, until July finally gave way to August. And even on into the month the story was the same. William felt little, if any, time for his mission. He wondered with the briefest of moments what the chief spy, Major Pearson, might be thinking. It mattered not and seemed like it would matter even less. The William Steele of duty and country seemed to be taking a long and well-earned break if he was ever to return.

The love that Cecile Huget felt for William had waned slightly during their time apart. She once again reminded him of the story of the sparrow with the broken wing. They were lying on the grass in a field just outside of the town together then. The summer sun released a more pleasant heat that day. She darted her hands over the place, imitating the flight of the sparrow before and after her wing broke. This time William grabbed her imitating hands gently and pressed them against his chest. She looked at him and though no words were uttered she knew what he meant by the gesture. Sometimes the rationale answer is not the right one. Sometimes all one needs is love or at least the feeling of not being alone to get through the day. The story had come full circle to William. He had learned.

William also played with the little child of only five years old, though his sixth birthday was fast approaching. The name bestowed on him by his loving mother was that of Charles, William learned. The reason for its choice was because it was the name of his father, who was given the name himself after that of the great Frankish king of Charlemagne. The father who had died in 1917 during the Great War was the little Charles's hero and thus the presence of William was not exactly appreciated but he warmed to the man and permitted William to be in his presence. William was not himself great with children, but he had allowed himself a fleeting thought about being some sort of father-figure even if he still was not sure he was the correct role-model. But Charles needed a father and William loved Cecile with all his heart.

They hardly ever talked about the on-going Civil War. The war itself had escalated but quietened for a time. Cecile informed William that to her knowledge no one on either side really had the stomach to fight. Men going back into trenches and firing on their own kind was just too difficult to fathom. Even the revolutionary zealots hardly fired a shot on the front which, according to a regular patron of Cecile's café, resembled more of a long and disgusting garden of flowers that looked like grubby men. The absence of a decent amount of artillery on the revolutionary side save those held by Petain's warriors were hardly used due to the scarcity of shells and Bonaparte's republicans were reluctant to use theirs because there was wide expectation that the rebels would just lose interest in the venture.

And so, with the lack of the use of loud guns the sound of war could not be heard in Epernay. Rather, what could be heard was that of young love, though William was thirty-four and Cecile was twenty-nine. They acted as though they were young lovers. They talked like young lovers, laughed like young lovers, loved like young lovers and they held hands through the streets declaring their young love to those who wished to look their way. William even took to helping out in the café himself. They struck up a semi-decent professional working life, though they were not exactly cut from the same professional cloth. William had desired never to act so regimented as he did in the army again, whereas Cecile constantly desired the discipline of the staff as one not far from the more military-like drilled style of service. She was always personable to those she served, and stern to the man who skipped and danced by her on occasion to clean, serve and take coin. But as soon as the aprons fell, so did their professional selves. The personal emotions pushed back, and they were in each other's arms once again. Even the poor Charles had to look away and could seldom be found around the house when William and Cecile were sharing the bed together.

Nature was beautiful around Epernay, and Cecile's house, though terraced, had windows overlooking a glorious meadow which stretched to the north-west, thus the windows in the house were bathed in the orange evening sun each sunny day. William, ever the keen eye for the glories of nature, took to gazing out of one of the windows overlooking the meadow. Living on the outskirts of the town had its benefits but also its downsides. He had to walk quite a way to re-stock the café. But for a view at the back of the house as glorious as it was, it made the journey worth it. He opened the window one day and peered out trying to smell the evening air which often brought with it the aroma of lavender and parsley. The breeze was not strong but it had travelled far, bringing with it more and more smells that softly invaded his nostrils. Though he sneezed once or twice as pollen seemed to still be in the air, he was nonetheless grateful for the feeling.

"Don't lean out too much or you will fall!" Cecile warned William who by now was teetering over the white window ledge with little regard for the possible consequences of being led further out. "It is a bit of a way down and I do not want to be scraping you off the grass. Blood stains on grass ruin the view so no thank you!"

"Were I to fall I would fall on a bed of nature's embrace" William defended himself playfully.

"Maybe, but I don't think nature wants you on her bed though, so she might give you a bloody nose. Now come on. I do not intend to wait here long. You, me and Charles will go for a walk. I am to meet Maxine today and you will keep Charles occupied until I am done with her, OK?"

This was a familiar order to William. Cecile had gathered over her years of living in Epernay a small collection of close friends, dotted around the town. They too had been in the town for a while, but they too were not natives. Most of them came with the war and stayed after it ended. Cecile herself was originally from Nancy, as were her parents. Her grandparents though came from Alsace, an area of France lost to Germany long ago, but this was not common knowledge. She only told this to William. She did not want locals thinking she was in any way German. He assured her of his secrecy. He also took the opportunity to assure her of his love and loyalty, which she admitted was a crafty yet romantic thing to mention at the same time and her love for him only grew.

August began drawing to a close, and with it the odd day of rain began appearing, but rain barely settled as the grateful land drank up the water with glee. The rain was warm and citizens of the town danced in the rain and the puddles on occasion. This would be almost always followed by angry shouts of concerned wives and mothers, and on occasion husbands and fathers, for them to come back inside and dry themselves. William never liked the rain as on too many occasions it had ruined his trench dugouts and the idea of rain reminded him of Flanders rain in Belgium making war an even more terrible affair. He had lost just one friend to drowning in mud, but it was one friend too many. He stayed indoors, preferring once again to stare out of the window and enjoy the smells the rain had to offer as it poured itself over the gorgeous plains of France.

"A letter for you. This is the first time I have seen a letter arrive for you. Aside from your mother, who else knows you are here?" Cecile pondered.

William shrugged. "It is most probably from my mother."

Cecile placed the next day's offering to future café patrons on the table and began sifting through the contents, tutting in passive annoyance that she had to brave the rain to carry that day's supply. "But what about friends, hmm? Do they not know you are here?"

William sighed softly. He had not been one to so easily make friends. His conversation skills had never been quite up to scratch. The only friends he knew were in the army and they were mostly consisting of those in the lower ranks, as those in the higher ranks, even officers that he commanded, did not take kindly to him so well. Even those he worked with in the French embassy never ever quite got past the fact that he was the farmer, son of a farmer and had he not been given a decent leg-up from his friend Henry then he might still be tending a farm that was never supposed to be a farm in the first place. The lower ranks had by the end of the war all dispersed back to their normal lives and so William was not quite friendless, but certainly more alone. But he had taken it somewhat in his stride. In fact, he was certain that he would not be chosen for the tasks of espionage had his ties to England been stronger. He did not respond to Cecile and instead opened the contents of the letter. He breathed in and slumped in his chair.

"Is your mother OK?" Cecile asked, pausing her sorting.

"It is not from my mother. It is from my boss. Well, I think he is my boss." He read its contents.

Dear Mr Steele. I do hope your stay in Epernay has been relaxing and enjoyable. But I think now is the time to do what is expected of you. I do not wish to recall you from your mission but I am minded to make you aware that I report to people higher up from me who are relying on you, and speed is of the essence. Don't think we aren't keeping an eye on you. We are rather good at doing that, you know. Ever yours. P.

"I need to go to Paris, probably very soon" William sighed with resignation.

"Oh, you aren't getting away from your duties that easily. I want proof" Cecile said semi-jokingly. William handed her the letter. She read it. "OK, this is a good enough excuse. But don't let this become a habit" she warned, giggling.

"Trust me, I intend to fulfil this final duty and I will return to you" he swore. She smiled and though the night was young and Charles was wandering outside they retreated to the bedroom and shared their time together as man and woman without a second thought until the night sky painted itself overhead and Charles nicked a few things from the table and took them with him to his bedroom for a make-shift dinner and tucked himself into bed. The night was fair. The night was plentiful.

William repeated his vow to Cecile as the morning light was beginning to rise. "I will return after this duty is done. If they ask me, I will go again and my time in Paris will be shorter and shorter until I never return there." The car which had been well-hidden from counteragents and Pearson's own spies was uncovered and was laden with provisions donated from Cecile's stocks.

"Return soon. This time my love for you will never wane. It will only grow" she vowed, returning the favour to William who smiled from ear to ear. Charles blew a raspberry and stomped back into the house, letting the two share a final laugh together. William took Cecile's chin and rested it on his finger, pulling it up to his as they shared a final kiss.

"And when I do, I will have to ask you a question" he said, drawing a confused look from Cecile's face.

"If it is to change the colour of the café, I won't entertain the question" she brushed off.

"No" William playfully sighed. A question you only ask once in your life, and maybe if you say yes, our life".

Cecile paused to take in the cryptic words. She understood what he meant, and she looked up and smiled. "Then return sooner." He nodded and got in the car, awakening the sleeping engine whilst trying not to waken the sleeping neighbours. He car whirred, the engine remembering its primary function as a car and not as an ornament which it had been masquerading as for the last month. The wheels turned slowly with a slight squeak, almost making more noise than the motor itself. William winced slightly as did Cecile but eventually the car purred its way-out carrying William, his eyes locked firmly on the calm woman, the love of his life.

Her eyes looked back with care and hope of his return. She was holding her apron in her arms as it wafted in the early-morning breeze. Her brown hair, lightened from the summer's sun, cascaded from her right shoulder as she waved at him as he waved back, apprehensive of when she might see him next. He waved back secretly sharing the same emotion. They both similarly shared a great desire to be reunited, and soon.

Chapter 26

"They either run away or cry the whole damned time!" Petain barked at Maurice. "Your fighters are no soldiers. They are just drunk or bored peasants with a gun!" The wily marshal was red faced and patrolling the room pausing briefly to slam his hands down on the central table to direct his ire at his strained partner. "My men have made progress up the west coast. Poitiers is seized and we want to make a sweep towards Nantes. But our damned flank is badly exposed because your people don't fight!"

The thin and tall figure of Maurice, sporting a beard that had advanced itself down his chin faster than his forces had move further north, cut a concerned face. His partner was outfighting him and his red revolutionaries had no stomach for fighting. In fact, neither did he. His pessimistic view of himself and the world, cultivated from an early age when he was bullied at school and shunned by his parents, had returned in force to make him a defeatist. He had learned to be a true defeatist during the Great War but this was on another level. He had command, control, power, and still to his dismay he was doubting himself. His will had taken him so far but the triumph of the will seemed to be ebbing away. Only his vengeful heart, wanting revenge on the world and the country which did not accept him, kept him going.

Maurice had always harboured a bitter view of the world. He had no desire to see it remain as it was when he was young. He felt that people like him were destined to never see the joys of life. His rejection from friends and family for his outspoken views on life seemed to push him deeper into his isolation and mental inner sanctum. Every time he made a half-hearted gesture at engaging with the real world it was as if he was trying to touch a scolding kettle. He never considered his own part he was playing, instead looking out and it had made him angry.

This was not to say that he was incapable of compassion. Something had always stirred within him; a hope that someone or something would take all of the pain of rejection away. Something would give his life meaning whether it was a woman or an idea or an opportunity. In a paradoxical way he believed the war would give him that opportunity. Fighting for a country and a system that had rejected him seemed to be a redeeming quality. He believed in something for once and though he was late to join up he genuinely enjoyed life. In fact, his ability to speak and be given the nickname of 'the goat' directly related to his newfound mission in his life.

He too was bitter at the events of the war. He shared that idea with Petain though he had a more specific and lower-level view. The surrender seemed to further validate his idea that the country and the system were so insufficiency and that the war proved that. The pressing of that little red book into his palm was like a lifeboat being flung to him in a sea of despair. He was given life-anew and it had given him something else to believe in, and it made sense.

This was what fuelled the young man and it was the only thing stopping him from flipping the table and walking away into obscurity. He remained rooted to the spot whilst the prowling Petain barked at him. He imagined the world he wanted to create, unfinished in its specificity but under construction in part down to the workings of Karl Marx and Friedrich Engels. A new system where people like him would always be welcome. An idea that craved freedom and support for all. He believed in it and thus concealed in his jacket, unseasonal still for that warm time of year, that little red book remained close to his breast.

"And yet you sit there and say nothing, nothing! Are you so incapable of decisions?" The marshal took to talking to himself. "Of course, he's incapable. He has never commanded anything more than a rabble of angry, starving peasants. I'm wasting my time with this hack".

Maurice snapped back into the room. "An angry, starving, rabble of peasants they might be" interjected Maurice, "but they carry with them the seeds of revolution inside them. Without them you would not have the people to run the factories of the new France. You need me." Maurice sat awkwardly but leaned over to d'Esperay and Frossard who were stood by the wall, too frightened to get in the way of Petain's meandering around the room. "You all need me."

"Our munitions are flowing in from Russia now, and you are getting a portion of the supply" Frossard indicated. "The Russian Civil War seems to be progressing so well that they are even willing to send men to train our forces and with a bit more coercion they might even send us some heavy weaponry. If we can sneak the supplies past marauding British vessels, we might even get our hands on some heavy artillery that could reach Paris."

The idea softened the brow of the famous field marshal. The idea of heavy weaponry enticed him as a fear tactic. He remembered its incredible use during the battle of Verdun. Shrieking volleys far behind the enemy lines proved devastating to the Germans. Many were destroyed or had been moved north after the war so his small but well-drilled fighting force had to rely on short range artillery pieces which slowed his advance.

"Heavy artillery, you say? When? When could they be made available?" d'Esperay asked on behalf of his commander.

"Russia needs certainty that we will win. At this moment it doesn't look obvious. They don't want to waste pieces for a cause they might think is lost" Frossard said with regret.

"But we are winning! I have taken miles and miles of land. As far as I'm aware we outnumber them eight to one!"

"We? That is the first time you have said that word in a while" Renaudin said wryly. "At any rate, we need a gesture. A big gesture the international community will rally behind. A big battle or crushing victory."

"Do you have the stomach for such an undertaking" d'Esperay asked with disdain in his voice. He had no respect for Renaudin, seeing him as a means to an end and nothing more. Renaudin looked over to him and smirked.

"With heavy artillery, I could be convinced". He winked at Frossard who in turn shifted nervously in place.

"Well maybe you can decide what kind of gesture you might like to provide. May I suggest actually fighting?" Petain tried to contain his rage by not speaking because each time he did he managed to say something insulting or provocative.

"We will attempt to push on the right flank" Maurice declared.

"The right? No! You must fight in the centre. Support my advance and cover my flank!" Petain protested.

"We will go up the right flank. That is our concern." Maurice finally spoke some words of resolute desire. The words seemed to throw the lion of Verdun into a fit of anger and despair greater than before. He stormed out of the room.

"He doesn't listen. None of them do. None of them!" d'Esperay followed closely behind as the door was flung open. Petain's adjutant Rolland was standing outside and was barged away by Petain's hand, causing him to fall to the floor. The door was shut behind d'Esperay. Frossard remained and now it was his time to furrow his brow.

"Why don't you support Petain's attack by focusing on the centre. It is the quickest route to Paris. Are you worried about the defences? I have been told that if we can get past them then it's a very easy walk through the centre towards the capital."

Maurice sighed, letting out air slowly as his chest deflated. "I want the east. I want to go there."

"Why on earth do you want to do that?"

Maurice looked over at his old friend Frossard. "Have you ever been in love?" The question seemed to baffle the already baffled balding man, exhausted from his too-ing and fro-ing to Russia. He scratched his head and spoke, but the question seemed too impossible to answer that no words came out. He huffed and looked away, choosing instead to gaze at the window which overlooked Bordeaux city.

"I was once. I had a wife" he revealed.

"What happened to her?"

"I happened to her. Idealism has no place in a marriage." The thought seemed to turn Ludovic into a shade of pale grey.

"I want to take the right flank because of love". Maurice did not say those words with any hint of doubt. "Epernay. That's what I want." Maurice had told no one about his love for a woman in Epernay, not even Frossard or Varine. He wanted to keep it a secret. In fact, he wanted his whole personal life to be kept a secret. If he returned to Sedan, which too lay in his field of vision for an attack up the eastern side of the country, he wanted records of his past to be burned. So that too, was a motivation. But the main reason was the love of the woman he still could not bring himself to talk to. The Englishman he saw with her was etched into his mind and he wanted to wipe the idea out. He wanted to ride into Epernay in glorious thunder so he could finally talk to her. He wanted her so much. Her brown hair, her modest features, her apron, all of the mental images he had created for himself were so strong in his mind that it almost drove him crazy. It almost, and in some cases overtook, his love for his political and philosophical mission. He would indeed, if he was honest with himself, throw it all away for her. It was a childlike love, with no hint of critical thinking or analysis. It was a simple desire and a desire so strong he was willing to throw Petain under the bus, and perhaps his whole movement, in order to achieve what he really wanted.

Frossard turned round with growing incredulity. "What? You are making tactical decisions based on love? Are you really that naive?" Frossard started making gestures similar to that of Petain's not a minute or two ago. "Are you losing your sight of our mission? Our goal is the liberation of the workers of the French people! We need to join with our Russian brothers. Two great nations throwing off the chains of country and capitalism to create a new world. Don't you understand that that is what we are doing?" He noticed with serious concern that his words seemed to wash over Renaudin with troublesome ease. "Love your fellow man, not one person or something like that. Love your mission. You make better decisions that way!" Those words seemed to cut into Maurice's mental forcefield as his gaze was finally met by the idealistic Maurice.

"The right flank, Ludovic. Give the word to Varine and the other leaders. I will make a speech before the offensive. That is my will." Frossard had not let Maurice's new turns-of-phrases go unnoticed. Maurice had taken on his own view that he was in charge and Frossard was worried that Petain's idea of leadership was rubbing off on the impressionable young man.

"You think you can make orders like Petain?" Frossard asked, irritated to the limit of his capacities.

"I give orders" Maurice replied calmly "to safeguard the revolution. If I believe that it is love that will be our guide, then I will have made the right decision. You understand, now go." Frossard paused before he left to see his friend transform himself into something very different to what he remembered over a year ago. Back then the man agreed to everything Frossard ever uttered, even the proposed union between the Russian revolutionaries and the French. The idea of two united peoples under one banner seemed an inevitability should Renaudin ever find himself in a position of power. The decision to join with Petain, the mannerisms of a leader and the dictation of safeguarding a revolution had all the hallmarks of a very different human being. Frossard vowed to himself that every time he found himself in Renaudin's presence he would try to turn his friend back on the right path.

The door closed behind him and Frossard exhaled. He had once again left Renaudin in splendid isolation and it worried him. Renaudin was unpredictable after spending time on his own. Frossard called for a nearby guard and asked him to keep an eye on Renaudin. "Do not let him out of your sight. I want to know where he goes and what he does."

"Sir" replied the guard. His name was Leon. He had volunteered in Paris with Renaudin's reds and was one of the infamous executioners. Renaudin had trusted him from the start and always had him around. Though never invited into the inner sanctum of the movement he was ubiquitous as a man with a rifle outside of the room Renaudin was in. So long as he was alive the leader of the Patriotic Communist Party of France was in safe hands. And though he was supremely loyal he too was concerned with the mindset of his leader.

And so, he became the unofficial informant of Ludovic Frossard, occasionally letting him know of the movements of Maurice Renaudin. There was no sinister element to this, and Leon was reassured by Frossard that this was merely to keep Maurice safe, and there was great truth in this. But the self-appointed leader seemed lost and Frossard wanted him found.

The lumbering and seemingly chaotic unholy alliance carried on turning its wheels and carried on cranking out communiques and propaganda pieces to the men at the front. Maurice hardly ever visited the front line. He chose instead to make recordings of his speeches available to his men and women fighting for his cause, though they were strictly banned in Petain's camp. Still, some recordings managed to get through. Renaudin's voice could be heard reminding his followers of their sacred mission with words that would hearten the troubled Frossard, but the sincerity seemed to be lacking, certainly when Frossard had other meetings with Maurice.

Petain's small and disciplined army carried on their slow march upwards as the republicans and Bonapartists, indistinguishable aside from the more professional behaviour of the regular soldiers of the republican state, seemed reluctant to check their advance. It would prove to be the most worrying part of the front for the republicans, and so they started taking elements of their vastly overstretched line to try and slow Petain's advance before Nantes. This would eventually play right into the hands of Renaudin, eager to put on a show for his ally and his supposed brothers far off to the east, themselves holding decisive military equipment bobbing in the waters outside Rostov on the sea of Azov.

As the September rains began edging ever closer into considerations by strategists on both sides the time for making decisive action was coming to a head. The time for Renaudin's move was nigh. As the Republican forces eventually slowed Petain, offering heavy resistance that ended Petain's momentum with staggering rapidity, Maurice moved his forces into position. The time for the red offensive was about to begin.

Chapter 27

The air seemed stale and serious despite the frivolity of the decorations around the grand hall. William's finger danced over the rim of his crystal glass, hardly drunk out of. The wine did not seem to be to his liking, but he did not want to offend his hosts with such a remark about the drink selection. He rolled awkwardly in his dining room chair as the conversation seemed to revolve more around the joys of life rather than the seriousness of the situation. He would not be surprised if the revolutionaries overran the palace, most of the assembled party around the long table would hardly have noticed. The choice of conversation, the choice of concern, seemed to feel more at home within the halls of Valhalla, the realms of heaven or the paradise of the garden of Eden. None of those places had ever suffered from the slings and arrows of misfortune. The food was adequate and provided the only redeeming quality to the evening. William was the only man in the room whose fate was not directly tied to the outcome of the civil war, yet he seemed the most concerned about it for the entire evening.

"Your wife agrees with me!" General Gouraud laughed with boisterous energy, slamming the table. "And I for one would agree with her on anything!"

"You have a habit of ignoring the fact that my wife agrees with me on everything, especially when it comes to the choice of hat for summer!" General Degoutte retorted, and in doing so lost his Pinz-nez to gravity, as it hurtled to the floor. He begged for forgiveness as he leant over to try to find it.

"Gentlemen! As you know the only hat that is acceptable in the summer is one that keeps the sun off your back, the colour does not matter" General Maunoury stated. "And I beg you to keep your voices to a minimum level of volume. There are ladies present.

Gouraud's wife, Helena, laughed at the thought. "I'll have you know that my husband Michel never agrees with me, so he must agree with someone else's wife." Laughter rang around the room.

"And we are quite capable of making our own noise". Madame Degoutte assured the mildly concerned General Maunoury. "If we wilted at the sound of noise, we wouldn't have married officers, now, would we?"

"On the contrary, French officers make the best husbands because they make noises at the wrong time, rather than the right!" snorted Helena. The women laughed whilst the men were dragged into polite silence. "But pray tell, how are any of you authorities on the subject of fashion? You are too logical to understand something that has no basis in logic in high society." William thought that an articulate riposte and started paying attention.

"The mysteries of what men and women find attractive extend to the length of the dress and the cut of their suit, madame" General Degoutte bravely informed the room. "Colours matter little if there is flesh on display."

"You men always see the most base and simple solution to anything remotely connected to beauty" Madame Degoutte said, rolling her eyes to the back of her head. She seemed to have consumed more alcohol than her slight frame might have allowed, and she was already swaying in her chair.

"It is because we have more important things to deal with, and thus must leave such unnecessary detail to those who have more time on their hands" General Gouraud noted, gesturing to the women in the room. All of the men winced at the words, indicating that such a statement was not in the best of taste for the assembled gathering.

"I think that concludes that portion of the conversation!" piped up the demure Princess Clementine, the astounding wife of Victor Napoleon. Seated at the head of the table opposite her quiet and ever-so-slightly inebriated husband, she had abstained from conversations that seemed crass and unnecessary. Raised herself in the palaces of the Belgian monarchy, she had seen her fair share of unnecessary conversation and chose to reserve her thoughts and her voice for more light-hearted topics that did not involve the harmless, or indeed harmful, barbs that accompanied more base discussion. She was the most well-dressed of them all, the insignia of the Belgian royal household pinned to her elegant ball-gown which glowed in a brightened yellow with black lines wrapping round her like small chains. She leant back and snapped her fingers together. "I think we will take the dessert wine now, and the whiskey. Bring it here so that we can pour different glasses for different conversations." She gestured to her husband. "I assume that will be alright, dear?" Victor waved his hand dismissively, caring little for the choice of drink at this late stage of the evening. "Then would you be terribly kind and fill the glasses as they come so we can take to our different roles for this part of the evening?" The manservant standing nearby bowed and did as he was told with the able help of the handmaid. William noticed that they too were elegantly dressed for their station but noted the uncomfortable nature of such attire.

"Ah, I can never be too long away from my wife. Return her to me post-haste!" declared the illustrious General Degoutte.

"Truer words...have been spoken constantly by everyone at every time. I don't believe you for a second" his wife retorted, prompting laughter from most of the party.

"Then who wants a trade?" he replied. The generals laughed and banged their hands on the table, which was followed by a mock bidding session, with bids of bottles of wine being used as currency. Clementine, once again choosing to abstain from an odd choice of conversation, noted William's similar abstention. She was impressed. She stood up, prompting the inebriated generals to end their bidding war to stand up also. Only Victor remained seated.

"Gentlemen, excuse us whilst we leave you to important matters. William? May I have a word in your ear?" Clementine gestured towards William. He nodded back. Victor's eyes darted between the two. "Good. Ladies, I will join you in the adjoining room presently." The wives of their respective generals retreated, taking with them the filled dessert wine which had been poured effortlessly without anyone noticing. The manservant and handmaid were exceptionally adept at performing their roles with a stealth-like panache. Victor and the generals remained seated, finishing their wine glasses before moving on to the whiskey.

"This is Glann ar Mor, the best from Brittany!" Victor boasted. "We had a new crate delivered in with last month's arms shipment. A delightful idea. I wonder what it is they want in return!" His remark was met with polite laughter. William made for the waiting Clementine in the corner to the hall closest to the door the wives of the generals had retreated through. She begged him close so her words might be private to all but William.

"You behave so well. I am honoured that you could join us" she remarked. "Though I am sure you are not here to sample our delights. You did not make your intentions clear and whilst you and I have talked before you have not met my husband. The lack of clarity of your intentions has been met with suspicion. I would advise you to speak softly with my husband. Speak directly. It does not do well to confuse him with indirect talk."

"My intentions are ones of curiosity" he replied. He had been ordered not to reveal his intentions by Major Pearson. None was to be aware that his mission was one of espionage. The British authorities did not trust Victor Napoleon and though his wife was a redeeming figure it seemed as if that consideration did not extend to her husband. And thus, she was to be kept in the dark also about the true reason for William's presence. He had in his mind what he needed to know. What was Napoleon's strategy? What did he think of the British? In what way would he steer the great ship of state? What would happen next? Many questions with sub questions rattled William's brain. He wished he could say more so he could confide in someone and hopefully receive some sort of help, figuring out how best to approach the questions. But he alone would have to find out. Major Pearson had purposefully left William to the mission on his own. The reasons were both practical, so as to avoid suspicion, and insurance based. If William was found out to be conducting matters of espionage, then he would be less likely to be traced back to the authorities of the British. William was still known as a lone man, shunned by Germany and ignored by England, certainly in the papers. "I am grateful for your action to secure me an audience".

Clementine bowed her head. "After the conversations we have had about the world, politics, philosophy, I feel as if I have owed you at least one favour. I can have no such conversation with my husband who is as empty as most wine bottles in this house." She seemed to look deep into

William's eyes, though he did not know if the gaze was one of admiration, perhaps even adoration, or a means by which she could find out what William was up to. But he would never know, as she smiled and turned away. "Until we meet again, Mister Steele". In a matter of two breathes she was gone. William did not know if he would see her again that night, but he felt that their paths might one day cross again.

"Where is our Englishman? Little Englishman! Return to us, if you would give us the honour" Victor shouted with sarcasm oozing from every word. "Would you like us to speak in English for you?"

William returned laughing nervously. "No, I am well-versed in French. And I return as your servant, your highness." The generals looked at themselves, noting William's use of the royal title that Victor was rarely referred to as. "But I must ask you of your view of the present situation." William was eager to steer the conversation towards something that would be useful to him.

"And what situation is this? The situation of the weather? William, it is late in September and the autumn rains always set in. Don't tell me you are surprised. Does it not always rain in England? I hear you have many words to describe it, don't you? The English have nothing to do but make up new words. It is a disease they all suffer from" Victor retorted, extracting pompous laughter from the well-dressed generals, though buttons were fast becoming undone in order to find more comfort within their tunics.

"But Mister Steele speaks French so there is hope for him" replied General Maunoury half defending William and half mocking him. "What conversation do you want to have? Would you like to discuss the delightful taste of this whiskey? Honestly, in times like these I would drink all I had made."

"It's the times like these which I would like to understand from you" William said, attempting to segue the conversation. He noted a glare of suspicion bounding hard for him. "You have hardly mentioned it and I am concerned. How on earth do you think you will win the war? I am worried that the revolutionaries are gathering momentum and I want you to win. So will you assuage my fears?" The ruse seemed to work as he seemed to massage their inflated egos with the desire to see them victorious. He had been in the army and had seen such a ruse work with terrific results before.

General Degoutte took the lead initially on the subject. "Ah, my dear sir. If we really must consider the current political and economic situation it is much prettier a picture than perhaps you are thinking, yes? Of course, there are setbacks but what you must understand is that we are supremely confident. Our host is exactly where our confidence emanates from." Degoutte repositioned his chair so that it faced William directly. He took his whiskey glass into his hand and struggled to cross his legs as he spoke, leaning back as if talking to a favourite son. "We here are all generals of the republic, but we all agreed, precisely after the Great war that the republic was doomed. It was a matter of when, not if, it would fall. No one, from the lowliest peasant to the richest factory owner, believed in the republic as it was any more. Our concern was primarily over the lack of a credible option that was radical in scope, but not radical in ideology. Marshal Petain and the younger officers thought differently, but it is because they are idealists. Ultimately, we needed an option and that is where our eminent host comes in. With some help from some of the pillars of French society and politics we created the Bonaparte movement." He bowed his head towards Victor who remained motionless and ever so slightly slumped in his chair. "With Victor's approval as the figurehead and inspiration, we created the new alternative to steer us into the next phase of the republic. And so, we have on our side continuity and the support of everything that is important, the government, the church, the army and to a great extent the people. Well, the people not stupid enough to throw everything away in a bid to gamble and start again."

The revelation, plainly spoken by the wily and experienced general who clearly had loosened his tongue with the contents of an oft-used series of wine glasses dotted around his part of the table, surprised William. The movement was a front, a tool used by what seemed to be the military. William asked "what about the Orleans Accords. It was proclaimed, by you, Victor, that after great negotiations you would take on the role of supreme commander and would spearhead the republic. I remember reading about the speech you made with great anticipation". William once again used the ruse of ego massaging to entice Victor into the conversation.

Once again, the generals seemed to come to his aid. This time it was the turn of General Maunoury.

"A magnificent exercise of pageantry, don't you think? It worked on you; I take it. And so, it worked on those prepared to defend the republic! Scores of men have taken to the barricades on Victor's magnificent call to action. Victor, you are enjoying your magnificent role, are you not? Perhaps you are imagining yourself in the shoes of your ancestor, emperor Napoleon! I think we could arrange for a battalion to chant 'long live the emperor' when they next face the enemy. The twelfth is a game division. I'll have a word with them, see if we can drum up some good old-fashioned chanting for you." The patronising words prompted Victor to dive headfirst into his whiskey glass. He remained silent, begrudgingly letting his generals do the talking for him.

"But, Victor, you are supreme commander. You are in charge, of course" William noted, once more trying to get some words out of the commander. Once again, his efforts were spurned by General Maunoury.

"Oh, yes, of course Victor is in charge. We advise but it is his decision whether he would like to win or lose!" The generals laughed though a hint of nervousness crept in. "There is a chain of command, just like in your army. You were a major, no?"

"Acting major. My commission ended with the war."

"It all still counts. Once a soldier, always a soldier" piped up the younger of the three generals, General Gouraud. He was succumbing to drink at a slower rate but even he too was beginning to feel the effects. The whiskey seemed to be doing its job. "Anyway, we will win because we have time on our side. We simply have to wait, show that we are not for turning and the angrier members of those extremists will start to ebb away and migrate to North Africa or Russia if we are lucky. We have better weaponry, better trained soldiers and now a peasant's army to more than rival that of those socialists."

"You see, Major Steele, and I hope you don't mind that I call you by your proper title, we secretly wanted this to happen. The civil war is regrettable, but it is hard to root out extremists and undercover saboteurs in peace time. In war all are out on display ready to be lined up and shot.

Those who run away will leave because they have lost and those who stay we have identified and arrested or shot on the battlefield. It is like a purge. The body needs to remove a virus, so it produces a fever. The body is sick, but it removes the far more deadly element. What you are witnessing is a fever, the virus will be overcome, and the body will become well again, with Victor as the great cure!" General Degoutte said, quickly remembering to include Victor in his speech, toasting the slumped commander-in-chief who looked to be finished faster than everyone else in consuming his share of whiskey.

William had come for information about a man and suddenly gained information about an entirely bigger picture. What Major Pearson would give to be told of this information. He might not get all the answers he was hoping for, but what William had been told quite candidly was more valuable than perhaps all that could be garnered from Pearson's network of agents in France at that moment. William, pressing his luck, tried one more time to gather any words from the man who would supposedly be the next president of France. He abandoned all pretence and tactics and went for the jugular. "Victor, what do you think about all this?" The only general with a few non-grey hairs left, General Gouraud cleared his throat to speak until the sound of Victor Napoleon's fist slamming the table interrupted him. A glass hopped off its feet and fell on its side, rolling off the table and hitting the ground with a cracking sound. The generals looked nervously away as Victor finally opened his mouth.

"I am the saviour of France. I will do all that is necessary so that she is alive and well." The words seemed defiant, but they lacked substance or detail. It was as if he was reading a political speech drenched in eloquence without the similarly necessary finer points. "There is no one else that will lead the republic. I received all those votes. They were all for me, my own." He struck his breast with pride. "I will lead as my house will always lead. And where I lead all will follow. The spineless cretins that make up the Parliament and the military know that they cannot get anywhere without me. I will remind them, like I remind you". He pointed at each of the three officers before slumping his arm back on his armrest. "I may sound like a puppet, Steele, but I am anything but. They need me as much as I need them." He stared at General Maunoury through his dark and husky eyes. "If they need to refer to me as emperor so that they remember

270

that then they will do so! When this war is over France will follow my fate, not yours." His words seemed to be enough for him and he returned to his slumped posture after saying all he seemed to want to say. It was enough for William. Victor Napoleon's view on the English could wait for another time.

Silence, the room was choked with silence. The generals had pushed too much, and they had realised it. Victor's words might have seemed hollow, but it reminded the Generals that they would not so easily get their way. It took William Steele, one who had found his voice from his ordeals in Belgium, England, and Germany, to break the silence. He ran his finger over the rim of his whiskey glass that he had not even taken a sip from. A lot of the success he had found this night had been thanks not only to the drink consumed but the drink not consumed by him. Victor had partly noticed this, as did his wife, but none had considered it to be a source of suspicion.

"I hear Petain's forces are advancing quite high up the west coast. Nantes is in his sights. It would be terrible for him to take Brittany too. Then you would probably run out of this delightfully bronze whiskey." William's words had a certain swagger, brought on by the deluge of incredibly useful information he had absorbed. So long as he was alive and permitted to travel, he was now one of the most valuable men for the English at that place in time, though the other men in the room weren't to know that. Their hubris, their pride in their plans and schemes, were just too great for them to be hidden by those willing and able to ask.

"We did plan on luring him away from the rest of the front, cutting him off and surrounding him" replied General Gouraud disdainfully, "but he had his flank well covered. He was always a cautious sort. Then we had trouble containing his advance but that's all been taken care of. He'll spend the rest of the war shacked up on the coast with nowhere to go." William wasn't convinced by the blasé attitude of the younger General. "As for the socialist hordes, all they've done is practised their digging skills. I could walk through their lines easily and not have a shot fired at me."

"All they've done is kindly prepare fields for some very nice irrigation for next year's harvest!" the eldest officer, General Degoutte, responded jovially. A more stifled chuckle was shared amongst the group. "Oh, and I

271

had almost forgotten. The Germans have sent a few Hussar regiments to the boarder of Picardy. A kind gesture but I have been assured that it is an insurance policy in case we run into any trouble. I've assured the commandant of Calais that they won't be needed, but they insisted". He shrugged his shoulders.

"Are the German authorities aware of all of your scheming?" William asked with genuine curiosity, also considering the value of the answer to Major Pearson.

"Lovers must have their secrets. My wife, god bless her, is in the next room and she knows nothing of most of my life including a few, you know" his arm nudged Maunoury's arm, giving him a wink as they shared a bit of laughter. "Secrets are good, no? We keep ours too." William was genuinely impressed with the scheme, the elements of deception, and though ethically he could never condone such behaviour it seemed thought through, and it gave him confidence that though the republic was not exactly a grand institution itself, it might indeed hold. Such continuity and the absence of a revolution that would undoubtedly rip up all of France itself and it would threaten the paradise of Epernay where he longed to return. He vowed not to choose sides to Pearson, Balfour or even himself. But then and there he found himself hoping for a republican victory, even if the republic was in the hands of a pseudo-military junta.

General Degoutte staggered to his feet, whiskey glass neatly tucked into his hand, and walked over to William's seat, slapping him hard on the shoulder. The inebriated state of this elderly officer enticed him to forget his still-able strength. The impact was enough to cause William's body to flinch slightly. "You're a good man, Major Steele. I like you, and undoubtedly you are a fine soldier as well. With that uniform you are wearing you are the perfect image of a modern English gentleman". William had adorned the only piece of smart and clean attire that he still had in France; his old Imperial War Graves Commission uniform. It dwarfed in comparison to the Generals who, though lacking their medals, had resplendent polished buttons adorning their splendid dark blue coats. "You are an ally to us and we would be honoured to have you in our ranks. What do you say? Make yourself a hero to France as well as England?" William felt the hand squeeze his shoulder tightly.

"I am grateful for the invitation, but I must sadly decline" informed William without a hint of consideration. "I must return to Epernay. I have business to attend to there. Personal and professional, and it must take priority at this time."

"Ah, don't get involved, Jean!" Maunoury leant forward, informing Degoutte. "The last time I involved myself in someone else's personal and professional affairs I lost my finest monocle."

"Ah, such is fate" mused Degoutte, letting go of William's shoulder. As he began walking back to retake his place at the table a loud rattling on the hall door cascaded into everyone's ears, causing the more inebriated individuals to wince in discomfort. The rattling continued unabated.

"Oh, for heaven's sake" shouted Victor, the rattling rising him from his waking slumber. "Come in! Someone let the man in. Quickly!" William, the more able of the gentlemen, rose to his feet, thinking that such a ruckus might be the perfect excuse to slink away having gathered enough information to fill an entire ledger in foreign secretary Arthur Balfour's desk. He opened the door to an exhausted red-faced officer, his peaked cap in his arms. He was so out of breath it was if he had decided to run a marathon before arriving. His tunic was stretched and beads of sweat poured from his brow. He was a sorry state for a high-ranking colonel in the French army.

"What is the meaning of this? Where is your sword? Why do you look like you have swum up the Seine River? Please compose yourself. You're sweating all over the floor!" Degoutte protested, staggering towards the exhausted colonel who looked as if he was about to succumb to a heart attack.

"Apologies, my general. It is urgent. I have returned from the signal corps." He saluted, dropping his cap which General Degoutte retrieved with disdain. "Excuse my state but you must know. The front is broken. There is a gap a hundred miles long or more from the Rhone. Dijon is open and will be taken without a fight. We have no strategic reserve between Dijon and Troyes." He began to shed tears. "What are we going to do General?"

"This is impossible. Any attack by the reds would occur in the centre, a route closer to Paris and to support Petain. The east is not important. It isn't true." Degoutte turned away in disbelief.

"It is true. The reds surprised our forces with overwhelming rapidity. They just ran towards our line." The colonel was in tears on the verge of falling to his knees.

By now the gravity of the situation was starting to hit. "Did our men not offer resistance?" questioned General Maunoury, his sense of bafflement conflicting with his diminishing dismissal of the situation.

"Yes General" the colonel nodded, "but they were too great a number concentrated in too small an area to contain. We followed your orders not to fire the artillery until it was necessary but by the time it was deemed necessary it was too late." The colonel began weeping into his elbow. William thought to try to console the disconsolate colonel but he too was rooted to the spot. Epernay was now well and truly in the firing line and if the colonel's words were true then there would be little to offer resistance before the town.

"My god, they'll be pouring through and romping around behind our line" Gouraud nervously said to himself, the first of the Generals to come to terms with the seriousness of the situation. "It's happening again." He quickly turned from disconsolance to anger. "We did not learn the lesson!" He pointed at the senior generals in accusatory anger. "You did not learn. You never learn! And we're now totally lost!" The words brought more tears to the colonel's eyes as he stood there crying into his hands.

General Degoutte, the only one of the three generals not seemingly losing his cool, looked around the room for help. He dared not look at Victor Napoleon who took this all in quietly. "It seems" Degoutte said slowly to William "That you will not be the only one flying to Epernay. I hope that your business there is brief and optional." The words seemed to be haunting to William.

"I must leave immediately" William said with enough seriousness to sink a ship.

"As will we" the old General indicated. "If you will excuse us all, your highness, we must attend to the breach without a moment to lose". Victor looked up at Degoutte with thinly veiled contempt.

"I cannot be emperor without a country" he said slowly. The generals bowed, General Degoutte indicating the blubbering colonel and William to do the same which they did with awkwardness. They all filed out, passing by the room housing the women who had until then enjoyed their splendid solitude, and indicated that the time was nigh to leave immediately. Despite protests that bordered on the offensive depending on the amount of alcohol consumed the dinner party was quickly disbanded and military matters became the soup of the day.

The various parties vanished into the night, the sound of their car wheels quickly disappearing into the silence of the city of lights that was Paris. The city seemed different now that it was unaware of a possible impending disaster. William had to pass by a couple of its streets in order to retrieve his car which had been kindly housed by a resident informant of Major Pearson. The city seemed quiet, unaware and in a state of similar indifference to what was going on to its south and, unbeknownst to all but William there and then, rapidly to its east. The war was coming to the capital and perhaps William was witnessing the final night of peace symbolised with un-boarded up windows, open cafes, dancing children and couples idling their nightly walks with talk of nonsense and love, often at the same time. Even the various flora and greenery seemed to indicate its temporary apathy as various flowers and trees were still basking in the glow of autumnal rain and autumnal sun which graced the nature of the city like a son returning to his family after years away at war. Little did they nor the scores of people within the city know that the son and the war were to return together.

So, to Epernay, William thought, to Cecile and to Charles. He did not know what to do when he was to return, nor what state it would be in on his return. He did not know the right course of action. It was a feeling that he knew so well during the war and soon after it. It had been the source of such angst, such internal suffering. Now it had returned. He thought he had seen the end of it but here he was once again confused, his heart racing, his head pounding. What was to be done? He found himself the victim of where he was and the feelings he had too. His love for the brown-haired girl with the brightening hair was too great a feeling to do something about then. He was consumed with saving her, his feelings for her, as if he was leaving the trenches back in 1918 going back to Emmanuelle. Funny, he thought, how history was repeating itself but in a different form and he was once again carried by its strong current, struggling to keep his head above the surface.

The republican generals spirited away to plug the gap and to prevent another military disaster. William spirited away to find a way to rescue his love.

Chapter 28

The train journey down to Munich seemed slow and draining, not only for Fritz but for the passengers on board also. The trains headed for Munich were often quiet and this one was no different. People did not want to travel towards a region that was mired in political turmoil. A quiet and unassuming quarantine had been placed around the most of Bavaria save Wurzburg which seemed to be spared the silence of visitors and businessmen. The smattering of souls on this train were mostly belonging to the official delegation headed up by the chief of the German General Staff.

The visit was widely publicised in newspapers all across the nation that deemed itself the new centre of the world. 'Kaiser sends in the big guns!' the Frankfurter Allgemeine Zeitung wrote on its front cover. 'Bavaria to be brought to heel by the army' wrote the Berliner Tageblatt wrote on its front pages. The liberal press corps was hitching its star to the delegation, as did general public opinion. Erich von Falkenhayn had support from up high and down low. His delegation boasting some of the Great War's most successful generals and even high-ranking liberal politicians leant an aura of majesty that seemed as if it could be rivalled only by the presence of the Kaiser himself.

Little space, if any, on newspaper pages had been dedicated to the goings-on in France. The Civil War was, to the Germans, an internal housekeeping problem. In the end, the economic union would commence as usual it did not matter who would turn up in Berlin to sign the proposals from the German government. There were some who voiced their objections fearing that a radical outcome would not be good for future peace and cooperation between the two countries. These voices were drowned out not only by general indifference that seemed to be the official policy of the German government but also by the goings on in the southern-most region of Bavaria.

Developments had not been swift but they were developing all the same. Just before and during the transit of the delegation the new Bavarian government had declared its support to the Kaiser, indicating that there were no plans to form any sort of wedge between them and the rest of the country. This official press release was contradicted by the swift passing of regional laws that seemed to curb some elements of press freedom, the forced closure of regional liberal publications and a new education curriculum review was to be taking place soon. What was being said and what was being done further churned the rumour mill. Who was in charge and who was not? The answer seemed no less clear with the passage of time. Bavaria seemed to be marching out of step with the rest of the country, figuratively and literally, as Bavarian divisions loosely amalgamated into the German army had been temporarily withdrawn and refitted with new uniforms bearing insignias of very different varieties. Helmets bearing a red, black, and white symbol on their sides were issued and though they did not differ too greatly from their non-Bavarian counterparts the symbolism was interesting. Military parades had been held in Munich city each day with high-ranking officials with no official ties to the high command nor the royal household taking the salute. The developments were worrying.

All of these worrying revelations of the new Bavarian regime served to pique the interest further. Otto von Lossow, the President of Bavaria, renamed his office 'minister-President' in a bid to affirm his subordinance to the central government of Germany, but the gesture fooled no one. He was ordered to accept the presence of the delegation heading his way and he had dutifully and publicly accepted, assuring those who were listening in the Parliament building that he intended to cooperate as much as possible to correct any undue fears and to fully process the new government following the abdication of the Bavarian monarchy. Yet all of his words were dripping with the sounds of the real architects behind the scenes.

No one knew of the whereabouts of the infamous duo that had all but telegraphed their roles in this internal matter. Paul Hindenburg and his lacky, Erich Ludendorff had been spotted but had not been implicated in the matter and therefore were not under any sort of arrest. But they were indeed running from the authorities as a pre-emptive matter and now in Bavaria they had become the authorities. And though their overt plans

278

seemed to be confined to Bavaria they had supporters all over the country. The idea of these two men as dynamic rulers, sitting at the top table of the country once again, seemed palatable to some sections of German society. This sentiment was growing, albeit slowly, because the legend of them as the two true victors of the Great War seemed to be carrying them into national reverence still. Perhaps developments in France had only served to fan those flames, emphasised by the reluctance to cover the story in the German newspapers. The idea of Germany's enemies beginning to resurface only favoured their cause, putting the Kaiser's plans of reforming the more liberal workings of German politics and society in jeopardy. It was a quiet divide amongst the German people but with every internal and external development the question became more and more important to answer; what next?

Seated by the back of the main carriage, his head resting against the pane of the glass window was that of Erich von Falkenhayn's son, Fritz. His head was rocking with the movements of the train in similar fashion to the rocking of his mind. He had not seen his wife since he had stormed out of the tearoom in Berlin. He had set off with the delegation party against is wife's wishes and had not told her of this. He had simply upped and left as quickly as he could. He was filled with regret. The sense of duty that had driven him to join his father had a sickening taste in his mouth. The duty to his wife, one he had routinely struggled to comprehend, fought its way into his mind but it had not the strength to overpower his internal decision-making. His duty to his father and his country and to the uniting desire for order had carried him to where he was, and it had broken him. Fritz was a passenger on the train and, seemingly, of his own life. He had become afraid to make decisions of his own merit, choosing instead the decision that seemed the most right, or perhaps the easiest to make.

He noticed Munich coming into view slowly. The city seemed different to when he was last there during the trials. Far less smoke was billowing from its roofs and streets. In daytime it threatened to look beautiful. Yet when the train drew closer and closer to the station within the city itself the sight was far more reminiscent of its former self when he last was a visitor here. Soldiers lined street corners, flags were waving, and all seemed very unfriendly. The atmosphere was less feverish, but the city seemed as if it was still in wartime, or perhaps ready to experience an invasion. Though his father had arrived with every intention to settle the matter peacefully it seemed as if Munich was preparing for an intention that was anything but peaceful. He was glad to be wearing civilian clothes and a jacket, for he felt that if he displayed any regalia that indicated his allegiance to the Kaiser, he feared he might be set upon. Perhaps this fear was unfounded, but Fritz was in no mood to find out.

The train pulled to a halt. "All change please. Train ready to depart for Berlin in one hour" announced one of the train operators outside on the station platform. The long time before departure indicated that those in charge of the train were not expecting large crowds. Perhaps no one wanted to leave as well as not wanting to come to Munich. Fritz leant back into his seat and asked for his legs to carry him. His energy had been sapped from his body thinking of his distressed wife. He did not even know where she was either. He hoped to see her soon. His love for her was still strong. He fiddled with the ring on his hand as his legs finally started making their movements.

The delegation party marched in close ranks as if marching through terra incognita, afeared if one of their party might be stolen away from angry citizens. Fritz lagged behind attempting to blend in to the sparse crowds of onlookers making their way to the Nymphenburg Palace. The meeting was scheduled for an hour ago, so time was of the essence for the delegation. General von Mackensen, his moustache bristling in the midday breeze, took the lead with Fritz's father in hot pursuit. Paul von Lettow-Vorbeck was not far behind also, as other adjutants numbering only five, fumbled behind. They walked down the city in a gesture that was designed to lend as much publicity to the spectacle as possible. They were the king's representatives and thus they needed to show off that they were, in some way, in charge. They had been offered an armed escort but declined, fearing too much military symbolism might give off the wrong impression, especially before any conversation was even to be had. The idea of military threat was to be only used as a last resort in order to bring the Bavarian government into line, with a view of incorporating the government further into the central authority.

Fritz lagged further and further behind. His mind was wracked with the guilt of abandoning his wife back in Berlin. He knew that he would be of little use to the delegation once the session was underway and so peeled off as they reached the palace to a nearby café where he ordered the same light desert and coffee that he had when he was last with his wife. It was an empty gesture that he thought might alleviate his mind from its guilt. He was mistaken and chose to sit idly by whilst looking at his watch. He was eyed a couple of times from passers-by, indicating to him his mistake for choosing to sit on the outside area of the café. He upturned his jacket collar and looked up as rain clouds circled overhead threatening to add rainwater to his quite-delicious coffee.

Time ticked by and he had anticipated the delegation party making its way out at some point soon. But when time carried on ticking on, the plan to keep the discussion brief as possible, Fritz started fumbling nervously with his watch. He looked around the pay for his gesture to his wife not with him but struggled to get the attention of a waiter working there. The café was wide and marginally busy. Delicious cakes and delicacies were spread across the inside of the window making for a delicious display, but also providing an unhelpful barrier to Fritz attempting to gather attention from anyone working inside. He carried on sitting, a few coins dancing in the knuckles of his hand, for a good few minutes becoming more and more impatient. How he would like his father to come out and see to the slow service, perhaps even lending Fritz a Mark or two to cover the costs. Fritz's father was strict but generous with money. Eventually, Fritz was seen to by a slow and lackadaisical waiter and he left the café with brisk speed.

He assured the multitude of guards, each one carrying a new and odd insignia on the sides of their helmets which seemed a bit smaller than those issued to soldiers during the war, that he was a part of the delegation that was closeted inside. Each soldier grunted with disdain at him and let him pass. The odd guard section held him up asking him for his papers. But eventually he was let in. The old palace had been renovated again, this time it had been kitted out not for a trial but for a political house of discussion and debate. Great chambers had been set up in the old palace of the now-vanished Bavarian monarchy. He asked where discussions were taking place and was directed by men, constantly in military regalia, to the rearmost hall. He made his way slowly, taking in the scene of a palace now seemingly used as a multipurpose plaything by those in charge of its contents.

He had reached the penultimate room, a long corridor with high walls and a high ceiling, housing a couple of the adjutants reading over documents of unknown quantity when the sound of a gunshot burst all around them. One man dropped the contents of his person to the ground as they all looked around with sharp attention, like rabbits in the night suddenly looking at light that had suddenly turned on. All in the corridor made for the door that was slightly ajar and rushed in. Fritz, the furthest from the door was the last to come to the door before he stopped suddenly, as if frozen to the spot, at the door. He peered through as if his mind had seen something, but he hadn't.

He couldn't see much as men were standing around blocking his view. What he could make out was a straight arm at around knee level waving about. The men in front of Fritz shuffled around and he could finally see what was going on. Slumped on the floor, blood pouring from his left breast was that of his father, Erich von Falkenhayn. His father's head was being held upright by Paul von Lettow-Vorbeck who was trying to shift him further up on his lap. The fallen father could be seen moving his mouth, but no words were coming out.

Everyone was speaking at once, with one or two men running to the rear window. Fritz looked up at the window. A windowpane had cracked and was all but smashed to pieces, save for a hole in the upper left-hand corner large enough for a bullet to pass through it. The adjutants rushed to the window pointing and shouting whilst General Paul was attempting in vain to push on Erich's chest to stop the bleeding. The elderly General Mackensen tried to do the same. The general noticed Fritz stopped still at the door and yelled at him.

"Run! Get out! It is not safe for you here! Go!" The general's shouting did little to pierce the frozen exterior of Fritz's skin. He could barely look at his father's face trying in vain to speak, blood trickling from the side of his mouth. "Thomas! Thomas! Get Fritz out of here! They could go for him next!" An adjutant by the window nodded and unholstered his pistol by his hip. "Fritz, get out of the city, now!" The general waved his hand in the air begging Fritz to go. Fritz took one final look at his father's limp and bloodied body, still rooted to the spot as he was taken by the arm and ripped from his spot by the adjutant.

The door was closed behind him and he was dragged by his elbow back down the corridor. As he flung open the corridor doors a couple of guards had made their way to them. "What happened?" asked one.

"One of our party has been shot! I am escorting Fritz to the station!" Lieutenant Thomas replied, waving his pistol. "Out of our way!" The two guards rushed through behind them and they carried on their way through the palace. They had all but reached the exit when two guards were standing behind their desks in alert.

"Open the door. We need to go. Orders from General Mackensen" the adjutant barked, waving his pistol.

"What is going on?" one of them asked.

"Erich von Falkenhayn has been shot. We don't know by whom. We just need to leave. Let us pass!"

The two guards looked at each other. They both drew their pistols and as they aimed it at Fritz and Thomas the lieutenant fired a couple of shots at the two men. They both fell to the floor, though one of them had been slightly grazed. He took a shot at Thomas, hitting him on the shoulder. Thomas was still holding on to Fritz's elbow and threatened to drag Fritz to the ground with him. Fritz managed to wriggle free and grabbed Thomas's pistol and fired back at the injured guard on the ground.

He stared at the man who now lay motionless and pocketed the pistol in his jacket pocket. He looked down at Thomas. The bullet had passed deep through up his right shoulder, blood pouring from his shoulder and neck. Fritz had seen this injury before. The jugular vein had been pierced and he had no first aid pack on him. Thomas was bleeding out. The stricken lieutenant held onto Fritz's elbow looking at him, panic etched across his face. He tried to speak but was suffering from the same affect of Fritz's father. No words came out. He was frantically holding his shoulder and neck trying to stop the bleeding. Fritz tried to help but knew it was all in vain. The grip Thomas had on Fritz's elbow slowly eased until Thomas's arm fell to the ground. Thomas tried one last time to speak but only blood poured out. His eyes closed and his mouth remained open but now motionless.

Fritz looked on in helpless fear and sadness. He let out a crying cough and stood up looking at the poor body. He saw not only Thomas but also the imagined body of his own father. He thought the worst and though his mind tried to reassure him he was once again rooted to the spot. He didn't know where to go or what to do. Should he go back and see to his father? Or should he turn and run?

His mind was made up when he heard fast-approaching footsteps from inside the palace rooms both nearby and upstairs. The sound ripped him from his quickly frozen spot, and he rushed to the fallen guards to frisk them for the keys to do the grand hall door. He fumbled the keys in his hands which were soaked in blood and unlocked the door unleashing him from the confines of the palace. Guards all across the otherwise-deserted compound were rushing towards the palace. One asked him what was going on but he couldn't make any words come from his mouth. He made nonsensical and frightened mumbling and carried on walking, almost running, towards the outer realms of the palace grounds. The guards rushed past him, and Fritz powered past, attempting to escape with speed. He dared not look back fearing it might slow him down and he might see men rushing after him. Though indeed eventually one or two did indeed attempt to chase after him he managed to get far from the palace so he could melt away into the city. His choice of clothing for that day were well-chosen and after a suitable amount of time had passed, he made his way back to the station with as much haste as he could without drawing attention to himself.

Luck seemed to be on his side as the train he had arrived on had delayed its departure due to the serious lack of passengers. Only thirty souls had taken their seats on the train and the train operator had deemed it sufficient for the journey to be a worthwhile venture. Fritz boarded the train and tried to inconspicuously take his seat at the rear of the train carriage keeping his head down as much as possible. His little seating area was vacant aside from himself and he eagerly awaited the train's departure. He would have to worry about two further stops of the train before he was safely spiriting away from Bavaria. A few hours would be all he needed before he could consider himself rather safer than he was at that moment. The great wheels of the train began to churn slowly and the familiar rattling and swaying of the lumbering locomotive struck up like a great band starting their long and loud symphony.

The train had made its long journey and had passed by the first stop with ease. No one had alighted from the first stop and a few had disembarked/ Fritz began sitting slightly better, the fear for his life slightly subsiding, allowing for an element of thought about what happened to his father to step into the mental breach. He sat back and looked away briefly from the view from the window to look inside his carriage. He noticed a man lumbering with difficulty down the middle of the train in a long, buttoned, trench coat. Fritz thought nothing of him and hoped he would pass him by with relative ease. Perhaps he would tell Fritz off for having his legs on the bench opposite him, so Fritz swivelled his legs round and placed them back on the floor in front of him. The figure approached by him and stopped. Fritz's heart pounded. He was so close to safety.

"You wouldn't happen to be Fritz, the hero of the final battle of France, would you?" the nameless voice asked. The voice seemed familiar, as if Fritz was hearing the voice of a relative or someone in Graudenz. He dared not look up and grunted dismissively. "Yes, yes, it is you. Ha-ha! I've found you. My friend, it is good to see you!" The nameless man sat down, thudding his body on the seat opposite Fritz. The man was larger, a round belly that betrayed the lifestyle of a man that enjoyed the tastier things of life. Fritz stared up to see the familiar face of his old friend from the war, Norman Gisevius. He stared blankly back at his beady eyes. Norman reached over and patted Fritz's knee with glee. "You old dog, you. Fancy seeing you here. Serendipity knows no bounds, does it not?" Fritz loosened up, a reunion with an old friend seemed bizarre but it was not the most bizarre thing to happen that day. He allowed his body to embrace the situation and he opened up his crumpled body that had been for so long shrivelling in terror.

"What on earth are you doing here, Norman?" Fritz asked with supreme confusion.

"I am on the way north to Wurzburg! It seems that I will be of use there!" Norman revealed, grinning like a Cheshire cat. "So, I am here on my way. And here you are, on your way! How wonderful." Norman chuckled as he spread himself on the bench. Fritz noticed his somewhat larger frame.

"I see you are making up for lost time at the dinner table" Fritz noted, indicating his interest at Norman's larger belly. Norman laughed and gave his tummy a couple of taps with his hands.

"Yes, I have developed a slightly sweet tooth in my time down south. We eat like kings down here, you know, and drink like kings, and love like kings! And what's better? There are no actual kings here any more to tell us we can't!" He laughed loudly, prompting a few passengers to glare at them for making so much noise. Fritz retreated back into the upturned collars of his jacket. Fritz looked at his old friend up and down, noticing the trench coat buttons had given up the pretence of being buttoned up. Norman's jacket slid open revealing a military uniform underneath. Fritz frowned.

"I thought you left the army" Fritz said, pointing at Norman's chest. "You said you wanted to return to your life on the Rhine." Norman laughed again, prompting more stares and glares.

"Ah yes, but times have changed and so has the Rhine, my friend." He glared and grinned himself, stretching to his side to rummage into his pocket. He pulled out a letter and handed it to Fritz. "Times have changed indeed." He stretched out his hand waiting for Fritz to take the letter. Fritz's body was crumpled up again, but he stretched his arm slowly to take the letter. Norman indicated for him to read it. He looked down and strained his eyes to make out its contents;

F. von Falkenhayn Esquire

It is with great pleasure that I write to you with the memory of our previous meeting so vivid in my mind. I hope this letter finds you well.

Events around you are happening very quickly, too quick for you to comprehend and too earth-shattering for anyone to stop. It is the inevitable march of progress hand-in-hand with fate. The wheels of state turn and those who step in its way are doomed to find themselves under its tracks. I regret those who find themselves under its tracks and so I write to you.

If you are reading this then the wheels are in motion, and you are in some way affected. I can only apologise that neither you or your father have seen fit to find yourselves on the right side of history, and the consequences of that decision. Though you, Herr Fritz, have a chance to correct your course. I saw in you the seeds of one who is understanding and that understanding may guide you towards progress yet still.

I beseech you, son of a noble and proud father who will be remembered within the halls of the great German heroes of the ages, to consider your part to play in this great game. Your name carries with it great weight and that weight would speed up the inevitable march of change. Not doing so would only delay what has been put into action. Reject the advances of those who wish to draw you into their sinking ship and indicate your support for the new Germany that will rise up from the old. I can promise you titles, land, legend, and power. A great reward for a simple shake of the head to the pretender of the throne.

If, however, you wish to reject my great and singular offer then I shall only regret further the fate that awaits you. And perhaps, if you are so inclined, to do all in your power to escape the fate meted out to those who wish to stand in the way of progress, then I am sadly dutybound to permit the passing of information about your personal conduct during the Great War to your illustrious and beautiful wife. She did seem so distraught on leaving the tea room in Berlin but as you said; duty must come first.

I advise you to do your duty to progress so that you might benefit and that your wife may never learn of your insatiable desires of the flesh, in the past though they may be.

I leave the choice in your capable hands, and the report of that choice in the hands of one who knows you, and your past, very well.

With regards

L.

The letter was poison to Fritz's mind. Even to the touch, it felt painful as if wrapped in barbed wire and glistening with the blood of dead men on a field of battle and death. His heart raced, his head throbbed and the whole world seemed to spin in front of him. The grinning glare of his friend, now turned into a harbinger of pain torture in his mind, washed into a sea of colours that swept towards Fritz in an attempt to bury him. He reached for his head to stop the spinning, but it only seemed to make it worse. Eventually, he was somewhat brought back down to earth by the hand of his old friend on his knee.

"It would do good to not delay a response" Norman said softly. "Time is of the essence and my stop is fast approaching".

"Have, have I been followed?" Fritz asked meekly through the dim of confusion, pain and sickness.

"No more than is usual for a very important man" Norman iterated, shrugging his shoulders. "I did so want to introduce myself before. You know, it's been too long since we had a conversation. The war seems like an age ago." His words seemed bizarre, as if he was speaking another language. Fritz held a letter full of threats and foreboding, holding the key to understanding what had just happened in the Nymphenburg Palace, and all Norman wanted to talk about was a friendly reunion.

"Norman, I, I need help. I, I need some air" Fritz gasped, holding his throat as if he was being choked.

"I'm afraid these trains are not well-equipped for every such luxury. Now, come on. The station is in view, and I must see to a gentleman about a letter" he said impatiently, winking in a friendly manner that only further pushed the needle into Fritz's heart. Fritz gazed into his mind for an answer, a sense of reasoning but could find none. His head rolled around and around as if it had lost all sense of time and space. The train started slowing down. "Now is a good time. Now is a very good time!"

Fritz, racked with the pain of causing further anguish for his wife, the anguish overtaking his heart and breaking it from the inside, caused him to drop his head, slamming his chin into his chest. He held the letter in his left hand and began crumpling it up slowly, gripping the ball of paper tightly, shaking his hand and then his arm. He wished to destroy it with his strength, obliterate it out of existence like an artillery shell hitting the ground. He could not do so, and remained silent as the train came to a well-timed halt.

"A shame." Norman sighed, slapping his hands on his thighs. He stood up breathing out slowly looking down on Fritz. "A really terrible shame". He hobbled off, his larger frame causing him to stagger as he moved out of view if Fritz had been looking up, departing the train and into the haze of Wurzburg's city outskirts.

The train did not stop there for long and even before Fritz had regained any sense of consciousness of the world around him the train had moved on and made for its next leg of the journey, easing its way out of the Bavarian region towards Berlin and home. What home might be awaiting the broken Fritz was his guess. He no longer felt safe, and felt like leaving a frying pan to enter the fire. Had he made this choice on his own, or had he just wilted at the mere thought of such a choice? So many factors, considerations and thoughts were rushing through his head. The sight of his father convulsing blood from his chest and mouth, the dying agony of lieutenant Thomas and the letter that still survived in his hand. He knew only one thing; the whirlwind had only just arrived in his mind.

Chapter 29

The train arrived back in Berlin's central station. The city was alive and electric with the news of scandal that had arrived also in hushed tones and whispers. They were only rumours for now but the story of scandal, the delegation sent to Munich in disarray, the story seemed to be ever-present in the city. People argued that the rumours had no basis of truth and that rumours were just that. Sensationalised stories were brushed aside by many, though they would soon learn of the validity of such hushed stories uttered discreetly at that evening's dinner table in private homes, restaurants and other institutions featuring a table.

The limp and crumped body of Fritz von Falkenhayn was retrieved, the young man breathing heavily almost wheezing. He was carried out, barely conscious, into an ambulance car. He was rushed away, groaning in the back, assuring those in attendance that he was not harmed or hurt. The attending medical personnel were concerned for the colour of his skin and the heavy breathing, but they too put it down just to shock and benign tremors of the heart. He was whisked away not to the hospital but to the imposing Berlin Palace, and though he would feel as if he was being taken straight there from the station, he had in fact rested in the ambulance car for an entire night. Nonetheless, he ambulance car jiggled harmlessly over the cobbled stones of Berlin, Fritz rocking in the back unable to stand or sit up for fear of falling once again into a daze.

The car made its way past the impressive, watered area surrounding the front of the palace. The glorious statue of Kaiser Wilhelm I looking down on the car which had at some point unknown to Fritz been given an armed escort. The back doors of the ambulance car were flung open and Fritz was brought round with smelling salts. He sat up with aid and attempted to get to his feet but failed, falling back onto the ambulance bed. Two medical orderlies jumped in to help him to his feet. He was brought out, his eyes wincing as it took in the lights surrounding the great statue to the kings of old. The windows of the palace were all alight as if a party was being held within. Figures could be seen looking out of the window at him as he was helped through to the palace door.

He was pushed through the doors and into rooms of unimaginable quality and splendour. He had quite enough of palaces but this one did indeed take what was left of his breath away. Gilded decorations and trinkets of state adorned the walls as far as the eye could see and though a murmuring of voices could be heard from unknown areas Fritz felt as if he was alone with the men carrying him in a palace fit for a god. Doors opened and closed as he was carried, staggering every so often, towards an area unknown. One of the men knocked on a door for Fritz and then went to spruce him up slightly. A button was fastened, a shirt was straightened, a collar's creases were creased further, and his sleeves were lengthened properly.

The door swung open and Fritz's head finally looked up to see the contents of this room. A man had just gotten up from behind a desk, his eyes looking straight into those of Fritz, with two soldiers standing beside a man seated in between. They too stared back at him. Fritz could hardly make them out until his eyes finally adjusted and his mind started coming to. Staring right into his eyes were those of Wilhelm Victor Albert; Kaiser Wilhelm II of the German Empire. His eyes, sloped at the edges, in full military uniform with the star of his office, his house and his power, dangling from his collar. His left hand firmly attached to his sword dangling from his side, clattering as he stood to his feet. Fritz coughed and spluttered, his Prussian body kicking in forcing him to bow. He struggled to return up right, doing so after great difficulty. As he returned to look at the room the Kaiser had approached him, looking him up and down. Fritz dared not speak and could not speak. Why he was there in the presence of the most powerful man in all of the world was anyone's guess. He stood motionless as if on parade being inspected. The Kaiser broke the silence.

"You are the son of Erich von Falkenhayn?" the Kaiser asked. Fritz nodded. He felt the right hand of the emperor rest on his shoulder, tapping it softly as he sighed. "To lose one parent is a tragedy. To lose another is a devastation." He looked deep into the eyes of Fritz. "You are a brave boy".

Fritz had no knowledge of the fate of his father. He pieced together the words that had jumbled themselves into his mind, breaking apart in his ears and reforming them as best as possible for him to make sense of. He had feared the worst and it had indeed come to pass. His assumptions softened the blow of the news, but it was nonetheless heavy on his heart. He had become orphaned in such a short space of time. He thought of his sister, sure in the knowledge that she would not know for some time. The news would crush her also and it filled his heart of even greater sadness. He stood to attention, but tears formed and rolled down his dis-coloured cheeks. His tears did not go unnoticed by the Kaiser, and he nodded to one of the men standing by Fritz, prompting Fritz to receive a dab or two of a handkerchief on his cheeks. He stood to attention, his skin hardening around him.

"I have said goodbyes to many men and I have caused many deaths" admitted the Kaiser with emotion that seemed insufficient for the information he revealed. "But in peacetime deaths hurt much more. Your father is a great loss to this country and to me on a personal matter. When the news breaks tomorrow it will be accompanied with word of a coming state funeral". The news did nothing to sooth Fritz's mind. He spoke up, trying in vain to search for good news.

"What of the rest of the delegation, my emperor?" he asked. The Kaiser raised his eyebrows and looked away.

"They are safe and well. They will return once it is safe to do so from where they currently are. I am assured of that." The Kaiser looked once again into Fritz's eyes. "I have a surprise for you. A surprise that might help with the pain you are feeling now". He stepped back gesturing at the three other figures in the room. Fritz looked up. Two soldiers were standing either side of an old man in a suit, a big silvery moustache adorning the face of a man who seemed very familiar. The curves of his wrinkled face seemed darker than what was usual on an old man. Perhaps the light was unflattering, but the face seemed more familiar by the second. The eyes of the old man were looking back at Fritz also.

It was the face of Paul von Hindenburg.

The infamous puppeteer was right in front of Fritz. The man who had supposedly ordered the assassination of his father during his wedding, was a suspect in Fritz's mind over the death of his mother, and the supposed chief culprit of his father's ultimate fate that very day, was right in front of him. His mind fantasised about the ways he might throttle the old man. But the tired old eyes, the slumped shoulders and the rather depressed facial expressions, dampened those fantasies. He felt nothing, or rather, he felt numb that this man was simply in front of him. He looked meek and contrite. There was nothing else to him.

Fritz learned that Hindenburg had been finally apprehended by the authorities. It turned out that not only had the delegation been sent to Munich to see to the crisis of the Wittelsbach abdication, it was also used as bait to force Hindenburg to make his move and so give the authorities an excuse to finally arrest him. The famous field marshal and one-time dictator of Germany had not been as good at hiding as he thought. Hindenburg had been bundled into a military truck and rushed off to Berlin without a moment's notice. The thought of fritz's father being used as bait angered him but what was left of his heart had been broken already, so the feeling of anger surrounded an empty breast within Fritz's body.

"I did not countenance a fatality, not for one second. And I would not certainly countenance the loss of a great man" the Kaiser stated with a grave tone. "But I am left in a quandary, a dilemma of fates. But I believe I now have my judge, jury and, perhaps, executioner." The Kaiser made his way back around his desk and using his right hand he seated himself steadily into his luxurious chair. He leant forward resting his chin on his thumb, his elbow neatly resting on his desk. "As this is a matter of murder, treason, crimes that are too great to fathom for the courts, I am left to deal with the fate of a man I once called my friend." The Kaiser looked with a harsh expression at the old field marshal. "Do you wish to make a case for the defence?" he said wryly.

The field marshal tried to stand up but one of the attending soldiers slammed his gloved hand on his shoulder and he fall back down on his chair with a thud. He collected himself and spoke, darting his head slowly from the Kaiser to Fritz and back again. "I assure you that I am just as regretful as you, my emperor. The incident was most certainly a tragedy and not one that I could have possibly sanctioned." Both the Kaiser and Fritz furrowed their brows. Hindenburg had not been a forced guest in the presence of the Kaiser for long. "I meant only to return to guide you, my emperor, away from the future perils from within our nation and outside of it. The civil war in France is evidence of that. My methods are regrettable, but I feared you were setting a regrettable course."

"You do not have the authority or the forethought to question me, Paul!" snapped the Kaiser, doing all he could not to slam his fest on his desk.

The old field marshal raised his arms in front of him to assure and to ask for a moment. "I meant no disrespect, my emperor. I am not an extremist." He looked into fritz's eyes with noticeable sincerity. "I really am not".

The Kaiser bristled with indignation. "Then why is his father lying dead on the floor of Munich's palace?!" The candidness of the Kaiser's words winded Fritz, though he once again remained stiff as a board.

"Against my orders!" pleaded Hindenburg. "Such an order could never come from me. My mission was always to persuade, not to assassinate, not to intimidate. Upon my life it is true!" His words seemed authentic, though who could possibly know.

The Kaiser sighed. "We will extract all the information we need from you presently. But the matter of your fate rests with me. You are ultimately responsible and thus you are responsible in my eyes for the death of Erich von Falkenhayn. How do you plead?"

Hindenburg's eyes looked as though he had been wholly ignored and pleaded once more. "Not, not guilty. I am an honest man!" He turned to Fritz indicating silently that his words were sincere. The Kaiser slowly joined Hindenburg's gaze, looking once again upon the broken yet upright man.

"What say you? What shall I do with him?" the Kaiser asked with his own piece of sincerity. The question seemed too awesome and great for Fritz to comprehend. His mind had already been filled with whirling and so it was in no fit state to pass judgement, especially if he could possibly pass judgement that involved the death of another. It seemed that nothing was off the table to the Kaiser who just as easily sent millions of men into a bloody war. Fritz stared back until he could take no more and stared down. He thought of his mother, her outstretched hand lifeless on the bed.

He thought of his father, blood pouring from his mouth and breast. He thought of his wife, beautiful but an unknown in her whereabouts or feelings for him. He thought of himself, his love of duty unravelling with each passing moment in his life. It was all he knew, the value of duty no matter the cost and no matter the outcome. He saw to his duty, but a duty to whom? To the Kaiser? To his father? To himself? He had not the answer.

And, at that moment, he thought of that Englishman. His words in the court room had not gone from Fritz's mind. They lay dormant under the bedrock of his mind, moving ever so slightly at this moment. Vengeance, the word that cuts through and infects the definition of duty until it eats up the host. That was what he seen his duty become; following bitterness and where did it get him? It had lost him the love of his wife. It had lost him his sense of honour with his infidelity in the war. It had lost him his sense when he confronted the Englishman. He was adrift, his mind followed suit, and his whole world had come to an end at that very moment. He rose his eyes to speak.

"The field marshal is led by his duty, but it is revenge he really seeks. I do not wish to pay him back in kind." His eyes slumped down, and he closed his mouth. The Kaiser leant back in his chair, Hindenburg looked puzzled at Fritz and then back at the Kaiser who pursed his lips and gazed at the contents of his desk.

"Extract what you can from him and then haul him in front of a private court" he ordered, waving the guards to take the fallen field marshal away. Hindenburg was hauled to his feet and escorted out. He turned back towards the Kaiser.

"With me gone, there is no stopping the true extremist. He is the man responsible for the extremism you have seen before you. Fritz! Fritz, he had your father assassinated. I assure you! I assure you. It was him. Now he has no checks to his schemes. You must believe me. On his own he is much more dangerous." The guards lost their patience and began dragging him by his arms, he staggered and fell, being hauled away by his arms. "Mark me. Beware of a man unbound by conscience or reasoning! Mark me well!" The Kaiser flapped his arm and a pair of doors further away were closed, banishing the sight of the field marshal from Fritz's' and the Kaiser's eyes. He tutted but kept his eyes on the closed doors.

"Curse him, he is right. We have cut one head off the snake, but he has a second and more venomous head. I would sooner have that scoundrel Ludendorff here. There's no telling what that man will do next. Whether I believe that the more sinister actions are down to Ludendorff alone is another matter." He stood up and looked at Fritz, his eyes fully on the broken man still flanked by two guards himself. "Needless to say, it is not safe for you here. It is not safe for you anywhere in this country. You are much better off dead to these fiends. I cannot have that happen to you. It would not do for public moral to say the least that anyone that crazy man deems necessary to die should be killed. You will be transferred to Calais where you will form a part of the light cavalry guard there."

"I had hoped, my emperor, that I may be allowed to return home to be with my sister" Fritz meekly asked.

"That is the first place they will look for you. Your sister will be hidden also, naturally. I would go to your wife and inform her that she must got into hiding. I leave the details of that up to you. You will leave on the morrow for Calais immediately. Do your duty and when this mess is done, and that scoundrel is brought to justice you may be able to return." The Kaiser was adamant.

As the word 'duty' was uttered Fritz once again winced in pain. He was once again cast down the strong current of duty, but he could hardly disobey his Kaiser. Though if he did it would be the ultimate display of defiance, he was in no fit state to do so, and perhaps he did not want to disobey the order. It was an escape, an escape with his life. What he thought his wife might think, he would not know. But he reasoned with himself that such extreme circumstances negated the ability to refuse such a command. He bowed his head and was led away from the presence of the most powerful man in the world.

He left the Berlin Palace, taking one last look at its surroundings and the great statue looking back at the building: that of Kaiser Wilhelm I. It was a glorious sight and one he would not perhaps see again for some time. He was given an armed escort to the recently purchased property nearby. He assumed his wife might still be there, arranging what had been delivered and what had been purchased to turn the house into their home. He was dropped off and assured of an armed guard outside of the property that night. He thanked those who had been ordered to stay and ascended the few stairs to the front door of his house. He saw no lights were on, though not all of the rooms had windows that faced the front of the house. He knocked on the door in hope that it would be flung open and that his wife would fling her arms around him once more as if they were young lovers once again. He hoped beyond hope that this would come true.

No such event occurred. He knocked the door, harder this time. One of the guards stationed outside of his house turned around to see what was going on. He knocked harder and the door swung open slowly. The door had not been locked. He peered through, the lights from the street flooding into the hall. He saw to the electricity switch and flipped it. The house was bare, save some token deliveries that had yet to be sorted. Chairs, a few paintings and such had been stacked in a corner. He walked up the narrow stairs to the bedroom which had been at least made up so the couple could at least stay overnight. He surmised that his wife would be in that room.

He crept upstairs, the night air as still as anything. He saw to the bedroom door and opened it and once again it was bathed in darkness, similar to the rest of the house. He turned on the bedroom light and saw the bed neatly made with a flower in the middle, with a little card resting against it. His heart sank as he walked to the side of the bed and took both in his hand. The flower was familiar. It had been picked from the fields of the old and broken ruins of the castle where their marriage had been held. Tears streamed from his eyes. He dared not look at the note. He had had enough of notes for a lifetime. He owed it to his wife to read it. He read it. It simply said;

I relieve you of your duty to me, so you may better do your duty to whatsoever you see fit.

She had been told everything and he knew it. His past had come back to well and truly haunt him and he was finally paying its terrible price. He sat on the bed; flower clutched tightly to his breast as he wept the tears of one who had lost everything and seemingly everyone. Everything he thought he had done right had turned itself on its head and now here he was, without a friend or a family member, or a wife, alone in a country where he was wanted dead, in a world that had no currency and, like him, might truly know no peace.

And so, Fritz would spend his final night in a country he had given so much to, schooled in the art of duty to one's country, knowing no glory to come of it, knowing no good to come of it, knowing no peace.

Chapter 30

Jubilation, elated disbelief, so many words of joy described the scene outside of Renaudin's bunker. Men and women were hugging each other, the song of the Internationale was sung boisterously, and rifles being fired into the air could be heard sporadically throughout the city. A chorus of joy not heard in France for so long emanated around Toulon, Marseille and many other cities that celebrated the great victory of the battle that came to be known as the Battle of Bourg-en-Bresse. The news had filtered through though slightly delayed, and two days later the news came in again that Dijon, the city housing the eastern-most republican command centre, had fallen also in a surprise assault.

But the Battle of Bourg-en-Bresse was the key and the door had been opened wide from the Swiss border to the Loire River. It was unexpected and though plans were made it had seemed to all and sundry that the offensive would fail with the first explosion of enemy artillery. The guns never fired and the 'red offensive' as Renaudin coined was able to go ahead with Renaudin's rag-tag army able to go into battle with their strength, their sheer numbers. The moral-sapping guns of the republicans and the Bonapartists watched on as the reds overran the defensive positions in a surprise advance that took the officers and soldiers completely by surprise. The hidden preparations had the desired effect and within sixty minutes of zero-hour Renaudin's forces had swept over the front lines and were running up the hills where enemy artillery was stationed, only then beginning to cause some, but little, effect on the battle. Scores of republican troops either surrendered or retreated to the point of desertion. With every push, every frantic advance of the offensive, more and more republican troops seem to peel away to the north in blind panic.

The Republican commanders had bet a king's ransom that the red offensive was going to take place at Vichy, in the central zone. Petain's advance had indeed stalled and was stranded just south of Nantes. Poitiers, on his right flank, had been retaken by the Republicans and were headed straight for La Rochelle on the west coast, threatening to cut off Petain's entire northern army and indeed himself, as he had travelled north also to provide a morale-boosting quality to his stalling offensive. A red offensive in the centre would have almost certainly saved Petain, allowing him to resume his offensive up the west coast. General Degoutte had personally seen to it that the central forces should defend in depth, forcing his already-stretched line to commit more forces to the centre at the expense of the eastern position. When he learned of the debacle and the part he played in it, he immediately resigned his command and was not seen in the general command centre at Orleans again. He had quite simply disappeared.

General Maunoury had agreed to replace Degoutte, promising to plug the gap that had been blown open. His strategic reserve consisted of the 'National Guard', the elite force that Victor Napoleon had grown, cultivated, and formed into a mythical force unstoppable to all. In reality, it was a small but well-dressed militia that provided security to him as well as providing good pageantry in photographs and propaganda. Nevertheless, they were deployed along with men from the defensive zone of the middle army to plug the gap. As Dijon fell without a fight the next defensive line was being made at Troyes and would be the final effective defensive zone in the east. The forces that were initially sent to check and halt Petain's advance were broken up and sent to reinforce the fast-depleting line. Regardless of the possible defensive solidity Maunoury genuinely now offered, the fact was clear that the republicans could no longer, for the time being, conduct any offensives of their own. The fact was slowly but irrevocably sapping the morale of the Republican forces, day by day.

Thus, the celebrations in Toulon were great and deserved. The revolutionaries knew that victory depended largely on a swift victory and now it seemed that they would achieve that very possibility. Renaudin was informed three days later as September waned, as did the number of good days for an offensive left of that year, that Petain was set to resume his march but not on Brittany, but on Le Mans, the last major city west of Paris to his position. Both Petain and Renaudin knew that they could not afford to be slowed to a halt for the winter of 1920 to set in. The spring of 1921 would be too late, the Republicans might find their strength and their courage again and who knows what international onlookers might do in that time. It would soon become common knowledge that Victor

Napoleon was due to travel to London and Berlin and perhaps even New York in the winter for aid. Victory had to come that year and before the rains made it impossible to send men and material to the front lines wherever they were.

Renaudin sat, brooding as much as ever, in his bunker whilst celebrations were still ongoing, not losing their vim and vigour with the passing of the days and the more inclement weather beginning to set in on the south coast of France. He sat pondering as more cheers rang out outside as heavy weapons were being unloaded from Russian crafts that had made their way from Rostov to Toulon. He sighed and rubbed his face as heavy artillery; the odd rusty armoured car and tank and munitions were dragged into the city along with new 'soviet volunteers' who made the city their temporary home. He paced slowly around the bunker as these new foreign brigades shared their stories about the successes of the Russian Civil War which was beginning to come to an end with the siege of Sevastopol.

Maurice had thought that the victory at Bourg-en-Bresse would bring him comfort. It was a seismic victory and it had brought the Soviet Russians into lending crucial assistance. Victory now seemed possible for the first time. But he could not find such comfort, he could not share such happiness. His bitterness seemed far too stubborn to push away in the matter of a few days because of a battle. He did not know why. Was it not enough? Was he just hungry for final victory? He did not know. But he started guessing. He was worried about the race between him and Petain. Now the tide seemed to be turning the race to Paris and to win the war suddenly became crucial again. Petain's forces were further north and though they were slower due to their heavier material they were more able to smash through hastily erected Republican defensive lines than he. The longer Renaudin's forces waited the more difficult it would be to overrun much better-prepared defences. The heavy weaponry only now making its appearance would take a while to arrive let alone to be taken up to the front. Perhaps this was causing him to feel no joy as all around him had been more joyous than anything for such a long time. Was he just smarter than them? He thought he was seeing a better and bigger picture and so distanced himself from all around him. Even the elated Frossard could not raise his spirits.

"Is it not wonderful? I get to practise my Russian language skills again" Frossard declared happily, almost dancing into the bunker in his wet overcoat. Rain had set in for a brief time and had only just eased, Frossard himself letting in the smell of recently fallen rainwater into Maurice's nostrils. "They await us. They await you. A picture with the Russian commandant and you together holding the banner of the Internationale. Send that picture all over the world and it will make you famous. Come, come!" he beckoned to Maurice with genuine enthusiasm and elation pouring down him along with the soggy rainwater. His bald head glistening with water allowed water droplets to drip down his face. It was almost as if he was crying tears of joy.

Maurice remained unmoved. He searched his feelings for a reason as to why he felt no joy, no excitement. Petain was a worry but who knew what miracles lay ahead for his own forces. Perhaps another well-timed offensive, another miraculous brainchild of his own making could occur again. He was celebrated for the tenacity and pig-headedness of his tactics and had now rocketed up to the nominal leader of the red movement throughout France without question. The battle had been a personal victory for him also, yet it did not seem enough.

"Allow me to refuse for now. There is a war I must win. There will be time enough for that sort of thing soon" he replied with nonchalance that irked the excited man.

"But it is important to show our solidarity with the Soviets immediately, as a token of thanks for their weapons and aid at least!" pleaded Frossard, breathless with anticipation. Maurice shook his head.

"There will be time enough for that." The corners of Frossard's smiling lips descended. Maurice seemed to retreat underneath his long coat, his tall and sleek body seemingly wrapped into a cocoon of greyish green wool. Frossard's concern with the course his friend was taking had grown and grown. Leon, his informal informant had reported back to Frossard that Maurice was increasingly erratic and had neglected to make any speeches to the fighting forces. Maurice had not once visited the front. The conversations Leon had overheard spoke nothing of the allegiance with the Soviets and any word of joining the Internationale never passed through Renaudin's lips. The man who once made it clear how envious he was of Frossard's ability to meet with Vladimir Lenin himself was nowhere to be seen. Now, with Maurice at the current height of his powers and the Soviets literally at his doorstep, the nominal head of the Communist forces of France was refusing point blank to meet with the Russians, sent over by Lenin himself. The transformation seemed all but complete.

"Then, what do I tell the Soviet commander?" Frossard asked, elements of despair creeping into his voice. Maurice shrugged, saying nothing. Frossard closed the door behind him slowly, watching his friend mumble to himself, and sighed as the gloss was well and truly removed from the joy he was feeling previously.

He walked off and decided to meet the commander on his own, and to the eventual consternation of Renaudin, decided to have the picture taken anyway but with Frossard in Renaudin's place. It was enough to turn Frossard into an enemy in Maurice's eyes. He saw Frossard as a man who would eventually stab him in the back and so he thought of ways that he might do it first.

With a copy of the photograph crumpled at the corner of the bunker a week later, Maurice searched once again for an answer. Why was he so bitter? Why could he feel no joy? By then, Petain's forces were at the gates of Le Mans having taken Nantes, Angers and Laval. Petain purposefully avoided the city of Tours as the Loire River it lay on was beginning to burst its banks causing havoc for defending and offensive armies alike. His own forces had torn over the Burgundian countryside, but he became visibly irritated when he learned that his forces had turned south of Troyes towards Auxerre, further south of Paris. He wanted to push north into the Champagne region. But why? It made no sense to go that way unless he wanted to take more undefended Republican territory.

Peeling back towards the centre seemed like the logical step, though that surely seemed the case to the Republicans noticing greater concentration of revolutionary forces threatening an encirclement of their defensive fortifications in the centre. They had pulled out of Vichy and the Auvergne region altogether and considered making greater defensive fortifications north of the Loire River where they could see out the rest of the year. In fact, the Republican forces were pulling each and every other way, General Maunoury had been found out as an incapable commander and was threatening to go the way of his predecessor, General Degoutte. Petain was halted once again and Le Mans but Maunoury could not find an answer for the marauding communist militia threatening his eastern positions which by now resembled heavily concentrated positions rather than long defensive lines.

Maunoury was given a great reprieve when Renaudin, himself declared supreme commander of the red forces with no equal after the success of the red offensive, ordered his forces to concentrate north, pursuing a direction towards to Marne River. No one could understand this move. All of the high-ranking officials in Renaudin's camp urged, with varying degrees of passion, for the supreme commander to change his decision. The central Republican forces were there for the taking. Petain himself sent telegram after telegram urging Renaudin to press home his advantage even though it meant handing the initiative over to him. No such reconsideration occurred and the boot that was on the neck of the Republican forces in the centre was lifted.

The stubborn Renaudin offered an explanation after a great deal of persuasion. He informed his commanders, which by now had increased three-fold in number due to the growing ranks of his forces now believing they were soon to be victorious, that the Champagne region would stretch the Republican line further, preventing a strong last-stand in the centre. With the Republicans forced to set up defences all along the Champagne region, including the defence of the city of Reims which was churning out much-needed weaponry for the Republican forces, Paris would be made easier to assault from Troyes which would be too difficult to defend. The plan seemed far too ambitious, and it would take too much time, but it seemed sensible enough to disperse the concerned commanders, giving Renaudin some respite.

They were not to know, however, that even Maurice Renaudin did not quite believe in the plan. Though he was unaware of the exact scale of ambition and genuinely believed that it would be effective, he knew that there lay better options ahead of him. So why did he believe in this plan so much above all else? The answer might indeed assist him in answering the question of his unrelenting bitterness. His bitterness had seemingly forced him to choose this most ambitious of options and though his orders were obeyed he had hoped that some form of common sense might prevail within him. It did not, and it only made him angrier.

In some ways, this plan allowed him to tear up more and more of France. He was content to see French cities, French countryside, French livelihoods and, if necessary, French people burned and ripped up, preparing the ground for a great restart. But even that idea only served to dampen his bitterness and hatred of the world. He was still consumed and even the thought of the entirety of France did not seem to be enough for him. He became afraid of his own vengeful heart, which seemed to feel like a great black hole as more and more of himself and all around him was being sucked into the eternal abyss awaiting inside his heart. Every notion of progress did nothing to change this.

Eventually, after waking up and splashing his face with water, a routine action he did every day to wake his mind and purge it from the troubled dreams he had endured that previous night, he latched onto a thought that might indeed rescue him from the vice that seemed to squeeze the life and soul out of his heart and mind. The desire to push northwards seemed to be the clue, so he raced from the town hall of Toulon to the bunker and studied the map. He dragged his hand along the large map, knocking down strategically placed flags indicating the positions of all of the major locations of forces across the entirety of France. Strategic officers frowned with confused watching the supreme commander, his sleek and slim long body dancing round the table, cause chaos on the map. His finger stopped at the spot and name of a town north of the central zone of the Champagne region. He grinned softly, allowing it to be seen only to those who stood just a matter of inches from his face. He dabbed his finger on the map a few times and stared at that spot for some time.

He looked up at the mildly bewildered strategic staff watching him and carried on pointing at the spot. "I want to go there" he informed them, receiving polite nods and the departure of one of the staffers. "I want to leave immediately and commence the offensive here now". Further silent nods followed. Maurice dragged his hand away from the map and left the bunker to prepare himself for the journey. It would be the first time he would visit the front and at such a volatile time in such a volatile area. None could make out why. They simply stared at the map and where he wanted to go. It seemed to be a town that at the moment lay just in Republican-held territory but was open to seizure.

The name of the town was Epernay.

Chapter 31

The roads north were teaming with people. Men, women, children, assorted belongings hastily stacked on horses and broken carts filled the paths, lanes and roadways heading towards the north coast. A huge mass of people almost moving in step together was pushing itself north slowly, lumbering on like nomadic people migrating from colder climates. Mercifully the rain of late September and early October had eased somewhat so people were not so badly drenched, the roads seemed good to take the strain of the weight of humans and human possessions. Children wept, women screamed, and men howled as the distant and not-so-distant sounds of explosions flashed through the huddled masses. Artillery shells were now in constant use and it only served to remind all that the war was reaching a final crescendo. The odd Republican soldier on Bonapartist militia member could be found at the edge of roads directing traffic as best they could but as explosions rumbled in the distance more and more of them fell into line themselves and made their way to the safe north.

There was no official word of safe havens north. Some had even fled to the German-held territory in the Franche-Comte and in the Lorraine region. The Nord-Pad De Calais had streams of refugees take cover behind the protective lines of German soldiers on the border. German soldiers even took to advancing their lines deep into Picardy to the Somme River in order to better solidify their lines against a potential over-zealous attack; but this was not expected. No orders were made for refugees to make their way north. The last time anyone had heard Victor Napoleon speak he had vowed never to surrender and would carry on the fight no matter what. "They shall not pass!", a phrase commonly known in the Battle of Verdun in the Great War, was invoked again, but at such a late and demoralised state of the war it served little purpose other than to sap further morale.

Word had been passed from town to town, from city to city, that the British Royal Navy was taking on refugees, those in genuine fear of their life, and ferrying them over the channel or perhaps to Canada, where they could naturalise in the French-Canadian quarter. These were not idle rumours, as those living or having reached the north coast could see the great battleships of the British Army, and even a giant portion of the demilitarised French navy docked at Le Havre, Abbeville, Cherbourg and Brest, taking on as many as they could. Women and children were prioritised but as it became more and more clear that the cause seemed lost for the Republican and Bonapartist forces companies of soldiers began finding their way onto the ships. Many refugees with the inability to prove that their lives were in immediate or passive danger were denied entry onto British ships and so relied on French ships to allow them on board, but this was no guarantee.

The refugees making their way from the Central region of France had been making their way north and so found their places on the ships easier. The refugees in the west too had found their ways to the north-west coast and onto boats as they had been affected by the movements civil war at a far earlier time. They were well prepared to jump ship. The refugees in the east, however, were the last to really get moving, and so the roads were particularly awful. The impending doom and slow progress forced many to take extreme means, pulling soldiers out of trucks and making their way north. Temporary barriers attempting to restrict refugee crossings to avoid stampeding were overrun. The scene was a mess with families either running to the German-occupied territory or the sea where there was no guarantee of safety. Arguments broke out all over the place over the correct course of action. The general consensus seemed to be taking a chance with the ships even if it seemed the riskiest.

The sheer desperation of people caused them to drag William Steele out of his car as he tried going the other way. William was forced out of his car at gunpoint as two men and their families forced themselves into the car; their rifles stolen from soldiers who had tried to halt their advance at a checkpoint further down the road. William was forced to set off by foot for most of the journey, coming across a stray horse that seemed on its last legs in an abandoned farmhouse. It had been tied to a wooden post and was screeching in desperation itself as it had been startled over and over again by artillery shells literally hitting all around the place in a completely random order. William freed the frightened horse, using his experience in his late father's farm to try to calm the poor creature. William cursed the shelling. It was indiscriminate and intending to cause as much fear as possible. Long range shells from long range artillery fired somewhere from the south peppered the ground as the revolutionaries signalled their intention to cause fear and distress all around the Champagne region.

To the bafflement of onlookers William rode towards the origin of the artillery shells, barely a soldier joining him in his journey south-east to Epernay. Without a saddle and a crudely-twisted rope he rode the horse as fast as it could, but the horse could not manage a great distance. It had been abandoned a while and so was not able to have the stamina required to make the greatest haste possible. It was probably why this horse had been overlooked by any refugees. To William it was the only option, and for the journey back it would be the only source of hope for a successful journey with Cecile and her very young son. Days passed, nights passed quicker and eventually after over a week of negotiating roads bursting to the brim with people and material he could see the silvery rooftops of the little town of Epernay. He crossed the field, the field he had looked over so long during his time in Epernay with his love from the window. The long lines of refugees started getting smaller and smaller as he went far off the well-trodden paths.

The horse panted and grunted, deciding after a heroic effort to take William no further. Its legs buckled, sending William to the ground with a sudden thud. William careered over the top of the horse's head and rolled onto the grass. William picked himself up and looked back. The horse had decided to go no further with its legs or with its life. It rolled onto its side, its eyes staring at William as the light began to dim. It thrashed its tail around until it finally went still. William shuffled up to it and placed his hands on its neck, patting it slightly. He wished it a good and speedy destination to the next life. He stood to his feet and started running towards the town, just over a mile and a half away.

The clouds seemed to roll in swiftly from the artillery guns far in the distance. The sun was obscured by the sounds and sights of death shrieking from the sky. It had all of the hallmarks of the memories of the Great War, only this was not really William's war to fight. He had fought in some way for his country, but as all soldiers did, he was also fighting for his own life. Here he was now fighting for a different reason, or rather running into the fight. He was fighting because of love, pure and simple. This was no fighting for a love deceitfully held within a photograph. His love was there, waiting for him. Tears threatened to push their way through his eyes but he begged for them to stay their journey for a while longer.

He was worried, or perhaps hopeful, that Cecile and her son had escaped anyway. They might indeed have taken the initiative and fled themselves, which would have been a good thing for them but finding them would be next to impossible. He feared though that they were still there. He had sworn to return and perhaps this would inspire them to remain and put themselves in potential danger. His mind raced as his legs raced and he was unable to know what he was hoping for. The town seemed still so far away. He could not see, due to the undulating plains, whether revolutionary forces were coming from the other direction. He just ran and ran, quietly enjoying the moments when he could not hear a single explosion for a time.

The town was deserted. People had either left or were cowering in their houses as artillery shells flew overhead or exploded a few hundred yards from them. It seemed incredibly odd to William why the revolutionaries should wish to shell this area when there were not fortifications of any sort. The only conclusion was that terror and fear were the primary reasons and they were having their effect with terrible success, even on William who had seen worse shelling before in his life. He wished to never relive those sights and sounds and here was smack bang in the middle of it all. Windows were either boarded up or smashed in. The cobble stones were still wet from the last spell of rain that fell a few days ago. The serene and heavenly nature of the town had been well and truly broken. It was a frontline town now, and it looked it. Luckily not one artillery shell had hit any part of the town, which seemed a miracle in some way. But the noise proved an equally effective deterrent for those who remained in the town to ever leave their houses.

His legs successfully took him into the town and he ran with great speed to the house of his love. The café façade was bare and the awning was tucked away. Cecile had done everything in her power to have her café open in sun, rain, sleet, or hail. It seemed incredibly odd to see it like this. He ran to the door and knocked loudly. The door remained resolutely shut. He banged on the door and shouted. "Cecile! Cecile! It's me! It's

William." His emotions got the better of him. "It's your William." He began fearing with dreadful joy that they had indeed fled.

This fear was broken when the door was unlocked and opened slowly. Charles stared up and smiled. "Steeley!" he said happily until he was whisked away from the door. Cecile's face then popped out and she stared at him. He looked at her, ashamed that he had taken so long to return. Though he had an excuse it paled into significance when considering how he had let her down so by being so long away. He stayed still, not sure whether he should hug her or apologise profusely and bid her good day. She did not let him ponder for long, as tears of joy fell down her beautiful face and she rushed through the door and flung her arms around his shoulders. She kissed his neck over and over again. She was elated, overjoyed at seeing his face. Her tears smudged gently onto his neck and he allowed a tear to finally be let out of his eye so it could roll down his face too. They kissed each other, slowly and smiling at the same time. It was a shared joy like no other.

"I feared you would not return" she whispered breathlessly.

"I feared you had left" he whispered back.

"I wait for you. We wait for you" she replied defiantly. "You do not get away from us so easily". They shared a stifled laugh and kissed again. The onlooking Charles made a familiar sound of childlike disgust, prompting the couple to stop kissing, both looking at Charles and smiling. A far-off explosion prompted the smiling to stop.

"We must leave immediately" he informed Cecile. "The revolutionaries could overrun the town at any moment".

"But, where do we go, William? We have more to lose from going, no?" She looked blankly at him, resting in his grasp around her waist and back.

"I do not know what the future will look like. Who knows what hell awaits this country, and you? We must go to England. I have a cottage there. Come, you must come with me. Both of you. It isn't safe here anymore."

"We cannot" Cecile replied with rueful sadness. "All we have is here. We cannot start again. I cannot start again after all I have built." She gestured around the house and the outside. "It would break me". William took her hands in his and held them close to him.

"You will not start again. You have me. You both have me. We will carry on and we will live together, be together and love together." Cecile looked at William and then looked away. Her eyes then opened, and her face seemed to light up. She looked up at William.

"You are asking me that question?" she asked innocently. He nodded.

"It's the question I've always wanted to ask you, since the moment I first saw you. I am ready to love, rather than to fix". He took out the feather made of newspaper from his breast pocket and showed it to her. The fact he had retained it all of this time filled Cecile's heart with joy and love. All she wanted to do was jump into William's arms then and there in the warmest and happiest embrace of all. She stroked the feather and looked up at him.

"How do you know that if you ask me to marry you that I will say yes?" she quietly joked.

"I don't" he whispered. "It is only a hope". She kissed him passionately as Charles had finally had enough and stepped back into the inner recesses of the house. For the first time in a long time, William's life finally felt complete.

The crackling of distant rifle-fire and a slight crescendo of artillery explosions prompted the two to follow Charles into the house. The house looked bare as always. Cecile informed William that ever since the Battle of Bourg-en-Bresse provisions had stopped coming, being redirected instead to supplying the army. She had to live on what she had stowed away for a rainy day and even that was running low. "I don't know how long we can hold out for" she said, gesturing to the low pantry stocks.

"Why have you not packed at all? Why are you not prepared to leave?" he asked, wandering why they had not even considered joining the great migration up north.

"There is nothing awaiting us up north. Our lives are here, until you returned."

"Then will you come with me?"

"You would not stay with us?" she asked with genuine wonder.

"Not when I can rescue you and take you with me".

"We do not need rescuing" she said stubbornly.

"I am rescuing what I love most in the world, save my mother" he informed her. Cecile nodded, appreciating the clever response. She pondered for a moment and then looked at him.

"It would not be an inconvenience? We do not wish to be a burden" she said. William approached her and wrapped his arms around her waist.

"It would be a burden to not have you join me". They kissed again but slower, taking a moment to enjoy the touch of each other's lips. Cecile noticed that William's lips were dry. She broke off and poured water from a bucket into a cracked glass, offering it to William. He dutifully drank the water, ever so grateful to end the thirst that had plagued him for days. Cecile nodded and moved to the stairs and shouted up to Charles.

"Charlie. Make a little knapsack. Take all that is near and dear to you. Only as much as I can carry!" she shouted. William cleared his throat. She smiled. "As much as William can carry!" A voice replied from the upstairs area.

"Then that will be everything!"

"Not everything!" Cecile retorted. "Excuse him, he has been very clingy to his personal things."

"We were all like that once, some still are in that phase" he joked. "Now hurry, it is a long walk up to join the crowds. I will lead in front, and you will lead behind. We hold hands in a chain so no one is lost. Understood?" She nodded her head. "It will take a while but if we hug as close to the German lands as possible then we may jump over the border if we are overrun. They will send us north with all luck but if we are very lucky the crowds will be our safety. We can get to the coast unmolested whilst the revolutionaries start converging on Paris. I say that gives us maybe a few weeks to arrive in Abbeville. That's the closest bet." He had thought this through on the long and arduous journey to Epernay. She was impressed and agreed with all he said, feeling reassured with the fact that the man she loved with all her heart had a grand plan. She held his hand squeezed. He squeezed back.

"Thank you. I love you." she said softly.

"I love you more" he replied.

"I love you most" she replied slowly and softly. He smiled, prompting her to smile and they shared another kiss.

Just then a knock on the door could be heard. Cecile had the forethought to lock the door beforehand which proved important when they could hear the doorhandle being twisted and turned in vain. They looked at each other, panic setting in on Cecile's face. She guided William silently to the stairs with her head and he nodded. He crept away but rather than going upstairs he hid behind the kitchen counter, behind the door frame to the kitchen. Cecile slowly crept to the door making no sound. The door banged louder. The sound of a car's engine running could be heard outside. The sound was forceful but not menacing. It seemed more inquisitive than anything. But no chances could be taken, not when all hell seemed to be breaking loose around them.

The door knocking seemed to stop and then start again. Whomsoever was outside did not seem to be persistent enough to want to break the door down. Cecile made for the door, breathing heavily no less nervous than one would be when about to confront an intruder. She dared not look and stayed by the door, hoping whoever was outside would eventually go away. They did not. She was concerned. Why did the visitor not assume no one was in? She looked around the house, noticing with an element of horror from the tiny cracks in the floorboards that Charles had turned the light on upstairs. No doubt the young boy was using the light to aid his search for the important things to take with him for the journey north. She did not grumble, bearing an innocent child no ill will for the follies and crimes wrought on his world by the adult world. She smiled, thinking of his inquisitive mind innocently believing that the world seemed safer with William around. Charles would not have made that mistake before

William's arrival. But it meant that she could not escape the visitor who had doubtless noticed the tell-tale signs of an inhabitant.

Against every desire in her body, she approached the door and slid the doorhandle to the left, unlocking the only barrier between her and the visitor. She hoped beyond hope that the visitor was just a frightened neighbour or a friend wishing to hide with her. Neither turned out to be the truth, as standing on the doorstep was the shape of an unknown man, tall and sleek with a ratty beard in an overcoat. He seemed to have a red lapel on his jacket. He was breathing heavily, similar to her own breathing. He seemed nervous, sharing a common feeling with her own. A car with three heavily-armed men in a running car could be seen behind him. They did not look happy but the man in front of her seemed overwhelmed as he took a brief moment to speak.

"My name is Maurice" the figure finally blurted out. Cecile noted that his accent indicated that he came from the North, not too far away from Epernay. "May I come in?" the figure asked. Cecile looked him up and down, noticing the indentation of a pistol in his left jacket pocket. She felt as if she had no choice. She wondered whether it might end the meeting quickly if she did so but she did not want to take the chance. She shook her head politely, but noticed his eyes light up with desire and passion. She did not know what to make of the sorry sight, but the man who had given his name as Maurice plunged his hand into the jacket pocket with the pistol inside it. She stopped her shaking head and nodded. He smiled and looked back nodding himself to the people in the car. Cecile retreated into the house, looking around to make sure the coast was clear.

Maurice stepped into the house and looked around. "Such a modest place. It is no less than perfect" he muttered, but Cecile was not listening. She placed wicker mats on the table in the sitting room, obscuring the map that she and William had forgotten to put away. She saw no sign of William, believing that he had gone upstairs, though the English fugitive was still taking his hiding place behind the cabinet on the kitchen side of the open-door frame. Cecile waited for Maurice to step coldly into the house and went back to close the door, locking it again. She took out what was left of her water and filled up a glass to offer the strange man.

"I'm afraid that I do not have any food to spare," said the frightened Cecile. "The war has made it- "

She was interrupted by the raised hand of Maurice, indicating that he wanted to speak. "I am well aware and all shall be well soon. All shall be well here most of all." His cryptic words bounced off the frightened skin of Cecile.

"Who are you?" she asked, his familiar voice and shape imprinted somewhere in her mind.

"The saviour of France. The saviour of people like you, neglected from the world. But no longer. And for you, my dear girl, I come to save personally." His words seemed to spook Cecile as it slowly dawned on her that he was talking to her specifically. "I am Maurice Renaudin."

Cecile stopped in her tracks. She knew the name. 'The Butcher of Paris', 'The Red Usurper of Toulon', 'The French Bolshevik', 'Lenin's French Chef', the titles she had heard of from people and newspapers had preceded the man's reputation both as forms of ridicule and forms of fear. His reputation as the man who killed the most people in Paris after the war was the most frightening of all, especially to her. The incident had placed his name in infamy across much of France and to her. She was frightened but in being frightened she felt herself being overpowered by his presence. She found herself sitting down, almost spellbound by his reputation and her body possessed by his wicked deeds she had read before. "Why are you here, Maurice Renaudin?" Maurice picked up a chair on the other side of the table and placed it right next to her, seated by her so his long legs advanced in between hers.

"I am here for you" he revealed ominously. "You have not known of me but I have known of you. I have seen you, here in your castle. I am your white knight. I have loved you and now I am here to rescue you and take you away from here." His words seemed sincere but overbeating.

"Where do you take me to?" she asked, dreading the answer.

"To Paris, with me. We are on the edge of victory. Soon, I am to be sat on the throne of the ancient kings, the old emperor and presidents past. I have loved you for years and now I wish to make good on the love I have felt with you. I wish to take you with me."

316

"As your queen or as your slave?" she asked with words finally coming out of her mouth in an effort to push him back.

"As my own, at my right hand, sitting atop this country."

"There is no sense in being atop a country that is just rubble and ash" she retorted, artillery shells exploding in the far-off distance. Maurice winced, and it seemed so audible a wince that it made Cecile think that this man was not used to being pushed back with words so much.

"It is a tactic of war to bring fear where there is no order" Maurice said reluctantly. "But they will soon cease and together we may build a new world from the old. A new France, with you as my love, the love I have had in my heart for so long." He pushed his hands out to her but she remained solid on her chair, unmoved by his gesticulation. She looked down and then straight into his eyes.

"This is not my France that you want to make. My France is being destroyed by you every day. You want to build but to do that you want to break. I will not let you do the same thing to me." Her categoric refusal shook Maurice into a dismissive temper. He leaned forward, hoping she might do the same so they might be able to kiss each other.

"Change is good. Change can take you from where you are now into something better. I offer you that not out of any other motivation than one of love. It is you and your people I love, for I am one of you. If nothing changes then you live and die here. Take my hand and follow the change I am going to make." He placed his hand on her knee, his palm facing upwards, hoping that she would place her hand inside. She did not.

"I do not know you yet you come in here saying all of these things. I do not believe you. You only come with death behind you, that is all." She clasped her hands together bringing them towards her. Maurice grunted and leant forward to kiss her but she moved her head away. He grunted and stood up abruptly, kicking back the chair causing it to fall on its back. Cecile, frightened to the core, stood up abruptly herself and backed away behind her chair. Maurice shot out his hand, grabbing Cecile's elbow. His eyes turned from passion to fire, fire brought on by his own inner rage.

"I come here triumphant. The whole of France lays prostrate at my feet. Her hordes of poor flock to my banner. What more do you want?

317

Do you want an empire? I will give you an empire! Do you want the world? I will bring it to its knees for you!" he said, raising his voice as if reaching the final punch of a political speech.

"No! I do not want that! I want my home. That is all! And you are intruding on my home. Get out and never return. Go back where you came from!" Cecile screamed, trying in vain to overpower his booming voice.

"This is no longer your home! It is mine and I will burn it down if I have to. You will come with me!" Maurice had turned into a creature of flame in front of Cecile's eyes. She backed away but could not escape is grasp. Her body awash with terror, she backed into the kitchen doorway, trying to reach the door to slam it in his face but his grasp rooted her arm to the spot. With every step she took back he took one step forward. She knew not what to do. She gasped, not wanting to call for William's aid so that he might continue to hide and be spared such a terrible fate. Her silence might also spare her child who had expertly kept silent during the whole ordeal. His grasp around her elbow seemed to dig into her skin. She felt faint as her mind contemplated her life as a slave to this man for her whole life. Were it not for her child, she would have certainly cut her throat with a strand of glass before she would succumb.

As her held body passed the kitchen door frame her eyes darted to the bottom left, to a figure behind the cabinet resting by the wall. It was William, crouched down. Her eyes darted quickly back to Maurice who by now was beginning to use his arm to reign her back to him. She gasped in sheer terror, wishing it would all be over. She closed her eyes hoping to wake up from the nightmare she had fallen into. "I love you!" Maurice bellowed "which is why you must come with me!"

William had concealed a broken table leg that had been leant against the cabinet. It had recently been snapped off the dining room table and replaced with a better one. He held it tightly in his grasp. He heard Maurice's voice and suddenly felt adrenaline coursing through his body. He stood up and clenched his open fist. "She's not coming with you" he hummed softly but aggressively and took the table leg in both hands and struck Maurice on his face, his grasp on Cecile released in shock and pain.

Maurice staggered back holding his face, his eyes darting back to the assailant.

"You. Englander! Get out of my way, you will be dead by the end of the hour!" Maurice exclaimed, taking out his pistol from his jacket and pointing it at William. William stood between Maurice and Cecile, unmoved, unbending.

"The lady asked you to get out. So, get out" William sneered, his heart beating fast as his eyes looked down the barrel of the pistol. Maurice shook his hand in anger, the pistol shaking up and down, indicating Maurice's inability to keep calm.

"This does not concern you! You are not welcome here in France! Get out yourself!" Maurice screamed wildly.

"Your reign of death has no power here. Not whilst I'm alive" he replied defiantly. His mind was filled with nerves but he let his heart lead, feeling no fear bend his body to the will of one who should have had the best of him. His feet were planted firmly to the ground.

"Then you will die!" Maurice growled and pulled the trigger to his pistol. The pistol clicked and for a moment William felt his soul leave his body. But this feeling was not due to a bullet piercing his heart, but just the final elements of fear leaving his body. The pistol clicked. It was unloaded. Maurice tried again and again but the pistol fired nothing. He glared at it with sheer anger as William took the initiative and used the broken table leg to swing with great force against Maurice's hand holding the gun. He smashed it against the pistol causing it to fly out of his grasp. William then grabbed Maurice's jacket collar, hauling him up from the floor, his long legs dangling behind him. William brought the hollow face of the wincing Maurice close to his eyes.

"You will have a burning France, but you will not have her" he whispered angrily. Maurice saw Cecile rest her shaking body against William's back, looking at him. Maurice's eyes darted between her eyes and his. His angry and vengeful mind whirred.

"Who are you? You are nothing. I have seen you before. You can give her nothing. You are a nobody!" Maurice said mockingly, trying in vain to release him from William's grasp on his collar.

"You will know me" William said, releasing Maurice causing him to slump to the ground on his knees. Maurice looked up angrily. "I am William Steele. Mark my name as one of many who defy everything you are and everything you stand for. William Steele." And with his last words he brought the broken table leg down and using all of his strength he smashed Maurice across the face, causing him to scream loudly in agony as he fell onto his back. He lay on the floor groaning in pain, his long legs writhing in agony. William breathed a bit, holding Cecile's waist to keep her close to him. They tried breathing slowly together, gazing with disgust at the writhing scourge of France on the floor.

They barely let out a few breaths when their heads darted to the locked front door. Banging could be heard again with voices shouting from outside. "Maurice! Are you OK? Leon! Break the door down!" The door creaked and strained as it did its best to hold against the shoulder of a strong man trying to get in. William looked around trying to think of what to do.

"Quick! Get Charles and bring him here!" He ran to the window. It was the same window he had spent many a morning, many an evening, staring out of in awe of the beauty of the field. He pushed the familiar latch and opened it. "We'll jump out of here!" Cecile nodded and whisked upstairs and grabbed Charles who had by now filled a knapsack expertly with his favourite things. She held Charles in her arms and carried him down the stairs as the door strained and cracked with every shoulder barge. William nodded at Cecile and jumped over the window ledge and held onto it as he dangled down and then hopped to the grassy ground below. The distance was about nine feet.

He turned around and raised his arms. Cecile then leant out of the window with Charles and dangled him out from the window. Charles's legs were just out of William's reach. "I'll catch him!" he shouted up to her. She nodded and gently let go of Charles. William caught the young boy, falling onto his back. Charles was alright and stepped off of William and looked up.

"Now you, mother!" Charles shouted up to Cecile. She nodded but was wary of the distance. She clambered onto the windowsill and as she did her eyes looked away to the horizon. She seemed to smile. William had his arms out. She pointed out.

"Look! Republican soldiers!" she shouted. William quickly gazed behind him. Not too far off around six soldiers in resplendent uniforms and helmets were running perpendicular to the town. She waved with her arms trying to get their attention. It seemed as if they saw her as they slowly broke off their line to start coming towards them. They were some way off, but the sight of them meant that perhaps there were more behind them. Republican and Bonapartist troops rarely travelled on their own without some sort of military support. To William, Charles and Cecile it was a godsend. The front door could be heard splintering.

"Quick! Jump!" William shouted. With as much strength and courage as she could muster, Cecile launched herself off the window ledge towards William. She fell towards him but just in front of him. She landed on the ground wincing in pain.

"My foot!" she exclaimed. She couldn't put much pressure on the leg.

"We must go. I will carry you. Towards the soldiers!" William barked softly, putting his arm round her to lift her on to his back. She shrugged off his arm and pointed to Charles.

"Help him, I will follow!" she exclaimed, shoving William away. He did as he was told, taking the young boy into his arms and hoisting him onto his left shoulder. He ran towards the soldiers who were running towards them. He looked back briefly to Cecile who, to his relief, was making good progress despite her painful foot. He turned around again and started running as fast as he could again through the shallow meadow up the gentle slope towards the soldiers who by now were just a hundred meters or so away. He looked round again and saw Cecile staggering a bit. He saw figures appearing by the window they had escaped from. He heard the sound of rifle shots coming from the house. He ran towards the soldiers and eventually got to within fifty meters. He set down Charles and told him to run to the soldiers.

"Help mummy!" he innocently ordered and ran towards the soldiers as fast as he could. William nodded and turned back. He ran towards Cecile who was lagging a bit further behind. He ran as fast as he could, hearing rifle shots now coming from the Republican soldiers, taking a few pot shots at the window. William jumped over a couple of little earth mounds with his eyes locked on Cecile. A rifle shot was heard and immediately Cecile seemed to fall face first into the soft grass of the meadow. William's heart stopped though his legs kept running. More rifle shots rang out from behind him as the figures in the window darted away. He reached Cecile who was lying on the floor. She mad managed to fall onto her side.

He looked her up and down. Blood patches were coming through her beautiful blue and white dress. She had been hit through one of her lungs, the bullet passing through her. Blood was pouring from the entrance and the exit wound. She was struggling to breathe until she coughed up blood. William fell to his knees pulling her up to his lap, letting her head rest on his lap. He tried to wipe away the blood streaming from the side of her mouth and took off his jacket, trying desperately to wrap it round her wounds to keep pressure on them to stop the bleeding. Her eyes rolled in their eye sockets looking up to him. The bleeding carried on unabated as she looked up at him trying all he could to save her. Tears were streaming down his face as he pushed heavily down on one of her wounds, using the other hand to wipe blood away from her beautiful flushed face.

With one of her hands, she raised it to his cheek. It did not stop him from doing all he could to save her life. She stroked his cheek a few times, managing to whisper ever so silently "It is ok". He looked down; his eyes bloodshot red with tears running like streams down his face.

"Don't. Don't. I will save you. Wait. The soldiers are coming" he replied through tearful gasps. He could not look at her face covered in blood from her mouth. His own hands were covered in blood so wiping blood away from her face would have no effect. He pushed down hard on her wound with all he could but it did not stop the bleeding. She carried on stroking his cheek. He fell onto her bloodied chest, sobbing into her dress. He leant back up and looked at her, clasping her hand on his cheek. He could do no more. "Don't go" he pleaded softly. "I need you here". She smiled and looked into his eyes with love that was insurmountable.

"My son stays with you. I am with him. Look after him" she whispered, the volume of her voice ebbing softly away. He nodded.

"I, love you" he whispered back to her, matching the volume of her voice. She smiled a blood red smile. He let a stifled smile out.

"I love you" she replied, returning the favour, stroking his cheek again and again.

"My life is incomplete without you" he softly pleaded, thinking one last plea might rouse her once more to live. She shook her head and looked into his eyes.

"C'est la vie" she uttered as her hand stopped stroking his cheek. Her hand went limp on his as her eyes slowly moved away from his to look into the sky. It was as if her eyes showed her soul the way to go. Her body stopped shaking as she finally let go.

William held her lifeless hand still, tears streaming from his face. His heart, which had been emboldened, was broken in two. He looked at her and caressed her cheek, wishing beyond all hope that she may come back.

A soldier shouted over to him, "Quick. We must go! It is not safe! We pull out to the North. Come with us. Quickly!" Rifle shots began to be heard as artillery shell explosions seemed to be coming nearer as if they were following the clouds of a thunderstorm. Indeed, even raindrops came from above, softly at first but the clouds overhead looked as if they were bringing with them a stronger and greater amount of rain.

William lay on his knees, finally letting the hand of his love fall beside her. He searched his feelings, wanting to know what to do. His mind and his heart tried with every sinew to regain some form of movement and feeling. He closed his eyes as the soldier nearby repeated his pleas. He opened them again and pushed his arms underneath the body of the woman he loved with all of his heart. He got to his feet with her body in his arms and staggered away, with the soldier letting a few rifle shots off into the town William had just fled from.

He staggered onwards, following the soldiers as they moved back up north themselves. He looked around for Charles who was being taken by the hand by another soldier. William knew not what to say to the little boy, whose mother's body he had in his arms. Cecile should be given a proper burial, he thought. She deserved that much.

"We came to pick up stragglers!" the soldier informed William. "We have cavalry support for this only. Anyone left after us is stuck here!" William looked around for the cavalry and noticed it not too far off in the distance. The riders were black. There must have been around seventy-five of them riding together. "Quick, we must go to them! They will take us to the trucks!" the soldier ordered. William continued to stagger forwards with tears unabated and the body of Cecile cradled in his arms, her head nestled into his chest.

As they approached the riders William noticed their uniforms, helmets and insignias. They were German cavalry units sent over to assist with evacuations. He looked into their faces and saw their blank expressions. They juxtaposed his emotions greatly and he was angered by them. Though they helped save him they were not the faces, the people, that he wanted to see at that time. He staggered towards them as they began circling round behind him to cover their escape. Some had rifles in their hands, some carried sabres. Their regalia rattled together as they expertly rode their horses around the small party. They seemed to belong to a larger detachment as William was told that this was one of several German cavalry parties operating in the area.

William staggered along as army trucks began to drive on the horizon towards them. He staggered towards them along with Charles and a few other straggling refugees, one or two from Epernay itself. Charles was now being carried by a soldier who had ditched his rifle in order to easily carry the small boy with his well-packed knapsack. William staggered more, the weight beginning to test his strength. He lurched to one side, turning his head to the ground to make sure he did not fall. He looked up at a nearby German horseman. He noticed familiar eyes. The rain began falling hard, bouncing off the helmet of this particular horseman. William gazed with his bloodshot eyes into this rider. The eyes staring back at him were those of Fritz von Falkenhayn.

William remembered the man easily. Those blue eyes were unmistakable. The helmet did nothing to mask the identity of the man who accosted him so greatly in that cell in Munich. William approached Fritz's whinnying horse and held up the body of Cecile to him. He shouted at him with utter anger and devastation. "Is this what you wanted?! Is this the peace that you wanted? Is this the justice that you wanted? Is this the order that you wanted?!" William shrieked the words towards Fritz who looked at him blankly. The horse writhed around as Fritz and William locked eyes furiously. The other German riders did not understand the Englishman's shouts but Fritz did. William held up the lifeless body of the once-beautiful woman to Fritz who stared with his eyes. Fritz rode away, staring back briefly before riding away, William staring back out of breath and exhausted, his heart bursting at the seams with emotion as the rain beat down faster and harder than ever.

At last, William, Charles and the soft body of Cecile were pushed onto a troop transport truck. William took Charles in his arms and they cried together as the countryside flew around them. The truck made its way north to Abbeville under German cavalry escort. Fritz von Falkenhayn lagged behind the trucks, looking into the one with William on board. He got a glimpse of William once more before he rode off, with a few tears falling down his own eyes as he rode off into a very unknown future of his own.

The truck did not stop until it finally coughed and spluttered to the coast where the British navy was waiting to take on stragglers, with many more refugees beginning to arrive from Paris where the final death rattles of the republic could now be heard.

Chapter 32

Ears ringing, heart pounding, eyes watering, the shots of pain running through the nerves all over the body. The excruciating pain seemed impossible to shift. The world seemed to spin and there seemed to be no way of stopping it. The floor was hard and cold to lie on. With every twist from side to side the pain seemed to throb with the regularity of a metronome. Such pain had not been felt in a long time. With every burst of pain, a convulsion of anguish escaped the lungs. The feelings of rage bubbling beneath the painful surface seemed to heat the body up and the pain only made it feel as if fire had enveloped everything from head to toe. For the body of Maurice Renaudin, on the floor of a house in Epernay, it was the final straw in a life that had been wrought with vengeful rage.

Hey lay prostrate for what seemed like an eternity. His eyes were closed and watering after the second strike to the head from a blunt object. His teeth gnarled and grinded together in a symphony of anger that would have torn the entire planet in two. After a minute or two his arms flayed around searching for something to hold on to that might help him get his bearings straight but nothing seemed to fall into his grasp. His arms bumped against random things but none were helpful to him. He felt as if he would never get up, perhaps even never see again. He felt hot liquid on his face, knowing it to be blood running from somewhere he could not feel, the numbness setting in quickly giving him a modicum of respite. He cried for help. "Varine! Leon! Somebody!" He could hear shouts and the breaking of wood. He heard the voice of the man who struck him shouting also and it made him grind his teeth further. "Help! Kill him!" he shouted before losing consciousness.

The scruffy leader of the communist forces was brought to after being brought to with water splashed over his face. He could only see out of one eye, the other refusing to let its eye lid open. The beams of light stung his barely-open eye as his brain struggled to contemplate the real world. His one eye darted around looking for something to help his head from spinning. He winced from the sounds of loud and obtrusive rifle fire. He looked over immediately to where the man who assaulted him had stood, seeing only Varine and another of his entourage firing their rifles out of the window. He looked at his saviour, the ubiquitous Leon, gazing down to him on bended knee. He looked up, knowing full well the shame of his vulnerable and bested state. He feared what Leon might think of him.

The long-time defender of Maurice cared little for the ups and downs of the man he had sworn to protect. Leon was unmoved and undeterred in his support for his commander. Though the two were never quite on the level of friends the undying loyalty of the grand and strong Leon had earned Maurice's unshakable respect. As a man of few words, he was the perfect man to listen to Maurice who never stopped talking during the less interesting times. And so, with his commander on the floor in agony, he did all he could to rouse Maurice at least to a state that allowed him to stand and walk. He wiped a trickle of blood away from Maurice's face and ear and got him to his feet. "The town will be secured very soon" Leon said in a bid to reassure and distract the incredibly dazed Maurice. The broken commander leant heavily on Leon, patting his arm coldly.

"Good. What of the Englishman?" The shots rang out again and again from the window. Leon helped Maurice to the window and he gazed above them, watching two figures running towards each other over a hundred meters away. He noticed enemy soldiers even further away, some on bended knee firing their rifles towards them, quite wide of the mark but getting closer with every shot. A rifle was fired and one of the figures fell to the floor. He looked expectantly, hoping with sheer venom that the Englishman had seen his last day. His one good eye did all it could to strain to see. He could not see far very well, but this was a hindrance that had plagued him for years. He never liked to wear his spectacles because he had believed that they demeaned his image. But right now, he could see little and wanted to, needed to see what had happened. He reached in his long jacket for his dusty old spectacles which had hardly seen the light of day in months. He pushed them to his good eye and strained again.

The sight seemed too gruesome for him to stare for any length of time. He saw the figure of a man, kneeling down. The sight gave him a breath of hope but it was dashed when the figure of a woman, convulsing with blood, lying on his lap. The woman he had loved for years, fantasised about for years, desired beyond all desires in the world, was dying in front of his eyes. He threw his spectacles to the floor and fell forward between the two men at the window and collapsed onto the window sill, gripping it tightly in mournful rage with his spindly hands. He wept, feeling the tears sting his eyes, the sorrow stinging his heart, as rifle shots pierced the brickwork around the window with increasing levels of accuracy. Maurice was hauled from his shoulder back as the bullets started flying and hitting the window frame, some making their way into the kitchen itself, smashing an empty pot and the door of a head-height cabinet, swinging the little latch open. Everyone crouched to the ground as more rifle shots pinged past. Varine took a few glimpses above but was forced back down.

Maurice wept with anger and hatred, soothed by the one solitary thought that the man who attacked him, William Steele, would be deprived also by the life of the woman he too loved. It was a solitary thought that barely brought any comfort, but it was a thought all of the same. Maurice looked around the place, noticing his discarded pistol that had let him down so greatly. He crept towards Varine as bullets carried on ringing around the window. "Why did you give me an unloaded pistol?" he screamed into his ear. The grimacing man looked back at him.

"I did not know it was unloaded" he shouted back, though the answer seemed insincere. Maurice stared at him and did not press the issue, pursing his lips and creeping away until the rifle fire seemed to stop. They waited for a few minutes before Varine once again popped his head back up. He stared over and saw the soldiers forming a rear-guard as the man could be seen carrying a body away with him. "Do not get up until our reinforcements take the town. There may be more of them!" Varine seemed overly cautious but with the leader of the reds only just managing to escape danger perhaps caution seemed to be the right thing to do. The party of four paused briefly until they heard scuffling and the sound of men running near the open window. Varine looked up again to see communist partisans, three of them, rushing up the now-vacated shallow meadow up the gentle slope of the hill.

Maurice stood up and placed his hands on the window sill. His hands shook as he reached for his spectacles. He once again put them to his good eye as he stared into the meadow. He saw grass marked in blood. There was too much blood there for the woman to have survived. He knew deep in his heart that she had been killed. Her body was not there though. He grimaced and banged the window sill with his fist. He turned away and stormed out of the house. "Start the car! Follow that man. Follow all of them! Get any car or truck you can find and bring me men to follow us!" he barked.

"No!" Varine shouted with sheer insolence that made Maurice growl loudly in anger. He ignored Varine and jumped in the passenger seat in the car banging the side impatiently as drops of rain began hitting the top of the car. Varine ran to the car and grabbed Maurice's shoulder. He looked with sheer contempt at one of the only men that had ever been allowed into his inner circle. "Leave them! The woman is dead! You must go to Paris!"

"No, no I want to catch them! We need to get them!" he shouted back, banging the side of the car again. Varine persisted.

"France is the prize! Not one random man, or a dead woman." Varine noticed Maurice wincing at the thought of his love being dead. He pushed on as the rain began falling heavier and heavier. "She's dead! Let her go. To Paris! The final battle. We need you there!" Maurice panted with rage, collecting himself, his one good eye darting around as if searching for his thoughts and perhaps his wits. He looked straight ahead, nodding. The other three clambered in to the car and they made for the most direct road to Paris. The final battle was about to begin.

The war had swung decisively and irrevocably into the revolutionaries' favour. Le Mans finally fell to Petain and he advanced with all speed to the west of Paris. Troyes fell two days later after fierce and costly fighting. The pyrrhic victory for the communist forces could be managed; there were more than enough replacements. For the Republicans, the sheer loss of men and resources was too much to replace. The central defensive line had held but at the cost of a great encirclement as on the second of October soldiers from Petain's thirteenth regiment met up with the advanced red guard from Lyon met at Orleans. The ancient city of the kings of France, where the Orleans Accords had been signed effectively giving Napoleon V supreme command of the Republic, fell without a fight.

The city was declared an open city. To the Republicans and even to Petain the thought of damaging the ancient and revered buildings of the city was just too great, even if it cost the Republicans over fifteen-thousand encircled men. General Maunoury had managed to extricate himself from Bourges just south of Orleans but the destiny of the republic seemed all but set.

The greatest prize of them all; the city of Paris, lay open to the revolutionaries. General Maunoury was ordered by Victor Napoleon, one of the first and last general orders that the puppet commander ever truly gave in military affairs, to defend the capital at all costs, if only to give the evacuation operations more time. The General was ordered to remain in Paris and go down with the ship if he had to. Maunoury replied to the hallowed telegram asking for powers of surrender should he be unable to repulse the enemy. He was granted the solemn privilege, holding in his hands the ultimate fate of the French Third Republic. He set up his city command in the Garnier Opera House with his advanced command base in Notre Dame. He believed that the revolutionaries, now holding the greatest collection of heavy artillery since the final days of the Great War, would never shell the city, especially not the great cathedral of Europe.

General Maunoury had just shy of ten thousand men and Bonapartist militia at his command, but he knew that he was greatly outnumbered and the wavering morale of his forces would not likely hold out for long without considerable help. He contemplated greatly on his strategy and made the decision to wire all of the bridges with high explosives in an attempt to greatly slow down the enemy. He hoped that it would never come to that, as the bridges themselves were of great historical reverence, and would no doubt be viewed as a terrible crime in the eyes of all of France. But he gave the orders all the same, believing that the city would forgive him were he ready to blow them up. He waited atop Notre Dame's high bell-tower for the hammer to fall, to the consternation of the deacon of the cathedral hoping to have the great building spared any part in the oncoming storm.

The Seine River lay in front of the revolutionaries and the city had prepared greatly for this coming battle. The great commanders, the great unlikely friends of the revolution, Marshall Petain and Maurice Renaudin were due to meet up before commencing the joint attack on the city. They met in a wooded area just outside Ollainville. Both parties had driven to the secretive location to finally meet and exchange pleasantries and discuss the strategy for the upcoming battle. The October rains were really setting in but neither party wanted to delay the meeting and especially not to delay the attack. The secret location in the wood was designed to be where both could feel safe in a land that was not exactly friendly to the presence of the revolutionary forces of both sides. However, both sides had in their mind's ulterior motives; chickens that were coming home to roost.

Marshal Petain arrived first with a small entourage of only two men. He did not want to appear too confrontational reminding himself and his aides that Varine, most likely to attend, was a keen ally of his and he had all the proof he needed to assure himself and others that Varine could be trusted. Renaudin drove later accompanied by Varine and Leon, the other man in the car from Epernay ordered to stay in the car which parked itself not too far away from the meeting point. Both parties were terribly suspicious of each other especially as the race to Paris seemed to be a draw, permitting neither party to declare themselves the more superior of the two. They would have to settle for an equal share of the glory and thus the power; a fact that seemed impossible to stomach when both were so close to the end.

Petain waited impatiently, but was in a jovial mood. He had the whip hand and the insurance policy of having three men he could trust at the meeting, one standing behind Renaudin ready to do away with the suspicious communist leader. He had grown weary of Renaudin especially after learning of the influx of Russian weaponry, Soviet volunteer forces and allowing for the destruction of many strategic and historic parts of France in his murderous advance northwards. He had still not forgotten the march that was stolen on him in the initial commencement of the civil war. What irked him even more was the fact that Renaudin had scored great and successful victories. The eastern offensive had stretched the Republican lines, caused havoc and terror both behind and within the lines of the Republicans. The offensive into the Champagne region rather than immediately making for Paris had stretched the lines further and had acted as a feint as the Republicans had taken forces off more vital areas to set up defences north-east of Paris, making the southern approach to the capital city a far easier venture. Renaudin was proving to be an adept commander, or so he thought. He was also wary of the sheer numbers of forces now at Renaudin's disposal. Petain's army was impressive, well drilled and professional, but it's finite numbers inevitable dwindled with each element of resistance against his forces. He had to slog it out with not many men whilst Renaudin's rag-tag rabble had allowed to rush through with relative ease, save the battle of Troyes which was bloody but impressive itself.

Petain consoled himself with a singular thought. No matter how strong the red snake was that wrapped itself around his legs one cut of the head and the whole body would go limp. Renaudin was impressive but vulnerable. He intended to make good on his thought. He had always intended to use Renaudin until he was of no more use, at which point he would be disposed of. The ace up his sleeve would be the insurance policy for the fate about to fall upon a man he held a bit of respect for in terms of his military prowess, but great contempt for what he stood for, and indeed what he looked like.

The battered commander, still looking worse-for-ware after the assault on him in Epernay, arrived half an hour later. Petain was sitting on a fold-out stool with his two adjutants, Major Rolland by Petain's side, close by. Renaudin was helped to the clearing in the wood until he was in eye-sight of Petain. He shrugged off Leon's assisting arm and walked upright towards the Lion of Verdun. His eye was still unable to be opened and chose not to wear anything to cover it. He preferred instead to wear the injury with pride. He walked over to Petain and bowed sarcastically. The wily marshal waved his hand courteously. "It has been a good few months since we have met, my dear Renaudin" the infamous voice of one of France's heroes said wryly. "And yet here we are on the edge of destiny". He looked the tall, bearded, slender man up and down. "I see you have been in the wars yourself. Not too badly afflicted, are you?" he asked with a smile, insincerity dripping from his lips.

"I am well enough" replied Maurice, returning the grin. They looked at each other, an awkward silence descending upon the party. Petain breathed in slowly, breathing out even slower.

"Shall we get down to the battle in front of us?" Petain asked, looking over to Varine briefly, Varine's eyes silently informing Petain that his man was still his. "I believe your men will need to attack in every direction whilst we seize the second-most eastern bridge in the city." He clicked his fingers for one of his adjutants who reached behind him, prompting a twitch from Leon, until he revealed a furled-up map. Major Rolland unfurled the map slowly, stopping abruptly as Maurice raised his hand.

"We intend to shell their positions until there is no defence to speak of in the south of the city" Renaudin said without emotion. "Our forces will sweep through the city after a suitable bombardment with short- and long-range artillery". The information seemed to wrangle in the ears of Phillipe Petain.

"You are presenting me with a *fait accompli*?" he asked, curious as to how Renaudin had come to negotiate the future proceedings.

"In more ways than one, Marshal" Renaudin stated, nodding at Leon who revealed a pistol discreetly concealed under his tunic. The ever-dependable bodyguard loosed off a couple of shots into Petain's adjutants, causing them to fall to the ground. Major Rolland squirmed for a few seconds before falling still, similar to the other man. Petain jumped from his stool and backed away, fumbling for his pistol that had been too-well holstered at his side.

"What is the meaning of this? You mean to double cross me?!" accused Petain, fiddling furiously with his holster in vain. He looked aggressively at Varine who himself was doing the same. But before Varine could reveal his pistol the barrel of Leon's pistol was pointed right at his own temple. His eyes moved quickly to Renaudin.

"Maurice? What is your man doing?" Varine protested, holding very still. Maurice walked over to Petain, flinging his arms from the holster latch which would not budge and forcing the pistol out himself. He turned back towards Varine standing perfectly still, Leon's pistol held cold against the side of his head.

"I know why you gave me an unloaded pistol. If there was a man with a gun inside that house, I would be dead, which is what you wanted, isn't it?" Maurice asked, coldly. Varine shook his head nervously.

"A mistake, I assure you!" Varine pleaded, something out of character for the otherwise assured man.

"The mistake was trusting you" Maurice replied, giving a slight nod. Leon pulled the trigger. Boris Souvarine, the dynamic man of Maurice's inner circle, dropped to the ground lifeless. Maurice stared at the body of his once-trusted friend and then turned towards Petain. "Your spy is gone. My spy remains, standing in front of you". Leon clicked his neck.

"You will be making a terrible mistake. My men will not follow you. France will not follow you. You will be cast out!" Petain yelled furiously, hoping his words might be heard somewhere from someone who might come to his rescue. "You need me!" Maurice smirked and sighed. His one good eye looking around the place as he placed his arms on his hips.

"You intended to steer France in another direction. I wish to burn her, and start again. Those who do not follow me will be burned themselves. In my new France will not need the likes of you. The world no longer needs the likes of you". He nodded once more, Petain put his hands in front of his head, but the erstwhile hero of France could not prevent his untimely fate. The Lion of Verdun, famed for his never-say-die attitude, was slain in the woods outside Ollainville. Maurice turned away, Leon looking at what he had done. He grimaced, having been the one to kill one of France's heroes. But he swallowed his pride.

"Do we bury him?" Leon asked. Maurice was already walking away back to the car.

"Take his body and put it in an open casket. We will parade him around the city when the battle is won. He died in battle, his final words being a message of support for us. Make it so". The body of the old field marshal was taken in secrecy outside of Paris once Petain's own car outside of the wood had been destroyed. With preparations set, Maurice returned to the outskirts of the capital by the large Russian artillery pieces. He nodded, commencing the final great bombardment of the war.

Paris was ablaze. The city seemed to be an anvil for the hammer of the Gods. The bombardment commenced at seven-thirty in the morning and did not stop until twelve-past-one in the afternoon. The Parisian inhabitants were either gone, dead, or cowering in what was left of their houses. Artillery shells rained down indiscriminately, obliterating old and famous buildings, statues and monuments. The Eiffel Tower itself was hit though it remained standing. One of Notre Dame's great bell towers had been smashed to pieces. The Arc de Triomphe was broken into two. The Palais du Senat was a smouldering crater and the Louvre Palace had giant gaping holes as if a giant had torn large chunks out of the grand building with its hands. General Maunoury looked on as the beauty of the city was razed to the ground. He watched helplessly as shells exploded all around him. He had counted on such a horrendous act never occurring, believing that even the revolutionaries would not stoop so low as to deal a terrible blow to the ancient city. Paris was bleeding, rubble cascading into the river causing the already full vein of mother nature to rise higher and higher. The rain did little extinguish the flames dotted all over the city beginning to grow and rise higher into the hazy and wet October sky.

The defences he had planned had counted on the absence of artillery shells. Great blockades, static defences, littered the city streets. He hoped to funnel the enemy forces away from the windy streets into the big high streets where they would face the heavier weapons at his disposal. All at once, those plans had gone and he could only sit and watch from his precarious vantage point in the damaged cathedral straddling the Seine Reiver as his limited forces were blown apart, the lucky ones eventually resurfacing from the smoke and the rubble either to reform ranks, retreat to the river or run away.

Though the ending of the sinister and morale-sapping artillery bombardment eventually did subside, respite was not awarded to the Republican and Bonapartist defenders. The awful noise of a rampaging enemy from both sides, south of the city, could be heard. The waves of the enemy were fast approaching from their jump-off points and the rattling of machine guns soon followed as the brave defenders remaining stead-fast at their posts around the outskirts let forth their volleys. Thousands, hundreds of thousands of Renaudin and Petain's forces descended on the city, infecting the city and festering amongst the small broken streets. The battle was well and truly under way.

General Maunoury, rings around his eyes betraying the look of a man unable to sleep in the slightest, pursed his lips as he watched defensive point after defensive point become overwhelmed with the sheer number of the enemy. "Take as many as you can with you!" he shouted down the poor-quality radios, his hands jittery at the prospect of signalling to the demolition corps to begin the destruction of the ancient bridges.

A stray artillery piece careered into the cathedral, shaking the entire structure to the core. Many inside feared the old building would not soon survive another blast. "It is best you retire to the Garnier, General" Colonel Eugene, closely and happily placed at the disposal of the commander of the city. Maunoury, reluctant to leave his post on the Seine, nodded, knowing that another major setback would require the bridges to be blown. Many of his forward command post retreated over the river, itself attempting to invade the city with its strong, surging, current. The rain soaked through his tunic as he rushed over to the north of the city which burned less but buckled under the great pressure of battle no less than its southern brother.

The Garnier Opera house creaked, spared a direct hit but crumbling under the pressure of explosions rattling its foundations. This was an affliction that plagued many of the bigger buildings in the city. Maunoury was anxious to get a good vantage point of the battle but the roof of the opera house was vastly inferior to that of Notre Dame. He had to rely more on what was being pushed through, or screamed through, the short-wave radio sets scattered around the central hall eagerly staffed by nervous and worrisome communications officers. It proved to be decisive, as the delay in getting a clearer picture of the situation only served to cause confusion and the loss of the initiative.

For, in truth, the Republican forces were successfully defending large parts of the city. All sectors, though crumbling slowly, seemed to be holding. The rubble made passing through roads slower and provided the defenders with adequate defensive positions from which to hold back the hordes of revolutionaries. A daring officer by the name of Major Felix even led a counter-attack down the Saint Michel Boulevard. Unfortunately, his advance was not met with much support and he was surrounded, cut off from retreating and cut down in the Luxembourg Gardens in the shadow of the smoking ruins of the Senat Palace. Maunoury only learned about the daring advance twenty minutes after it had been snuffed out.

"The bridges are not to be destroyed until as many as can be withdrawn from the southern part of the city are successfully withdrawn" Maunoury barked down the phone radio. He had been pleading to keep avenues open for retreating troops so they could carry on the fight, but as the rainclouds further obscured the sun's light as it began to set for the last time on the city the situation seemed to be reaching a terrible climax. Isolated reports of revolutionaries successfully crossing bridges in small packs reached the Garnier Opera House. Blowing the bridges seemed to be the only thing left to do to try to rescue the battle.

General Maunoury ran over to the phone with a direct link to his demolitions corps. He gave the order he wanted never to give. The situation seemed hopeless as artillery shells seemed to fall even faster on the northern part of the city hampering the necessary rapidity of reinforcement and redeployment in the southern parts of the city. The noose seemed to be tightening. His orders were obeyed and he waited anxiously for the minute hand to reach five-past-eight in the evening. The second-hand danced past and he closed his eyes, imagining the whole of French history descending in upon him to swallow him into a dark and unending abyss.

Explosions, one after another, could be heard. The grand opera house waved and shook with every shockwave passing underneath it. Paris felt as if it were about to fall into a chasm of its own making. Maunoury counted the explosions in his head. One...two...three...four...five...six... seven...eight. Each explosion shook the hall again and again. Paintings and decorations not taken down during the hasty withdrawal of civilian life days before fell to the ground with the sounds of great thuds, the sound of smashing and the sound of creaking from wooden beams and bricks both old and new. But the explosions were not complete. At least four more should have occurred. Maunoury opened his eyes again and barked down the phone. "Is it complete?" he asked. There was a long pause until a shaky voice replied from the dark abyss of the radio.

"No, General. Three, perhaps four, failed demolitions. The fuses must have been compromised by artillery strikes. Please advise!" What could Maunoury say? That was his last gamble. He dropped the phone in blank astonishment, the voice coming from it repeating "Please advise!

Please advise!" The General was seen walking away to the Green Room of the opera house and was not seen again for some time.

Maurice Renaudin arrived at the outskirts of the city. He saw the broken spire of Notre Dame, the Eiffel Tower leaning over itself like a man punched in the stomach. His one good eye was joined by his other eye recovering slightly but still hazy in its sight. The city was ablaze and though he felt nothing but pain and anger inside the sight made him smile for the first time in a long time. The car stopped when it came to the first main road blocked by rubble. Renaudin had been assured that most of the southern part of the city had been secured.

The lone commander of the revolutionaries got out of the car. He was noticed by dozens of his men passing through to the front. They began cheering wildly. More and more men peered round and popped up from where they were to look at the source of the commotion, joining in with their cries of joy soon after they noticed Maurice. Renaudin would not usually be so close to the action of a fight. He feared for his life too much. He feared death too much. But this time he clambered out of the car and walked slowly but assuredly towards the front himself. Leon got out of the car and jogged close by him. The cheering grew and grew until it threatened to drown out the sound of artillery shells screaming overhead. He was cheered like a hero returning to his people. He was a hero in their eyes.

Swarms of revolutionaries ran to the bridges, preserved by fate. A few remained, oddly giving the defenders only a few areas to defend in. Their stout defence held up the rampant attackers until they began to be flanked by marauding revolutionaries who had either taken a long and winding route through one of the bridges on the outskirts of the city or had waded over the high river of the Seine, clambering to the other side. Eventually the fighting reached the inner ring around the Garnier Palace itself. The artillery fire had stopped as the fighting had reached the last lines of defence. Republican and Bonapartist forces fled to the north of the city, shedding their weaponry and tunics as fast as they could run. Those who remained found themselves enveloped by the attackers who encircled the inner ring until they pushed their way to the Garnier Opera house itself.

Rifle fire was exchanged in furious flurries from each side. The edifice of the opera house was sprayed in lead until it was barely recognisable. Eventually, Renaudin's forces pushed with sheer recklessness to the doors of the opera house. The locked doors were pounded with shoulders, splintering the barrier between the hell outside and the victims inside. The door splintered open after a good twenty minutes of fighting. Defenders inside the building flung their weapons to the ground and their hands in the air as Renaudin's forces swarmed all over the building dragging anyone they could find into the street to parade to the hordes outside or dragging anyone to be shot against a Parisian wall. Many chose the latter as a massacre of modest proportions occurred with gruesome regularity.

Three men rushed in. One carried the red flag of the Internationale. One carried the tricolour with the red star in the middle; the emblem of Renaudin's communist movement. They made for the roof and when they reached it, they unfurled the flags and waved them above the baying crowds lining the streets in sheer delight. General Maunoury was hauled from his hiding spot in the Opera House Green Room and paraded through the streets. He was pushed with force through the streets as he was taken with two aids to the steps outside of the smouldering Elysée Palace where he was pushed in and taken to the balcony where he could be seen by the masses of revolutionaries, Petain's and Renaudin's own men and women pouring into the courtyard and nearby streets, some firing rifle shots into the air, complimenting the delirium within the ruined city. He was forced to wait for the arrival of the hero.

Maurice Renaudin strode through the broken streets of the city in a symbol of masterful pageantry. He managed to find a horse and cart and on it he placed the body of the Lion of Verdun. The horse and cart rolled on behind him as if he was leading a solemn but grotesque funeral procession. Those who belonged to his camp cheered in delight at the triumphant march of their leader. Those who followed Petain removed their helmets in respect and bowed their heads. To all there the great marshal had died in battle, his dying words articulating his unwavering support to his great friend, Maurice Renaudin. After a long and costly battle all desired to believe the lie, and in the minds of all revolutionaries Renaudin was declared the great leader of the revolutionaries.

Renaudin's grotesque funeral procession reached the Elysée palace. The victorious mob gave way as the procession reached the steps of the palace and Renaudin entered, making his way to the balcony. As he passed through the palace, climbing the steps of the great presidents of the nation, flags of the republic being cut from their hanging positions, statutes of the past destroyed or pulled down and dragged away, he felt the weight of destiny on his shoulders. It was as if the heavens had opened for him to ascend into the realms of the great men of history. The choirs of angels rang in his ears amidst the cheers he could hear outside. Flags fluttered down, great monuments to the France of old desecrated and destroyed, as he made his way to greet the adoring crowds.

As he made his way to the great doors to the balcony, flanked by a few of his trusted followers, he heard the sound of a familiar voice. Ludovic Frossard, the oldest of Renaudin's collaborators, had made his way also to the palace. He had only a pistol in his hands though he too looked as if he had done his fair share of fighting. He looked desolate though, and worried.

"Maurice. Remember, this is for all of us! The people of the world. The workers, the peasants, the downtrodden. This is for them! Tell them that! You must! Send a message to Russia and the world! Tell them that we are here for their freedom as well as our own!" Frossard exclaimed, thrusting his fist into the air. Maurice stared back at him blankly, his hurt eye giving in once again to its pain. He shook his head.

"I will break our people before I look to the world, and when I do it will be our people who will make them bend the knee". Frossard watched as the megalomania finally gripped Maurice's body whole. "This is for no people. This is for destruction. And what emerges from that destruction will be one that you and France will be proud of". Frossard looked at Leon who stared back blankly also, revealing no emotion himself. Frossard lowered his fist a broken man, watching his once-good friend turn away to lead France into a very different future to the one had they both talked about years ago.

He threw open the doors to the grand balcony to the great roar of his victorious followers. He let them greet him with sheer ecstasy. The vagabond straggler from Sedan was now revered at the top table of France.

He raised his arms and another roar rose to his ears. He looked over at General Maunoury with contempt. He raised his arm to quieten the crowds as they struggled to hold themselves together. Renaudin nodded his head slowly at General Maunoury who was released temporarily from the grasp of his captors and he spoke.

"I, as the commander of the garrison of the French Republic, officially surrender the city to you. May God have mercy on the people of France". He was booed and jeered at as Renaudin raised his head and once again quietened the crowds, who did so quicker.

"So ends the final moments of the Republic that so ashamedly became the whore of Germany. So begins the dawn of the French Commune, and the glorious new dawn of a new people from the ashes!" shouted Renaudin, raising left fist as his right hand reached into his jacket pocket for the pistol of Phillipe Petain. He raised it to General Maunoury and fired a shot straight into his heart. The body of the General fell back before being shoved over the side of the balcony to the ground. The crowd burst into great cheers of joy as Maurice once again took the cheers and applause with showmanship, though in his heart he still felt utter hatred and disdain.

He looked over the people, shouting and screaming his name. The flags of the tricolour with the red star in the middle was waved all around and the delirium sweeping in front of him dragged his head into a drunk stupor. His chest broadened more than ever before. He was on top of the world, and yet he still felt no joy, only hatred, only revenge. Even now, with the country at his feet, he did not feel it was enough. He thought of the woman he lost, dead to him and the world. He thought of the man who took her away. His teeth gnashed together behind his lips. None could see his anger and fury remain despite the great victory attributed to him that day.

He turned his back on the crowd, the great doors re-opened, as he set to return back inside to sit atop the throne of emperors, presidents and kings. His rabble had pushed him there so he dutifully accepted. Though as he stepped through the doors his eyes darkened, his snarling face twisted further in agony and vengeful hated as it finally dawned on him that now nothing stood in his way; he could now wreak his revenge on the people, the country, and the world.

Chapter 33

It was a very packed deck onboard the familiar face of the Carmania. The old ship, redirected from her dull route to Germany, looked more resplendent and taken care of since William saw it last. The turret guns had returned to her bow and stern and she had a nice and new coat of paint. The ship returned to the state of its former glory during the war. Yes, she was once again used as part of a ferry service, but she was now armed to defend herself. Even Captain Fitzroy seemed to have a new coat of paint over himself too as his uniform and hat, and even his skin, seemed to sparkle in the light, even when the clouds rolled in for a seemingly eternal time. The smoke billowed from her exhausts as she was expertly looked after by the gallant and re-energised crew.

The passengers, however, were more depressed, more desolate, greyer, than any passengers previously stowed away on or underneath the decks of the Carmania. Hundreds of families, huddled together so as not to lose any of their own, were so great in number that the great iron decks heaved under the weight of those making use of the ship's body. They were grumbling, some audibly wailing, as most cursed their luck that they should have to live through two great disasters of their country. Those who had been displaced by force or by choice were now being forced out of their own country for what seemed to be forever once again. Men, women, children, and young babies, cooing or crying in their mothers' arms, hobbled, and swayed as the waves of the English Channel lashed with impressive strength against the ship's strong sides. She had been reinforced with stronger armour which made her heavier, dropping the ship further in the water but allowing her to better break the stronger waves of October's torrents at sea.

The command area of the top deck had been reserved for her crew and for more important souls on board. A detachment of army personnel, battle-ready seamen and dignitaries of note made their way above the huddled mass of refugees below. They were few in number, ready and waiting for any potential threats to occur. The waves seemed unknown.

The French navy had pledged their service to the Republic but the chaos slowly enveloping the whole of France threatened any trust that remained between the French people and Britain. Everyone was suspicious, which was evident by the fact that ports in the north and west coast of the country housed either British or French ships committed to the evacuation operation, never both in the same port.

The Carmania left port from Abbeville and was one of the last to leave the French port. Reports of marauding revolutionary forces making their way with lightning speed towards the north coast prompted a more rushed approach. The Carmania was not due to leave for another two hours but was ordered to make for Portsmouth as soon as was possible. The orders seemed to be made aware to the huddled masses awaiting their turn with hope and the officials were somewhat overpowered by civilians taking the matter of who was allowed on and who wasn't into their own hands. Captain Fitzroy, reluctant to see chaos occur on his redeveloped ship, invited all aboard and this was met with great appreciation. Thus, when the ship did eventually depart, leaving those who had unsuccessfully approached the ship stranded with little hope of reprieve, the journey was peaceful. Those aboard gratefully kept the peace themselves for the journey that was to take a good few hours to complete.

On the top deck leaning against the railings, taking few chances to wander anywhere than to the side of the ship for fear of succumbing to the rocking of the ship's body, was the shattered and grieving William Steele. His glum and depressed expression gave away his emotions greatly, with even the admiring Captain Fitzroy deciding to leave the man alone. The five-year-old boy Charles was close at hand, choosing occasionally to visit the little room housing the body of his mother. Charles was permitted to hold his mother's lifeless hand. He ran her cold fingers against his cheek like she did when Charles was worried, sick, or unhappy. The sensation seemed to calm him, as if she was trying to assuage him from the mourning of her own death. Charles had never understood the concept of death, even though his father had not returned. He had never come to terms with his father's death, but with his mother succumbing to death's terrible sting he was slowly understanding the concept and its terrible price on those left behind to mourn. He remained in attendance to his mother's body throughout the journey, in the full knowledge that soon she would take her final resting place underground away from his eyes forever. Cecile was still beautiful, and she lay as if she was in a deep and wonderful sleep. The sight was too serene for William, but just enough for her only son.

William looked out to the horizon, choosing not to look back at the land enveloping itself in fire and destruction. In truth, part of him enjoyed France because it was an escape from the trials and troubles of England. The emotional distress of Emmanuelle, of the monumental shock of his father's death and the betrayal of his once best friend, had turned the taste of William's home into bitter ash. But it could not remain that way, his life would not be content for that taste to remain. His mother remained, his house remained, and it was there that he would too remain; at least for a while until he might know peace. It was the idea of peace, built from that very ash in England, that allowed him to return without protest.

He gazed out into the view of the sea, itself seemingly not at peace. The wash of the waves whirred up the water underneath and spread over it again to sooth the little torrents. That dance would happen again and again, and his eyes would follow the white foam popping up and disappearing in a few blinks of the eye. Mother nature had a way of creating and dispelling chaos with every gust of wind or mighty push of a current. The ship's journey through nature's torrents seemed to resemble that of a man trying to push his way past the world of fate, forces beyond its control billowing around, and William felt jealous. Would it take a man similarly covered in reinforced metal, armed with great big turrets, to successfully navigate through chaos though powerless to do anything about it? He thought of his own surname; thinking that if anyone could do just that then they better have steel in their name. He wanted to live up to the strength of his family name, though his mind did not quite let him believe that a surname made a man. What makes a man are the choices he makes, the knowledge that he speaks and the truth that he seeks. It was a fanciful idea but to William the presence of such a desired idea would be enough to help a man navigate the rough and unpredictable seas. Though if it would be William, he would have to learn to not get so seasick at the same time.

He looked down at his hands, clasped together as his elbows rested against the handrail. They were still wet but not from the sea but from the tears that fallen off his chin and splashed onto the skin bellow. Cecile's death had not escaped his mind and he feared it might never do so. But life was like that, and William knew it. You can't escape your past; you must build yourself up with it. William wished that such a life lesson did not have to come at the cost of a life that he had loved so much. He was more than content to have learned such lessons from a book or from great stories overheard in the late evening in a bar from an old and wise man. He sighed, finding sighing a regularity, as he carried on looking over the great blue of the English Channel.

"She's beautiful, and the sight can make sailors mad with love" a voice uttered nearby. The Scottish accent allowed William to guess the identity of the owner of the voice. "It is why some men choose to live on the ocean waves and it is why they are forever content with being buried at sea; it is the final embrace of a love they have succumbed to". Major Pearson, in a large-rimmed hat and indistinguishable garb, matched the pose of William. "Have ye ever fancied a life out here?"

William rolled his shoulders and slowly shook his head. "If I did then I'd never hold down another meal again". The reply caused Pearson to grin and look away.

"A good enough reason as any."

"Why are you here, Major? Did you guess that I would be on it?" The spymaster let his grin remain etched on his face.

"I'm in the business of knowing things, William" he replied. He took out a cigarette case and opened it, taking a long cigarette out and lighting it with relative ease despite the whistling of the wind threatening to extinguish his little flame. He inhaled deeply and offered the case to William who raised his hand to politely refuse. "You didn't smoke during the war either?"

"I gave up after the war. I saw no need for it" William replied. Pearson sniggered and packed his cigarette box away into his trench coat pocket. There was a quiet and dignified silence as the two men gazed into the sea. "Why are you here?" William asked, breaking the silence.

"To offer my thanks, William. You have been helpful to me and the men I answer to. Your correspondence, rushed and hard to read as it was, proved invaluable. What with Victor Napoleon at Horse Guards and at court, we now know how to deal with him. As France's soul leader of the resistance, he is a man we are going to have to deal with for a very long time." Pearson seemed to sneer with sarcasm at the mere mention of the Frenchman's name.

"What about the President?"

"Don't know. He may be down there below deck; he may not be. Hopefully he's done the honourable thing" Pearson mused with a sigh. "Napoleon is our man now, which makes you valuable to us still, perhaps more so. His wife is an admirer of you, that we have noticed. Worse luck has befallen a man." William rolled his eyes.

"I'm done with your games" William replied with a hint of disdain. "I could have saved Cecile if I wasn't playing espionage for you in Paris" he pierced his lips as he uttered her name. Pearson straightened his back, his arms still similarly resting on the handrail.

"Best not look in the past for revenge in the present. You said that, or words to that effect. Do you remember? In Munich? You're a post-war hero to us, William. A man like that is very useful and remains so until only time allows him to retire." Pearson looked at his watch on his wrist with comedic subtilty. "And that time is quite a long way away".

"I just want to be left alone to live in peace" William stated, figuratively putting his foot down on the matter. Pearson subtly had no notion of allowing William the satisfaction.

"I'm afraid ye will not be allowed either" Pearson sniggered softly. "Nobody will, I suspect." William finally looked at the Major, creasing his forehead in confusion. Pearson stood up, keeping one hand on the handrail to keep him steady. "Oh no, to the contrary dear William. France's story is done, for now. Britain's story is just about to begin. And we are preparing for that very story. All men with previous combat roles will be invited to return to their posts, including your war commission, William. Though, we can dispense with the 'acting' bit of your title. You've earned that much." The news forced William to turn his body fully to the Major. "So, I'm afraid ye will not be left alone, and there is no peace to be found, certainly not unless we are very lucky".

"Are you planning on going to war?" asked William, forcing Major Pearson to plead for a quieter tone to the conversation.

"Hush, now. But yes. We've learnt vital lessons from the French. We intend to be well prepared, and we won't be quite so accommodating." Pearson leaned into William's ear, holding his elbow tightly. "It's going to get quite messy, William." Each word seemed to be filled with a haunting feeling, and William felt every part, Pearson withdrew himself from William's ear. "But you have done much and suffered greatly. You will have what you want, temporarily of course. Eventually you will be needed." The master of spies turned back round to once more gaze upon the sea which seemed a bit wilder than before. "I'll see to it that you may find some peace, along with your mother and the little boy. That child is owed that as much as anyone else down on those decks. See to it that he is granted that peace". William had wanted to protest about his continued use to Major Pearson and now the army, but the mention of Charles and his right for peace softened William's mind. He looked at Pearson and extended his arm. He took the cigarette out of Major Pearson's hand and turned back towards the sea himself, inhaling the familiar warm and inviting smoke, letting it caress his lungs in a slow ecstasy of comfort. He exhaled, letting the smoke billow slowly out of his nostrils with ethereal ease.

"What are you going to do?" William asked, letting his curiosity get the better of him. Pearson laughed softly and after a pause he stood up and straightened his sleeves.

"Enjoy the rest of the voyage, Major Steele" he replied, walking away, and disappearing into the depths of the ship. William looked on as the figure fell out of view. He held the half-burned cigarette in his hands as he once more gazed upon the deep blue sea caressing with force the side of the ship, rocking him into a mental haze that allowed him to glide over his mind until the Carmania eventually chugged its way through the winds to Portsmouth, and home.

The Salisbury plains looked crisp and brown. Though autumn had well and truly set into the land it remained inviting and glorious. The cottage and estate had been impressively seen to. Niamh, William's lonely mother, had spent a diligent amount of time restoring many parts of the secluded paradise to some element of a former glory. Much had yet to be done, mostly amongst the extremities of the estate's land. There was still much to do within the cottage also, though great strides had already been undertaken. The last drop of rain had fallen a few days ago which meant that the road to the estate had recovered from a slightly mirky state, allowing for much to be taken up and down the road, including provisions and, eventually, the returning William.

Cecile's body was finally laid to rest at the far north-eastern corner of the large garden. Her gravestone had been inscribed with her name, the stork acting as the symbol of her family home in Alsace, and three simple words underneath; 'Life well loved'. William's contacts at the Imperial War Graves Commission had, as recompense for abandoning him before he was whisked away for the trial in Munich, prepared the gravestone in good time and had delivered it to him before he made the journey back to his house. It was placed upright at the head of Cecile's final resting place, itself overlooked by a great oak tree.

William, his mother, and Charles, stood in silence before Cecile's final place of rest. The October winds rustled gently through the trees, indicating mother nature's assurance that the grave would be forever honoured by the elements of sun, water, and wind. William held Charles's hand, silently reminding him that he was not alone and that he was, in some way, home. His mother would always be close at hand and that if he ever wanted to visit the grave to be with his mother, or to look after it, he would always be welcome to do so. Charles squeezed William's hand back, silently thanking him for everything. Niamh stood a few steps behind them, retreating silently back to the house to let the two share a solemn moment together.

William gazed up at the evening's stars, looking up as they began opening their bright and twinkling eyes. The stars seemed beautiful and radiant that night in an oddly clear evening. Small and wispy clouds barely covered the slowly growing multitude of stars above. He thought of the time he was in the jail cell in Munich with Johanna. He remembered the story of the bright stars in the sky, the brightest stars belonging to those departed with the greatest love for those staring up. He stared into the sky, and he allowed himself a smile. He did not have to look long as up to the left he noticed two great and twinkling stars in his eyesight. He knew beyond all doubt that those two stars were the loving souls of his father and of Cecile. He chuckled in his mind at what they might be talking about. The farmer and the café owner disagreeing on the best way to make money, he wandered if Cecile's star might be found somewhere on the other side of the sky after giving up on hearing his father go on and on about ruthless crop rotation.

He gazed at them, reminding himself of their location so that one day he would tell Charles where to look when he would tell the story to the young boy, now without a mother and a father, loved by William with all his heart. The stars seemed to shine with heavenly grace as William remained with his head to the sky. He could almost hear Cecile's calming voice, his father's reassuring speeches at the dinner table, her laugh. Through the gentle wind's breeze, he felt as if he could hear the wind once more brushing through her soft light-brown hair, becoming brighter with each day of sun. Even her apron, as infamous as her beauty, fell into William's imagination, imagining it billowing softly in the breeze hung up as it frequently was with that day's washing. It was as if she was standing in front of him. His imagination briefly gripped his body as he raised his arms to hold her but as they found no such body they returned to his sides.

William's wandering mind was brought back down to earth by the sound of Charles slowly succumbing to tears. The little boy wanted desperately to feel his mother's hand on his cheek one last time. He gripped the boy's shoulders as he turned away wiping tears from his eyes again and again. Charles stomped softly away and stopped by the foot of a tree, his tears overwhelming his body. William turned and approached the crying boy and knelt, so his face was level with Charles's own.

"Why do you furrow your brow?" asked William, noticing Charles's face reveal a tinge of anger underneath his mournful expression.

"I want to find and get the man who took my mum away" he sobbed, gripping his fist, bringing it up to his mouth as he closed his eyes. "I want to get him" he vowed. William sighed and wrapped his arms round Charles, the little boy sobbing and leaning into William's chest. He kissed the boy's forehead as reached into his inner jacket pocket. He took out the beautiful feather made of newspaper and put his hand on Charles's gripped fist, caressing the fingers to open themselves. He placed the feather in Charles's palm.

William pulled Charles into his lap and whispered softly "Let me tell you a story of the time a little girl met with a sparrow with a broken wing."

Epilogue

A lark landed on the lower branch of a young and newly planted tree. He danced on its little feet taking in the sights and sounds of all that was around him. The lark was worried that he had been too slow to fly to warmer climes as autumn was fast giving way to a very familiar winter, though perhaps a winter that was not that cold. The lark did not know that winter's teeth were not to be so sharp and danced on the tree branch trying to regain his strength, ready for the next leg of his journey. He brushed off one leg and then the other. Then he flapped one wing, and then the other. He was quite alone and felt quite lonely. But he consoled himself with the knowledge that the warm destination might soon cure his lonely heart.

The surroundings were very unfamiliar, but they were only to be a temporary view for the little lark who had only desired to stay on the branch for a short while. The next stop would not be for a good while, so the longer he waited to recover the longer he might be able to fly that day, especially as flying at night was now too cold to handle at that time of the year. He looked around in simple curiosity at where he landed. He saw many bricks of resplendent white, slabs of white bricks that were dotted around. The surroundings seemed most peculiar. This sight was very odd and not one a little bird like him would usually see in a wooded area.

His curiosity got the better of him. He hopped off the branch and flapped his little wings a bit further, landing with supreme grace on top of the white bricks. They seemed to be smooth and well treated. His little feet rested with delicate ease as he gazed out even more, finding more and more white bricks to jump on and flutter around. He did so, taking care not to make too much noise for an unfamiliar place to a small bird is always a place of suspicion and potential danger. But with every hop further into the growing field of large white stones his worry and suspicion seemed to wane more and more. It seemed more peaceful as if he had arrived at a protected area of woodland just for larks to rest and play.

A

He took a closer look with his tiny eyes at what lay under his feet. Many white bricks had little indents and carvings on them. He could make out little, but he tried his best. 'A soldier of the Great War, known unto god'. That phrase was written on quite a few of the bricks and stones, as the lark flew between rows and rows of them. How many of these stones were there? His wings brushed against the top of some of the stones as he flew by them. He decided to fly higher into the sky. The stones seemed to keep going for miles and miles. He flew up and hovered against the incoming breeze and looked down.

Rows upon rows of stones, gravestones, lined in close ranks below him. The flowers beautifully dotted around the gravestones brought colour into the growing sea of white stone resting on a green bed. He swooped back down and gazed at the walls of etchings. Names, names upon names, too many to count, were carved into these big stones. Alphabetical order, so many names in alphabetical order, cascaded down each wall. The lark hopped to other walls and saw more of the same. He hopped and read a few. These names looked so solemn and full of mournful grace. The names, the lark surmised, of those who had gone too soon, and some perhaps gone together.

The sight of the names began to fill the lark's heart with great sorrow. He spread his wings and flew away to other parts of the growing gravesite, beautifully quiet with just his flapping wings making the only sound. He stopped at a gravestone and strained his eyes to read it.

'295145 PRIVATE A.H. ALDOUES, 4TH BN. LONDON REGT. R. FUS., 21ST SEPTEMBER 1917 AGE 28'. A cross lay underneath that inscription. His heart grew too great with sorrow, and he launched himself into the air, not yet fully recovered for the next leg of his journey. But he did not want to stay there long. The lark made his way further south, crossing to the east to follow a helpful breeze. He dived again, feeling his energy sap a bit quicker than before. He had to wait a bit longer to recover. He dived into a flock of trees and again he found himself surrounded by a sea of white brick and stone. He hopped in front of another stone to see what these ones meant. He read the inscription.

'200201 PRIVATE BERTIE JAMES CHAMBERLAIN, LEICESTERSHIRE REGIMENT, 1ST OCTOBER 1917 AGE 19'. So

B

young, the lark thought. So young. He found an inscription further down the stone. 'O LORD WHEN THE ROLL IS CALLED IN HEAVEN MAY HIS NAME IN THEY BOOK BE FOUND'. The words seemed to haunt the lark's very soul. He flapped away, further, and further he flew until once again his energy seemed almost completely spent. He begged for his fate not to find him once again amidst a sea of mournful rock.

He swooped down again and found a smaller sea of white rock, daintily tucked away in a corner of a field with grass growing all around it. He begged for his curious eyes to stay their gaze. He looked down, hopping from stone to stone trying with all his might not to read another inscription. He hopped to the ground and looked to his right. He allowed himself to reach the inscription on the base of this gravestone in front of him. It ended up being the most haunting words he would read that day.

'WE CANNOT LORD THEY PURPOSE SEE, BUT ALL IS WELL THAT IS DONE BY THEE'.

The lark could stomach no more. He flapped his wings and begged his body to carry his far, far away from these dotted lines of pure white stone. His eyes closed lest he gaze upon a single white stone once more. A welcome breeze was found, and he stretched his little wings, thanking the mercy of nature of helping him escape the terrible sights that he saw that day. He followed the breeze south for the warmer embrace of air and the less mournful sights and sounds that he had seen and felt on that fair but mournful evening.

So left much of nature's children as autumn grew wearier of is presence in that year of 1920. It appeared as though the beauty that might return after years of absence would have to wait a while longer to reappear for many in Europe. The clouds of war that parted to the sheer relief of millions seemed to be closing once again. The peace that allowed so many to at least breathe seemed to be a chimera, in Britain, France and Germany at least. That realisation that the peace that was afforded the world was just a momentary respite seemed to also be shared by many other nations from one corner to the other. Just as it seemed as if all the world had achieved some bit of peace it looked to all the world as if the mere notion had just been loaned by the fates for a time. It turned out to be a very short loan.

C

The Kaiser, the leader of Pax Germania, rushed around along with his allies in the army and the Reichstag to keep the order within his country in a bid to retain the supposed domination of the world. The new ruffian, taking charge of the ancient nation of France at gunpoint, held the fate of so many souls within the palm of his hands without anyone knowing what was to happen next. Britain's king and is government prepared for the worst as they did all they could to steer their country from a similarly chaotic fate, though the price of such a course was great. The other nations both old and new would have their turn in the limelight of history, but many awaited the fate of the great nations to play out. The world would turn on the great choices or the great agonies of fate of the major actors and players in the months and years to come. Then again, were they ever really in control?

People began to take more breathes of their own, for they might never know breathes in peace again, and for a long time at that. Breathing, a common occurrence to all permitted to live in the new era of Pax Germania, was becoming more and more strained by the growing advance of conflict and chaos. Perhaps none had won the peace, and thus none had the right to breathe easily. The world might soon choke, as it did for several years before, until it convulsed the new and frightening world yet to come. The fear of the future was settling back in.

As for those resting under their own gravestones, besides the sword of sacrifice, they might be the only ones to really know true peace. Those designated to carry on with the turning of the globe seemed to be further away from it though they had the privilege to remain alive. Those who rested amidst the immaculately kept cemeteries of the Great War lay with expectations that their deaths would forever mean something within the hallowed halls of human history. Their final resting places might act as reminders of endeavours of human glory, bravery, and folly. Their wishes that they may be remembered as men who died in the war to end all wars were wishes clung to by those who wished to see such magisterial wishes followed through.

The peace that the soldiers resting in the fields fought and died for seemed a long way away. Who would be so brave enough to go and tell them that their deaths had brought about no lasting peace, no end to a world that seemed to be content with eating itself up again? Who amongst

D

the people who visited the cemeteries in what was left of Belgium, what was left of Germany, what was left of France, what was left of Britain, would be brave enough to kneel by the names of those departed and reveal the failure of those left alive to win the peace?

And so, as France burned, as Germany began to break itself in two, as Britain tip-toed along the edge of the abyss, those final resting places, thousands upon thousands in rows upon rows up and down the old Western Front, looked on as the peace was fought over with such ferocity. Perhaps, if one visited those hallowed grounds and listened to the breeze on the wind, people might hear the groans of the fallen and the musings, the painful wondering, of whether things might have ended up so differently.

E

Printed in Great Britain
by Amazon

23097844R00209